the Cheetah Girls

the Cheetah Girls

Livin' Large!

Volumes 1–4

Deborah Gregory

SCHOLASTIC INC.

New York   Toronto   London   Auckland   Sydney
Mexico City   New Delhi   Hong Kong   Buenos Aires

ISBN 0-439-70100-7

12 11 10 9 8 7 6 5 4 3 2 1   4 5 6 7 8 9/0

Printed in the U.S.A.   40

First Scholastic printing, October 2004

This book is set in 12-point Palatino.

Acknowledgments

I have to give it up to the Jump at the Sun peeps here—Andrea Pinkney, Lisa Holton, and Ken Geist—for letting the Cheetah Girls run wild. Also, Anath Garber, the one person who helped me find my Cheetah Girl powers. And, Lita Richardson, the one person who now has my back in the jiggy jungle. Primo thanks to the cover girl Cheetahs: Arike, Brandi, Imani, Jeni, and Mia. And to all the Cheetah Girls around the globe: Get diggity with the growl power, baby!

Contents

✿ ✿ ✿ ✿ ✿ ✿ ✿ ✿ ✿ ✿ ✿ ✿ ✿ ✿ ✿ ✿ ✿ ✿ ✿ ✿

Introduction

O nce upon a rhyme, there were two beautiful, bubble-icious girls named Galleria
and Chanel who were the best of friends and
the brightest wanna-be stars in all the land.
One night, they looked up in the sky at all the
real, glittering stars and dreamed of a place
where they, too, could shine forever. Under the
spell of the moonlight, they made a secret pact
that they would find this place no matter how
long it took, no matter how hard they had to
try. Then they would travel all over the world
and share their cheetah-licious songs and supa-
dupa sparkles with everyone who crossed their
path.

But it wasn't until Galleria and Chanel banded together with three other girls and unleashed their growl power that they discovered the jiggy jungle: that magical, cheetah-licious place inside of every dangerous, scary, crowded city where dreams really do come true. The jiggy jungle is the only place where every cheetah has its day!

The Cheetah Girls Credo

To earn my spots and rightful place in the world, I solemnly swear to honor and uphold the Cheetah Girls oath:

- Cheetah Girls don't litter, they glitter. I will help my family, friends, and other Cheetah Girls whenever they need my love, support, or a *really* big hug.

- All Cheetah Girls are created equal, but we are not alike. We come in different sizes, shapes, and colors, and hail from different cultures. I will not judge others by the color of their spots, but by their character.

🐾 A true Cheetah Girl doesn't spend more time doing her hair than her homework. Hair extensions may be career extensions, but talent and skills will pay my bills.

🐾 True Cheetah Girls can achieve without a weave—or a wiggle, jiggle, or a giggle. I promise to rely (mostly) on my brains, heart, and courage to reach my cheetah-licious potential!

🐾 A brave Cheetah Girl isn't afraid to admit when she's scared. I promise to get on my knees and summon the growl power of the Cheetah Girls who came before me—including my mom, grandmoms, and the Supremes—and ask them to help me be strong.

🐾 All Cheetah Girls make mistakes. I promise to admit when I'm wrong and will work to make it right. I'll also say I'm sorry, even when I don't want to.

🐾 Grown-ups are not always right, but they are bigger, older, and louder. I will treat my teachers, parents, and people of authority with respect—and expect them to do the same!

🐾 True Cheetah Girls don't run with wolves or hang with hyenas. True Cheetahs pick much better friends. I will not try to get other people's approval by acting like a copycat.

🐾 To become the Cheetah Girl that only I can be, I promise not to follow anyone else's dreams but my own. No matter how much I quiver, shake, shiver, and quake!

🐾 Cheetah Girls were born for adventure. I promise to learn a language other than my own and travel around the world to meet my fellow Cheetah Girls.

the Cheetah Girls

Wishing on a Star

For Sabie, the original
Miss Cuchifrito.
And Toto, too.
I miss you both.

Chapter 1

Toto must think my toes are dipped in Bark-B-Q sauce, the way he's trying to sneak a chomp-a-roni with his pointy fangs. I have just painted my toenails in a purply glitter shade called "Pow!" by S.N.A.P.S. Cosmetics and am lying on my bed with my feet dangling to the winds so they can dry.

"Guess what, big brother, you're gonna have to get your grub on somewhere else," I coo to the raggedy pooch with dreadlocks whom I love more than life itself. "I, Galleria Garibaldi, supa divette-in-training, cannot afford to have Toto-tugged tootsies."

Mom isn't sure what breed Toto is, because she and Dad adopted him from the ASPCA before I was born. But when all the hair-sprayed ladies on the street stop and ask me, I say that he is a poodle instead of a "pastamuf-fin" (that's what I call him). It sounds more *hoity-toity*, and trust: that is a plus on the Upper East Side, where I live.

I stick the bottle of nail polish in my new cheetah backpack. I hold up my hands, and it looks like a thousand glittering stars are bouncing off my Pow!-painted tips. "Awright!" I tell myself. "This girlina-rina is gonna get herself noticed by first period, Toto. High school, at last!"

Tomorrow is my first day as a freshman at Fashion Industries High School, and I'm totally excited—and scared. I figure it can't hurt to make a big first impression—but painting my nails is also a way to get my mind off being so nervous.

I'm real glad Chuchie is coming over for dinner tonight. That's Chanel Simmons to you—she's my partner-in-rhyme (aka Miss Cuchi-frita, Chanel No. 5, Miss Gigglebox, and about a gazillion other names I call her). We've known each other since we were in designer diapers. Chuchie, her brother, Pucci, and her mom, Juanita, ought to be here any minute, in fact.

Chuchie's going to Fashion Industries High, too. Thank gooseness—which is my way of saying thank you. She's about the only familiar face I'll be seeing come tomorrow morning.

Chanel is a blend of Dominican and Puerto Rican on her mother's side, Jamaican and Cuban on her father's side—and sneaky-deaky through and through! She lives down in Soho near my mother's store, Toto in New York . . . Fun in Diva Sizes. It's on West Broadway off Broome Street, where people are a lot more "freestyle" than in my neighborhood.

Down there, you can walk on the sidewalk next to a Park Avenue lady, or someone with blue hair, a nose ring, and a boom box getting their groove on walking down the sidewalk. Up here, hair colors must come out of a Clairol box. It's probably written in the lease!

"Galleria?" I hear my mom calling me from the dining room. "You 'bout ready, girlina? 'Cause your daddy's getting home late, and I'm not playing hostess with the mostest all by myself!"

"Coming, Momsy-poo!" I shout back. But I

7

don't move. Not yet. Plenty of time for that when the doorbell rings.

Thinking about Chanel has put me in mind of my music. I start singing the new song I have just finished writing in my Kitty Kat notebook: "Welcome to the Glitterdome."

I have to get my songs copyrighted so no one will bite my flavor before I become famous—which is going to happen any second. I have a drawer full of furry, spotted notebooks filled with all the words, songs, and crazy thoughts I think of—which I do on a 24-7 basis. I will whip out my notebook wherever I am and scribble madly. There is no shame in my game.

I pick up my private notebook, on which my name—Galleria—appears in peel-off glitter letters, and turn to a blank page. I start writing notes to myself and working on the "Glitterdome" song some more.

What I love the "bestesses of all" (as Chanel would say) is singing, rhyming, and blabbing my mouth. It's as natural to me as dressing for snaps (that means, for compliments). I can make up words and rhymes on a dime. Not rap, just freestyle flow. I also spell words "anyhoo I pleez"—as long as they're different from other people's spelling.

The doorbell rings. "Galleria!" my mom shouts. "You'd better wiggle you way over here. The 'royal' family has arrived!"

I slip into my cheetah ballet flats and hurry to get the door. Tonight's a big night for Chanel's mom, Juanita: She's introducing us to her new boyfriend. He's some kind of mysterious tycoon or something, whom she met in gay Paree, aka Paris, France, no less! From what Mom tells me, Juanita thinks he might be her ticket to the Billionaire's Ball, if there is such a thing.

"She met him in Paris, and he supposedly owns half of the continent or something," was how Mom put it. "She's trying to get him to marry her—so we've gotta make a good impression."

Well, okay. I guess I know how to make a good impression. Hope he likes purple glitter toenails, 'cause I am me, y'know? Like me or don't, I'm not fluttering my eyelashes like Cleopatra!

"Chuchie!" I say as I open the door. "Wuzup, *señorita?*" We do our secret handshake greeting—which consists of tickling each other's fingernails—and give each other a big hug.

Juanita looks like a glamapuss. Poly and Ester must have been on vacation. She's still as thin as she was when she was a model (unlike my mom, who is now a size-eighteen, class-A diva). Right now, Juanita's wearing this long, flowy dress encrusted with jewels, like she's the royal toast of gay Paree or something. Like I said, it looks good on her, but it's kinda weird if you ask me.

"Hey, Galleria!" she says. Then she steps sideways so I can see her new boyfriend. "This is Monsieur Tycoon," she says, laying on the French accent.

"Pleased to meet you," I say, offering my hand. But he doesn't take it. I guess over there they don't shake a girl's hand if they don't know her. "His Majesty" just smiles this teeny little smile and nods at me.

"Come on in, y'all," I say, and they do, Mr. Tycoon last of all. Juanita gives me a little wink as she passes and I can tell she's happy and nervous all at the same time. Pucci hugs my waist.

I look at Chuchie, and she rolls her eyes at me. I bite my lip to keep from giggling and wonder how Chuchie's managing not to giggle herself. She's always the first to lose it, not me. But that's because she's met the tycoon before.

He's good-lookin', all right, with a big black mustache and black eyes that make him look like he's an undercover spy. And he's wearing a pinstriped suit that's probably hand-sewn— every stitch of it! He comes in and looks around the place, nodding like he approves. I'm so glad he thinks we're worthy of his royal highness. *Not*. I mean, I am not used to being scrutinized, you know? I wonder how my mom is going to react.

"*Bon soir*," Mom says, flexing her French and gliding into the room from the kitchen, six feet tall and looking every inch the diva she is—still ferocious enough to pounce down any runway. The tycoon gives her a little bow and puts his hands together like he's praying, but I think it's because he's impressed.

"I hope you're all hungry," Mom says. "I've been in the kitchen all day, whipping up a *fabulous* feast."

I know she's fibbing, but I stay hush-hush. Mom *always* goes down to the Pink Tea Cup for dinner when she wants to serve soul food. Their stuff is greasy but yummy.

Me and Chanel give each other looks that say "We've gotta talk!"

"'Scuse us for a minute?" I ask the grown-ups. "I want to show Chanel my new cheetah backpack."

"Go on," Mom says. "We'll call you when dinner's served."

We hightail it into my room and shut the door behind us. As soon as we do, Chuchie explodes into a fit of giggles. "I can't take it anymore!" she gasps.

"Is he for real?" I ask. "Shhh! He'll hear you laughing and get insulted. You don't wanna mess things up for your mom!"

"She is so cuckoo for him!" Chuchie says.

"Chuchie, you're gonna be a royal princess one of these days, and I'm gonna have to bow down and throw petals at your corn-infested feet every time I see you."

"Stop!" Chuchie says again, dissolving into another fit of giggles. When she's finally done, she says, "Seriously, Bubbles. I'm worried about Mom. I mean, his 'His Majesty' is so weird. I'm not even allowed to talk when he's around! He thinks children are supposed to be seen and not heard." Chuchie calls me Bubbles because I chew so much bubble gum.

"Children?" I repeat. "Miss Cuchifrita, we're in high school come tomorrow! We are not children anymore!"

"Tell me about it! Are you ready for the big time?"

"Ready as I'll ever be—I've got my nails done (I flash them for her), my new backpack, and attitude to spare. How 'bout you, girlita?"

"I guess," she says, not sounding too sure of herself. "It's gonna be kinda strange not knowing anybody else but each other."

"Hey, we don't need anybody else," I tell her. "We are the dynamic duo, yo!"

Me and Chanel have been singing together since we were six, but not professionally, because Chanel's mom does not want her to be a singer. A talent show here or there is "cute," but after that she starts croaking.

What Juanita doesn't know is that me and Chuchie made a secret pact in seventh grade. We are going to be famous singers despite her (or maybe to spite her) because we can't be models like she and my mom were.

The Cheetah Girls

My mom is a whopper-stopper six feet tall. I'm only five feet four inches. Juanita is five feet seven inches. Chanel is five feet three inches. Do the math. We're both too short for the runway sashay. (My mom was a more successful and glam-glam model than Juanita—and sometimes I think that's why they fight.)

Unlike Juanita, my mom is pretty cool with whatever I'm down with. She wanted to be a singer really bad when she was young. She had the fiercest leopard clothes, but she just didn't have the voice. Then she went into modeling and sashayed till she parlayed her designing skills.

The only reason *I* haven't become a famous singer yet is because I don't want to be onstage by myself. Being an only child is lonely enough. I would go cuckoo for Cocoa Puffs, for sure. With Chuchie around, it's like having a sister. Like I said, we are the dynamic duo, bound till death. But, still, there's something missing—and I'm beginning to think I know what it is.

"You know what, Miss Cuchifrita?" I say. "I think we need to find us some backup singers and make a real girl group."

"Yeah!" she says right away. "Girl groups always become famous. Look at the Lollipops. They were finger-lickin' large."

"Or the HoneyDews," I say. "Their bank accounts are ripe with loot."

"Or Karma's Children, or The Spice Rack Girls!" Chuchie adds. "They are not even supa-chili anymore, but they once were, and that is what counts."

The kids in junior high school used to say that I look like Backstabba, the lead singer of Karma's Children. That is probably because I'm light-skinned (dark butterscotch-y) and wear my hair kinda long in straight or curly styles. (My hair is kinky, but I straighten it.) I don't think we look alike. I have bigger hips and tommyknockers (that means boobies). I also wear braces.

Karma's Children are four fly singers—Backstabba, Greedi, Peace, and Luvbug—from Houston and they must have instant karma because they had a hit record right out the box, "Yes, Yes, Yes." From what I can see, you don't have to have a lot of lyrics to be large. The Spice Rack Girls had a hit song with even fewer words—"Dance!"—and they live in a castle, I think, somewhere in Thyme City, Wales, which is far, far away from the jiggy jungle.

"Hey, if we get in a girl group, we could travel all over the world, singing," Chuchie says.

"We could go to London," I say, getting in the groove. "Drink Earl Grey tea with the queen."

"Yeah, and shop in the West End district." That's Chanel for you. Her idea of geography is knowing every shopping locale worldwide!

"We could go to Paris, too," I say. "Eat croissants with butter—not margarine!"

"Yeah, and shop at French designer saylons," Chuchie adds, stretching the long "a."

"Like Pouf," I say, "where they sell the *très* fiercest leopard-snakeskin boots. Then we can go to Italy to see all my aunts and uncles on my father's side."

"And shop at Prada! That's where I'm headed. 'Prada or Nada,' that's my motto for life!"

Chuchie picks up my hairbrush and starts singin' into it like it's a microphone—doin' Kahlua and Mo' Money Monique's "The Toyz Is Mine." I pick up my round brush and join her, both of us bouncin' on the bed as we sing and do our supa-dupa moves in perfect har-mo-nee.

Chanel kinda looks like a lighter version of
Kahlua—with the same slanty, exotic brown eyes,
and oodles of long micro-braids falling in her face.

When we're done, we both dissolve in giggles. Then I roll over and say, "We're gonna do
it, Miss Cuchifrita. Alls we gotta do is find the
rest of our girl group."

"Uh-huh. But where we gonna do that?" she
asks me.

"I dunno," I say. "But one thing is for sure:
It's gonna happen." We give each other our
secret handshake and a fierce hug.

That's me and Chuchie: always hatchin' big
dreams together. At first, we wanted to open a
store for pampered pets—and now we have a
game plan for becoming starlets. And you
know what? One day, they're all gonna come
true. Trust me.

"Hey! What are you two 'high school' girls
doin' in there?" I hear Mom calling. "I got din-
din on the table and I know you don't want
cold pork chops and black-eyed peas!"

"Coming!" we both yell.

"I'll page you later," Chuchie says as we go
to join the grown-ups. "We can 'dish and tell'
later."

"You got it, girlita," I say. "'Cause I know I won't be able to sleep tonight. I'll log on when I get your page, and we can hog the chat room all night long."

Chapter 2

It's 10:45, and Chuchie, Pucci, Juanita, and Mr. Tycoon are long gone. Mom is cleaning up in the kitchen. My dad walked in about half an hour ago, and he's waving a piece of corn bread in the air as he talks. Talking with his hands comes with his heritage. Signore Francobollo Garibaldi is Eye-talian—from Bologna, Italy—but he loves soul food. I guess it comes with lovin' my mom.

Dad runs the factory in Brooklyn where the clothes are made for Mom's store, Toto in New York, and sometimes he gets home real late. Like tonight.

I give him a kiss, or *un bacio*, as he calls it, and say, "I got school tomorrow and I gotta get my beauty sleep, okay?"

"Okay, *cara*," my dad says, kissing me back. "Luv ya. Just make sure your skirt is longer than twelve inches!" He smiles at me and gives me a wink. *Cara* means "precious one" in Italian. That's my dad for you: behind me all the way, as long as I keep my knees covered!

I get washed up and get into bed, knowing Mom will be coming in to say good night any minute. She never misses. Sure enough there's a soft knock at my door, and she comes in and sits by my bed.

"You have a good time tonight?" she asks.

"Uh-huh. I guess," I say. "Mr. Tycoon's kinda different, though."

Mom laughs. "I know what you mean, sugah. You and Chanel didn't say two words the whole time, but I bet you were kicking each other under the table!" Mom knows us too well.

"Yeah." I giggled. "Better kicking than talking— I got the feeling he wouldn't like it if we did!"

"You're right about that," she says. "But Juanita's crazy 'bout him, so we've just gotta play along and hope she gets what she wants— and likes it when she does."

"Uh-huh," I say.

"You ready for school tomorrow? Just don't roll up the waistband of your skirt!" she says.

"Okay," I say, and fake a yawn. "G'night, Mom."

"Good night, baby. Don't be scared, now— stay fierce. Show 'em who you are, and they'll love you just like I do." She kisses me on the forehead and goes out, shutting the door behind her.

Mom is so cool. When I am rich and famous, I am going to buy her the one thing she wants more than anything else: Dorothy's ruby slippers from *The Wizard of Oz*. Mom is a *serious* collector. She wants whatever nobody else has, or almost nobody. There are only five pairs of ruby slippers in the whole world, and the last pair was auctioned off at Christie's for 165,000 duckets. I will find the anonymous mystery person who has bought the ruby slippers and buy them for Mom as a surprise.

Mom has seen *The Wizard of Oz* more times than I care to remember. She boo-hoos like a baby every time, too. I don't know why it makes her cry. It makes me laugh.

There is something Mom isn't telling me

about her family, but I'm not supposed to know that. She never talks about them, and I don't have any relatives on her side.

In the living room, there is a very old, gray-looking picture of *her* mom, a brown-skinned lady who looks sad. She says her mother died a long time ago, before I was born. Chanel says my mom is a drama queen. I think she is just larger than life. Diva size.

I have a lot of ruby slipper stickers, which I have put on my school notebooks and dresser drawers and my closet doors in my bedroom— the "spotted kingdom." I also have ruby slipper cards. I keep them in the leopard hat boxes by the bed.

Inside the ruby slipper card, it says MAY ALL YOUR DREAMS COME TRUE. I keep one pinned on my busybody board and open it sometimes because it gives me hope that my dreams will come true, too. I don't want to let my mother down and live in this bedroom forever.

My Miss Wiggy alarm clock reads 11:00, and suddenly, my beeper is vibrating on the night-stand. Got to be Chanel. I roll over, hop out of bed, and log on to the Internet on my swell Ladybug PC.

Toto is hunched on his front paws and staring at me with his little black beady eyes. My poor little brother can't accept the fact that he is simply a fluffy pooch. Toto is fifteen, (which is 105 in human years), and he sleeps in my room, in his very own canopy bed, with a leopard duvet. "Oh, Toto, you always make me smile," I tell him as I type my greeting to Chuchie.

"Chanel, Chanel, you're so swell. What are you wearing tomorrow, *mamacita*, pleez, pleez, tell?"

No answer. Hmmmm . . . she beeped me, but she isn't in the chat room. That's strange. There is plenty of cyber action, judging by the number of on-screen entries. Everybody must need a 'Net break since it's back-to-school "D day" for anybody under eighteen with a brain.

"Oh, if I only had a brain, I wouldn't feel so lame, and I'd jump on the A train when it rained, because there'd be no shame in my game . . ." I hum aloud while plotting my next move.

"My name is Dorinda," flashes on my computer screen. "I'm pressing my khaki boot-cut pants right now and shining my Madd Monster shoes. I'm wearing a black sweater, right. Do you think it will be too 'that' to wear a tube top underneath it?"

Oh, this girl is mad funny, I think, cracking up as I type a response. "Hi, my name is Galleria. September is the time for the belly button to go on vacation and the brain to come back in full effect. Unless you want Serial Mom to corner you in the girls' room and cut off your top with a rusty pair of scissors, you'd better leave the 'boob tube' at home! Where are you going to school, anyway?"

"Galleria, the Joker, thanks. Tomorrow's my first day at Fashion Industries on Twenty-fourth Street. I'm going to major in fashion design! Guess I can't 'cut' class. Ha. Ha."

Hip-hop, hooray. This girl is going to the same school I am, even though our majors are different!

"I'm gonna be checking for you, girlita. I'm there tomorrow, too, or I'll be a T square. I'm majoring in fashion merchandising and buying—I've got a passion for fashion but can't cut my way out of Barbie's cardboard wardrobe. I leave that to my mom. She's a majordomo dope designer. You scared about going to high school?"

"No. I'm cooler than a fan, baby. Well, okey-dokey, a little," Dorinda replies. "It's farther away from my house than I'm used to traveling in the A.M., if you know what I'm saying. And it'll take away from the time I used to spend helping my mom get everyone ready for school."

Another entry flashes on my screen. "Hey, Bubbles! Let's wear our leopard miniskirts with berets, but with a different-colored turtleneck. Which do you want to wear, red or black?"

Chuchie is finally in the house. "Gucci for Chuchie! No diggity, no doubt. You're late. This is Dorinda and she's going to be in the house with us tomorrow. Where you been?"

"Pucci lost one of his Whacky Babies—Oscar the Ostrich. That beaten-up thing was his favorite, too. *Ay, caramba*, I was so glad that he finally fell asleep on top of Mr. Mushy. Now he'll be crying when he wakes up tomorrow and sees he's got a crushy Mr. Mushy, but I'm not moving him!"

Pucci is Chuchie's younger brother. He is nine, pudgy, spoiled to death, and has the biggest collection of Whacky Babies stuffed animals in the jungle. I call him "Eight

Ball" because his head is shaven clean like a pool ball.

I type back, "Ooh, that's cold, Chanel No. 5. Dorinda is majoring in fashion design. Ain't that dope?"

"Cool, Miss Dorinda. Where do you live?"

"116th and Lenox Ave."

"Uptown, baby, you gets down, baby?" Chuchie writes.

"I try. I can move. I can groove. I'm gonna take dance classes at the YMCA on 135th 'cause I'm in the Junior Youth Entrepreneur Leadership Program there, so I get classes in everything for free."

"We got skills, too. We take dance and voice classes at Drinka Champagne's Conservatory on Saturdays. You think you got more skills than us?"

"No! I'm not flossin'."

"Correct, *mamacita*. Me and Galleria sing, too. What you know about that?"

"Nothing. But I think I can sing, too—a little. I would like to, anyway. I'll check for you two tomorrow and show you!"

"Bet, Dorinda. Bubbles, don't try to get out of it. What color top are you gonna wear? 'Cause you better not wear the same color as me, *está bien?*"

"Bubbles? That's funny," Dorinda types.

"Chuchie calls me Bubbles because I love to chomp on gum. Something I cannot do in public because my mom says it's tick-tacky," I type for Dorinda. "I'll wear the red top with the black scribble, okay?" I type to ease Chuchie's mind.

"Dorinda, where did you go to junior high?"

"I went to Wagner," Dorinda types back.

"You really are a hoodie girl, huh?"

"Guess so. It was two blocks from my house. Easy breezy on the traveling tip."

"That's cool. It could be worse."

"Word?"

"Word. At least you don't live in the suburbs!" Chanel types, proud of her snaps. "Galleria is a boho because she is so 'that,' and I'm a Dominican bap, I guess, and proud of it. We'll see if you can hang with us!"

What does she mean by I'm so "that"? I'll fix her. "You're a burp!" I type back. "Boougie, undone, ridiculoso, and princess-y to the max. Don't deny it."

"Don't let me read you from cover to cover or you'll never recover, Secret Agent Bubbles, okay, *mija?*" responds Chanel. "I'm going to wear the black turtleneck top with the leopard skirt, so you can go ahead with your red top." I can just see her giggling. She is a majordomo gigglebox and can't be stopped.

"Maybe we can be a crew. You never know," I type for Dorinda's assurance.

"Let's meet outside the cafeteria at 12:00 sharp. But we're not going in. I don't want to get food poisoning my first day of school. You know what we'll be wearing, so you can't miss us!" Chanel signs off.

"See ya and I'm tryin' hard to be ya!" Dorinda retorts.

This girl is quick. Maybe she *can* hang with us, I think, as I sign off, "Powder to the People!"

"Powder to the People!" is a joke between me and Chanel. I'll tell Dorinda about it tomorrow. For now, I log off and get back into bed.

Toto is lying on the floor now with his nose pressed to the floor.

"Toto, watcha thinkin'?" Cheez whiz, I wonder what it's like to be a dog. One thing is for sure. They don't have to get up at the crack of dawn and go to school.

Wishing on a Star

In the darkness, my fears dance around like Lotto balls. So I sing out loud to all the twinkle-dinkles like me, trying to sparkle in this crazy place called the Big Apple. A real deal jungle. We don't have the grass and trees, but we do have some of the animals.

"Twinkle-dinkles, near or far,
stop the madness and be a star.

Take your seat on the Ferris wheel,
and strap yourself in for the man of steel.

Welcome to the Glitterdome.
It's any place you call home.

Give me props, I'll give you cash,
then show you where my sparkle's stashed.

Glitter, glitter. Don't be bitter!
Glitter, glitter. Don't be bitter!
Glitter, glitter. Don't be bitter!"

I drift into sleep, and I'm sure the fears have all been chased away. Not by my singing, but by Toto's snoring, which is louder than the backfire from the Cockadoodle Donuts truck that passes by our street at four A.M. every morning. My songs are my secret weapon, though, for shooting straight to stardom. . . .

Chapter 3

Mr. Drezform, our new homeroom teacher, has trouble pronouncing my last name, like all the other teachers I've had since kinder-garten. "Galleria Gareboodi?"

"Here!" I yell out, smiling and raising my hand in the air like I just don't care. "It's Galleria Gar-i-bald-i."

This boy in front of me turns around and heckles me. "Gar-i-booty!" he says, and laughs. Then *everyone* else in the class turns to look at me.

"*What?*" I ask, challenging him. "What's your name, yo?"

"Derek," he says, still smiling.

"Derek what?"

"Derek Hambone," he says. "The new brotha in town—from Detroit."

"Derek *what?*" I ask. "Did you say Hambone?" Now the class is laughing at him, not me. "Hah! You'd best not be laughing. Your last name sure ain't no Happy Meal."

I snarl and squint my eyes. He turns away, busted. Now I'm looking at the back of his head, which has the letters "D U H" shaved into it. "Duh?" I say to Chanel, mouthing the words without sound. "What are we on— *Sesame Street?*"

Derek is featuring a red, blue, and white Johnny BeDown shirt with matching droopy jeans covered with logos like a roadrunner map. Johnny BeDown clothes aren't made by the Joker, if you know what I'm saying. You have to shell out serious duckets for them. They just *look* like the homeless catch of the day.

There are three things I hate. 1. Cock-a-roaches. 2. Math tests. 3. Wack-a-doodle clothes. The first I can't avoid unless I move out of New York City. The second two are *kinda* like roaches because they're everywhere.

I, Galleria Garibaldi, will never dress like everybody else. I write this in my freshman notebook using my purple pen. It's true that I get my animal instincts from my mom, but I have my own flavor, 'cause I'll wear cheetah prints in hot pink or lime green, and Mom sticks to the old-school ones.

I remember I was only four years old when she bought me my first furry leopard coat with a matching hat. My father nicknamed me Miss Leoparda because I wore that coat to pieces. I also had a stuffed leopard animal named Cheetah Kat, which I took with me everywhere. And Toto now has seven leopard coats, thanks to me.

As for Chuchie, her taste in fashion runs to berets. She is wearing one today, with her braids hanging down into her face.

"Gimme one of your pens," she groans. "Mine stopped working." Chuchie must own about fifty of these French pancakes (that's what I call them). The beret she is wearing today is black with a gold-braided edge. Her mom brought it back from Paris. Chuchie is sitting next to me, drawing silly faces in the margins of her notebook and giggling quietly.

Attendance is taking a long time, and my mind wanders to Dorinda. We're meeting her at noon, outside the cafeteria. I wonder what she'll be like. . . .

Mr. Drezform blows his nose, causing Chuchie to giggle real loud, and Derek Hambone turns around and grins at me, giving me a big wink. Heavens to Bootsy—Derek has a gold tooth in front!

Chuchie dissolves into giggles, and I give her a hard elbow to the ribs.

"Hey, Derek," I say, "what's with the haircut?"

"Oh, you mean the letters?" he asks, giving me his goofy, gold-tooth smile again.

"Yeah."

"It's my initials," he explains proudly. "Derek Ulysses Hambone."

I bite down hard on my lip to keep from losing it completely. "You know, Derek, it also stands for something else."

"It does?" he asks, clueless. "What?"

"Figure it out, *scemo*," I quip, using the Italian word for idiot.

"Okay, I will," he says. "And *shame* on you back—even though, you know, you are cute." Another goofy grin, and he turns away again.

Great. Just what I need on my first day in

high school: a fashion disaster with a geeky smile and a gold tooth who *likes me*.

I can tell it's only a matter of time till he asks me out. Someone call 911, please.

"It's time for *lonchando*," Chanel says as we wait outside the cafeteria for Dorinda.

"I've got an idea for our Kats and Kittys Halloween Bash," I tell Chuchie. The Kats and Kittys Klub, which we belong to, does all kinds of phat stuff, and me and Chanel had been talking about the Halloween Bash ever since the Fourth of July. "We should throw it at the Cheetah-Rama, where Mom goes dancing. What do you think?"

"*Está bien*. I forgot to tell you. I saw those girls from Houston on Sunday down in Soho."

"What girls?"

"'Member the twins who were at the Kats Fourth of July Bash? What were their names?"

"Oh, I don't know. You're the one who was talking to them," I say, feeling a twinge of jealousy. She's talking about those wanna-be singers who showed up and sang when nobody asked them to.

"Aquanette and Anginette Walker," I mumble.

Of course, I do remember, because I remember everything.

Despite my flinching, Chuchie adds, "They can sing. They said they're coming to the Kats meeting on Friday. They moved here to go to LaGuardia Performing Arts High. That's where we shoulda went."

"We didn't go because you were too scared to audition, 'cause of your mother, remember?" I point out.

If Chanel didn't go, I wasn't going to audition by myself, but yeah, I'd wanted to go there, too. I wonder if the twins had to audition to get into LaGuardia. Or maybe they had "connects." They sure had the nerve to floss by singing at the Fourth of July barbecue grill, with the mosquitoes flying in their hair.

"True. They can sing," I say.

"And they can eat, too. The one in the red top ate seven hot dogs," Chanel says with a grimace.

"Which one has the name like the hair spray?"

"I can't remember, but they both had on a lot of that," Chanel says, giggling. "I thought maybe the one in the red top and white shorts had a television antenna up in that hairdo, it was so high."

Dorinda waves as soon as she sees us. I see she has taken my advice and is wearing a black turtleneck top with the khaki boot-leg pants. "Hi!" she exclaims, all excited. "I'm really, really *hungry*."

She is so tiny and pretty. I mean munchkin tiny. She doesn't look like a freshman at all. (She looks about twelve years old. For true.) She is also about the same color as Chanel— kinda like mochachino—and her hair is corn-rowed in the front, then the rest is just freestyle curly. From what I can see, she doesn't have a weave, unless it's an *unbeweavable* one, as Mom would say. Mom can "spook a weave" from the other side of the tracks. And I don't mean the ones in the subway, hello.

"Oh, word, I get to feel even shorter now," says Dorinda, squeezing between me and Chanel. "And I'm wearing heels!"

"We're three shorties," giggles Chanel, trying to make Dorinda feel better. Dorinda is even shorter than us. I feel so much taller with her around. I could get used to this.

"Here comes Derek," I mumble under my

breath. "Don't look at him," I plead with Dorinda.

Derek dips down the hallway and smirks in our direction as he passes. "Hey, Cheetah Girl," he hisses, winking at me. "I'm workin' on that puzzle you gave me." Mercifully, he keeps going.

Dorinda doesn't miss a thing. "Who's that?" she asks, squinching up her little nosy nose.

"That's Derek Hambone from our home-room class."

"He's got on enough letters to teach Daffy Duck the alphabet," Dorinda says, chuckling.

"You are funny." Chuchie giggles. "You should see the way Galleria was looking at Derek in homeroom."

"Oh, don't try it, *señorita*," I counter. "Duh!"

"*Cheetah Girl*—that's kinda cool. You two are definitely blowing up the spots." Dorinda chuckles, fingering my cheetah backpack and reading the metal letters on the straps. 'Toto in New York'? What's that?"

"It's my mom's boutique—Toto in New York . . . Fun in Diva Sizes—down in Soho," I say. I notice that her tapestry backpack with happy faces is fly, too.

"What street is it on?" she asks me.

"West Broadway, off Broome Street," I tell her. "My mom makes these and sells them in her store."

"Really?"

"Really. She's a dope designer. Nobody makes clothes in diva sizes like she does. See how fat his stomach is?" I add, patting my backpack's paunchy stomach, "and the straps are leather, not pleather, like they put on the cheesy backpacks they sell on Fourteenth Street."

"How do you know it's a he?" Dorinda asks, her slanty brown eyes getting even slantier. Definitely Cheetah material.

"'Cause he eats more." I laugh, stuffing my textile design book into his fat paunch, then zip it up.

Dorinda has intense eyes, which she now focuses on Chuchie's cheetah. "You got one, too, huh?"

Chuchie nods her head and grins. "Whatever Secret Agent Bubbles gets, I get."

"You wish, you bumbling bourgeois detective!"

Chuchie hits me with her backpack.

"Oh, that's the top you said you were gonna wear," Dorinda says, turning to me. "What's it say?"

"Powder to the People. Grace is on the case. Will is chill. Sean is a fawn. I'm Fierce, You're Fierce," I say, pointing all over my top. "Whatever supa-licious things we come up with. Me and Chanel marked up a lot of tops this summer and sold them at our lemonade stand."

Dorinda really looks impressed.

"People were loving them. Bubbles's mom made them in bigger sizes and sold them in her store, too," Chuchie chimes in, bragging about our designing bite.

"Diva sizes," I say, correcting Chuchie.

"*Lo siento, mija.* I'm sorry!"

"My mom says there are no large sizes, just sizes that are too small!" I explain.

"I want to do some," Dorinda says.

"You gotta use black fabric marker so it won't wash off in the washing machine. But you can't put it on synthetic fabrics like poly-ester," I explain to her. "You could write on that with a blowtorch and it would bounce off."

Dorinda giggles ferociously. "That's funny.

How long you two been best friends?" she asks.

"Oh, this dish rag? I've known her since we took our first baby steps together. Both our mothers were models back in the day," I explain.

"Were they, like, in *Essence* magazine?" Dorinda asks me.

"My mom was. But the only modeling Juanita ever did was for *Chirpy Cheapies* catalogs, and Chanel has a lifetime supply of those wack-a-doodle-do clothes to prove it." I giggle.

"Yes, my mother was the diva of the discount catalogs, I confess, but it paid the bills, and now I got skills, okay?" Chanel snaps her fingers in Z formation. "My mom just wrote a book," she tells Dorinda. "She went all over Europe and Japan to write about the history of Black models since back in the day."

"Really?" Dorinda is hugging her books to her chest as we walk outside, cross the street, and slip into Mikki D's.

"Uh-huh. It's called *They Shoot Models, Don't They?*" Chanel says. "Get it? Photographers take pictures of models with cameras."

"Word. I got it."

"I just wish she would hurry up and get the money for it so she could give me some," Chanel whines in her best Miss Piggy voice as she orders from the Mikki D's counter clerk.

Chuchie is a shopaholic waiting to happen. Even I know that. Even worse than me. Getting ready for high school has left us pretty busted, though.

"These twenty-five duckets a week ain't stretching very far at the S.N.A.P.S. counter," Chanel says with a sigh.

"They are definitely drizzle duckets."

"What's that mean?" Dorinda asks.

"It means, 'If it rains, we poor!'" I giggle. "Stick with us and you'll learn a lot of words."

"I want to be a writer, too," Dorinda says. "I read a lot. My mom says I should open a library so I won't have to go there all the time."

"You go just for fun?" Chuchie asks in disbelief.

"Yeah. I take out books all the time. You should see how many books I got under my bed!"

"Like what kind of books?"

"You know. *Sistah's Rules. Snap Attacks. I'm Fierce, You're Fierce.*" She giggles, making fun of us.

She is mad funny. I didn't want to ask

Dorinda how much allowance she gets, because that would be rude. Our moms pay the bills for our cell phones, beepers, bedroom phones, Internet service, blah, blah, blah, but there are still so many other things that we want but we just have to "cheese" for it.

Chanel, of course, is much nosier than I am. She will ask anybody, anything, anytime—while she bats her eyelashes and acts all cute. "How much do you get?" she asks Dorinda, biting into her hamburger.

"For what?" Dorinda responds.

"For allowance, *mamacita*."

"Oh, I don't really get allowance. But I work at the YMCA Junior Youth Entrepreneur Leadership Program three nights a week, so I make about twenty dollars. If I was sixteen, at least I could get my working papers. That's how I could make some real bank."

"What classes you taking?" I ask Dorinda, changing the subject. I don't want her to feel like she can't hang with us just because she doesn't have duckets. Me and Chanel aren't with that.

"Sketching. English composition. Textile design. Biology. Computers—I love that. I'm gonna learn new technology applications like cyber rerouting and building databases."

"Computer nerd. You go," Chuchie smirfs. I have to laugh. Chuchie only uses the computer to get on the Internet and do her homework, otherwise she could care less about it.

"At least I got the dance class I want," Dorinda continues. "Dunk the funk. That's the move. I've had enough modern for a while."

"I heard that, *señorita*. We're taking it, too! What period you got?"

"Seventh."

"We're in the same class! That's dope," Chuchie exclaims.

Suddenly I remember something. "Check out this song I wrote last night," I say excitedly. And then I sing it for them:

"Twinkle-dinkles, near or far,
stop the madness and be a star.

Take your seat on the Ferris wheel,
and strap yourself in for the man of steel.

Welcome to the Glitterdome.
It's any place you call home.

Give me props, I'll give you cash,
then show you where my sparkle's stashed.

Glitter, glitter. Don't be bitter!
Glitter, glitter. Don't be bitter!
Glitter, glitter. Don't be bitter!
There's no place like the Glitterdome!"

"I like it, Bubbles!" Chanel says, then starts harmonizing with me. "There's no place like the G-l-i-t-t-e-r-d-o-m-e."

She is always down for bringing on the noise. There is nothing we love doing more than singing together—and Chuchie is better at putting music and melody to words than I am.

"Glitter, glitter. Don't be bitter!" Dorinda suddenly belts out, hitting the notes higher than even Chanel does.

"You *can* sing, *mamacita*," Chanel coos.

Chanel is like my sister, but I didn't choose her. We were bound together by lots of Gerber baby food and our diva mothers. Dorinda is different. She is just *like* us, and we only just met her!

"You should come with us to Drinka Champagne's Conservatory on Saturday,"

Chanel says excitedly. "That's where we take vocal lessons."

"How much is it?" Dorinda asks nervously.

"No duckets involved, Do'," Chanel counters. "We're on special scholarship."

"Do'. I like that," I remark, pulling out my Kitty Kat notebook. "Do' Re Mi. That's your official nickname now."

"Okay." She giggles, then scrunches her munchkin shoulders up to her ears. "I'm Do' Re Mi. My sister is gonna like that."

"What's her name?"

"Twinkie. She's nine."

"Like my brother, Pucci. Maybe we can hook them up," Chanel heckles on the mischief tip.

Then she gets an idea. "Oh, Bubbles, you know what would really be dope? Bringing Do' Re Mi to the Kats and Kittys Klub!"

"What's that?" Do' Re Mi yuks.

"Me and Bubbles belong to this 'shee, shee, boojie, boojie, oui, oui' social club—'for empowering African American teens!' Chanel chimes in, imitating the Kats president. "Before, they let us come for free because our mothers were members. Now we have to pay membership fees, but we can go by ourselves—finally!"

"How much does it cost?" Dorinda asks.

Clearly, Dorinda is all about the *ka-ching, ka-ching*. She is so smart. I really like her.

"It's about six hundred dollars, or is it six hundred fifty dollars a year for us till we're eighteen?"

"I think it's six hundred fifty dollars now."

"But don't worry, Do' Re Mi. We got you covered. We want you to sing with us, right, Galleria?"

"Uh-huh," I say. Chuchie doesn't make a move without asking me first. That's my girl-ita! "We're getting together a girl group, like The Spice Rack Girls, only better."

Dorinda brightens. "Awright! Where we gonna sing?"

"I don't know. We'll figure it out," I say. "We were thinkin' of singin' at the Kats and Kittys Halloween Bash. My mom's already makin' us Halloween costumes, anyway. I bet I can get her to make one for you, too."

"What does *your* mother do?" Chuchie asks Dorinda on the nosy tip.

"Nothing," she answers nervously. "She stays at home."

"How many brothers and sisters you have?"

Chanel asks, fluttering her eyelashes. Nosy posy just won't quit.

"Ten," Dorinda says.

"That's a lot of kids!"

"I know. But they aren't really *her* kids. I mean, she's a foster mother—and she's our mother, just not our *real* mother."

For once, Chanel stopped batting her eyelashes.

"Really? Are they your 'real' sisters and brothers?"

"No, but she's nice, my foster mom. She lets me do what I want, as long as I help her and stuff."

"You gonna come with us Friday, right?" Chanel says, not waiting for an answer. "We're on the party committee and we get to help plan all of the events."

I can tell she really likes Do' Re Mi. She is acting like a big sister. Just the way she acts with Pucci, her little brother. I wonder where Do' Re Mi's real mother is.

"You know we're the Kats, not the Kittys, right?" I say to amuse Do' Re Mi, then do the handshake wiggle with Chanel.

"I heard that. What's that you two are

doing?" she asks, extending her hand, too.

"Do it like this," Chanel says, showing her. The three of us wiggle our fingertips together. "All right! We got growl power, yo!"

I can see it coming. Now that we've found Dorinda, all our dreams are gonna come true. All we need now is another backup singer or two, and we'll be ready to pounce.

Chapter 4

With seven dollars in my cheetah wallet until Monday, there is only one filling solution before the Kats and Kittys Klub meeting: the Pizza Pit on Eighty-fourth and Columbus. When we step to the cash register to pay, much to our dee-light, Do' Re Mi makes a donation into the collection plate. "I got it," she says, giving the clerk $7.85 for our pizza slices and Cokes. "You're definitely crew now," Chanel says, giggling to the ka-ching of the cash register. One thing about Dorinda: She is generous with her money, even though she's got to work for it herself. I've never known anybody like that before.

We walk to the back of the Pizza Pit so we

can sit away from all the mothers with road-runner kids. The last time we sat up front, one of them threw a Dino-saurus Whacky Baby right into Chanel's large cup of Coke and knocked it over.

Chanel is sitting facing the entrance. "Look who just walked in," she says, talking through her straw, then quickly adds, "Don't turn around yet!"

It's too late. I already have—just in time to catch the grand entrance of those fabulous Walker twins from Houston. They are about the same height and size, but one of the twins is a chocolate shade lighter than the other. You can tell they're not from New York. The lighter-skinned of the two has on a hot pink turtleneck with a navy blue skirt. The other one has on an orange coatdress with ivory on the side. They look sorta church-y—at Eastertime.

"Heh, y'all. How y'all doin'?" one of them says. The twins are kinda friendly in a goofy sort of way, and their Southern accents just sorta shout at ya, "Y'ALL, we in the house!"

"Wuzup? You two coming to the Kats meeting?" I ask them, knowing full well they ain't here for a lobster cookout.

"Yeah, we're going over there. What we talking about tonight?"

"It's time for general elections. And we have to begin planning our next event. Me and Chanel are on the party committee. What committee are you on?"

"Volunteer services. We wanna plan something for a Christmas drive at a church or a women's shelter."

"We're planning to throw a dope Halloween bash," I counter. "Y'all missed our Christmas party." All of a sudden, I notice that I am trying to talk like them.

"Is that right?" one of the twins asks with a smile. She has nice lips—what we call juicy lips. Her eyes are big, too, like Popeye's.

"What's your name?" Dorinda asks her.

"Y'all, forgive me. I'm Aquanette," exclaims the twin with the pink acrylic nail tips. Okay, pink acrylics tips means Aquanette, I tell myself so I don't forget who's who. I wonder if Aquanette puts the rhinestones on her Pee Wee Press-On Nails by herself.

"You belong to Kats, too?"

"No. I'm just visiting. I'm Dorinda. Dorinda Rogers."

"They got good slices?" Aquanette asks Dorinda. She can't help but notice how quickly Dorinda is eating her food.

"Don't ask me if they're good. I'm just hungry," Dorinda says, smiling at her. Dorinda is s-o-o nice to everybody.

"We'd better order. We'll be right back," Aquanette says.

Anginette, it turns out, is the more vocal one in the ordering department. "Can we get a slice with anchovies, extra pepperoni, mushrooms, and sausage?" she asks the counter guy.

Chanel giggles at me, looking down at her pizza and kicking my Gucci loafers under the table.

"Watch the Gucci, Chuchie! It's leather, not pleather—like yours!"

Recovering from her laugh attack, Dorinda politely says to Anginette, who has returned with two slices and a Coca Cola, "I hear you two can sing."

"Yes, ma'am. You, too?"

"Well, sorta. I haven't been in any talent shows or anything, like Galleria and Chanel, but they're gonna take me to Drink some Conservatory with them for vocal classes."

"You mean Drinka Champagne's," Chanel says, cutting in. "It's the bomb for vocal and dance classes."

"Dag on, they got everything in this town," Anginette says with a tinge of know-it-allness in her voice. "That's why we came up here to go to LaGuardia, 'cause they have the best vocal department in the country."

My first thought is, okay, was that supposed to be a one-up, two-down? My second thought is, she'd better not come for me or I'll read her like the Bible.

"We wanna be backup singers in a group," Aqua explains earnestly, slurping up the cheese from her slice.

"Forgive my sister. She hasn't eaten in five years," giggles her unidentical half. "Actually, we came up here because there ain't enough room in Houston for Karma's Children *and* us!"

Aqua is definitely the funny one. Karma's Children still live in Houston even though they're now famous.

"How old is Backstabba now?" Aquanette asks Chanel.

"They try to say she's eighteen, but I heard she's just sixteen. They still have a tutor who travels with them on the road, so it must be true, 'cause she ain't finished high school."

"I like Jiggie Jim," Angie says. "That falsetto voice, all that screeching—'Aaaaah got to know where you stand, gi-r-r-l,'" she sings, then gasps, "it just gives me goose bumps!"

Hmm. Angie is quite theatrical once she gets her pepperoni quota. She sure isn't biting off her twin sister's flavor.

"Jiggie's groove is cool, even though his voice is a little too high for me, if you know what I'm saying," I counter, smirking, "and I personally am not into guys who wear black sunglasses—at night, thank you."

"I heard there's something wrong with his eyes," Chanel offers, trying not to smirk. "His left eye doesn't talk to his right one."

We all howl. Chuchie *loves* to invent fib-eronis.

"Are you Spanish?" Anginette asks Chanel, whom she obviously finds amusing.

"Dominican, *mamacita*, and proud of it," Chanel says.

"You can call her Miss Cuchifrita," I offer bitingly. "She's going to give out *piñatas* around midnight."

"One week of Spanish and you ready to do show-and-tell," gasps Chanel, batting her lashes at me. "You know what a *piñata* is?" she asks the twins.

"Nope," say Anginette and Aquanette like a chorus.

"They're animals made out of papier-mâché and glue, then stuffed inside with candy," Chuchie explains. "When you hit the *piñata*, all the candy falls out!"

"Oh! I know what they are," Angie says. "They have them in the Santa Maria Parade in Houston."

"Are you Spanish, too?" Aquanette asks Dorinda.

"Nope, I don't think so."

"Is that right? You are so pretty. Ain't she cute, Angie?"

"Thank you," Dorinda says matter-of-factly. "Actually, I don't know my family. I live in a foster home."

Oopsy doopsy. That should keep our Southern Princess of Extra Pepperoni chomping quietly for at least a few minutes.

"We came up here to live with our father," Anginette says, trying to rescue her sister from putting another *"piñata"* in her mouth. "Our mother is a district manager for Avon, so she travels all the time. Our father felt we weren't being properly supervised since they got dee-vorced."

Their mother is an Avon lady. No wonder they're so nice. I am not gonna tell them that I only like S.N.A.P.S. Cosmetics. They've probably never heard of it.

"What does your dad do?" Do' Re Mi asks them.

"He's the senior vice president of marketing at Avon. He was my mom's boss. That's why he moved up here. They got any hot sauce here?" Aquanette asks, turning to her sister.

"Nope," Anginette answers.

"Well, then, gimme yours," Aqua says.

Out of Anginette's purse comes a bottle of hot stuff. We all burst out laughing.

"So it's like that?"

"Y'all laugh, that's okay. If our mother saw us, she would start some drama," Aqua says, pouring the Hot Texie Mama sauce on her slice.

Okay, this is hee-larious.

"They don't have this in New York, girls, so you have to bear with us. We is homesick!"

"Our mom won't let us use hot sauce because it's not good for our vocal chords. Our father don't say nothing, though," Anginette says, waiting for the bottle to come back her way.

"I didn't know that. See, Bubbles, you eat all that hot stuff. I'm glad I don't," Chanel says, acting all mighty.

"We're not supposed to drink soda, either, but I love it," Aquanette adds, slurping her Coke.

"Chanel drinks enough soda to do Coke commercials," I counter. These girls don't even drink Diet Coke. "Is it bad for your voice, too?"

"Yup. Y'all sing in a choir?"

"No, but we go to Drinka Champagne's Conservatory on Saturdays, religiously. We take voice, dance, and theater."

"Y'all should come up to Hallelujah Tabernacle on One Hundred Thirty-fifth and Lenox. We sing in the junior choir on Sundays."

"Well, I'm usually getting my pedicure at that time," I say, giggling. Aquanette has on too much white lipstick. Against her brown skin, it looks like a neon sign, I think, as both Chanel *and* Do' Re Mi kick me under the table from opposite sides. I am gonna make both of them polish my Gucci loafers, I swear.

"What's y'all's range?" I ask, imitating that cute Southern drawl. Okay, so I am jealous. They sing in a choir, which means they can raise the roof off Jack in the Box.

"Mezzo, mostly," offers Anginette.

"Mezzo, too," adds Aquanette. "The gospel stuff is cool, but we want to sing pop, R and B-style music."

"So do we," Chanel says, nodding her head.

"Well, let's sing together sometime. Y'all can come over to our house!" Aquanette screams. "What y'all doing tomorrow night?"

"Well, we sure aren't going to the movies, because the duckets have run out," I say with a sigh.

"Nah, y'all can't be as broke as us. We are more broke than a bad joke! We need to make some money, doing *something*."

Now she is speaking my language. "Last summer, me and Chanel sold lemonade right on Second Avenue and Ninety-sixth Street near the big Duckets 'R' Us Bank, and we made some serious bank. How much did we make last summer, Chanel?"

"Lemme see. About four hundred dollars.

We may have to dust off my Mom's Tiffany pitchers and set up shop again, I swear," she says, giggling.

All of a sudden, I get a brainstorm. "Hey, y'all—we should perform at the Kats and Kittys Halloween Bash. You know, like charge admission. There's five of us—shoot. We could put on a show, we'd be, like, The Black Spice Rack Girls! And wear costumes with, like, spice leaves hanging off or something. I'd pay five dollars to see that!"

"Five dollars? How 'bout twenty-five dollars?" says Do' Re Mi, egging us on.

"Oh, my G-O-D, girl, that's a good idea!" yells Aquanette.

"My mom can *make* our costumes," I offer, bragging about my designing mom once again. She is gonna kill me. No, she'll probably charge me. But I'll worry about that later. "Last year, over one thousand Kats and Kittys came to our Christmas party. And they came from all over the country."

Okay, so I am exaggerating. But they did come from New Jersey, Philadelphia, Connecticut, Westchester, and even D.C., aka Chocolate City. There are over a hundred Kats and Kittys chapters across the country, but New York is the dopest one, and we throw the "dopiest dope" parties. Everybody comes to jam with us.

I'm not sure yet if I like these girls, but I know a ka-ching when I see one. Me, Chanel, and Do' Re Mi have got the flavor, but these two have the voices, and together we can at least put on one show. But first, I know we better get a few things straight before we go blabbing before the committee.

All serious, I say to the twins, "We're gonna go in there and ask the board members to let us do this. How come the two of you don't want to sing by yourselves? What do you need us for?"

"Me and Angie aren't about drawing attention to ourselves. That's not how we were raised," Aqua says, moving her acrylic tips to her chest, then turning to look at her sister. It's crystal clear which of these two operates this choo-choo train.

"We sing in the church—that's one thing— but we're about being humble," Angie says, looking at me earnestly.

Then, like she's on the *True Confessions* talk show, Angie says, "I honestly don't think we are flashy enough to be in a group by ourselves."

I have to give it to them: There is more to these fabulous Walker twins than hot sauce, tips, and chedda waves. They seem serious. "So you think that the five of us together could do some serious damage?" I ask, smiling at Chanel and Do' Re Mi.

"I think we should try it. If it don't work out, at least we'll have had a little fun with the show, then split the money and keep on searching for the rainbow," Angie says, fingering her arts-and-craftsy earrings.

Do' Re Mi steps to the home run plate. "We'll have to agree on the costumes and stuff, because we are not gospel kinda girls."

"We know that. We can see!" Aqua claims. "You three have that New York style. We are not going to come into this and take over. We *want* to be in a group."

"Okeydokey, then. The committee will go for it, right, Chuchie?"

Chuchie nods her head yes.

"All right, then," I say. "It's time to get busy in the jiggy jungle—no diggity, no doubt."

Chapter 5

C hanel and her family, Pucci and Juanita, live in a cheetah-certified loft on Mercer Street in Soho. (Yes, Mom helped decorate it.) In one part of the loft, Juanita has built a dance-exercise studio completely surrounded by mirrors. She likes to look in the mirror when she's exercising, which she does a lot.

Today she is in the studio giving herself exotic dance lessons and listening to some music that sounds *très exotique*. Maybe Juanita thinks moving her middle will make her a riddle to Mr. Tycoon.

"Hi, Galleria," Juanita calls out to me when I peek into the loft. Juanita hasn't gained an ounce since her modeling days. She brags about it all the time. Today she has on a crop top, and a sarong (like you wear at the beach) wrapped around her waist. She is moving a leopard scarf in front of her face right below her eyes, like she thinks she's the Queen of mystery.

"You girls want to come in here?" she asks me without missing a beat.

"No, we're going into the den," I yell back, trying to keep a straight face. Juanita thinks it's cute that we are performing at the Kats show. She has been in a very good mood lately, thanks to Mr. Tycoon.

The way she is wiggling her hips is too much for me. I run into Chuchie's bedroom and start wiggling my hips with my hands over my head. "I know, *mami*," Chuchie says, giggling, then rolling her eyes to the ceiling.

We have been rehearsing for a week, and everybody is getting on everybody's nerves. We can't seem to agree on what music to play for the show, but now it's show time—or, I should say, a showdown. Aqua and Angie are already waiting in the den with the records they want to use for the show.

Me and Chuchie walk into the den prepared to battle. See, our music tastes are exactly the same. We both like Kahlua, and we both like my songs—simple! Right now, I'm ready to throw down for my songs, and I must figure out how to get my way.

Do' Re Mi is sitting there quietly, reading a book called *The Shoe Business Must Go On*. She's very into shoes lately—especially the kind that make her taller! And, of course, she's always into books. I guess that's why she's so smart. Well, I hope she's smart enough to be on my side now.

"Okay, y'all," I begin. "We gotta figure out what we're gonna sing at the bash."

"I love Prince," Chuchie says, starting the negotiations. "Can we do his song 'Raspberry Beret'?"

"No," I say without even thinking. I can't believe her! I mean, what is she thinking? And didn't I just get through saying our tastes were the same in music? Yaaa!!!

"Who gets to choose the music, anyway?" Do' Re Mi asks, getting right to the point.

"We all do, but can't we pick songs by girls?" I say, stumbling. This is not going well. I need a mochachino.

"Who do y'all like?" Chuchie asks Aqua, imitating the twins' accent.

Aquanette says, "I told you. Karma's Children, Jiggie, Ophelia—"

"Uh-uh. No gospel!" Do' Re Mi says, sucking her teeth.

"I brought some house records from my mom," I say. "They're tracks without lyrics, so it will be easy to put my music to them."

There. I've slipped it in. Let's see if anybody has any objections.

"What do you mean, *your* music?" Aqua counters.

Dag on! I think to myself, imitating her. Why can't she just accept that I'm the leader of this pack?

"The songs I write," I explain patiently, pulling out my Kitty Kat notebook. "Don't act like you haven't seen this. I'm writing in it all the time!"

"Oh, *those* songs," Angie says, snuffing me.

So it's like that. I realize I'd better be quiet, before I go off. I guess it's my own fault. What with all the excitement about formin' a group, I hadn't mentioned to them that we would be performing *my* songs, too.

On the other hand, what's wrong with sin- gin' my songs? What do they think we're gonna sing: "Amazing Grace"? See, I'm 'bout to go off, so I'd better shut up for a change.

"What about that group, the Divas?" Angie says, trying to be the peacemaker. "Why can't we do one of their songs, like 'I'll Crush You Like a Broken Record' or 'I Will Defy'?"

It turns out that Angie and Aqua only like gospel singers. I say, "Good as we are, we aren't good enough singers to pull *that* off."

I knew I shouldn't have flapped my lips. I can see them looking at me like, what's she all mad about?

"Me and Chuchie like girl-group types of songs," I say, moving on to another point. "Do' Re Mi is partial to rap—plain and simple."

"Okay, what about 'Nothing But a Pound Cake'?" Aqua asks. This is her idea of compromise? That song is by Sista Fudge, who is a powerhouse singer. She *can* raise the roof off Jack in the Box.

"Aqua, can you just get it into your head that the rest of us can't carry a song like that? We don't have the vocal range!" I scream at her. "And can you pleez think about something else besides eating, okay?"

Oops, I went and restarted the Civil War. Aqua gives me a look that shoots right through me.

"Yeah, that's right. We're so used to singing together or with the choir, I forget y'all can't sing like us," she says, showing off, no doubt. "We definitely need to pick pop songs so y'all can stay in the middle notes."

After two hours of fighting, we finally pick two songs we can all agree on.

The singer we *all* like is Kahlua. We choose two of her songs: "Don't Lox Me out the Box," and "The Toyz Is Mine," which is a duet Kahlua does with Mo' Money Monique. It actually is perfect for five-part harmony because it has lots of choruses and refrains.

Of course, I still want to add some of my own songs to the mix. What is wrong with Aqua? I ought to clock her. And Angie, too. She is more sneaky. She'll smile in your face, then go along with her sister. First thing I'll do is drill right into Angie's chedda waves!

I can't deal with this drama today, not until I talk with Mom and figure out how to tell Aqua and Angie (without going off) that we are singing at least *one* of my songs. I know we are only doing this for a Halloween show, but it would make it so much more fun.

Forming the group (at least for the bash) has inspired me to write a song about it called "Wanna-be Stars in the Jiggy Jungle." I've been dying to let them hear it for days now.

Well, later for them. I know my songs are dope. They are probably jealous. They can sing, but they can't write songs. Angie and Aqua already told us that. They are gonna have to give it up.

"Okay, girls. Time to go home! I'm expecting company, and I don't want a bunch of kids hangin' round when he gets here," Juanita yells. Chuchie and me look at each other and stifle a giggle. We know who "he" is, all right. Juanita and Mr. Tycoon are doing the tango. Pretty soon, she's gonna be showin' off the rock—and is it ever gonna be a boulder! It'll probably topple her over.

"I have to go, anyway," Do' Re Mi says. "I've gotta go baby-sit my brothers and sisters while my mom takes one of the kids down to the foster care agency."

"Why, wuzup?" Juanita asks. "Is everything okay at home, baby?"

"Um . . . uh-huh," Dorinda says, pasting a

smile on her face. But I know, and so do Chuchie and Juanita, that things at Do' Re Mi's house are always in crisis. Kids comin', kids goin', all the time. I feel bad for her. It really makes me and Chuchie appreciate all we've got: two parents who love us (even though Chuchie's are divorced), and plenty of duckets for whatever we need (even if we do have to do a lot of cheesin' to get it).

I'm glad we got Do' Re Mi into our girl group. Once we perform, we're gonna get her into the Kats and Kittys for free. We already arranged to get her into Drinka Champagne's for nothing—Drinka calls it a "scholarship." Well, Do' is sure a scholar.

"Bye, Miss Simmons," I hear Angie and Aqua yell to Juanita.

Now that the others have gone, me and Chuchie have to go look at a few spaces. As the officers on the party committee, it's our job to find a club to hold the event.

We need to find a majordomo club, too, because a lot of Kats and Kittys will come to a party as laced as this one. Mrs. Bugge, the club president, will then work out an arrangement with the club owner after we choose a space.

That's the one thing I like about being an officer at the Kats and Kittys Klub: We get to feel large and in charge—even though we are "minors." (Yuk. I hate that word.)

"Let's check out the Cheetah-Rama," I say to Chanel, who is lost in her own *Telemundo* channel. I can tell there is something on Chanel's mind because she is real quiet, and Chuchie is not a quiet girlita, if you follow the bouncing ball.

Chanel leans on the refrigerator door, twirling one of her braids for a second, then takes a deep breath and blurts out, "Who's gonna be the lead singer of the group?"

"Me and you, *of course*," I answer, trying to be chill. "Look, Do' is the best dancer. No doubt. She can harmonize with us. Aqua and Angie are the background singers. That's cool, right?"

"*Está bien, mamacita.*" She breaks out into a smile. I know she wants to sing lead on "The Toyz Is Mine." And that's fine by me, 'cause when we sing *my* songs—and we *are* gonna sing my songs—there's only gonna be one lead singer: and that's me.

Chapter 6

Seventh period, every Thursday, dance class is definitely the highlight of our week. Me, Chanel, and Do' Re Mi are a crew now. We meet during lunch and after school every day. Then we go over to Chanel's loft in Soho and practice our vocals with Aqua and Angie. (Things are still touchy between us, but I'm not touching it—for now.)

Today, I'm wearing a calfskin black blazer with a matching miniskirt and a cheetah-print turtleneck. Chanel has on leopard jeans and a red top. Do' Re Mi is wearing a black denim jumper. She has it zipped down a little so you can see her red tank top.

I want to surprise Do' Re Mi with a cheetah

backpack when we go to my mom's boutique on Saturday, so I've been really nice for a change. I've helped clean the kitchen every night and I've been reorganizing my room.

Last night, me and my mom watched a special on chimpanzees as we hand-sewed some new leopard pillow shams for the bedrooms. Dad says the best tailors in Italy still sew by hand, and he said he was proud of me. When we got ready for bed, I rubbed Mom's shoulders. She told me to stop tickling her. I'll get better at it. I'm sure Do' has a book I could read on massage.

In the locker room, Dorinda takes off her top. She always wears a white training bra, but she doesn't have much to train. She is flat-chested like Chanel. Ouch. I don't know if it bothers Do' Re Mi, so I don't have jokes about that. I wear a regular 34B bra already, and I've got the big hips to go with it.

Do' Re Mi hums to herself all the time, now that we are singers. She is so tiny, she easily could have been a ballerina. She has a perfect little body. She is really muscular.

"I took gymnastics all through junior high," Do' Re Mi tells us while she is changing. "I miss it."

"You have to have perfect balance for that, right?" Chuchie asks.

"No doubt," explains Do' Re Mi. "That horse is no joke. Once I came down hard on it. I was about six—and bam! I hit my thigh. I was crying. Mrs. Bosco—I mean my mother—had to come to school to take me home."

Mrs. Bosco. That is the name of her foster mother, I realize. Do' Re Mi never told us that before. I wonder if the kids in school ever made fun of her for having a foster mother instead of a real mom.

"Did you tell your mother about the show we're doing?" Chuchie asks her.

"Of course, silly. She says it's cool," Do' Re Mi explains, stuffing her clothes in a locker. "But she really wants me to be a teacher. I don't want to do that."

I wonder where Do' Re Mi's real mother is, but I'm not going to ask her that. I hope one day she will tell us.

"Where did you get your, um, last name from?" Dorinda asks me, hesitating. "It's so different."

"My dad is Eye-talian." I giggle. "He's from Bologna, Italy. There was a guy named

Garibaldi in Italy. He was a hero because he freed the country."

I change into the new leopard bodysuit I just got that I'm going to wear with black tights. "My dad says he saw his first opera when he was nine," I tell Do' Re Mi, because she is very into me talking about my family, anyway. "It had a Black opera diva from the United States, and that's when he knew he would come to the United States."

I wonder if my dad's dreams have come true. He says he wanted to marry a Black opera diva, but that Mom is the closest thing because she looks like one. When they joke around, she mouths opera for him, and he sits in the chair and watches her. I try not to laugh.

Me and Chanel like to stay in the back of the gymnasium, just in case we feel like doing different dance steps or making up new moves. Dorinda likes to stay in the front. She is the best dancer in the class, and Ms. Pidgenfeat smiles at her as she walks around to correct our movements.

"Everybody watch Dorinda," she yells whenever she wants us to get a dance step down. Do' Re Mi has all the moves down to jiggy perfection. I'm kinda jealous, but then I think about how much I like her. She is definitely crew forever.

Today we go back to Drinka Champagne's Conservatory for our vocal lessons. They were closed for a very long summer vacation because Drinka was on tour in Japan. She is a famous singer from the disco era, who founded the conservatory for divettes-in-training like me and Chanel. (After practicing with Aqua and Angie, I do realize how much practice *I* need.)

Drinka had an ultra-hit disco song back in the day called "Just Sippin' When I'm Not Tippin'." It was number one on the Billboard Dance Charts in 1972 for thirty-seven weeks. I know this because she has told us about the same number of times.

Drinka is finishing a class and standing by the receptionist. She is wearing silver spandex pants with a matching top, and a silver apple-jack hat that almost covers her face. Her pointy sequined slippers (yes, they're silver) curl up at the toes and make her look like Tinker Bell. "I think it looks like she's got tinfoil on her feet!" argues Do' Re Mi.

Everyone at the conservatory is excited about our singing at the Kats and Kittys Halloween Bash.

"Get paid, girls!" Miss Winnie, the receptionist, says, cheering us on. She is so nice. "You girls are gonna have to work hard together," she explains, giving Do' Re Mi her very own card stamped VOCAL 201. Do' Re Mi is supposed to start with Beginners Vocal 101, but because we're performing together, Miss Winnie lets her join our class.

For the first thirty minutes of class, we do scales. Wolfman Lupe plays the piano to guide our vocal warm-up. Doing scales means singing from the upper to the lower chambers in the voice to help loosen it up. It's kinda like stretching before dancing.

After warm-up, Drinka comes into the studio and teaches the vocal class. "Okay, pretty girls, show me what you can do," Drinka says, clapping. She tells us, "You have got to have a theme and a dream and a mind like a money machine."

We are lucky, no doubt, to be getting such primo vocal training for free. For the past two years, we've also gotten to take dance classes here, too. I mean we've learned all the global moves. Caribbean, Brazilian, and African are my favorite dance classes because we get to stomp around to the beat of live drummers. In salsa class, we dance to musicians playing conga drums.

After Drinka's, we have to hook up with Angie and Aqua at the subway station. I call them on my cell phone to make sure they're on the way. Angie and Aqua are coming from Ninety-sixth Street and Riverside Drive, where they live with their father. We meet them at the end of the platform at the Times Square station.

We have to take the N train to the Prince Street station to go to my mom's boutique. Aqua, Angie, and Do' (Do' Re Mi's shortened nickname) sit huddled together on one subway seat while me and Chuchie sit on a parallel one. I think the three of them—Angie, Aqua, and Do' Re Mi—feel more relaxed together, even though we are *all* a crew. I mean, Do' Re Mi loves to cook and sew, and so do Angie and Aqua. They all cook at home, too. They're huddled together peeping at a recipe for "Dumbo Gumbo" in *Sistarella* magazine. Like me, Chuchie is not interested in cooking. It takes her an hour to boil Minute rice. (She cooked it once. Yuk.)

The officers of the Kats and Kittys Klub were excited about our upcoming performance at the Halloween bash. "Why didn't you two think of this before, Galleria?" asked Ms. Bugge, when we told her our plans.

I told her, "Me and Chanel never wanted to perform by ourselves. That's not our idea of a show."

Now there are five of us. Five fab divettes. Hmmm . . . maybe that would be a good name for the group. . . .

I pull out my Kitty Kat notebook and start to dawdle and diddle. Five Fab Divettes. Nah. It sounds like a set of dining room chairs.

See, you have to have a catchy name for a group, and a theme that comes from the heart. That's what Drinka was tryin' to tell us.

Do' Re Mi looks at us and asks if everything is okeydokey. She is always looking out for her peeps. I like that about her.

"We're chillin'." I smile. "You like house music?"

"Some of it," Do' Re Mi says, shrugging. "Why?"

"We can borrow some of my mom's records to use as tracks for the show." Now that we have memorized the lyrics to both of Kahlua's songs (a small miracle), we can concentrate on my songs. And my songs need tracks. That's where my mom's house music comes in. All music, no words. Angie and Aqua still haven't given in on singing my songs, so I expect another battle on this. But I figure if I have Do' Re Mi on my side, that will make three against two.

"Sometimes my mom cranks up the house music in the store and dances. She says it's like going to church," I tell her.

"That's funny." Aqua laughs, hearing me. "She should come to our church. She'd have a good time, then. 'Cause we get down."

We are planning a trip to Aqua and Angie's church, but not until after the show, because we are all mad hectic. I pray that Aqua and Angie don't suggest we use gospel music tracks for the show. For now, it's too noisy to talk about it. That's the subway for you.

We are going down to my mom's store to see if she will make our costumes. Of course, I know my mom will make me sign an IOU—

which really means, pay now *and* pay later. Pay later in duckets, and pay now by cleaning my room. Not every day, mind you, but every hour.

I also want to give Do', Aqua, and Angie a surprise. The question is, will my mom cough up three more cheetah backpacks so we can look like a real crew? (Stay tuned, Kats and Kittys, to find out. . . .)

My mom's boutique is the brightest store on the block. You can see it all the way down West Broadway, which is a five-block-long strip of boutiques. A lot of famous divas come to my mother's store to shop.

We climb the five steps up to the big glass door entrance of Toto in New York. "If my mom offers you anything to eat, take it or she'll think there's something wrong with you," I whisper to Do' Re Mi.

Chanel presses the buzzer so we can get buzzed in. All the dope boutiques in New York have buzzers because a lot of shoplifters, or boosters, try to come in and "mop" stuff. That means shopping for free. Boosters don't usually come into my mother's store because they are more scared of her than of the police.

"Ooh, Toto in New York, that is so cute," Angie says, looking up at the lime green and hot pink sign flapping in the wind.

"Ooh, look at all the leopard clothes. They got clothes to fit us?" Aqua asks all excited when we get inside.

"You keep eating like you do and they will," I smirk as we plop down on the big leopard-print love seat and wait for my mom. We can't interrupt her because she is doing her leg lifts against the counter. A house music song, "You Think You're Fierce," is playing on the sound system.

"See, that's house music," I mumble to Aqua. Bet they've never met anyone like my mother in Texas. Aqua and Angie are watching my mother in awe. (Their mouths are open.)

Mom weighs 250 pounds. That's 120 pounds more than she did as a model—something "Madame" Simmons loves to make digs about—but she is as beautiful now as she was back then. And I'm not saying this because she is my mother. My mom was and is a real diva— not just "back in the day," but today.

"We can't walk down the streets without some man goospitating and whistling at her," I tell Do' Re Mi proudly. "One guy stopped us right and asked my mom, "Girl, is it your birthday, 'cause you sure got a lot of cakes back there?" She hit that bumbling Bozo over the head with her leopard pocketbook. "I'm sure he's still recovering, somewhere over the rainbow." I smirk at Do' Re Mi.

Get me through this show, I pray silently to Mom's Josephine Baker poster. (See, an old-school diva like Baker, who used to have a leopard for a pet, understands what I'm going through.)

"Where's Toto?" I ask.

"Toto, come here, cream puff. I said come here!" Mom screams. Poor Toto comes charging out of the dressing room, where he was sleeping on the cushion, and makes a beeline under the couch because he doesn't see me. His hair is matted on the side like mine is when I first get up in the morning.

"Galleria, look at Toto! He gets so scared when I yell at him—he looks like a dancing mop!" Mom screeches.

"Come here, Toto. I want you to meet my

friends," I coo, trying to comb out Toto's hair with my fingers. I like when his hair is perfect like cotton candy, but Mom likes the untamed look, so he only goes to the beauty parlor every two months. Toto is ignoring me and he starts walking on his little doggie booboo.

"Toto, that's enough. Stop dragging your furry butt on the floor. I just got it waxed!" Mom yells, then starts pinning some burgundy velvet fabric on a dress form.

"These your friends from Kats and Kittys?" she asks.

"Yup."

"Where are you two from?" Mom asks, looking at Aqua.

Turning to look at me, then back to my mom, Aqua asks, "You mean me?"

Chanel kicks me. I kick her back.

"Yes, you, darling. You see anyone else here I don't know? You can call me Dorothea, by the way," Mom says.

"Oh, I'm sorry, Ms. Dorothea," Aqua says. "I didn't know you were talking to us. Um, we're from Houston."

"Houston. They have the best shopping mall in the world." Mom swoons. "And I should know. I've been to every shopping mall from here to Hong Kong. Did Galleria tell you I named her after the mall there?"

"The Galleria? Is that right?"

"That is right," Mom says, all pleased with herself. I've heard this story a ca-zillion times. "I was in Houston modeling for a fashion shoot. I was so bored because I didn't know anyone there—well, anyone I wanted to see— so I went shopping at the Galleria. That's where I bought my first pair of Gucci shoes," she goes on. "I was pregnant and I wanted to remember the moment forever. Most beautiful shoes I've ever had. Burgundy-sequined pumps with little bows in front."

"Kinda like Dorothy's ruby slippers?" Do' Re Mi asks, perking up.

"*Exactly*." I smirk. "Mom still has the shoes in a leopard keepsake box, along with my baby pictures and a personal ad that she answered before I was born."

Now why did I say that? I have *such* a big mouth.

"Personal ad, what's that?" Do' Re Mi asks.

"It's for meeting people," Chuchie snips.

"You mean, like, for dating?" Angie asks.

"Yes. Like, for dating," Chuchie says with her *boca grande*.

"'Lonely oyster on a half shell seeks rare Black pearl to feel complete,'" Mom explains with a giggle.

"Galleria's mom answered the personal ad out of *New York Magazine*, and that's how she met her dad. Get it?" Chuchie explains some more. I am gonna get her later.

Aqua and Angie look at each other like they have just met the Addams family, then "chedda waves" catches herself and goes to pet Toto. "Wait until he meets Porgy and Bess," Angie coos, trying to pat his head, but he looks at her and yawns.

"Oh, how cute," Chanel says. "What kind of dogs are they?"

"Oh, they're not dogs," Angie chimes in.

"They're our guinea pigs from home. We couldn't leave them behind," Aqua explains, waiting to see my mom's reaction. I move my feet from Chanel quickly because I know she is going to kick me, but Aqua notices. "What's the matter?" Aqua asks me.

"Oh, nothing," I lie. "I thought I saw a roach."

"A roach!" My mom huffs. "There better not be any roaches in here or I'll go to that exterminator's office and exterminate him!"

"I was just joking, Mom," I say, quickly realizing that I don't want to endanger some poor man's life and leave his wife a widow. Mom would do it. Trust me.

"There's nothing wrong with guinea pigs for pets," Mom says, coming to Aqua and Angie's defense.

Why is she doing that, I wonder?

"Josephine Baker had a pet leopard. That's her," Mom says, pointing to the poster of Josephine. "She was the most famous Black singer and dancer in the world."

"She danced in banana skirts," Do' Re Mi says excitedly. "I know all about her. She was so famous, they shut down Paris just for her funeral."

"That's right, darling," Mom says, approving of Do' Re Mi. "Say, what are you divettes going to wear for the show?" Mom asks.

My mom knows full well the Whodunnit and the Whodini: 1. Why we are there. 2. How cheesy I will get to have her help us. 3. That I am desperate.

What she doesn't know is, I know how to turn the tables.

"Mom, you gotta give us some ideas!" I whine, even though it kills me. Mom loves to give "advice."

"Leopard is always the cat's meow, darling. How about some leopard cat suits? Then you can go to Fright Night on Prince Street and get some leopard masks with the whiskers, like you used to wear for Halloween when you were little. Some little leopard velvet boots or something, and the five of you would look fierce."

"I love it!" says Do' enthusiastically.

"That sounds fabbie poo, darling," I say, imitating my mother, then add for good measure, "Mom, can I get a weave for the show?"

"Do you have weave money?" Mom asks, then continues with her investigation before I get a chance to respond. "What are you going to call the group?"

"We haven't decided yet." I yawn, then pull out my Kitty Kat notebook, where I have written down a few names. "We thought of names like The Party Girls, The Ladybug Crew, A Taste of Toffee—that was Aqua's idea. The Ruby Slippers."

"Oooh, I like that," my mom says, smiling, then she hesitates. "But that's not for you girls."

"Why not?" Do' Re Mi asks.

"Darlings, I've been in this jungle a lot longer than you. Why don't you just stick with what you are instead of looking all over the place for answers?"

Mom then turns and looks at me. "The spots worked for Josephine Baker. They've worked for me. They'll work for you. Don't turn your back on your heritage."

"Your mom is funny," Aqua whispers in my ear. I can't believe it, but somehow the twins are getting along better with my mom than I am!

"'Member what that boy Derek called you in the hallway once?" Do' Re Mi asks me.

"What on earth did that Red Snapper say that was so deep?" I ask her.

"He called you a Cheetah Girl," Do' Re Mi says, then squeaks, "maybe we could all be the Cheetah Girls."

"Do' Re Mi, you are so on the money," Chuchie says, all excited.

"Yeah, we could be the Cheetah Girls," Aqua chimes in.

Angie claps her hands in delight.

Mom had been right. I was trying to be something I wasn't. I guess I can live with the Cheetah Girls, even though it wasn't my idea. Actually, I kinda like it!

"I love it!" Chuchie screams. We hug each other and scream so loud, my mom threatens to gag us and tie us up with fabric.

I catch Mom's eyes, then point to the back-packs, then to my friends, and mouth the word, "*Posso?*" which, in Italian, means "Can I, please?"

Mom doesn't even put up a fight. She walks over to the cheetah backpacks and gives one each to Do', Aqua, and Angie, like it was her idea. "Now, would you please settle down so I can take your measurements for the costumes," Mom says with a smile and a sigh.

"Omigod!" Do' Re Mi gasps, and runs over to give Mom a hug. There is something special between those two already. I'm glad.

Do' Re Mi turns to Angie and Aqua and says, "Y'all are okay with wearing cheetah cat suits, right?"

"That's right," Aqua says with a smile. "Dag. It's just a costume, Dorinda. We do have

Halloween in Texas, you know!"

"Hey, we gotta have a costume for Toto, too!" I say, in a sudden burst of inspiration. "He can be, like, our mascot!" This gets howls of approval, and an okay from my mom. Awright!

When we leave, Toto runs to the glass door and stares at us with his begging, beady eyes. We all wave at him. "Bye, Toto!" "Bye, boo-boo." "See you at show time, doggie-poo!"

Chapter 7

I need to resolve this music thing with Aqua and Angie, today. We have to begin practicing the songs I've written, now that we have the other two down.

Today, Dad drives me down to Chanel's house for rehearsal. He is late getting to the factory, so he is lost in his own world. "How are rehearsals going?" he asks me.

"Don't ask," I groan.

Dad wants me to be a singer, too. I think secretly that my singing has kept him and Mom together. Whenever they fight, I always start singing, and it makes them laugh.

"*Ciao*, Dad," I say, blowing him a kiss as I get out.

I'm glad that my parents are not coming to the bash. It's for Kats and Kittys only, thank gooseness. Between school, rehearsals, dance classes, and vocal classes, I am about to explode like microwave popcorn.

We have two hours to rehearse our vocals before we have to do our dance moves with Drinka.

"Listen, can we just do this?" I say to Aqua and Angie. I am holding my breath because I don't want to fight with them anymore.

Do' Re Mi is going along with the program. She kinda likes my songs. But the "Huggy Bear Twins" (me and Chuchie's secret nickname for them) are hard to please.

"All right," Aqua moans.

"We'll just start with the first verse today," I say, "so that Chuchie and Do' Re Mi can join in. You two listen up and try to come in where you know the words."

We start to sing:

"Some people walk with a panther
or strike a buffalo stance
that makes you wanna dance.

The Cheetah Girls

Other people flip the script
on the day of the jackal
that'll make you cackle.

But peeps like me
got the Cheetah Girl groove
that makes your body move
like wanna-be stars in the jiggy jungle.

The jiggy jiggy jungle!
The jiggy jiggy jungle!

So don't make me bungle
my chance to rise for the prize
and show you who we are
in the jiggy jiggy jungle!
The jiggy jiggy jungle!"

Why are Aqua and Angie leaning so heavy on the chorus? You can't even hear the rest of us! I wonder if they are doing it on purpose. Sure, they are better singers, but they don't have to sing like they're at the Thunderdome.

"Aqua, Angie, maybe you should sing the chorus a little softer so we can hear the harmony more?" I suggest.

"Oh, okay," they both say.

Chanel doesn't say anything. For someone who can run her mouth like she's doing a TV commercial on *Telemundo*, I can't get a squeak out of her when I need her to represent me. Why do I always have to stick up for us? And why is Do' Re Mi singing so softly?

"Do' Re Mi—you need to sing louder after the first verse, I think, no?"

"'But peeps like me got the Cheetah Girl groove,'" Do' Re Mi sings—this time with more gusto. "Like that?"

"Yeah," Aqua answers.

I'm wondering if anyone will boo at us at Kats and Kittys. Could they be that cold?

After dance rehearsal, we are standing outside of Drinka's building. By now, I've had about all I can take. Not only did the singing rehearsal go badly, but the dancing rehearsal went even worse. Especially Chanel—she was so busy giggling she couldn't even get through the numbers!

"Why don't you pay attention to what you're doing!" I scream at her now, losing my cool completely. Angie, Aqua, and Do' Re Mi get real quiet.

"What happened?" Chanel yells. "What did I do?"

"Chanel, you better not mess this up. You have to try to pay attention to what we're all doing so we look like we're doing the same moves."

"I'm not the one messing it up. You are, with your big mouth!" she screams at me. Chanel never screams. Only I do. We argue right there on the street.

Angie, Aqua, and Do' Re Mi wait on the sidewalk while me and Chanel are fighting. "I hate when you act so stupid and you don't listen to me!" I tell Chanel.

"You don't know what you're talking about, you chocolate-covered cannoli!"

No, she did not go there. So what if I was half Italian? She is Black and Latin. I never make fun of her. Well, almost never. I run all the way to the corner and put my arm up to get a taxi back home. It is my last ten dollars till Monday, but I don't care. I just want to run far away.

Do' Re Mi runs after me. "Y'all need to stop! Hold up, Galleria."

"No. I'm going home. I need to chill for now. I'm sorry, Do' Re, okay? I'll see you all tomorrow."

Once I am inside of my safe cheetah palace, I grab a box of my mom's Godiva chocolates. She keeps it hidden in the back of the kitchen cabinet. I don't care if she gets mad at me. So what? Everyone else is.

I take the Godiva box and get as far as I can under my blanket. I cry myself to sleep, slobbering on my leopard velvet pillow while I'm chomping on the candy. How could Chanel call me that? I feel like dragging her by her fake braids right down the street. I didn't even know she knew what a cannoli was.

I miss Toto. He's out at the dog groomer's—finally. Oh, well. He's probably just as glad I'm not suffocating him to death right now. Here I am, just fourteen years old, and my life is finished, I think, as I doze off into a deep sleep.

Chapter 8

What's harder than hiding a spotted cheetah in the desert? Trying not to speak to
your best friend when the two of you go to the
same school! By the time I left homeroom to
make a mad dash to my color theory class, I
was seeing spots from trying to keep my eyes
glued on my desk so I would never look up and
make eye contact with Chanel.

As I walked down the hallway, I concen-
trated on the answers for my quiz on primary
colors: Red and yellow make orange. Blue and
red make purple.

Hmmph, I hiss to myself. Chanel No. 5 can
get on the stage by herself and eat Meow Mix
for all I care.

"Galleria, Galleria!" Chanel yells, puffing down the hallway. She finally catches up to me, even though I still try to ignore her. "I just wanna know. You still want me to do your hair today after school?"

I am so mad, I forgot all about that. My mom is finally gonna let me get a weave, and Chanel is supposed to put it in.

"*Ciao-ciao*, chinchilla, cheetah," I snarl, shooing her away with my hand. "Pretend I'm not here. It's a mirage."

Breathing really hard, Chanel chokes on her words. "I had a bad dream last night, Galleria, for real. Please talk to me. *Per favore*, pleez."

Cheez whiz, Chanel No. 5 has finally learned something in her Italian class. I open my mouth to begin reading her the riot act when all of sudden I hear the word "Okay" slip out of my mouth.

"I dreamed we were on the stage, and you were screaming at me to dance faster, and I was so scared that I was gonna fall because the heels were so high on my shoes," Chanel says without breathing. "I tried to dance, but I fell so hard, and somehow—this is the weird part—I fell right into the people off the stage.

So I started screaming, right, and you, Do' Re Mi, Aqua, and Angie kept on singing. You acted like you didn't hear me scream. Then I tried to run because the people started chasing me and I just wanted to get away."

By now Chanel is giving tears for fears—real drama. So we hug. This was supposed to be fun for us, and it is turning into a *Nightmare on Broome Street*.

"My mom gave me fifty dollars for my weave. You think I could get two strands of hair for that?" I ask.

Chanel blinks at me. She can't believe I'm letting her off the hook this easy. I've got to admit, it's not like me. But I can't be mad at her. She's been my best friend forever, and I was acting kinda bossy and mean.

"Three at least!" she says, giggling. Then she gets serious. "I'm sorry for what I said," she confesses. "You made me mad. I didn't like what you said in front of Aqua that time."

"What time?" I ask.

"When we were at the Pizza Pit and you said I would be giving out *piñatas* later."

"Oh, I'm sorry," I tell her. "I was just playin'."

I was showing off in front of Aqua and

Angie. Now I see that Chanel did the same thing in front of them.

By the time school was out, we were rollin' like usual. First, we had to pick up leopard paper masks with gold whiskers from the Fright Night shop on Prince Street. Then we had to take the subway to Harlem to pick up Do' Re Mi at the YMCA, since she works so close to "It's Unbeweavable!," where they sell hair by the pound.

Do' Re Mi works at the Junior Youth Entrepreneurship Leadership Program Store in the Harlem YMCA. The program is designed for teens who need jobs and it's supposed to teach them leadership skills. Do' Re Mi had to complete a twelve-week curriculum on Saturdays, attend workshops during the week, and work in the store. I don't know how she does it all. She is yawning till the break of dawn half the time.

Because we never miss an opportunity to harmonize, and I am determined to get Do' Re Mi's voice at least a tidbit stronger in the soprano department, we start singing on Lenox Avenue as soon as we pick her up.

"Let's take it from the last verse," Chanel

says to Do' Re Mi, taking charge for a change.

"To all the competition, what can we say?
You better bounce y'all 'cause every Cheetah has got
its day.

You better bounce y'all
'cause the Cheetah Girls are 'bout to pounce, y'all
and get busy in the jiggy jungle
no diggity, no doubt.

Get busy in the jiggy jungle.
The jiggy jiggy jungle.
The jiggy jiggy jungle.
The jiggy jiggy jungle!"

We are stylin' again—and more important, we are crew again—now and forever!

"I've never seen you with hair so long, Miss Thing," my mom says, touching my new Rapunzel weave. "But I still prefer to take my girls off at night and scratch my head."

Mom is, of course, referring to her wig collection. Angie and Aqua get a giggle out of this. They both have gotten their hair done—on the press and curl tip—and I think they're amused by my mom's wild and woolly wigs.

"Is it me, or is it hot in here? I'd better open the door and get some air in here." Mom doesn't wait for us to answer: she just opens the glass door and puts down the stopper hinge to stop the door from closing on its own. We are so excited because we are getting our final fitting for our cat suit costumes for the show tonight.

"Let me see your nails," Mom asks Aqua, who is definitely growing into the supa-show-off of the two. "What is that? Dollar bills?"

"Uh-huh," Angie answers proudly, flossin' about the gold dollar-bill sign decals she has put on her red tips.

"You trying to stay on the money, huh?" my mom says, smirking. "Well, you gotta make some first."

Angie and Aqua only get twenty-five dollars a week allowance apiece from their dad, but he also pays for them to get their nails done twice a month. I wonder if Angie spends as much time on her homework as she does on her nails.

"Fabbie poo," Chanel exclaims as she slips into her cat suit. "This is so phat!"

"Chuchie, you are gonna be over the leopard limit tonight, girlita!" My mom giggles.

The cat suits are all that. Each one has a mock turtleneck collar and zips up the back. Do' Re Mi's has a tail, too, because we thought that would be cute. Do' Re Mi puts on her cat suit, then flosses.

"You know how to work it, Miss Thing," Mom snips. "Not too tight?" Mom asks Do' Re Mi, who is prancing around like she's the cat's meow.

Do Re Mi's cat suit looks really tight, but when Mom asks her again, she just shakes her head sideways, smiling, and answers, "Cheetah *Señorita, está bien!*"

Mom smiles, then holds out a plate of Godiva chocolates for us to munch. She is being so nice to us. I poke Aqua, who excitedly takes a piece of chocolate and smiles. "Thank you, Mrs. Garibaldi. I mean, Miss Dorothea!"

Mom has told them more than once, "Call me Miss Dorothea, but just don't call me Heavy D!"

Aqua and Angie are so used to being formal around grown-ups, sometimes you can tell they don't know how to act normal.

I thought again about Chanel calling me a "chocolate-covered cannoli." I wouldn't tell Mom or she would make Chanel eat a whole box of them.

Chapter 9

The beauty mark Do' Re Mi paints right above her upper lip looks less fake than mine. I decided to try painting one smack-dab in the middle of my cheek.

"She's a fake!" Do' Re Mi hums.

I rub off the cheesy dot of brown liquid liner and try it her way.

"Pa-dow! That's the dopiest dope one," Do' Re Mi says after I'm finished. She has dimples for days. I didn't think there was anyone cuter than Chuchie. I didn't think it was possible. But Do' is running a close second.

We have each painted on a beauty mark and put Glitterella sparkles around our eyes. Theme is everything, I keep repeating to myself. We are starting to be very meow-looking. (Even Aqua and Angie. It's amazing what a little makeup can do.)

"Harmony check!" yells Aqua.

"Welcome to the Glitterdome.
It's any place you call home.

Give me props, I'll give you cash,
then show you where my sparkles stashed.

Glitter, glitter. Don't be bitter!
Glitter, glitter. Don't be bitter!
Glitter, glitter. Don't be bitter!"

We were on point and almost finished "beating our faces," as Mom calls it. She says she thinks we may have a future. She came to one of the rehearsals at Chuchie's and watched.

"Dag on, Galleria. You should just give me this lipstick," Angie says, outlining her full smackers with my lipstick. Actually, we were splitting the one tube of S.N.A.P.S. lipstick in Flack between the five of us, but I was holding on to it.

"That's enough!" Chuchie yells. Flack is this metallic purple-blue color that may give mad effects under the Cheetah-Rama's strobe lights when we are onstage.

"It's not blue, Galleria. It looks more purple in the light," Aqua says, holding up the tube.

"If you get hot sauce on it, it'll be red!" Chanel blurts out, then snatches Aqua's backpack. "Let me check your bag! You can't carry a bottle of hot sauce in your bag anymore. It could break and ruin everything. Just carry packets!" Do' Re Mi giggles.

"That's a Cheetah Girls rule!" I yell out. "Now, come on. We've got one hour to get to the club before show time."

"Do' Re Mi, you sure your cat suit isn't too tight?" Chanel asks, poking Do' Re Mi's butt and pulling her tail.

"No. I'm fine!" Do' Re Mi growls. "You think we'll be able to see onstage with these masks on?"

"We just ain't gonna move too close to the edge so we don't fall off!" says Angie.

Truth or dare be told, Angie and Aqua are lookin' more relaxed than the rest of us. They have more experience singing. And, besides, anyone who could get those church ladies to fall out in the aisles has serious skills. The only experience we had was talent shows and vocal lessons.

"Maybe we should just let Angie and Aqua sing for real, and we lip-synch into the mikes," I turn and say to Do' Re Mi and Chanel, 'cause I'm getting cold feet fast.

"Last dance. No chance," Do' Re Mi says, wiggling her matchstick butt.

We are gonna sing four songs—two of mine, and two of Kahlua's—"Don't Lox Me out the Box" and "The Toyz Is Mine." In the end, we decided to use tracks from all house music tapes to perform to, and sing the lyrics over them.

I can't believe this is happening. Not the performing part. I can believe that. Me and Chanel have been singing long enough into plastic hairbrushes to win the unofficial Wanna-be Stars in the Jiggy Jungle Award. I just can't believe we are actually going to make some money on the d.d.l. (the divette duckets license).

We walk over to the Cheetah-Rama in our outfits. "Cheetah Girls! Cheetah Girls are in the house!" Chuchie yells down the block. It's Halloween, so everyone is looking at us and smiling.

The Cheetah Girls

We are only five blocks away from the Cheetah-Rama, which is at the end of West Broadway near the Mad Hatter Lounge. My mom goes there for tea on Sundays. The Cheetah-Rama is the dopiest dope club. They have cheetah couches and curtains, and my mom has been here a few times to dance because they play house music on special occasions. She drags Dad along, or sometimes Juanita, but sometimes she'll come by herself because she has a lot of old school friends who are still single and who still like to hang out.

This isn't the first time I've been in a night-club, because last year we had the Kats and Kittys Klub Christmas Egg Nogger at the Hound Club in Harlem. But this is the first time I've hung out at a club that my mom the diva has danced at. I feel like it's the jointski, and I'm glad that no grown-ups are allowed here tonight—except for the Kats and Kittys Klub's staff and treasury committee.

Me and Chuchie have only been to the Cheetah-Rama in the daytime. It is kinda dark inside now, and I step on Aqua's foot because I don't see the decline of the ramp inside the entrance. I stumble for a few steps, and Chanel grabs my arm.

"Oh, snapples, Chuchie, 'member that dream you had? Well, it's not a dream!"

I don't care if I fall on my face. We've agreed to make our entrance wearing our masks, but my eyes haven't adjusted to the darkness.

You can tell it's Halloween, all right. The Cheetah-Rama is definitely haunted, with hundreds of Kats and Kittys wearing some pretty scary costumes.

"Hi, Mrs. Bugge," Do' Re Mi yells out. Her costume is hee-larious. She is wearing a green Afro, baseball uniform, and sneakers.

"Who is she supposed to be?" I ask, poking Aqua, who is staring at her.

"Menace Robbins!" she snips back.

"Oh, that guy from the Houston Oilys basketball team?" I ask.

"It's the Oilers!" Aqua snips.

Okay, so I never watch basketball games. Apparently, sports are a very big thing down south, according to the twins.

This is definitely a live party. It is wall-to-wall thumpin'—the music, the crowd, the lights. The excitement in the air is thumping, too.

The Cheetah Girls

People turn to look at us. The Cheetah Girls have definitely made an entrance. It was worth almost falling on my face!

"Cheetah Girls come out at night, baby!" I scream, throwing my hands in the air like I just don't care. Every eye in the house is on us, including some I can't see.

"Bubbles, don't look now," Chanel whispers. She is in back of me, pulling the tail on Do' Re Mi's cat suit, causing Do' to squeal. I turn, and Chanel whispers, "Don't look. Don't look."

I look, anyway. There is someone grinning in a Batman mask. "Holy, cannoli!" I giggle to Chanel. "Batman has big feet." Batman starts walking toward me, but his cape isn't flapping in the wind.

"Hey, Cheetah Girl!"

I know that voice. Oh, no, it can't be. The Red Snapper turned into a Caped Crusader? Gotham City is in deep herring. "Derek?"

"That's me. *C'est moi!*"

"Since when did you become a member?"

"Since you are, *ma chérie.*"

"Oh, it's like that," I say, smirking. His family has the duckets. Why am I surprised that he joined? Copycat.

"Are you taking French in school?" Chanel asks him, poking fun at him.

"*Oui, oui, mademoiselle,*" Derek says, grabbing Chanel's hand to kiss it.

"We're glad to see ya, Mr. *Oui, Oui!*" Chanel says, choking, taking her hand back and wiping it on her cat suit.

Derek seems so different without his Johnny BeDown hookups.

"Where's Robin?" I ask, referring to his friend Mackerel, who also goes to Fashion Industries High with us.

"He's not a Kats and Kittys member. He thinks it's mad corny."

"Too bad. You coulda been the dynamic duo."

"I got a Batmobile outside. Wanna ride later?"

"I don't know."

"Well, if you decide to, just give me the Batsignal." Derek laughs, pointing a flashlight in my face.

"*Au revoir*, Batman." Chanel says, wiggling her fingers.

"*Ciao,* Cheetah," he says to me. "Remember—you could be my Catwoman."

He does have good comeback lines, even if he was super-nervy right out of the box. Maybe Chanel is right—maybe I do think he's kinda cute, even if that gold tooth of his makes me laugh. *Not!*

Mrs. Bugge is signaling us to go backstage. It's show time. We run backstage and pick up the cordless mikes on the floor waiting for us. Then we line up five in a row behind the curtain, just like we rehearsed. Me and Chuchie are in the center. Do' Re Mi is standing to my left, and Aqua and Angie are together, next to Chanel.

"May the Force be with you," I tell Chuchie. This is something mystical, from a Star Wars movie, I think, but my mom always says it. I say it over and over again to myself.

Chuchie squeezes my hand. "Your hands are freezing, Bubbles," she whispers.

I almost wish Mom was here, because I am so scared.

I'm definitely on my own now. With my crew. Not in Mom's shadow. Me and Chuchie have followed the Yellow Brick Road just like we said we would. We made that promise to each other when we were seven years old. We would follow the Yellow Brick Road until we were independent and on our own—and, yes, had money of our own in our cheetah purses. We are never gonna work at Mikki D's.

"We'll always be crew. No matter what happens," I whisper to Chuchie, winking at her. I really do love Chuchie, my ace *señorita*. My fairy godsister.

Do' Re Mi is sniffling. "Do' Re, you're not crying, are you?" Chuchie asks her.

"No!" she giggles. I swear she cries more than the Tin Man. (I'm not supposed to know this, but Chuchie told me.)

My heart is pounding through my ears. At least I know I have one. Deejay Doggie Dawgs is lowering the music. That means it is definitely show time. No turning back.

"Are y'all ready, girls?" Mrs. Bugge asks, sticking her head behind the curtain.

"Ready for Freddy!" Aqua quips. "Freddy Krueger, that is."

Aqua loves her horror movies—and her horror-scope. I can't help but laugh. Freddy is probably out there. And Aqua probably invited him.

"Kats and Kittys. It's show time, and we have a very special treat for you tonight," Mrs.

Bugge announces to the crowd. "It's Halloween. How many of you are scared out there?"

The crowd boos. She is so corny.

"Well, I'll tell you the truth. I'm scared of the girls that I'm about to introduce you to. You may know them as Galleria Garibaldi, Chanel Simmons, Dorinda Rogers, and those singing twins from Houston, Aquanette and Anginette Walker, but tonight they are THE CHEETAH GIRLS, so give them a hand!"

I want to remember this night, forever. Absolutely forever. That is all I keep repeating to myself as the curtain goes up.

The strobe lights blind me in the face if I look too far back into the crowd. Now it is all about the beat. On three, we begin to sing, as if we've done this a hundred times—and the truth is, we have, in rehearsals.

"Don't lox me out the box, baby,
because you'll never know what side I'm buttered on.
My taste is sweet.
I can feel the heat . . ."

Wishing on a Star

The Kats and Kittys are live. They are clapping along to Kahlua's song, and we are really getting into it. Everything is going just as we planned. They won't stop clapping. We wait before we go into the next song, and I try not to look into the audience. There are too many people, and I will lose my concentration.

It's time to sing "Welcome to the Glitterdome." On this song, we are facing the curtain, then we are supposed to turn to sing from the side profile as the strobe lights flash on and off to imitate stars in the sky.

Even out of the corner of my eye I can see that Angie and Aqua are still seconds off from the dance cues. They don't turn as fast as the rest of us do! I do not let this distract me, but I pray that no one notices.

Oh, I could just die, I'm thinking, when it's Do' Re Mi's turn to take center stage and do her split. This is when I see people I know smiling at me. Kats and Kittys who live in Manhattan. They are all in the house!

I am smiling from ear to ear, then pouting on cue as the song goes along. My mike is going in and out, but I can hear a sound as distinct as the sweetest melody—it is the sound of Do' Re

Mi's cat suit splitting. A sound I will never forget! She is giggling, and so is everyone else. The people closest to the stage are pointing and giggling at her. They not only heard it, but they saw it happen, too!

Bless her little heart, as Aqua would say. Do' Re Mi keeps dancing, she doesn't stop, but she cannot do the somersault at the top of "Wanna-be Stars in the Jiggy Jungle" or everyone would see the split in her cat suit—and her leopard underpanties. "Go Cheetah Girls! Go Cheetah Girls!" the crowd is chanting.

By this point, me and Chuchie are laughing, but the show must go on. Everyone is clapping at us, and it doesn't matter that Do' Re Mi's cat suit is split, or that Aqua and Angie don't turn on the right cue. We did it! We did it!

The clapping doesn't stop. "Wanna-be Stars in the Jiggy Jungle" is the song the audience loves best. We can tell by how hard they clap at the end. We take our bows, and lift our masks off, and throw kisses, just like we planned.

When the curtain comes down, we scream. "Oh, my gooseness, lickety splits!" Chanel shouts, grabbing Do' Re Mi's booty as we scramble into the dressing room.

"That's what you get for showing off!"

When we get into the dressing room, Do' Re Mi chews out Aqua and Angie. "Aqua, Angie, you two gotta turn faster when we do that pivot step. What were y'all thinking about?" Do' Re Mi gets all bossy as she changes into her velvet leopard leggings. We stay in our costumes as planned and take our masks off. I'm sweating like crazy.

"We about to get paid, baby," Chuchie yells.

"We don't get our money till next week," I call out.

Chanel sighs. "I know. I'm just sayin'."

There is a knock on the door. "Go away. We're not ready to come out!" I shout.

Mrs. Bugge sticks her head in the doorway anyway. "There is someone who wants to see you girls, so hurry on out."

"It's probably Batman!" Chanel quips.

"No, it's the Joker." Do' Re Mi clowns, and spreads her lips.

"It's the Penguin!" I snap. "And he wants to dance with me." We all squeal and laugh.

"Seriously, though," I finally say, "we're gonna need more practice."

"Yeah," says Do' Re Mi. "And I'm gonna

need a bigger costume."

"Oh, snapples!" Chanel giggles.

"You should have told my mom," I say, trying to be nice to Do' Re Mi, because I know she must feel bad. "She would have made you a bigger one."

"I didn't want to say anything," Do' Re Mi says softly.

"Why not?" I ask.

"You don't understand," she says, blinking back tears. "You'll never know what it's like to have to take everything that people give you just because you're a foster child. Nobody ever made me anything before. I didn't think I deserved it, and I didn't want to screw it up. I'm sorry," she whispers.

"That's okay, baby. Next time, you better open up that little mouth of yours and speak up!" Angie says.

There will be a next time—that's for sure.

"We still coulda served seconds. They were loving us!" Aqua says, lapping up the victory. "Now everybody knows the Cheetah Girls are ready to pounce."

"*You* are, that's for sure," Chanel says, smirking.

Then I say what I cannot believe, but know to be true. "I want us to stay as a group, no matter what happens. Even if we don't make any money."

"Oh, I'm definitely buying a ranch back home," Angie says, snarling. "I don't know about y'all."

"You know what I'm saying."

"We know what you're saying," Do' Re Mi says sweetly.

I spread out my hands so we can form a call-of-the-wild circle. "Let's take a Cheetah Girls oath."

I make up the oath right on the spot.

"We're the Cheetah Girls and we number five.
What we do is more than live.
We'll stay together through the thin and thick.
Whoever tries to leave, gets hit with a chopstick!
Whatever makes us clever—forever!!!"

Then we do the Cheetah Girls hand signal. Stretching out our hands, we touch each other's fingertips, wiggling them against each other.

"None of us ain't ever gonna drop out of the

group, like Rosemary from The Spice Rack Girls, right?" Aqua jokes.

"*Riiight,*" Do' Re Mi says with a drawl.

"And none of us are gonna burn down our boyfriends' houses if we get famous, *riiight?*" Chuchie yells out.

"*Riiiiight,*" we all chime in as we head out of our matchbox dressing room to get our groove on.

The music and screams are loud. Really loud. Mrs. Bugge is standing in the hallway with a tall man wearing a yellow tie and a red suit. I don't think it's a costume. But you never know.

"Girls, someone wants to meet you. He's a manager, and a business associate of Mr. Hare, the owner of the club. Mr. Johnson, I want you to meet the Cheetah Girls."

"How you doin'? I'm Aquanette and this is my sister, Anginette. Did you see us perform?"

I clear my throat so I can talk. "Hi, I'm Galleria, and this is Chanel and Dorinda," I say to Mr. Johnson. I wonder what he thought of our performance.

"Nice to meet you," Mr. Johnson says, shaking my hand. "Well, you girls are cute. I came down to pick up a check from Mr. Hare, and I thought I would stick around and check out your act."

Our act. That sounds pretty cool.

"I heard the name of the group—the Cheetah Girls, and it sounded cute. I was wrong, though," Mr. Johnson continues.

"What do you mean?" I ask him, feeling my cheeks turn red.

"You were splendiferous. Fantastic. Marvelistic. You know what I mean?" Mr. Johnson says.

He sure has a way with words. We all laugh and get excited. A manager! I wonder what that is.

"What do you do?" I ask him.

"Oh, I'm sorry. My name is Jackal Johnson, and I have a company called Jackal Management Group. I think you girls need a good manager like me to get you a record deal. You understand?"

"We understand," Do' Re Mi chimes in.

"Here is my card. I'll expect to hear from you soon. I think, with the right management and direction, the Cheetah Girls can really go places—and I'd like to take you there. We can set up a meeting for next week."

"We'll call you," Chanel says, holding my arm.

"Next week," I add.

When we head down to the party, it's like a dream. Just the way I've imagined it a thousand times. Now it's really happening!

"I have one thing to say," says Do' Re Mi, sashaying to the dance floor. "The Spice Rack Girls had better bounce, baby, 'cause the Cheetah Girls are 'bout to pounce!"

No diggity, no doubt!

"Wanna-be Stars in the Jiggy Jungle"

Some people walk with a panther
or strike a buffalo stance
that makes you wanna dance.

Other people flip the script
on the day of the jackal
that'll make you cackle.

But peeps like me
got the Cheetah Girl groove
that makes your body move
like wanna-be stars in the jiggy jungle.

The jiggy jiggy jungle!
The jiggy jiggy jungle!

So don't make me bungle
my chance to rise for the prize
and show you who we are
in the jiggy jiggy jungle!
The jiggy jiggy jungle!

Some people move like snakes in the grass
or gorillas in the mist
who wanna get dissed.

Some people dance with the wolves
or trot with the fox
right out of the box.

But peeps like me
got the Cheetah Girl groove
that makes your body move
like wanna-be stars in the jiggy jungle.

The jiggy jiggy jungle!
The jiggy jiggy jungle!

So don't make me bungle
my chance to rise for the prize
and show you who we are
in the jiggy jiggy jungle!
The jiggy jiggy jungle!

Some people lounge with the Lion King
or hunt like a hyena
because they're large and in charge.

Some people hop to it like a hare
because they wanna get snared
or bite like baboons and jump too soon.

But peeps like me
got the Cheetah Girl groove
that makes your body move
like wanna-be stars in the jiggy jungle.

The jiggy jiggy jungle.
The jiggy jiggy jungle.

So don't make me bungle
my chance to rise for the prize
and show you who we are
in the jiggy jiggy jungle!

The jiggy jiggy jungle.
The jiggy jiggy jungle.

Some people float like a butterfly
or sting like a bee
'cause they wanna be like posse.

Some people act tough like a tiger

to scare away the lynx
but all they do is double jinx.

But peeps like me
got the Cheetah Girl groove
that makes your body move
like wanna-be stars in the jiggy jungle.

The jiggy jiggy jungle.
The jiggy jiggy jungle.

So don't make me bungle
my chance to rise to the prize
and show you who we are
in the jiggy jiggy jungle.

The jiggy jiggy jungle!
The jiggy jiggy jungle!

The Cheetah Girls Glossary

bank: Money, loot.
boho: An artsy-fartsy black bohemian type.
bomb: Cool.
bozo: A boy who thinks he's all that, but he's really wack.
cheese for it: Manipulate.
cheez whiz: Gee whiz.
chomp-a-roni: Trying to catch a nibble on the sneak tip.
cuckoo for Cocoa Puffs: Going bonkers.
diva size: Dress size fourteen and up.
divette-in-training: A girl who can't afford Prada or Gucci—yet.
don't be bitter!: Go for yours!

duckets: Money, loot.

flossin': Showing off.

goospitating: Looking at someone cute like they're lunch.

growl power: The brains, heart, and courage that every true Cheetah Girl possesses.

jiggy jungle: A magical place inside of every big city where dreams really come true—and every cheetah has its day!

majordomo dope: Legitimate talent.

nosy posy: A person who is nosy and can't help it.

one up, two down: One-upmanship.

pastamuffin: A dog with wiggly hair.

peeps: People.

powder to the people!: Never leave home without your compact.

raggely: In need of beauty parlor assistance.

smirfs: Smirks.

wack-a-doodle-do: Very corny.

wanna-be: Not a real player—yet!

Shop in the Name of Love

For my fluffy,
smoochy, barky
boo-boo Cappuccino
I wuv you.

Chapter 1

Princess Pamela does *la dopa* braids, thanks to me. When I was ten years old, I taught her how to do all the *coolio* styles—frozen Shirley Temple curls, supa dupa *flipas* that don't flop, and even unbeweavable weaves. Of course, I was too young to go to beauty school, but sometimes, *tú sabes que tú sabes*—you know what you know—as my Abuela Florita says. *Abuela* means grandma in Spanish. And my *abuela* knows what she knows, *está bien?*

Doing hair and singing are what *I*—Chanel Coco Cristalle Duarte Rodriguez Domingo Simmons—know best. (You don't have to worry about remembering all my names, because everyone just calls me Chanel, Chuchie, or Miss

Cuchifrita—except for my Abuela Florita, who now calls me by my Confirmation name, Cristalle, because, she says, I'm a shining star—*una estrella*.)

Now that I'm part of the Cheetah Girls—a girl group that is destined to become *muy famoso*—one day I will have lots of *dinero* to open my own hair salons. Miss Cuchifrita's Curlz—yeah, there'll be two of them, right next door to both of my dad's restaurants, so that I get to see him more.

"Chanel, you musta wear the braids bigger, like thiz, from now on. Don't you think you look so boot-i-full?" Princess Pamela coos in her sugar-cane accent. I love the way she talks. She is from Transylvania, Romania, home of Count Dracula and a thousand vampire stories. Her native language is Romanian, which is one of the romance languages—like Spanish, my second language. Now me and Bubbles, my best friend since the goo-goo ga-ga days, say "boot-i-full," exactly the way Princess Pamela does.

My mom doesn't know that Princess Pamela braids my hair. She thinks that Bubbles does it. *Qué broma*—what a joke! Bubbles (aka Galleria Garibaldi) does not have a "green thumb" for hair. She knows how to write songs, and how to make things happen faster than Minute Rice—but I would look like "Baldi-locks" if she did my hair, *comprende*?

I think that once you find out who Princess Pamela is, though, you'll understand why a smart *señorita* such as myself must resort to "fib-eronis" (as Bubbles calls them) just to keep *poco paz*—a little peace—in my house.

"Oooh, they do look nice bigger like this," I coo back at Princess Pamela, looking in the mirror at my longer, fatter braids and shaking them.

I'm so glad I got my hair done today. I usually wait three months, or until I have collected "fuzz balls" on my braids—whichever comes first. But this time is different. We, the Cheetah Girls, have a very important *lonchando* meeting coming up, with Mr. Jackal Johnson of Johnson Management. He was at our first show: at the Kats and Kittys Halloween bash at the world-famous Cheetah-Rama nightclub. We turned the place upside down, if I do say so myself—and we even made four hundred dollars each after expenses, *muchas gracias*!

Anyway, Mr. Johnson came backstage after,

and said he wanted to be our manager—and take us to the top! *Está bien* with me, because the top is where I belong.

Now back to the real-life Spanish soap opera that is my *vida loca*—my crazy life—and why I have to make up stories about who does my hair.

Five long years ago, when I was nine years old, my dad left my mom for Princess Pamela. I still see him every once in a while, but I miss him a lot. So does Pucci, my younger brother.

Back then, when my dad first met Princess Pamela, she had a "winky dink" tarot shop around the corner from our loft in Soho on Mercer Street. It was so small, if you blinked or winked, you missed it, get it? Back then, her name was Pasha Pavlovia, or something like that, but we just called her "the psychic lady."

My dad's name is Dodo, but he is not a dodo. His nickname is short for Darius Diego Domingo Simmons. He was only four years old when he and his sister had to get out of their beds in Havana, Cuba, and escape when Fidel Castro took over. They were sent to relatives in Jamaica, but my dad says he misses his father every day. He misses the smell of the grass, too, and more than anything else, the water. There are no beaches like the ones in Havana, my dad says.

In that way, he and Princess Pamela have a lot in common. She had to leave Romania as a child when the Communists took over there, too. They both know what it's like to lose everything you have and never see your home again. They both have that sadness in their eyes sometimes.

Princess Pamela says when she saw my dad it was "love at first bite." He came into the shop for a reading and I guess he fell under her spell. Princess Pamela is a *bruja*—a witch—who can see the future. Mom hates her, but I think she is a good witch, not a bad one.

"Let me see how it looks with the headband!" I exclaim excitedly, and jump out of the beauty salon chair, hitting myself in the forehead with the red crystal bead curtains that divide the psychic salon from the beauty salon in the back.

"Ouch," I wince as I separate them to go to the front. See, thanks to my dad, Princess Pamela's Psychic Palace on Spring Street is now *muy grande* and beautiful. He built the whole place with his own two hands. He also helped Pamela install her Psychic Hotline, where she gives advice over the phone.

And thanks to her nimble fingers (and me), she now has a hair salon in the back. She even changed her name to Princess Pamela—because "it is a very good name for business—Pamela rhymes with stamina. It can unleash the secret energy into the universe."

Princess Pamela also loves music with flavor—*con sabor*—reggae music, rap, salsa. Sometimes I bring her cassettes, and we dance around if there aren't any customers. She likes Princess Erika, Nefertiti, and Queen Latifah the best. "Why not the Black people here should be like royalty? They can make their own royal family," she jokes, her accent as thick as ever.

My dad also built two other stores for Princess Pamela—Princess Pamela's Pampering Palace and Princess Pamela's Pound Cake Palace—both on 210th Street and Broadway. *The New York Times* rated her pound cake "the finger-lickin' best in New York City."

I am proud of her, and I think Princess Pamela is going to be Pamela *Trumpa* one day, and take a huge bite out of the Big Apple!

"Which headband do you think I should wear, the pink one or the green one?" I yell back to her, as I pull them out of my cheetah backpack. I just got these headbands from Oophelia's catalog—my favorite un-store in the entire universe.

Pink is my favorite color. Or sometimes red is. I like them both a lot. So does Princess Pamela—her whole place is covered in red velvet. Leopard, which is a "color" the Cheetah Girls use a lot, is my third favorite.

"*Ay, Dios mío*, what time is it?" I shriek. "I've got to get home!"

Bubbles, Dorinda Rogers, and Aquanette and Anginette Walker—the other members of the Cheetah Girls—are coming over to my house at seven o'clock so we can practice table manners for our *lonchando* meeting with Mr. Johnson. It may be the most important meeting I ever have. My mom is making dinner for us, and she doesn't like it if I'm not around to help—even though she won't let me get near the kitchen when she's working in there.

See, my mom is very *dramática*. She likes to have her way all the time—and know where I am *all the time*, which is right about now, so I'd better get home.

"I have to go!" I yell to Princess Pamela, who is on the phone fighting with someone.

"No! For that money, I can order flour from the King of Romania, you *strudelhead!*" she huffs into the phone. Then she wraps herself in her flowered shawl and comes toward me, with a little blue box in her hand. "Before you run off—this is for you, dahling," she says, smiling.

My heart is pounding. It is a present from Tiffany's!

"Chanel, this will bring you good luck with your meeting, so you will get many royalties," Princess Pamela says, kissing me on my cheeks and handing me my present. "You get my joke, no?"

"Joke?" I repeat, squinching up my nose.

"When you have a record, you get the royalties. You understand now?"

"Yeah," I giggle. "Besides, maybe I am going to be royalty for real, soon, because of my mom's new boyfriend, Mr. Tycoon, right?"

"Right, dahling. And how is he?"

"He's in Paris right now, and Mom's going crazy waiting for him to get back," I say, rolling my eyes. "You should see her—she's on my case all the time."

I don't want to get into my problems with my mom in front of Princess Pamela, so I keep my mouth shut and open the box. "*Ay, Dios mío!* Real diamonds!" I cry, and hug the princess. I hold up the diamonds to the light to admire them, and then I put my beautiful little diamond studs in my ears.

"Diamonds are a Cheetah Girl's best friend!" Princess Pamela sings, in such a funny voice that I can't stop laughing. "You think I could be a Cheetah Girl, too, and be in your group, Chanel?"

I just giggle at her, wishing I could stay longer. Princess Pamela is so dope—being with her is just like being with my crew. I wish it could be like that between me and my mom, instead of things always being so tense.

"*La revedere*—I gotta go!" I kiss her on the cheek, and hug her tight.

"*La revedere*," she whispers back, saying good-bye in Romanian, and kisses me on the cheek.

When I get outside on Spring Street, it is really crowded. On the weekends, thousands of tourists and native New Yorkers come down to

Soho to shop. They will do the Road Runner over you, too, if you happen to be walking by one of the boutiques where there is a sale! One lady gets a little huffy, like Puff the Magic Dragon, when I don't walk fast enough in front of her—but that is like a breath of fresh air compared to the fire my mom is puffing down my back when I get home.

She is standing in the kitchen, with a spatula in her hand and an Yves Saint Bernard facial mask on her face. It covers her whole face except her eyes and mouth, and it is this putrid shade of yellow-green.

Cuatro yuks! She does the mask thing every Sunday afternoon. She thinks it keeps her looking young for her tycoon, and it must work, too, because he seems pretty gaga for her.

"Do you know what time it is? I'm not here to cook dinner for you and your friends, and to entertain them while you're out somewhere having fun, you understand me?"

"*Lo siento, Mamí.* I'm sorry. I know I'm late!" I exclaim.

"Why aren't you wearing a sweater?" Mom drills me.

"I'm not cold," I squeak.

"Wear a sweater anyway. And what is that on your head?" Mom waves the spatula at me, then uses it to stir the pot of Goya *frijoles* for our Dominican-style *arroz con pollo* dinner.

"It's a headband. Isn't it cute?" I exclaim.

"It looks like a bra strap!"

"It's not a bra strap. It's a headband, *Mamí*."

"Well, it *looks* like you're wearing a bra strap on your head, okay? And where did you get those?" Mom asks, pointing to my diamond stud earrings.

Uh-oh. Where is Bubbles when I need her? She'd be able to come up with something. She always does.

But I'm not that quick, and anyway, this is not the time to tell a real *mentira*—a lie that will come back to haunt me like *Tales from the Crypt*. So I decide to be honest. Why should I have to lie just because Princess Pamela gave me a present? After all, she is my dad's girlfriend, so she is *la familia* to me, I think, trying to get up my courage.

"Princess Pamela gave them to me as good luck for the meeting with Mr. Johnson. Aren't they boot-i-full?" I squeak, hoping to tap into Mom's weakness for "carats."

"She did *what*!?" she screams at the top of her lungs. Her facial mask cracks in a dozen places, and her eyes are popping big-time. Suddenly, she looks like The Mummy. Even through her tight lips, her voice is loud enough to send coyotes running for the hills.

"*When* did you see her? *Cuándo?*" Mom demands, standing with one hand on her hip and the other holding the spatula straight up in the air.

"I just stopped by there on my way home," I whine.

"Don't you *ever* take anything from that *bruja* again. Do you hear me? *Me sientes?*" she screeches, squinting her eyes. The Mummy is walking toward me. I think I'm going to faint.

"And if Bubbles did your hair, how come she didn't come back with you?" my mom asks me suspiciously. "That *bruja* Pamela does your hair, doesn't she? You think I'm stupid." She pulls on one of my braids. "You try and lie to me?"

I have not seen my mom this angry since my dad left and she threw his clothes out the window into the street, and the police came because she hit a lady on the head with one of his Oxford wing-tipped shoes.

"I'm sorry, *Mamí*," I cry, praying she will stop. "I won't do it again!"

"I know you won't, because I'm gonna hang you by your braids!" says The Mummy who is my mom.

I run to my room, grab the red princess phone by my bed and beep Bubbles, putting the 911 code after my phone number. Me and Bubbles have secret codes for everything. She will understand. I sure hope she gets the message, but I know she's probably already on her way here for our dinner together.

I listen to my mom clanging pots and pans in the kitchen, and I let out a big sigh. See, me and Mom fight a lot, especially now that I am a Cheetah Girl. It seems like everything I want, she's against. She does not want me to sing. She says I should get a real job—be a department store buyer or something—because if I keep chasing my dreams of being a singer, I will get my heart broken by living *la gran fantasía*—the grand fantasy. And most of all, she does not want me to see Princess Pamela.

I sit on the edge of the bed, waiting for Bubbles to call back, and I look into the sparkly eyes of my kissing-and-tongue-wagging Snuggly-Wiggly stuffed pooch. Abuela Florita gave him to me as a joke for Christmas, because I always wanted a real dog like Toto, who is Bubbles's "big brother." (Mom won't let me have a dog because she says she is allergic to them.)

Snuggy-Wiggly Pooch is sitting on my night-stand with his tongue hanging out, next to the *Book of Spells* that Princess Pamela gave me (my mom doesn't know about that either).

I sit on my frilly canopy bed and stare at all my dolls. I have twenty-seven collectible dolls. They are *muy preciosa*—very precious—and come from all over the world.

"Charo is from Venezuela and she never cries. Zingera is from Italy and she never lies. Coco is from France and she smells so sweet, *huit, huit, huit*," I repeat to myself, like I used to do when I was little. *Huit*, which sounds like wheat, means eight in French. It's a silly rhyme, but I like it. And right now, I just want to get my mind off my misery.

When I was little, I used to lock my bedroom door, use my hairbrush as a microphone, and sing into the mirror, thinking about all the people who would love me if they could only hear me sing. That's all I ever dreamed about—me and Bubbles singing together, and Abuela Florita sitting in the first row clapping and crying joyfully into her handkerchief.

I have always felt closer to Abuela than to my mother, because she understands me. She would never try to get in the way of my dreams the way my mom does. I know Mom's just trying to protect me from the heartbreak of failure, but why can't she believe in me the way Abuela Florita does?

I can hear Abuela's voice now, telling me what a great singer I am. She says, "*Querida Cristalle, tú eres las más bonita cantora en todo el mundo.*" I know it's not true, because Chutney Dallas is the best singer in the whole world, but it makes me want to sing just for her. Why, oh why, can't my mom see me the way Abuela does?

I let out a big yawn. Suddenly, even though Bubbles hasn't called back, even though it's not even dinnertime, I cannot keep my eyes open anymore.

Chanel is so sweet, *huit, huit, huit.* . . . I think, as I fall asleep, just like a real-life mummy. . . .

Chapter 2

The sound of the doorbell wakes me up out of my deep sleep. I'm still too scared to come out of my room. I can hear my mom talking with Aqua in the hallway. Aquanette Walker is one of the "Huggy Bear" twins (that's my and Bubbles's secret nickname for them) from Houston, Texas. We met them at the Kats and Kittys Klub barbecue last summer. They were singing, swatting mosquitoes, and eating hot dogs all at the same time. We *had* to have them in our group!

My little brother, Pucci, is running down the hall to the door. "Hi, Bubbles! I'm a Cuckoo Cougar! I'm a Cuckoo Cougar! You wanna see if you can outrun me?"

So Bubbles is here, too. I crack the door open and sneak out, to see if I can get her attention without my mom seeing me, and before Pokémon-*loco* Pucci drags Bubbles into his room to floss his Japanese "Pocket Monsters."

"I know you can run faster than me, Pucci. You are 'tha man,'" Bubbles says, hugging Pucci back.

"Are you singing, Bubbles?" Pucci whines, holding Bubbles by her waist. She is like his second big sister.

"We're all singing, Pucci—we're the Cheetah Girls—me and Dorinda and Aquanette and Anginette—and Chuchie, too," Bubbles says, pointing to our crew, who have all assembled in the hallway.

Pucci looks up at Bubbles with the longest face, and asks, "Why is it only for girls? Why can't there be Cheetah Boys, too?" Leave it to Pucci to whine on a dime.

"I wanna be a Cheetah Boy!" Pucci says, yelling even louder, then hitting Bubbles in the stomach. Pucci is getting out of control. When I see my dad, I'm gonna tell him.

"That's enough, Pucci!" Mom yells. I can tell she is still mad, by the tone of her voice. My crew can tell, too, and Bubbles looks at me like, "What's going on, *girlita?*"

"Hey, *Mamacitas,*" I yell at them in the hallway. I pop my eyes open real big when my mother turns her head, so my crew knows there is something going on. *Ayúdame!* Help me, my eyes are screaming.

"Go on, sit down at the table and I'll bring your dinner in." Mom sighs with her back turned. "I'm not eating now because I'm expecting a call from Paree."

She means Paris, of course. These days, Mom uses her new French accent "at the drop of a *croissant,*" as Bubbles says. I can tell Mom is still mad, but I also know she's not going to yell at me in front of everybody. So for now, at least, I'm safe.

As we file into the dining room area, I squeeze next to Bubbles. "What's going on?" she whispers in my ear.

"You got here just in time. I think my picture was about to end up on a milk carton!" I say, bumping into her.

We hightail it to the long dining room table, so we can eat dinner and practice the "soup-to-nuts situation." That's what we, the Cheetah Girls, call table manners.

My godfather—Galleria's dad, Mr. Garibaldi—is from Bologna, Italy, and he can cook like a chef. He says Europeans have better table manners than we do, so Bubbles knows everything. I have good table manners, too, because Abuela taught me. Dorinda, on the other hand, has table manners like a mischievous chimpanzee. That's why we are doing this dinner. She eats too fast and never looks up from her plate. One day, Aquanette, with her *boca grande*—her big mouth—blurted out to Dorinda, "Girl, the way you eat, you'd think you wuz digging for gold!"

Dorinda wasn't even embarrassed! She just giggled and said, "You gotta get it when you can." Do' Re Mi, as we call her, looks the youngest of all of us, and we all kind of treat her like our little sister. But in a lot of ways, she's lived through more than any of us.

Do' Re Mi's had kind of a hard life. She lives in a foster home uptown, with a lady named Mrs. Bosco and ten *other* foster kids. Dorinda says that sometimes they even steal food from each other's plates if Mrs. Bosco isn't looking.

So now that she is one of the Cheetah Girls, we're teaching Do' Re Mi how to "sip tea with a queen and eat pralines with a prince," as Bubbles says.

"*Mamacita*, the braids are *kicking*," Bubbles whispers to me, then touches my new headband and snaps it back into place.

"Ouch," I whimper, then giggle, adjusting my headband again.

"They got any leopard ones? How much was it?" Bubbles asks as we sit down at the table, on our best behavior.

"Eight duckets," I reply. "They came in green, and pink, and I think, black." Bubbles *loves* animal prints. She'd be happy if she could buy a headband that growled.

"You're gonna be broke and that ain't no joke," Do' Re Mi says, cutting her eyes at me. "How much money do you have left from what we earned at the Kats and Kittys show?"

"Not enough to buy an outfit for the *lonchando*," I say, cutting my eyes back. Compared to her, I've always had it easy—Mom and Dad always got me lots of things. Even now that they're not together, I can usually get what I want, up to a point. But see, I guess Princess

Pamela was right about me being "royalty," because nothing ever seems to be enough for me. I never met a store I didn't like, *está bien*? I never had a ducket that I didn't spend first chance I got. And now, my first "duckets in a bucket" for doing what I always dreamed of doing—singing with Bubbles onstage—are drizzling away *fast*.

"I didn't buy *anything*," Do' Re Mi grunts back at me. "I had to give all my money to Mrs. Bosco to help pay for her doctor bills."

"But we gotta look nice for the big meeting, don't we?" I moan. "We can't have you showin' up in old clothes from Goodwill!"

"Shoot, don't worry about it," Aqua huffs. "We ain't gotta impress nobody yet. Let's see what Mr. Jackal Johnson can do for *us* first."

"What do managers do, anyway?" Do' Re Mi asks.

"Nowadays, they just get you record deals and book you on tours," Bubbles explains to us. "You know, back in the day of groups like the Supremes and The Jackson Five, managers taught you everything, just like in charm school. How to talk, dress, sing, do interviews. That's what Mom says."

"Word. Well, maybe Mr. Jackal Johnson is just a jackal who'll make us cackle!" sighs Do' Re Mi, making a joke from one of the lines of Bubbles's song "Wanna-be Stars in the Jiggy Jungle."

After we stop giggling, I add, "Yes, but they are still talking about our show at the Klub."

"That's right. We are all that, and Mr. Jackal Johnson knows it." Aqua pulls out a nail file from her backpack to saw down her white frosted tips, which are covered with dollar-sign rhinestone decals. It's her trademark. She's "on the money"—get it?

"Aqua, you are not filing your nails at the table. That is so ticky-tacky!" screams Bubbles, then slaps her hand. "We're supposed to be learning table manners here—this is a big meeting and greeting, Miss 'press on.'"

"At least she ain't whipping out a Big Mac from her backpack," Do' Re Mi quips, making a joke about the twins because they always carry food or hot sauce with them.

"No Big Macs in my backpack, just got room for my dreams," Galleria says out loud, grooving to her own rhythm. Then she whips out her Kitty Kat notebook and starts writing furiously. "That's a song!"

"Shhh, my mom is m-a-a-d!" I whisper to her, then turn to Do' Re Mi. "To answer your question, I only have about thirty-seven duckets left!"

"That's all!?" the four of them say, ganging up on me.

"I knew you went and bought those Flipper shoes! You didn't fool me, Miss Fib-eroni!" says Bubbles, who is always supposed to be on my side but hasn't been lately.

"I don't care if you don't like them, I think they're *la dopa!*" I protest, talking about the sandals I bought the other day behind Bubbles's back. See, we were hanging out at the Manhattan Mall on 34th Street, and I saw them at the Click Your Heels shoe store. They are made out of vinyl, and have a see-through heel with plastic goldfish inside.

"I don't know why Auntie Juanita wants you to be a buyer, 'cuz you are a shopaholic waiting to happen," Bubbles quips. She calls my mom "Auntie" even though we aren't related. But we are just like sisters. Bubbles has a big mouth, but I'm used to that because she always used to back me up when my mouth wrote a check I couldn't cash. "Now what are you gonna do for a dress for our big *lonchando* with Mr. Johnson?"

"I don't know," I say, feeling like I want to burst out crying. "I've got these great diamond earrings Princess Pamela gave me, and those great shoes . . . but no dress. Bubbles, you still got some duckets left?"

Bubbles whips out her cheetah wallet to show us that she still has the money we earned from performing at the Kats and Kittys show stuffed inside. "I got all the duckets in this bucket, baby," she says, flossin'. "I'm not buying *nada*—and definitely no Prada!"

"Word, Galleria. Your wallet looks like it's having triplets," Do' Re Mi quips. She *would* be impressed.

"Maybe you could lend me some till our next gig?" I start to say, but Galleria cuts me off.

"No way, Miss Cuchifrito!" she says, putting the wallet back in her bag. "Duckets just fly through your fingers, *girlita*. I'd never see mine again. Maybe you ought to just borrow a dress from somebody—or make one, even!"

Just then, my mom comes into the dining room, so we all shut up about money. My mom puts the piping hot *panecitas* and butter on the table. These little rolls are my favorite. Do' Re Mi grabs one and starts spreading butter on the whole *panecita*, then does a chomp-aroni like Toto, and eats the whole thing!

"At least you're using a knife," I say, being *sarcástico*, then giggle. Everyone looks at me, because Do' and I are very close now. We talk on the phone a lot, and I even help her with her Spanish homework. So I guess I'm the one who's supposed to get this choo-choo train in motion.

"Do' Re Mi, watch this," I say, trying to be nice to her. "Break off a piece of the roll, then butter it and put the knife back across the plate like this."

"Word. I got it." Do' Re Mi giggles, then makes fun and starts spreading butter on the bread—oh so delicately, like a real phony baloney.

"You're on a roll, *churlita*!" I crack, then cover my mouth because I'm talking with food in it— and my mom has walked back in the dining room with the platter of *arroz con pollo*. She gives me a look that says, "I'm not finished with you yet." Aqua and Angie are giggling up a storm, like they think it's funny Do' Re Mi has to learn how to eat butter on a roll.

"Don't you two worry, we're gonna steam

roll over *your* choo-choo train, too," Bubbles warns them.

See, me, Bubbles, and Do' Re Mi have *tan coolio* style. We all go to Fashion Industries High School. The twins, who go to Performing Arts, dress, well, kinda corny, and act even cornier.

"Now, assuming Miss Cuchifrita here can make herself an outfit, all we have to do to get the Cheetah Girls on track is get you two some new do's—and outfits you can't wear at church!" Bubbles loves to tease the twins, who are unidentical but very much alike.

"Oh, and I got some virtual reality for you two," I add.

"Virtual reality?" Aqua says, taking her pink-flowered paper napkin off her lap and patting her juicy lips.

"I got the *Miss Wiggy Virtual Makeover* CD-ROM. It has one hundred fifty hairdos we can try, and one of them has just got to be fright, I mean, right for you!"

"We could do a sleepover here the night before our *lonchando*, right, Chuchie?" Bubbles asks. "That way we could take care of the do's right before the luncheon."

"I don't know about that," I say, croaking. "My mom's kinda down on me even *bein'* a Cheetah Girl. Maybe we better do it at your house." I roll my eyes at Bubbles, then toward the den next door, where my mom is talking on the phone to Mr. Tycoon in Paris.

I'm scared for my crew to leave, because then I will have to be alone with her. I take a deep breath, which is what Drinka Champagne, our vocal coach, tells us we have to do to help our singing voices stay strong.

After today's craziness with my *madre, lonchando* with Mr. Jackal Johnson will be a piece of cake. A piece of Princess Pamela's pound cake . . .

Later that night, I'm on the Internet chatting with my Cheetah Girls crew, when I hear my mom yelling over the phone to my dad. "I have a prediction for that *Princess Pamela*," my mom says all *sarcástico* into the phone receiver. "If *she* doesn't stay away from *my* daughter, The Wicked Witch of the Yeast is gonna slice her up like that cheesy pound cake she sells!" my mom snarls, then hangs up the phone. Mom always has to have the last word. I hear her bare feet pounding down the hallway.

"*Ciao* for now!" I type furiously on the keyboard. That's the signal we use when a grownup is coming. I run to my bed and open up my history book. All I need is for my mom to see what I'm talking about with my crew on the Internet, and she may figure out a way to stop that, too.

I know she's about to come in, and I'm dreading the screaming fight we're about to have. But to my total surprise, the knock on my door is so low I almost don't hear it.

"What!" I yell, pretending that maybe I think it's Pucci.

"Can I come in?" Mom asks, in a voice so soft and sweet I barely recognize her.

"Sure, *Mamí*," I say more quietly.

When she walks into my room, she is smiling at me. Now I feel guilty for thinking bad thoughts about her. I've been assuming she was going to get on my case about every single thing in my life, and here she is, being sweet and nice.

"Hi, *Mamí*," I say, trying to act normal.

"Hi. What are you up to? You and the Cheetah Girls have been talking in the chat room, right?"

She is still smiling! Weird.

"Yeah." I giggle, shutting the cover of my history book. No use pretending now. Besides, it doesn't seem to be necessary. She's obviously not mad—but why? *Qué pasa?*

"I've been wondering—what are you going to wear for the lunch meeting with Mr. Johnson, Chuchie?" Mom asks me, plopping down on my pink bedspread. She then crosses her legs, like she is practicing a pose for the Chirpy Cheapies Catalog. My mom used to be a model, you know. Right now, she has put her wavy hair up in a ponytail. She almost looks like she could be my big sister instead of my mother.

"*Yo no sé,*" I answer. "I don't know. I really don't have anything good to wear."

"Well, why don't you go ahead and order that green leopard pantsuit from Oophelia's catalog," she says with a satisfied smirk.

"Well, I can't buy it, because I only have thirty-seven dollars left from the money I got from the show," I say, kinda nervous. Don't get the wrong idea—I didn't just buy shoes and headbands, okay? I also bought a new laser printer for my computer, so that we, the Cheetah Girls, can make flyers for our shows—if we have any more.

"I know you don't have any money left, but I'm glad you bought a printer. So the outfit is on me. A little present. Here," Mom says, holding out her credit card. "You can use my credit card and order that one outfit."

I sit there frozen, not even able to breathe. This is like, unbelievable! My mom offering to let *me*, the shopaholic deluxe, use her credit card? What is up here?

"You sure?" I ask nervously, not daring to take it, for fear I'll be struck by lightning or something like that.

"Yes, I'm sure. I've been thinkin' about it all day. You and I haven't been spending enough time together lately—what with me bein' with my new boyfriend, and you hangin' with the Cheetah Girls. I miss bein' close."

I smile. "Me too, *Mamí*."

"And I know how much this lunch meeting means to you and the girls. So I decided I want you to look your very best."

"Wow" is all I can say. I can feel the tears of gratitude welling in my eyes.

My mom looks up at the ceiling. "And it just bothers me that that *bruja* Pamela has been pushing her way into your heart, trying to buy your affection with diamond earrings and such. If anybody's going to buy you nice things, it's going to be me."

So *that's* it! "But, *Mamí*—"

"Now, you just tell her you can't accept them, and that she's to stop giving you expensive gifts. It puts a wedge between you and me, baby, and we don't want that."

"But—"

"Now, now," she says, stroking my braids. "I can afford to get you even nicer earrings, if that's what you want."

"I can't return them, *Mamí*," I say, holding my ground now that I know what she's after. So, all this niceness is just a trick, to try and turn me against Pamela! Well, it won't work. If people I like want to give me things, I should be allowed to accept them. "I can't and I won't!"

"All right," *Mamí* says, seeing she can't win on this one. "You can keep the earrings. But from now on, no more gifts from that *bruja*, you hear?"

"Yes, *Mamí*," I say, grabbing the compromise when I can get it. "Can I still buy the outfit?"

"Of course, baby," she says, smiling again,

although it looks more forced now than it did before. "I want you to look beautiful for your big meeting."

"But I thought you didn't even want me to *be* in the Cheetah Girls!" I point out. Then I want to kick myself for bringing it up. Why couldn't I just keep my *boca grande*—my big mouth— shut for once?

Incredibly, it doesn't seem to bother her. "I think it's just a phase you're going through, *mi hija*," she says, still smiling. "But since you insist on this singing nonsense, you may as well go all the way with it." She pushes the card into my hands and squeezes them. "Buy yourself the outfit. And remember who bought it for you—*me*, not Pamela—*está bien?*"

"*Sí, Mamí*," I say, giving her a big hug and kiss. I'm still mad at her for not believing in me, but at least she's showing me she loves me.

"Now, you know the rules, Chanel. You only order that one outfit. You give me the card back as soon as you're done. And don't you ask 'that woman' for anything ever again. *Entiendes?* You hear?"

Now she is wiping imaginary dust off my

altar table right next to the window. My altar table is covered with a pretty white tablecloth. On top of it, there are candles and offerings to the patron saints—fruits, nuts, and little prayer notes.

"I didn't ask Pamela for anything," I whine, making the cross-my-heart-and-hope-to-die sign across my chest. "She just gave the earrings to me!"

"Well, *don't* accept anything else. And if your father asks you anything, don't tell him what I told you. *Entiendes?*" Mom asks me—again. Now I'm really getting annoyed.

"*Está bien.* I won't. I promise," I respond. Anything to make her stop being such a policeman. "And thank you sooooo much! Letting me charge a new outfit is the best present anybody ever got me!"

I give her another hug, and that seems to do the trick. She flashes me a big smile, kisses me on the forehead, and heads for the door.

When Mom finally leaves my room, a sudden feeling of total bliss comes over me. The credit card feels sleek and powerful in my hand, and I'm anxious to get my shopping groove on. Prada or *nada*, baby! Okay, so I am

rolling more with the *nada* than the Prada—
but that is all gonna change with one phone
call!

As I flip through the catalog, looking at all
the dozens of things I'm longing to own, I hum
to myself, "Oooh, Oophelia's! I'm feeling ya!"

Chapter 3

I have never held Mom's credit card in my hot little hands before. Never. And now, the hologram on its face seems to wink at me, casting a witch's spell over me. I dial the 800 number and follow the computer instructions, punching in numbers here and there until I get to speak to a real-live person.

Meanwhile, I am thinking about poor Dorinda. She must feel so down about not being able to keep the duckets from our gig. It's so unfair that she had to give the money to her foster mom. My heart goes out to her. Surely, my mom wouldn't want us to lose out on making a deal with Mr. Johnson just because Do' Re Mi came dressed in rags!

I decide then and there to make one tiny little exception to Mom's rule. After all, she said I couldn't buy anything else—but that meant *for me*, didn't it? When the operator picks up, I order two of the green leopard outfits—one in my size, and one in Dorinda's. I give the credit card number to the lady on the phone, and as I do, my gaze wanders to the pages of the catalog. So many other great things, things I've always wanted, and will never have another chance to get . . .

What would it hurt to borrow just a little of Mom's credit to stock up on stuff? When we sign with Mr. Johnson, it will be no time till we're making big duckets from gigs, maybe even a record deal! I can pay my mom back before she even knows I've spent the money!

"Will that be all, ma'am?" the voice asks me.

"Uh . . . no," I hear myself say. "No . . . just one or two more things . . ."

Do' Re Mi looks so "money" in the new outfit I bought her. And on top of that, Bubbles's mom, who is my *madrina*—my godmother—since birth (and the best godmother in the whole world) made *her* a green leopard pantsuit to match ours for our meeting with Mr. Johnson!

Aqua is wearing a black-and-white-checked blazer with a red shirt and black skirt. Angie has on a denim suit with a hot pink turtleneck.

"At least they don't look like they're going to church," Bubbles giggles to me, sneaking a look in the mirror that covers one whole wall of the Hydrant Restaurant on Fifteenth Street, where we are meeting Mr. Johnson.

When we first tried to tell Angie and Aqua what to wear for the meeting, Aqua got all huffy and said, "*We* are saving *our* money to go home to Houston for Thanksgiving!" The twins are headed south for the holidays—in more ways than one!

"I feel so large and in charge, I'm loving it—and you all, too!" Bubbles says. "That was so nice of Auntie Juanita to let you buy Do' Re Mi a pantsuit, too, Chuchie!"

Okay, so I told Bubbles a little fib-eroni. I didn't want her to think that I did . . . well, what I actually did. I'll have to straighten her out soon, though, before she opens her *boca grande*—her big mouth—and spills the refried beans to my mom.

The Cheetah Girls

The table is covered with a bright red linen tablecloth, and six red linen napkins placed perfectly apart. Right in the middle of the round table is a big glass vase with lots of pink roses, my favorite *flores*.

"You nervous?" I ask Do' Re Mi, then I add giggling, "I feel like I'm at a seance and the table is gonna lift up any second!"

Mr. Johnson has gone to check our jackets. Yes, we have it like that. There is a waiter dressed in white, standing near our table. He smiles at me when I look in his direction.

"Somebody pinch me, pleez, so I can wake up!" I giggle, then look around at all the people who are having lunch at the Hydrant. I take the book of matches with the name of the restaurant out of the ashtray, and stick it in my cheetah backpack for a souvenir. All around us are grown-ups, and they are all dressed *adobo down*. The lady at the table next to us is sitting by herself.

"She must be waiting for *El Presidente*," I whisper to Bubbles. The lady is wearing a big hat with a black peacock feather poking her almost in the eye! She looks at us and smiles. Then the peacock lady puts on lipstick without even looking in a mirror! "She definitely has the skills to pay the bills," Bubbles quips.

Do' Re Mi looks like she is getting nervous, too, because she is reading the menu like she is studying for a test at school. Then all of a sudden she whispers to me, "What should I order?"

"Just don't get spaghetti marinara," I whisper back.

"Do' Re Mi, try the *penne arrabiata*—that's the pasta cut on the slanty tip with red *pepperoncino*."

"What's *that*?" Do' Re Mi quizzes Bubbles.

"Those crushed red pepper flakes that Angie loves to put on pizza. You can hang with that!" Bubbles blurts out.

"Here he comes," whispers Angie.

"Ladies, order to your heart's delight," Mr. Johnson commands us, as he sits down and puts the napkin in his lap. We all do the same thing. Do' Re Mi flaps the napkin really loud when she opens it, like it has wings, but we act like we don't notice. Mr. Johnson is wearing a yellow tie brighter than a Chiquita banana, and his two front teeth don't talk to each other. He has a *really* big gap.

"This place is majordomo dope," Bubbles exclaims, looking around once more.

"Yeah, and I've done some pretty major-domo deals here, as you would say," chuckles Mr. Johnson, looking at Bubbles. "So you're the writer of the group, huh?" he asks her.

"Yup," Bubbles says, smiling. Bubbles isn't afraid of anything. She just acts like herself. He obviously just looks to her as if she is the leader. Which *is* kinda true anyway. We wouldn't be a group, I think, if it wasn't for Bubbles. But I don't want Bubbles to be the *only* leader, because it was my idea too to *be* in a group, so that counts for something.

Today Bubbles is wearing her hair really straight and parted down the middle. I put her extensions in myself, so I know they won't come out even if Hurricane Gloria flies in from Miami!

"Pucci would love this place," I giggle, looking at the red brick walls. My mom says the Hydrant is a one-star bistro. I don't know what that means, but now that she has Mr. Tycoon for a boyfriend, she goes to places, she says, where they don't even have prices on the menu. I guess this one doesn't count, because it does.

"You know, this place used to be a fire-house," says Mr. Johnson. "Lotta action coming down that pole." Mr. Johnson is looking over in the direction of the big metal pole that goes all the way up the ceiling. "Back in the day, there were some pretty bad torch jobs in the city. Buildings burning down all the time. It kept firemen pretty busy, but things have gotten better, and they closed the firehouse down two years ago."

The waiters are sliding down the pole now, bringing food from the kitchen above. "Tourists love that," Mr. Johnson chuckles.

"I wonder if the waiters get scared," Aquanette asks, touching her pin curl, which is laid down and fried to the side of her face.

"Well, let's clear away the okeydokey and talk some bizness, here," Mr. Johnson chuckles. He definitely has more rhymes than Dr. Seuss. He looks at all five of us and says, "As your manager, I want you to know that I'm going to forego all production costs for a demo, and get you in the studio with some real heavy-hitting producers, arrangers, and engineers."

"Can we do some of my songs?" Bubbles asks, always looking out for *número una*.

"Not right away, Galleria. Now, I know your songs are smokin', 'cuz I heard you girls singing them the night I saw you perform at Cheetah-Rama, but let's start with the producers' songs." Mr. Johnson takes a sip of bubbly water from his glass, then licks his lips. "Pumpmaster Pooch has worked with some really big artists, so he knows how to turn a song into an instant hit," he says.

I hope the water doesn't make me burp, I think, as I sip some from my glass, too.

"Who has Pumpmaster Pooch worked with?" Do' Re Mi asks.

"Well, I don't want to say right now, because none of the songs have gotten picked up just yet. You girls have to understand. There is a one in a million chance for a record to turn gold, but if you go into the studio with producers who've got the Midas touch, you're likely to turn that song into gold."

"What happens to the songs after we finish them?" Angie asks.

"We—that means I—have to get your demo to the record companies. It takes a lot of wheeling and dealing, but don't worry about it, 'cuz it ain't no thing like a chicken wing."

We look at each other like we've just eaten some Green Eggs and Ham, or something.

Mr. Johnson catches on to our confusion. "What I mean is, I have a serious setup at Hyena Records. Me and the A&R guy—that's the artist development person, who goes out scouting the country for talent just like you— go way back. *And* I've been doing business with Mr. Hyena, the company president, for years. After he gets a taste of that growl power y'all got going on, he'll be chomping at the bit to sign some superlistic talent such as yourselves. Just let me handle it."

I sit there wondering how Mr. Johnson can talk so fast without even taking a breath. I wish Drinka could see him in action.

"Hyena Records. Who do they have on the label?" Do' Re Mi asks, all curious. When Mr. Johnson turns his head toward her, I motion quickly to Angie with my hand. She has a piece of green something stuck on a tooth in the front, and she is just smiling her head off.

"Now, they're not what they used to be back in the day," Mr. Johnson says, his pinky finger dangling to the wind as he sips his water. "But nothing is like it used to be in the music biz."

"Ooh, this is bubbly," Aqua says, her eyes popping open as she puts her glass down.

"Bubbles. That's me," Galleria says, starting to sway. "The Cheetah Girls are cutting a demo, so take a memo, all you wanna-be stars trying to get a whiff of what it feels like," Bubbles giggles. She is flossin' for Mr. Johnson.

"That's very good, Galleria." He chuckles. "You do that off the top of your head?"

All of this is going to Bubbles's head, I think. I wish I knew how to make up songs like her. Then Mr. Johnson would like me, too.

The waiter comes and takes our orders. After he leaves, Mr. Johnson whips a manila envelope out of his pocket and opens it. Inside are five pieces of paper.

"Listen, before our food gets here, I want each of you to give one of these to your parents. Have them look it over, then sign it. You can give it back to me the next time we meet, in the studio."

"What is it?" Do' Re Mi asks.

"It's no big deal—just a temporary agreement—a standard management contract, so we can get started right away on your demo. It's your time and my dime—so let's not waste it, Cheetah Girls!" Mr. Johnson quips.

Shop in the Name of Love

He sure is making moves like a jackal. Just like his name. I guess I'll have my dad look it over. He is good with business. I wish I could give it to Princess Pamela, too. She is smart like that. But Mom would really go off on me if she found out I did that.

"Enough business for now," Mr. Johnson says with a big, gap-toothed smile. "Why don't you girls tell me all about yourselves?"

And we do . . . oh, do we ever!

Chapter
4

Things went really well today at our first business *lonchando*, I think to myself as I'm lying on my bed, clacking the heels of my black patent leather loafers together. I have the keyboard on the bed, and I'm yapping on the Internet with Bubbles, Angie, and Aqua. Dorinda is coming over so we can do our homework together. Meanwhile, I'm trying to get them to help me with this Princess Pamela situation, and end the frustration.

"I just don't think it's fair that you can't see Pamela, and I'm not being square," Bubbles says.

Angie has an idea: "Dag on, we got so many problems. We better have Cheetah Girls council meetings, so we can give each other advice, instead of rehearsing all the time and talking about being wanna-be stars!"

"It's a done wheel-a-deal," Bubbles types back, imitating Mr. Johnson. "Let's have Cheetah Girls council meetings once a week!"

My bedroom door is open, so I don't hear when my mom walks right in. "Chuchie," she says, almost scaring me.

"Oh, hi, *Mamí*," I say, hoping she isn't trying to peep my chat.

"You forgot to give me back my credit card," she says.

"Oh! Right!" I fall all over myself going to my dresser drawer, and take it out. Handing it to her, I say, "*Mamí*, that was so generous of you letting me get that outfit."

She smiles and gives me a kiss. "The meeting was good, huh?" she asks. Then she sits down on my bed.

"*Sí, Mamí*. Thanks so much."

She hands me back the management agreement form that Mr. Johnson wanted us to sign. "As long as you do your schoolwork and finish high school, *then* go to college, you can stay with this little group of yours. Just don't get any ideas that this is for real, okay?" she says, taking my comb and starting to comb her hair.

"Okay, *Mamí*," I growl back.

My mom just won't get it into her head that I am very serious about being a Cheetah Girl, or that it means everything to me. I know I will do whatever my mom wants me to do, but on the other hand, I have to do what's right for me.

"You better let your father see that agreement, too, or he'll have a fit," Mom adds, while she looks in my mirror and combs out her hair.

That's how she gets when she talks about my dad. It makes me so sad that they fight all the time. I'll tell you one thing, though. She is not going to keep me away from Princess Pamela.

"Yes, *Mamí*," I reply.

Deep in my heart, I know what I want. I want to be a Cheetah Girl and travel all over the world. Then I'm going to buy Abuela Florita a house away from Washington Heights and near the ocean so she can dream about the D.R.—the Dominican Republic, where she was born. I'm gonna live near her, so we can see each other more often.

Mom interrupts my *gran fantasía*. "So. You're going to the studio tomorrow, huh?" she asks.

"Yeah, I'm kinda nervous about making a demo tape," I explain.

"What's that?" she asks me, then looks at herself sideways in the mirror.

"It's a tape of songs that shows how we sing, so a record company will give us a deal. Maybe it's not a whole tape, but it's something."

"Mmm," Mom says, getting up off the bed. "You and your crazy dreams."

She leaves my room and goes back to the exercise studio. Lately, she has become an exotic dancing fanatic. She says it's great exercise, better than jogging. Her tummy is as flat as my chest, so it must be true. She's looking good, and she's got a boyfriend with *mucho dinero*, so why is she so worked up about Princess Pamela?

I ponder the situation. What am I gonna do? I love Princess Pamela, and she is so nice to me, but I know it makes my mom unhappy that I am close to her.

Our Cheetah Girls crew council is a good idea, for starters. Maybe I could ask Bubbles's mom, Dorothea, my *madrina*, who is super *simpática*, what I should do. But, then again, she and Mom are friends since their modeling days, so maybe I can't trust her with everything.

Then it hits me! I get *un buen* idea. I can call Princess Pamela's Psychic Hotline, disguise my voice, and ask *her* what to do!

I dial the 900-PRINCESS number and hold my breath. I can feel my heart pounding through my chest like a secret agent on a mission. "I like truffles, not R-r-u-ffles," I hum to myself, rolling my Rs. Everybody at Drinka's voice and dance studio is so jealous because they can't roll their Rs like I do.

That is my *cultura* for you, I smile to myself, as I take a piece of Godiva chocolate from the box Bubbles's mom gave each of us for Halloween. I've hidden the box from Pucci's little grubby hands.

A voice machine comes on, telling me the Princess is out, and to call back later. Great. There's never a psychic around when you really need one.

I get off the bed, and put a few oranges on my little altar table as an offering for Santa Prosperita. I don't know if she is a real saint, but she is *my* saint, and if you want something bad enough, you can get it, Princess Pamela says. She should know.

"I know it's not right to ask for anything

material, but *por favor*, I need just one little thing," I whisper to my Santa Prosperita. "Just one little Prada bag!"

See, the Kats and Kittys Klub is selling raffle tickets for community service. Each of the members has to sell as many raffle tickets as possible, and all the proceeds are going to the needy. The best part: the grand prize is two Prada bags! I have got to have them—at least one of them! The only problem is, I'm not too lucky at these kind of things. So I figure I'd better buy a *lot* of tickets.

Of course, that could be a problem, since my pile of duckets is now down to just fourteen. But hey—no *problemo*! I go to my math notebook and open it up to the last page. There, I have written the number and expiration date of my mom's credit card!

I know what you're thinking, but it's not true—I only wrote it down just in case I lost the card, or forgot the number or something! And I *meant* to cross it out when I gave the card back, but I haven't had the chance. And now . . .

Well, look. It's a worthy cause, *está bien?* All those poor needy people in the world—how could I not reach out to help them?

I'm sure my mom won't mind, especially since, if I win, I'll definitely give her one of the Prada bags. Besides, I'll pay her back for everything, once the Cheetah Girls hit it big—which we're sure to do, now that we're signing on with Mr. Johnson and making a demo tape! I mean, how long could it be before we're rolling in *dinero*?

I call up the Kats and Kittys Klub. Mrs. Goodge, the secretary, gets on the line. "Oh, hello, there, Chanel! What can I do for you?"

I tell her.

"A hundred tickets? Why, Chanel, that's very generous of your mother!"

"Yes it is, Mrs. Goodge," I say. "My mom is one of the most generous people there is, and she really cares about needy people, too!"

"How will she be paying? Cash or check?" Mrs. Goodge asks.

"Um, she gave me her credit card number to give you," I say.

"Oh. I see . . . well, I suppose that'll be all right," she says.

I give her the number.

"That's one hundred raffle tickets at two dollars each, for a total of two hundred dollars.

Thank you so much, Chanel—and be sure to thank your mother for us!"

"I'll do that, Mrs. Goodge," I say.

Yeah, right. Sure I will. That would not be a smart thing to do, now, would it? I hang up, feeling guilty but excited. I'm sure to win the Prada bags, with odds like these. A hundred tickets! How can I miss?

I flop back on the bed and flip through my Oophelia's catalog once again, even though I know every page by heart. How can I pass up these lime green suede boots? I wonder. . . .

My mom is gonna kill me. Well, at the rate the group is growing, the Cheetah Girls will probably be rich soon, so I can pay my mom back then, I tell myself. I pick up the phone and punch in a number, and I hear my own voice ordering the lime green suede boots from the Oophelia's catalog operator.

Then I spot something else I just have to have. Ooh, this rug is so cute. It has a big *mono*, monkey face on it. I love monkeys! Ooh, it has a matching blue stool with a *mono* on it, too! I guess it won't hurt if I order just one more thing. Mom won't mind, I tell myself. She knows my old daisy area rug has seen better days. It looks like someone has tiptoed through the tulips on it.

Mom *did* say not to use her credit card, but I don't think she will mind, since it's something for my room. At least that's what I tell myself. And if she does mind, too bad. I deserve a new rug, and the stool matches, so I just have to get that, too.

I am so good at making my voice sound grown-up, the operator never asks me anything. The stool is $156, and the rug is $38. Mono better do some tricks with a banana for this kinda money, I think, giggling to myself as I place the order. "Does it come in any other color?" I ask.

"No, just blue with the red monkey design," the operator replies.

The stool is real leather, not pleather, so I decide to go for it. But I have to have the cheetah picture frame, too, I suddenly realize. I *need* a new frame for my Confirmation picture sitting on the dresser. It is my favorite picture, not counting the one of me at my sixth-birthday party, standing with the piñata that I busted open all by myself. In it, I am making a face because I got a terrible stomachache after I ate everything that fell out of the piñata.

In the Confirmation picture, I'm wearing the holy red robe for the ceremony. This is the color that symbolizes the fire of the Holy Spirit. Abuela has her arm around me and she is smiling. My silver cross is draped across the picture frame, which is supposed to be silver, but it has changed colors and looks old. My mom picked it out. I wonder if she knew it was fake silver. Surely she'd want me to have a better one if she knew. A picture like this one deserves the best frame there is!

So I order it, along with everything else. I'm feeling dizzy from my little shopping spree—dizzy and happy, and a little bit scared. What if my mom finds out before I get enough money to pay her back?

Well, she won't, that's all, I tell myself. I'll just make sure she doesn't. I quickly shut my math notebook and put it away.

"Will that be all, ma'am?" the operator asks. Just as I'm about to say yes, I realize that I really need a new outfit to go to the recording studio, so I make the operator wait until I pick one out of the catalog. She adds it to the total, and when she reads me back a list of what I've bought, I almost chicken out, it's so much money.

But then, I think to myself, Why should I care if Mom gets mad? She's always mad at me anyway. No matter what I do, it's wrong— "Don't talk with that witch Pamela! Don't take the Cheetah Girls too seriously! Don't do this, don't do that . . ." Well, too bad for her. I'll do what I want.

"Yes, that will be fine," I tell the operator.

That's what you get, *Mamí*, for trying to control every move I make!

I have just hung up, when Pucci comes into my room without even knocking. "Get out, Pucci!" I yell at him. I hate when he does that. We aren't little anymore, you know? "What do I have to do to get rid of you?" I blurt out.

"Get me a dog. I want a dog!" Pucci giggles. "How come we can't have a dog?"

"You know *Mamí* isn't gonna let us have a dog, Pucci. Why are you bothering me?"

And then it hits me. Why *can't* Pucci have a dog? *I* want one, too. Nothing against Snuggly-Wiggly Pooch, but a real dog would be *la dopa*! Mom's always complaining how allergic she is, but there must be some kind of dog that doesn't shed. Why can't we get one of those? Yeah . . .

now, there's a great idea! Right away, I start to cook up how to get us a real-live dog.

Meanwhile, I don't feel like doing my ballet exercises, but I know I've got to, to help keep my body strong. Changing into my pink leotard, I groan to myself. All this shopping is exhausting, but hey—a Cheetah Girl's day is never done!

Chapter 5

These days, the Cheetah Girls are really living *la vida loca*—the crazy life. Rehearsals, school, homework, and, for me, fighting with my mom, and spending secret nights on the Psychic Hot Line with Princess Pamela, or shopping on the phone and ordering from Oophelia's catalog.

Thank goodness, history class is the last of the day. At four o'clock, we have to meet Mr. Johnson at Snare-a-Hare Recording Studios in Times Square. He has arranged for us to have a recording session with this Big Willy producer, Pumpmaster Pooch.

We did find out about Pumpmaster's "credits." He did the rap remix for the Sista Fudge single, "I'll Slice You Like a Pound Cake." That's something, huh? That song is one of Princess Pamela's favorites. It makes her giggle and makes me wiggle.

Speaking of Princess Pamela, I've been running up the phone bill calling her 900 number. I've been getting some pretty strange advice, too—she's been telling me to watch out for animals. I wonder what she means by that. . . .

Maybe I should forget about the dog I've been planning to get Pucci. Or maybe it's the Cheetahs I ought to stay away from. No, that can't be. Maybe Princess Pamela is off the mark this time. After all, she doesn't know who she's talking to. I've been disguising my voice, so maybe that's throwing off her predictions. Still, it's been bothering me, and I just can't figure it out.

I almost asked Princess Pamela about it yesterday, when I gave her the management agreement to pass on to my dad. But that would have been giving myself away, and I didn't want it getting back to my dad that I'd been running up the phone bill to get advice I could have gotten for free!

I also wanted to tell Princess Pamela about

all the money I've been spending, and get her advice on that, too—but I knew it would make Mom mad if she found out I'd been asking Princess Pamela for advice, let alone that I'd been using her credit card and running up her phone bill!

"How much did Mr. Johnson say it costs for an hour at the recording studio?" Do' Re Mi asks, bringing me back to reality. We are at our lockers after school, getting ready to go over to the studio for our recording session.

"The studio? It costs a lot, but we don't have to pay for it," I answer.

Me, Bubbles, and Do' Re Mi are looking *muy caliente* today—hot, hot, hot! We're all wearing matching red velvet jeans and crushed velvet leopard T-shirts from Oophelia's. Bubbles's mom paid for hers. I bought mine and Do' Re Mi's on my mom's credit card (surprise, surprise).

"Chuchie, you are lost in your own soap opera channel. What's the matter, *mamacita*, Snuggly-Wiggly Pooch ate your homework?" Bubbles chides me, putting her arm around my shoulders. "What's wrong? You're not giggling, and that's kinda like Toto not begging for food. Ya know what I mean, prom queen?"

I poke Bubbles in the side, because Derek Hambone and Mackerel Johnson are standing by their lockers across the hall. "Duckets in the bucket alert!" I whisper in Bubbles's ear.

Like the Road Runner, Bubbles makes a bee-line to hit up the dynamic duo, and make them buy Kats and Kittys raffle tickets.

"Hit 'em up, Galleria!" Do' Re Mi says, egging Bubbles on.

Derek is this new "brotha from Detroit," as he calls himself, and the word is, he comes from a family that owns the biggest widget factory in the East—*mucho dinero, mamacita!*

"Derek, my Batman with a plan. Buy a raffle ticket for me and part with two dollars for a good cause. You, too, Mackerel. Come on, I'll let you two touch my vest—it's national velvet. Feel the pile!" Bubbles urges them.

"Awright," Derek says, reaching for the ticket, but then he looks at it, reads about the Prada prize, and says, "Cheetah Girl, you expect me to get jiggy in the jungle with a *Prada* bag? I'm not going out like that."

"Oh, come on, *schemo*, you ain't gonna win the raffle, anyway, just part with the two duckets!" Bubbles says, pouting. Derek is such a *pobrecito*—a real dummy. He doesn't even know Bubbles is calling him a dodo bird in Italian. I *know* Derek isn't going to win, because I *better* win. No one else deserves that Prada bag more than I do! *"Prada or nada"* is the motto I live and die by.

"Awright, I'm gonna let you hit me up this time, Cheetah Girl, Derek says, like he is a loan officer at Banco Popular, "but you owe me *big-time* for this one." Reaching into his baggy jeans, I wonder if Derek is ever gonna find the bottom of his deep, baggy pockets. I wonder how the "Red Snapper" is gonna get his money off the hook.

See, Derek likes Bubbles—and he's always snapping at her bait—that's why we nicknamed him "Red Snapper"—and also because his best friend is Mackerel Johnson. Derek is the only one of his posse who is large enough to become a member of the Kats and Kittys Klub, though. It costs $650 a year.

Mackerel smiles at me while he's bouncing to some tune in his peanut-sized head. He is so hyper, he looks like a Chihuahua bobbing his head up and down.

Oh, snapples, that's what I could get Pucci! "My mom can't say *nada* about a Chihuahua—they are so little, who could be allergic to them?

Meanwhile, Bubbles is still closing the deal. "Thank you, *schemo*," she smirks to Derek and Mackerel, stuffing their duckets into her chubby Cheetah wallet.

"Shame on you, too, Cheetah Girl. Just be ready when it's time to collect, awright?" Derek says, winking. Then he walks away with Mackerel.

"You got one of them dog books from the library, right?" I say to Do' Re Mi. I'm on a bowwow mission now.

"Yeah, why?" Do' Re Mi replies.

"Look up the breed Chihuahua and see if they shed hair."

"Word. Wait, they ain't got any hair," Do' Re Mi counters. She is so smart. The most book-smart of all of us.

"Look it up anyway," I giggle. "I think Miss Cuchifrita just got lucky. See, if Chihuahuas don't shed, then I can buy Pucci one for his birthday!"

"If you buy Pucci a dog, *you're* gonna end up at the dog pound for sure," Bubbles quips to me.

"And where you gonna get that kinda money?"

"It's three o'clock, y'all!" Do' Re Mi says, setting off down the hallway in her size zero velvet jeans. "We better get over to the studio, and start gettin' down!"

"Oh, snapples, I forgot to get the agreement back from Princess Pamela," I sigh to Bubbles.

"What's she doing with it?" Bubbles asks me, like she's saying, "Don't play with fire."

"I gave it to her so she could give it to my dad," I said. "I didn't have time to go all the way uptown, baby, okay? My mom is watching me like a hawk when she isn't doing her exotic dancing!"

"Mr. Johnson won't mind if you don't have the agreement. Just tell him we'll bring it to him the next time," Bubbles says, grabbing my arm and pulling me along. "Come on, *señorita*. We've got some singin' to do!"

Recording studios have more gadgets on the control board than I've ever seen in my life. "They got so many buttons, how do they know which ones to push?" I exclaim to Do' Re Mi, who is *muy fascinado* with anything *electrónico* or *en la Web*.

"That's why he's making the duckets," Bubbles smirks to the engineer, who is sitting at the board with headphones on.

Bubbles's mom, Dorothea, has come with us to the studio, but the twins haven't arrived yet.

"This is Kew, the engineer," Mr. Johnson says, introducing us as the Cheetah Girls. No matter how many times I hear our group's name, it sounds like *la música* to my ears. I love it!

"Mr. Johnson, can I speak to you for a minute?" Dorothea says. The two grown-ups go into another room—so they can talk business, I'm sure. Dorothea is all about the "Benjamins" and she doesn't play. She looks *la dopa* today, too. She is wearing a big leopard hat, and leopard boots that make her look taller than "The Return of the Fifty-Foot Woman"— even though she is only six feet tall. I wish *I* was that tall.

At last, the huggy bear twins have arrived!

"You know the Cheetah Girls rule: don't be late or we'll gaspitate!" Bubbles says, warning the twins as they hurriedly throw their cheetah backpacks on an empty chair in the studio.

"Dag on, y'all, just when we think we know how to get somewhere, they change the subway line on us!" Aqua laments, fixing her pin curl in place. Aquanette and Anginette still haven't learned their way around the Big Apple yet.

"You're 'Westies' now like me, so you'd better get with the IRT program," Do' Re Mi grunts. She lives on 116th, on the Upper West Side, and last summer, the twins moved from sunny Houston to 96th Street and Riverside Drive.

Like mine, their parents are "dee-vorced" (as Angie says in her Southern drawl), and the twins live with their dad. He must be kinda cool, 'cuz he pays for them to go to the beauty parlor twice a month to get their hair *and* nails done. I think they should pay me instead because I would give them *la dopa* hairstyles instead of the "shellac attack" curls they like so much. Sometimes less is more!

Today, the twins are wearing makeup, so they look kinda cute. Aqua and Angie are *café sin leche* color, and they love that white frost lipstick on their big, juicy lips. They are screaming for a Miss Wiggy! virtual makeover.

Mr. Johnson and Dorothea come back into the room. His beeper goes off, and he looks at it nervously. "I got a situation I gotta take care of," he says. "That is Mr. Hyena—I told you about him—he is the Big Willy at Hyena Records. Mrs. Garibaldi, Kew will look after you. And Pooch will get with you girls when he gets through," Mr. Johnson adds chuckling, never too nervous to get a rhyme out.

Pumpmaster Pooch is in the other room on his cell phone. We can see him through the big glass partition. He waves at us with his five-carat fingers. I mean, he is wearing enough gold rings to start a gold mine. Kew is busy fiddling with the keyboard, so the five of us sit and watch the music videos on MTV, which are playing on one of the monitors over our heads.

"*Ay, Dios mío*, Krusher's latest music video!" I whisper.

Dorothea goes into the room with Pumpmaster Pooch, so we relax a little. I feel so nervous!

"Krusher's got it going on," Do' Re Mi says, looking up at the monitor and grooving to Krusher's new single, "My Way or the Highway."

"Look at Chanel getting all goo-goo-eyed!" Do' Re Mi says.

"I'm saving my first kiss for him," I giggle to my crew.

"You better hope it ain't the first 'dis!'" Do' Re Mi sighs.

"Oh, *cállate la boca, Mamacita*. Be quiet." I sigh, then hum aloud, *"Yo tengo un coco* on Crusher."

"What's that mean?" Do' Re Mi asks, smirking and squinting her eyes.

"Look it up!" I heckle. "I'm just playing with you, Dor-r-r-inda, *Mamí*," I say rolling my Rs like I'm on a choo-choo train. "You won't find it in *el diccionario*. It means I have a crush on Krusher."

"Coco is cuckoo for Krusher," Bubbles heckles, making a play on my middle name.

"Watch out, Chuchie, this may be your last dance, last chance," Bubbles says, pointing her finger excitedly at the monitor.

The Krusher music video has ended, and now there is a commercial for a Krusher contest. "Are you the lucky girl who will win an all-expenses-paid date with R&B's hottest singer, and spend two fun-filled days and nights with Krusher in sunny Miami? What are you waiting for? Call 900-KRUSHER right now!"

"*Ay, Dios mío*! I'm gonna enter," I squeal, jumping up and down.

"Okay, Cuckoo Coco, get over it, because here comes the man," whispers Do' Re Mi, secretly pointing to Pooch, who is on the move toward us.

"Ladies, ladies, I'm sorry to keep you waiting," Pumpmaster Pooch says, rushing into the engineer's booth. He has on dark sunglasses and a hat, and a black windbreaker. I can tell he thinks he's kinda *chulo*, kind of cute, too.

"Now, I got a song you are gonna love. I've picked out some material for you—the type of songs that will get you a record deal, so just trust me on this," he says, talking with his five-carat hands the whole time. "Okay, let's do this."

Pooch tells Kew what tracks to put on, then takes us to the recording booth. The five of us stand in front of the microphones and put headphones on our heads. "We're gonna practice it a bit, then take it from the top when we're ready," Pooch says.

"Where are the musicians?" Angie asks, like she's been in a recording studio before.

"We're just gonna lay down some lead vocals

over the tracks first so you can get the hang of the song, ya dig?" Pumpmaster says, looking at Bubbles mostly, and the twins. The twins have been singing in church choirs since they're nine, so they always seem like they know what they're doing. "Then we lay down the background vocals and arrangements later. That's my job. We ready, Cheetah Girls?" Pumpmaster Pooch says, flashing a grin.

"We're ready!" we say together. I am so excited—I cannot believe that we, the Cheetah Girls, are already in the studio, recording. Okay, it's just a song for a demo, but you know what I mean, jelly bean.

"'I Got a Thing for Thugs'?" Bubbles says, scrunching up her nose as we read the lyrics off the sheet music that Pooch has handed out to us. "That sounds radickio!"

"Bubbles, let's just listen to them, okay?" I say, trying to calm her down because I know we are lucky to be here in the studio and not paying for it.

But after we finish rehearsing the same song fifty thousand times, we are so tired I never want to hear that song again. Bubbles is right. The song is *la wacka*! Bubbles looks like she is about to explode. I guess she thought we would be doing one of *her* songs.

Mr. Johnson, who has returned, comes in and congratulates us. "Ladies, you did a wonderful job. Now the car service is gonna come and take all of you right to your door."

"That song was wack-a-doodle," Bubbles says, pouting, when we are finally in the car with Dorothea. "It just wasn't *us*."

"Maybe once we do some of their songs, they'll let us record some of yours," I explain to Bubbles. She is *caliente* mad.

"What did you think, Mom?" Bubbles says, putting her head on Dorothea's shoulder.

"There is something about that Mr. Johnson that I don't like," Dorothea says, then leans back into the car seat. "I told him that I have to have the agreement looked over by a lawyer first, and that made him kind of nervous. If anything isn't right with that agreement, I'm gonna be so shady to Mr. Jackal Johnson the sun is gonna go down on him!"

Yawning, I put my head on Dorothea's other shoulder, and sigh. "Bubbles, you're right—that song *was* wack-a-doodle!" We giggle, then get real quiet for the rest of the way home.

I can't wait to get home and call 900-KRUSH-ER. I'm gonna call a hundred times if I have to, because I'm going win that date with Krusher and make my dreams come true.

That's what me and Bubbles always said when we were little. We would follow the yellow brick road no matter where it led us. Well, Miami, here I come!

Chapter

6

It's time for me to head uptown to Drinka Champagne's Conservatory. All five of us are now taking vocal lessons and dance classes there. Aqua and Angie don't need it, because they go to Laguardia Performing Arts High School and they get *la dopa* training all week, but it helps us to sing better together as a group. We also practice songs that Bubbles wrote—"Wanna-be Stars in the Jiggy Jungle" and "Welcome to the Glitterdome"—just in case Mr. Johnson and Pumpmaster Pooch decide to let us record them for our demo. Hey, you never know!

If I don't leave now, I'm gonna be late. Class starts at eleven o'clock, and Drinka does not play. If you walk in one minute late, she will stop everything and read you like *La Prensa*, our local Spanish newspaper, right in front of *everybody*. Now I'm mad at myself because I wanted to get to class early today, so I could show Drinka and the Cheetah Girls how much work I'm doing on my breathing exercises.

I spritz on my favorite perfume—Fetch, by Yves Saint Bernard (Princess Pamela bought it for my thirteenth birthday last year). I also spritz some Breath-So-Fresh spray in my throat. It makes me feel better, even though Bubbles says buying that stuff its like throwing "duckets down the drain."

I'm the one with the sensitive vocal chords, so I have to try whatever I can. Bubbles has a throat like the Tin Man. She can eat a plate of *arroz con pollo* with a bottle of hot sauce, sing for three hours straight, then still be able to blab her mouth on the phone till the break of dawn!

I look at the clock again. Hmmm. Maybe I can get one more call in to 900-KRUSHER before I go. I pick up my red princess phone, and start sweating as soon as I hear Krusher cooing in the background of the taped recording. I *have* to win this contest. My *corazón* would be broken if some other girl gets a date in Miami with my *papí chulo*, my sugar daddy. No—I can't think like this, or I will faint for real.

I listen to the recorded message for the tenth time in a row. The instructions are simple: you have to tell, in your own words, why you think you should win the date with Krusher.

I have a *buen* idea! I'll *sing* to Krusher on the phone. One of the Cheetah Girls songs! I betcha none of the other *mamacitas* calling could do that. It'll be my ace to first base.

"Hi, it's Chanel Simmons *again*," I say, giggling into the phone. Then I get kinda nervous. "I think I should win the Krusher contest because I know all the words to every song you've ever done. Right now, I'm gonna sing you one of the songs from my own group, the Cheetah Girls. . . . "

My *gran fantasía* is fumbled, though, because all of a sudden, I hear my mother hang up the phone in the hallway and scream my name really loud. "CHANEL! Get out here! *Apúrate!*" I almost faint for real, and I get a knot in my stomach like when I know I'm in *trouble*.

"*Ay dios, por favor, ayúdame*—oh God, please

help me!" I say, doing the trinity sign across my chest, then kissing my Confirmation picture. I look really hard at Abuela's smiling face.

"Chanel, you better get out here!" Mom yells again.

Taking a deep breath, I walk out of my bedroom. My knees are shaking more than the Tin Man's in *The Wizard of Oz*.

If looks could kill, I would be dead, judging by the pained expression on my mother's face. Her dark brown eyes are breathing fire. She is wearing black leotards and tights, and she is sweating because she has been exercising.

"That was the credit card company on the phone. They were calling me because of the excessive charges made on *my* credit card. But I don't have to tell *you* who's been making them, do I?" Mom challenges me.

"No, *Mamí*," I whimper. I know I am *finito*. It is time for my last rites, and I wish Father Nuñez was here to read them.

"Why did you do it, when I told you not to?" Mom screams. "I give you an inch, and you take a mile. *Por qué*, Chanel? Why? *Por qué*?"

I start crying. I feel like such an idiot for thinking I could get away with charging all that stuff on my mom's credit card. "I don't know why I did it," I stutter. "I was just mad at you."

"*You* were mad at *me*?" she says, turning up the volume another notch. "Are you kidding me? I give you my credit card—I trust you—and you're mad at me?"

"You won't let me be close to Pamela," I complain, letting it all hang out. I figure at this point, *que será, será*, as they say in the old movie. What will be, will be. "She's not a *bruja*, like you always call her. She's nice. She's nicer to me than you!" I'm really crying now, and so is my mom. I don't know who is angrier at who.

"Oh, yeah? Maybe you'd like her for a mother instead of me?" she says, half sobbing. "I let you buy a new outfit, and this is how you repay me?"

"At least Pamela wouldn't complain about me being in the Cheetah Girls!" I say, really letting the hot sauce fly. "You don't want me to go after my dreams—you only want me to give up on them, like you did!" Years ago, Mom gave up on being a model when she got to "a certain age." I know what I'm saying is unfair and mean, but I'm so mad now that I just can't stop myself.

"I want you to get out of my face until I talk to your father about this, but don't think for one second you're gonna get away with it!" Mom screams. "You can forget about all your stupid Cheetah Girls, too. *Tu entiendes?* You understand?"

No way. She can't do that! The Cheetah Girls is all I care about besides Abuela and my dad and Princess Pamela and Pucci and *arroz con pollo* and Prada! The Cheetah Girls and my dreams to travel all over the world are my whole life! Without them, I have *nada. La odia mi mami!* I hate my mother.

"I have to go to Drin-ka-ka Conservatory," I say, so nervous I can't even get the words out. "I promised everyone I'd be there."

"All right. You can go to this one last class," she says. "But you come right back afterward and wait for me here. *Entiendes?*"

"*Sí,*" I whimper, then grab my jacket and run out the door.

After vocal class, I am slobbering like a baby to my crew.

Bubbles is so mad at me, she won't even talk to me. "You have broken a sacred rule of the

Cheetah Girls, Chuchie, and I am so disgusted with you, I cannot even look at you," she yells in front of Angie, Aqua, and Do' Re Mi.

I do not know what sacred rule Bubbles is talking about, but I am sure she will tell me, and anyway, I'm too afraid to ask. Drinka, who runs the conservatory, has left us alone in the rehearsal space, because big mouth Bubbles has told her what happened. We are sitting on the hardwood floor in a circle.

"How come you didn't tell me what you were doing with that credit card, Chuchie? You were always so sneaky-deaky, even when we were little!" Bubbles blurts out. She won't stop.

"Is your mother really gonna make you leave the group?" Do' Re Mi asks me, looking worried and scared.

"I don't know. That's what she says!" I cry. I am so scared of going home. I want Bubbles to help me. She's always helped me when I get in trouble, ever since we were little.

"I have no idea why Aunt Juanita wants you to be a buyer. You would end up wearing all the clothes yourself! Like I said before, you're a shopaholic waiting to happen!" Bubbles yells at me.

"Dag, now you've *really* given your mother a good reason not to let you stay in the group," Angie clucks, looking down at her skirt, then pulling it past her knees.

"Yeah, and now she's gonna say that *we* are a bad influence on you. You better let her know we didn't have anything to do with this—and you can take back all those clothes you bought me. I don't want them!" Do' Re Mi yells at me. Her eyes are watering.

Dorinda is a big crybaby. I know because she calls me on the phone and tells me secrets that Bubbles doesn't even know about. Like the stuff about her first foster mother, who was really mean to her and gave Dorinda up, but kept her sister. That's how she got put in Mrs. Bosco's house when she was almost five years old.

"Chuchie, the Cheetah Girls are all we have," Bubbles says. "We are not like some other stupid group. We don't just sing. We are more than just some singing group, okay?" She waves her hand at me, rolls her eyes, and pulls out her cell phone. "Let me call my mom at her shop. Auntie Juanita will be there, too, Chuchie, and my mom will know what to do."

I cover my face with my hands. I just want this bad dream to go away. Everybody is real quiet while Bubbles talks to her mom on the phone.

"Keep Juanita there, Mom. *Please* help us. Think of something!" Bubbles pleads to my *madrina* on the phone.

She listens for a minute, then says to me, "Mom says get your compact out and powder your nose." I know that this is *madrina*'s way of saying "sit tight and get ready for Freddy, 'cuz anything could go down."

"Juanita is still in the store screaming, so Mom is gonna call me back," Bubbles explains to all of us. "She's gonna calm Juanita down and think of what to do. And you know my mom can think on her feet, even if she's wearing shoes with ten-inch heels that are too tight," she adds, flossing.

"I know that's right," quips Aqua.

Dorothea is no joke. She can wheel and deal and, hopefully, she will save me from being the subject of a missing person's report.

"You're gonna pay for this one, Chuchie. In full," Bubbles says, putting away the cell phone. "Your mom is *caliente* mad!"

Angie hands me a pack of tissues out of her backpack. I take one and hand it back to her. "No, keep the whole thing, 'cuz you're gonna need 'em by the time your mother gets through with you," Angie clucks, then unzips her backpack and takes out a sandwich. "I'm sorry, y'all, but I'm hungry. We didn't have time to eat breakfast."

"I hope you're burning a good-luck money candle, Chuchie, because you're going to need all the luck you can get," Bubbles says, rolling her eyes at me. "Even though those candles look like a bunch of green wax to me, I don't see any duckets dropping from the sky to save you right now!"

It's a good thing Bubbles's cell phone rings, because I want to crown her like a queen for being so mean to me. Bubbles pulls up the phone antenna and hops on her Miss Wiggy StarWac Phone like it is a Batphone or something. Then she says, "Hmm, hmm," all serious—at least ten times, and keeps us waiting in suspense like a soap opera. My godmother is obviously giving her the *super ataque*, the blow-by-blow report.

When Bubbles hangs up, she lets out a sigh.

"You are so lucky, Chuchie," she says, pulling one of my braids. Then she gives us a blow-by-blow of the soap opera that is filming at Toto in New York . . . Fun in Diva Sizes, *madrina*'s boutique in Soho.

"Chuchie, your mom came into the store screaming so loud that Toto ran into the dressing room and scared a poor customer who was getting undressed," Bubbles explains.

The twins laugh, but I don't. Neither do Bubbles nor Dorinda. "We have to go to the boutique right now. *All* of us," Galleria says.

We all look at each other and swallow hard. It's high noon. Time for the big showdown. Ready or not, here we come!

Chapter 7

Dorothea is yelling at a man outside the boutique when we get there. Toto in New York . . . Fun in Diva Sizes is a *muy famoso* boutique, and many famous divas shop there, including Jellybean Nyce, the Divas, Sista Fudge, Queen Latifah, and even Starbaby, the newscaster who wears so much gold you have to wear sunglasses when you watch her on television. Dorothea does not play hide-and-seek with all the riffraff that comes to Soho looking to pickpocket all the tourists.

"You see what the sign says? It says, 'Toto in New York . . . Fun In Diva Sizes,'" Dorothea says with her hands on her hips, drilling the man, whose clothes look rumpled and crumpled. "This is a clothing store, not a toothless-men-who-love-big-women dating service, so get outta here!"

The man grins at Dorothea, then smacks his lips like he hasn't eaten *lonchando*. Then he hobbles away with his bottle in his hand, babbling like a parrot.

"He doesn't have any teeth," I mumble to Bubbles.

Because the door of the store is wide open, Toto comes running out. He is probably still afraid because of all the commotion. He looks so cute and fierce in the little cheetah-print suit Bubbles made for him, and he's as fierce as a cheetah, too! He jumps on the back of the legs of the man who has never had a visit from a tooth fairy.

"Toto, come here! Don't go running after him like he has treats for you!" Bubbles yells, then grabs Toto and carries him back inside the store, rubbing his stomach. Toto likes to get attention from anybody.

"Hi, Toto," I say, giving him a rub, too. I love him so much. I guess I'll never get a dog of my own now, though. . . .

"Dag, it must be hard having a store in New York, because there are a lot of crazy people here," Angie says.

The Cheetah Girls

There are a lot of people in New York who are cuckoo, but maybe not as "loco as Coco," I think, feeling sorry for myself. I climb up the stairs and inside the store, like a prisoner going to the electric chair. There is my mom, sitting on a stool with her arms crossed in front of her, and her eyes shooting bullets at me.

Luckily, my *madrina* takes over the situation, as usual, as soon as I get inside. "Chanel, I'm going to lay out the situation for you like the latest design collection. Juanita doesn't want you to be in the group anymore. And in many ways I don't think you deserve to be," my *madrina* says.

Now both my mom *and* my *madrina*, who I love so much, are ganging up on me! I haven't eaten anything all day, and I feel really dizzy, but I don't say anything. I just stand there.

Dorothea, wearing a dalmatian-dotted caftan, has her hands on her hips and is looking at my mom but standing over me, which makes me feel smaller than Dorinda. I know I'm not going to be a Cheetah Girl anymore. I'm so sad, I burst into tears.

"Now, I don't think that making you leave the group is going to teach you anything,

Chanel, and I know how much this means to Galleria, so we've worked out a solution," Dorothea continues. "You are going to work part-time in my store and pay back every penny you charged up on Juanita's cards, even if it takes you till you're a very old Cheetah Girl!"

Gracias, Dios! I say to myself. Thank goodness! My prayers have been answered! I don't have to leave the Cheetah Girls after all!

"Thank you, Dorothea! Thank you, *Mamí!*" I gush, the tears streaming down my face. "I will pay back all the money, *te juro*—I swear! And thank you s-o-o-o much for letting me stay in the group!"

All the other girls let out a shout of sheer relief, and hug me tight. But a word from my *madrina* makes them quiet down.

"We're not finished with you yet, *señorita*," Dorothea says, looking at me and getting more serious. "You know, Chanel, we all love to shop. It's fun, but it is not something you do when you are unhappy, or mad at someone, or looking for *love*, or for approval from kids in school. Love you get from your family, your friends—your mom—not Oophelia's catalog. If you are shopping with money you don't have—whether you are a child or a grown-up—then you have a problem, and you've got to own up to it, and change your ways."

Even though I don't say anything, I nod my head so Dorothea and my mom know that I understand.

"Mom, I like that," Bubbles says all excitedly, then whips out her notebook.

"Like what, darling?" Dorothea says, not at all amused.

"What you said about shopping for love. I'm going to write a song about this!"

"That's nice, darling, just don't act like you're large and in charge with *my* credit card."

"Yes, Mom," Bubbles says meekly.

"Mrs. Simmons, I wanna give back the outfit Chanel bought me. Is that okay?" Do' Re Mi asks quietly.

"No, Dorinda, you keep that. Chanel is gonna pay for it, so you might as well wear it," Mom says.

Nobody is stupider than I am, I think to myself. Why couldn't I be smart like Bubbles, or Dorinda? "When do I start working?" I ask.

"There's no time like the present," Dorothea

quips, then looks at Bubbles and the rest of our crew.

"I got a Spanish quiz tomorrow, so I'd better study," Bubbles says, then picks up Toto and gives him a kiss on his nose. "Bye, Boo-boo—you be a good boy, and help Mom chase away all the bozos!"

"Knowing Toto, I'm surprised he didn't ask that man for a sip of wine from that bottle he was carrying!" Dorothea says, opening up the cash register.

Do' Re Mi picks up her backpack and puts it on her munchkin shoulders, saying, "Guess he's just tippin' when he's not sippin'!" She is making a joke on the Drinka Champagne's disco song from back in the day. I can see we're all feeling a lot better—most of all, me! Good old Dorothea—she is the best!

"It's gonna be all right," she tells my mom. "Don't write Miss Cuchifrita off yet. She isn't crazy, just lazy, but she'll learn that duckets don't drop from the sky. Trust me."

They both laugh. It's the first time I've seen Mom smile since we got here. But then, Dorothea could make anybody laugh. She is *tan coolio*.

"Come here, baby," my mom says. I do, and she throws her arms around me. I hug her tight. "You know I love you so much. I've just got to be able to trust you, that's all."

"You can, *Mamí*," I tell her, meaning it with all my heart. "I'm gonna play it straight with you from now on." I hug her back, really tight. "And thanks for letting me stay in the Cheetah Girls."

"I know how much it means to you, baby," she tells me, as Dorothea and my crew look on, smiling. "After all, I've had dreams, too."

She and Dorothea smile at one another, and just for a second, I can imagine them when they were our age. Young, full of dreams, and chasing *la gran fantasía*.

"I love you, too, *Mamí*," I whisper, smiling and crying at the same time. "And from now on, you can trust me one hundred percent!"

"That's my Miss Cuchifrita!" Dorothea says, smiling. And we all share a laugh together.

Chapter 8

Mr. Johnson called us with good news this morning. Not only has he booked us, the Cheetah Girls, for the Amateur Hour contest at the world-famous Apollo Theatre on 125th Street, but he has talked Hal Hyena, the president of Hyena Records, into coming to see us perform!

"He says he called in a favor—'cuz we got the flava!" Bubbles types to me on the computer screen.

The Phat Planet chat room on the Internet has become my hangout, because, as Pucci so loudly announces to everybody, "*Loco Coco* is grounded!" But Aqua's idea about forming the Cheetah Girls Council and having meetings sure comes in "handy dandy" for a grounded *señorita* like myself.

I only get to go out to go to school, to work at Dorothea's boutique, and take classes at Drinka's. So, of course, our meetings have to be on-line, but that's okay. They really help.

I am not sad anymore about what happened, because I've learned a good lesson. I'm only sorry that I caused everybody so much trouble. I like working at the store, of course, because I love Dorothea. And slowly but surely, I'm paying back the money I owe my mom. Of course, at the rate I'm going, it's gonna take me about a year, but like they say, I made my bed, now I've gotta lie down in it.

"Loco Coco is grounded, *Papí*!" I can hear Pucci on the phone with my dad in the kitchen, which is way down the hall from my bedroom.

I'm finally going to see my dad tonight, and I'm going to tell him everything. I know he must have heard the whole story by now, though, and I'm sure I'm going to get yelled at big-time.

"Do me a flava. Who's gonna come with me to see my dad?" I type on the screen.

"I want y'all to hear the lyrics I wrote for this

song," Bubbles types, ignoring my request. "Guess what the title is?"

"'You Think You Large 'Cuz You Charge'?" Do' Re Mi snaps.

"Cute, but no loot, Do' Re Mi! Anybody else want to take a crack at my new song attack?"

I have a title idea, so I type it in: "'Chanel Ain't So Swell'?"

"That was true when you broke one of our sacred commandments, but now it isn't, because you're working for the 'Benjamins.' Give up yet?"

"What's the sacred commandment, any-way?" Do' Re Mi types.

At least somebody had the nerve to ask.

"Um, let's see," Bubbles types in. I can just see her making up a snap on her feet. "'You can only do so much fibbing to your friends who've seen you in your spotted pj's before you're so far backed up in a corner, you come out boxing like a cuckoo kangaroo'? How's that?"

"Galleria, you're a mess!!!!" Angie types in. "But that is the truth you're preaching, because the Lord don't like lies."

"Or flies!" Do' Re Mi types in.

Oh, just what I need—for the gospel hour to begin. When Aqua and Angie get started, you never know when it's going to end.

Bubbles isn't having it, though. "Okay, back to name that tune? Y'all give up yet?"

"Yes!" we all type one by one.

"It's called, 'Shop in the Name of Love,'" Bubbles types.

Leave it to Bubbles. Nobody is better with words than she is.

"Come on, Bubbles, let's see the Cheetah-licious lyrics!"

"Not now, brown cows. I want Mr. Johnson to hear it first when we go to the studio again. Maybe he and Pumpmaster Pooch will let us record it for our demo tape!"

"What time do we have to be at the studio?" Do' Re Mi asks. "Mrs. Bosco has got to go down to the agency with Twinkie, another one of her foster kids, so I'm on baby-sitting duty."

"We have to be there by ten o'clock," Angie responds.

Basta. Enough. I need help here, and nobody's paying any attention. "Listen, I feel like a *holograma* because no one is answering me! I have to go my dad's store tonight—who's gonna come with me?" I type, hoping Bubbles will take the steak bait. She loves my dad's Shake-a-Steak sandwich.

"We'll go with you," Angie types.

"I'll come, too, but I gotta drop Toto off to Dr. Bowser, the doggie dentist, first," Bubbles types.

"Maybe if you didn't give him so much Double Dutch Rocco Choco ice cream he wouldn't have to go to the dentist," I type. I mean, Toto eats too many treats.

"I'm gonna let you slide the read ride this time, Chuchie, since you are seriously grounded, but we'll be there to back you up," says Bubbles.

"*Está bien!*" I type back. That's my crew for you. Always down for the 'do. And not just hairdos either.

We are really pouting on the way to my dad's store. It's a good thing we've still got Amateur Hour at the Apollo Theatre coming up, because our session at the studio did not go well at all. If the song Pumpmaster Pooch and Mr. Johnson had us singing the first time was *la wacka*, you had to hear the one he gave us the second time around.

"It was called 'Can I Get a Burp?'" Bubbles

moaned as soon as she read the title. "What are we now, cows? she asked. "I don't think these guys get our image, and I'm not going out like that. Did you hear how they responded to my 'Shop in the Name of Love' lyrics?"

"Word, I noticed it. When you showed him the song, he looked at you like you were a stray dog or something," Do' Re Mi says.

"Let's sing some of it together before we go in to Killer Tacos, yo?" Bubbles says, looking at us.

"We're always down for the singing swirl, Bubbles!" Do' Re Mi says, leading us on as we start to sing "Shop in the Name of Love."

"Honey may come from bees
but money don't grow on trees.
When you shop in the name of love
you gotta ask yourself
What are you dreamin' of?
What are you schemin' of?
What are you trippin' on, love?"

By the time we get to the refrain, we are on 96th Street and Broadway, two steps from my dad's store. Then we do the cute "call and response" refrain that comes at the end of the song. We're groovin' from all the people watching us sing.

> *"Polo or solo.*
> *Say what?*
> *I want Gucci or Pucci.*
> *Say what?*
> *It's Prada or nada.*
> *Yeah—you got that?*
> *Uh-huh, I got that.*
> *Excuse me, Miss, does that dress come in red or*
> *blue?*
> *Oh, no?*
> *Well, that's alright 'cuz the cheetah print will*
> *always do!*
> *The Cheetah Girls are large and in charge*
> *but that don't mean that we charge up our cards!*
> *The Cheetah Girls are large and in charge*
> *but that don't mean we charge up our cards!"*

We finish with a big dance flourish, and all of a sudden, people all around us on the street are applauding, whooping it up, and shouting for more!

"I don't care how many pound cake remixes

Pumpmaster Pooch did for Sista Fudge, nobody writes *más coolio* songs than my Bubbles," I exclaim.

"Yeah, but how are we gonna get in a studio and do the songs *we* love?" Do' Re Mi adds, hitching up her backpack.

"Yeah, 'cuz we sure don't have songs-we-love money for no studio time," Bubbles says sadly.

"Maybe I could ask Princess Pamela," I say excitedly.

"Sure, Chuchie, as if you aren't in enough trouble for two lifetimes!" Bubbles says, then pulls my braids. "Excuse me, does that dress come in red or blue?"

We are laughing, right up until we see my father standing by the door. He is obviously waiting just for us, and I can tell he is grass-hopping mad.

"*Ay, Dios mío*, Chuchie, his eyes are breathing fire hotter than his Dodo Mojo Salsa Picante," Bubbles says, trying to make a joke. Nobody laughs, though. We all get real quiet.

"Hi, *Papí*," I say, squeaking. I have a little knot in my stomach, even though I want to hug him. I decide not to say one more word. I'm in enough *agua caliente*—hot water—as it is.

Then I see the anger go right out of his eyes. He takes a handkerchief out of his pocket and wipes his forehead. "You girls are late. I was getting worried. I don't like you walking around the city at night, *tú entiendes?*"

"*Sí,*" I say softly.

He takes us inside, and we sit down in one of the red plastic booths. Both he and Princess Pamela have red chairs in their stores—hers are velvet, though. Dad looks right at me. His eyes look very sad. Then he reaches into his pocket, takes out my copy of Mr. Johnson's agreement, and lays it on the table.

"Now, listen," he says, lowering his voice. "I don't have an opinion one way or the other. But I just got off the phone with Pamela, and she says you girls shouldn't sign this agreement."

"Why doesn't she want us to sign?" I ask.

"You mean because she got a psychic feeling, or something?" Do' Re Mi asks.

"Yes, I guess that's what you could call it," he says, pulling on his salt-and-pepper goatee. "But if I know one thing about Pamela, her premonitions are not to be played with, *entiendes?*"

We all look at each other like we've just seen a monster.

"Pamela said, 'Tell the Cheetah Girls to stay away from the animals.' She said Chanel would understand," my dad explains, looking at me again.

"What animals?" I respond, acting all innocent, nervous that the spotlight is now on me. I realize she must have known it was me on the phone all those times. How embarrassing!

All of a sudden, *la lucha*—the light—goes on inside my head, and I see what Princess Pamela was trying to tell me over the phone. "Beware of predators who run in packs," I remember her saying to me. "They will prey on your good fortune. They will circle around you like vultures and steal what is yours."

It wasn't the Cheetah Girls she was trying to warn me about! "Oh, snapples—Mr. Jackal Johnson and Mr. Hyena!" I gasp. "Jackals and Hyenas. *Those* are the animals!"

"What should we do?" Angie asks, nibbling on one of her Pee Wee Press-On Nails, then tapping her hand on the table nervously. "I mean, it's only a premonition . . . and we've got this big gig comin' up at the Apollo. . . ."

"Let me see what my mom thinks," Bubbles says, acting large and in charge, and taking her cell phone out of her backpack. These days, we are depending on Dorothea *más y más*—more and more.

"My mom can't see the future, but she can smell an okeydokey from the OK corral a mile away!" Bubbles quips. Over the phone, she explains the situation to her mom.

When she hangs up, Bubbles has a satisfied smile on her face. She says, "Mom says she has a call in to Mrs. Eagle, her lawyer, to see what she thought about the agreement. She'll let us know as soon as she gets a peep."

"So," Dad says, turning to me like a secret agent. "Did you at least *win* that Prada bag?"

"Nope," I say, looking sheepish, because my dad obviously knows everything, thanks to the Mummy, aka my mom. "Can you believe Derek Hambone did—and he only bought one ticket!"

Shaking his head, Dad asks, "What about that date with Krusher?"

Ay, Dios! He really does know everything.

"Nope," I say, all sad, so at least my dad will feel sorry for me. "Can you believe some DJ from WLIB radio won? It's so unfair!"

All of a sudden, Dad lets out a roar of a

laugh, showing his big, big teeth. "That contest must've been rigged!"

"And you *know* Chuchie made more calls to that 900 number than the rest of us make in a year!" Do' Re Mi says.

We all laugh. Then me and my dad do something we haven't done in a long time. We hug each other real tight, and I start crying. "I love you, *Papí*."

"I know, *mía princesa*," he says, stroking my head as I lean against his shoulder. "I love you, too—but you really can't 'shop in the name of love.'"

I look at my dad in surprise.

"I heard you girls singing outside," Dad says, raising his thick eyebrows. "A deaf man could hear you down the block. I think Pamela is right, though—the Cheetah Girls are gonna make a lot of people happy—especially *my* Cheetah Girl!"

Chapter 9

I am humming to myself on the way out my front door, when I stub my toe really hard on a case of Pucci's Burpy's soda that is sitting in the hallway. "Pucci, could you put this box in the kitchen, *por favor!*" I yell out. "It's in the way! I just tripped right over it!"

"I don't care, just do it yourself!" Pucci says, running into his room. He has been mad at me all day because I got to see Dad and he didn't.

"You know, for all that money I spent on ballet lessons for you, you are *clumsy*," Mom yells at me from the kitchen. She is wearing a turban on her head with a big diamond broach in the middle, and is all dressed up to go meet Mr. Tycoon at the airport.

"Mom, how come Pucci gets to order Burpy's soda from the Internet?" I yell back at her.

"Your ordering days are over till you can buy it yourself, that's why!" she says.

"Mom, I'm going to the meeting at Mr. Johnson's," I say. Bubbles's mom has called the meeting, but she won't say why. Only that her lawyer called her back, and she wants to straighten things out with Mr. Johnson. I'm worried about it—I know Princess Pamela warned us about him, but he's the only manager we've got—and we've got our demo coming out, and the gig at the Apollo—if it doesn't work out with Mr. Johnson, what are we gonna do?

All Mom says is "Be back in time for dinner, Chanel. And tell Dorothea the Dolce & Gabbana sample sale starts at ten o'clock tomorrow."

"*Está bien.*" Too bad I won't be going to the sample sale, I think to myself as I close the door. But these days, and until I pay off what I owe my mom, shopping and me are total strangers.

Everyone is quiet when I walk into Mr. Johnson's office, and they all turn to look at me.

They must be early, because I know I'm not late, I think. Nervously, I look at my Miss Wiggy! watch.

"Let's cut to the paper chase here, Mr. Johnson. This contract is not going to work," Dorothea says, looking up from her leopard brim and right into Mr. Johnson's eyes.

"Mrs. Garibaldi, I can assure you this contract is pretty standard," Mr. Johnson says, smoothing down his bright red tie. "We're only talking about production costs."

"According to my lawyer, at the royalty rate you have written in this clause, the only game the Cheetah Girls are gonna be able to afford for the next ten years is jumping jacks!" Dorothea snaps at Mr. Johnson, then leans over his desk.

Bubbles looks at me and puts her finger over her mouth. I can see that I have walked right into another soap opera.

"I am footing the cost of the demo tape, wheeling and dealing to make everything happen for the Cheetah Girls, so it's only fitting that *I'm* sitting on the throne and seeing my girls become stars," Mr. Johnson says, slamming his hands down on his desk.

The Cheetah Girls

"You're going to be seeing 'stars,' all right—
right after I clunk you with my purse!"
Dorothea says, her dark brown eyes getting
squinty. "You are no longer going to manage
my girls. And, if you ever come sniffing around
them again, Mr. *Jackal*, or if you try to release
any of those songs with their vocals on it, I'm
gonna come back and be so shady the sun is
gonna go down on you. Do you understand?"
Dorothea says in that scary voice she gets when
she is mad. Leave it to my *madrina* to throw her
weight around and show who is the conductor
on this choo-choo train.

"What about the girls' gig at the Apollo? I
hooked it up so Mr. Hyena can be there. I mean,
I'm digging your concern, Mrs. Garibaldi, but I
think you're making a big mistake," Mr.
Johnson says, swiveling in his fake leather
chair. There are little beads of sweat on his forehead, like I get when I'm scared.

"The only mistake I'm making is that I don't
hit you over the head with my pocketbook, you
hungry scavenger!" Dorothea says, then
motions for us to get up with her.

We all walk out of the office behind

Dorothea, and bigmouthed Bubbles says to Mr. Johnson, "See ya around like a doughnut!"

Why can't I think of the kinds of things that Bubbles says? I start smiling and looking at my crew, but Angie and Aqua look sad.

"It would have been nice to perform at the Apollo. What are we gonna do now?" Aqua says, popping her gum.

"Don't pop gum in public, darling, you're too pretty for that," Dorothea says, then puts her arm around Aqua.

"I'm sorry, Mrs.—I mean *Ms.* Dorothea. I was just kinda nervous in there," Aqua explains. She puts the pink blob of gum in a tissue and throws it in the garbage receptacle by the elevator.

"Now we don't have a demo tape. We don't have a show. We don't have nothing. What *are* we gonna do, Ms. Dorothea?" Angie says, crossing her arms and pouting like a Texas Tornado cheerleader.

"Maybe we missed our last chance, last dance. Was the contract really that bad, Ms. Dorothea?" Do' Re Mi asks, looking up at my *madrina*, who is more than a foot taller than her, especially with her high heels on. They are bright-red patent-leather pumps that look good enough to eat.

Eat? Suddenly, I realize that I'm hungry.

"Some Dominican-style *arroz con pollo* would be great right about now," I say to Bubbles.

"Darlings, I know this fabulous Moroccan restaurant we can go to around the corner. My treat!" Dorothea says, pulling out her compact. "Listen, Cheetah Girls, don't get so nervous you're ready to pounce at the first opportunity that comes along. We're gonna figure out something, okay? It takes more than one shifty jackal to chase us out of the jiggy jungle, am I right?"

Dorothea looks at us, extends her hands, and does the Cheetah Girls handshake with all five of us.

"You got that right, Momsy poo—we are gonna do what we gotta do!" Bubbles says, egging her on. "Even if we did miss the opportunity of a lifetime, and even if it takes us longer, we're still gonna get diggity, no doubt. It's just a matter of time."

"I hear that," Do' Re Mi says, then sighs. She's trying to keep her spirits up—we all are—but it's hard not to keep thinking about everything we've just lost.

Because we are so down in *la dumpa*, after our *lonchando*, Dorothea asks us to come to her store so she can give us a surprise. When we get to the store, my mom is there! I wonder what's going on.

"What are you doing here, Auntie Juanita?" Bubbles asks my mom. I'm thinking, I hope Mr. Tycoon's plane didn't get hijacked! Mom puts her sunglasses on her head, and holds up a newspaper. It's the latest issue of the *Uptown Express*. "Did you see this?" she says, handing Dorothea the newspaper.

"Hmmph, the hyenas are circling after all!" Dorothea says, showing it to us. "'Hyena Records Sings Its Last Note, And Its Founder Is Singing Like a Crow to the Feds!'" We all gather around the newspaper, as Dorothea reads us the article blow by blow.

"Seems that Mr. Johnson and Mr. Hyena were in cahoots all along," Dorothea explains.

"What's a cahoot?" Angie asks.

"That means they were the okeydokey duo,

get it?" Bubbles says. "They were flipping the flimflam together."

"Oh," Angie says, shaking her head. "They weren't doing right by us. I get it."

"Angie, they were crooks!" Do' Re Mi blurts out, then plops down on Dorothea's leopard love seat.

"Seems Mr. Johnson would steer artists to the record label," Dorothea says.

Before she can continue, Bubbles blurts out, "Signing them to these *radickio* deals, like the one he was trying to perpetrate on us!"

"That's right, darling," Dorothea says, reaching for one of the Godiva chocolates on the counter. "Then Mr. Hyena would cover the royalty tracks, so that the artists never knew how much they were making, and the two would skim the profits out of the company."

"So Princess Pamela was right after all!" I blurt out, then realize that I should buy some Krazy Glue and stick my lips together permanently.

My mom looks at me like she is already picking out the color of my coffin.

"Juanita, I'm gonna side with Chanel on this one," Dorothea says, putting her arm around my mom as she explains Princess Pamela's predictions to her. "She may not be your cup of tea, but she sure knows how to read tea leaves!" Dorothea says, doing the Cheetah Girls handshake with us.

Mom thinks for a minute, her face all serious. "I don't mind if you see her," she says to me all of sudden. "You just cannot take any presents from her, or call her Psychic Hot Line—I don't care if she invented the crystal ball!"

"I told you, *Mamí*, I won't take anything from her again," I say nervously.

"You know what mothers are?" Mom asks me.

"What?"

"Psychics who don't charge—you can get all the advice you need for *free!*" My mom smiles, slapping Dorothea a high five.

"Well, I'm glad you all are happy—but we still don't have a demo," Aqua says, reaching into the box of Godiva. She must be getting very comfortable around here, because she used to always ask Dorothea first.

"Help yourself, darling," Dorothea says.

"Oh, I'm sorry, Ms. Dorothea!" Aqua blurts out.

"That's all right, just enjoy yourself," Dorothea says, smiling.

"Chanel, are you sure those Chihuahuas don't shed hair?" Mom asks me.

"I'm very sure, because Do' Re Mi looked it up in a book!" I say.

"That's right, Mrs. Simmons, I did," Do' Re Mi says, helping me out.

"Maybe next weekend, we'll see if we find one for Pucci's birthday," Mom says.

I can't believe my ears. "Oh, *Mamí*," I say, and run over to hug her.

"Don't hug me yet. If he sheds one hair, he's going right back to the dog pound," Juanita quips.

"Why do you have to get a 'he'?" Do' Re Mi quips.

"Because Pucci hates girls—except for Bubbles," I volunteer with a giggle, then sit Toto in my lap. "He's not like you, Boo-boo, right?"

Ms. Dorothea motions for all of us to sit down. "Now, the reason why I wanted all of you to come back to the store . . ." She breaks out in a big smile. "I have a little surprise for you, Cheetah Girls." Dorothea brushes her wavy wiglet hairs out of her face. "Remember I told you Jellybean Nyce was in here shopping?"

"Really!" Angie says. "Omigod, we love her!"

"I know. And I told her about your predicament, and she is gonna hook us up with the producer who did *her* demo, Chili Dog Watkins."

"*Really*?" Bubbles blurts out.

"Really," Dorothea counters. "But I'm not finished. I, Dorothea Garibaldi, have secured the fabulous Cheetah Girls a spot on The Amateur Hour at the world-famous Apollo!"

"No way, Jose!" I say, my mouth hanging open. "How did you do that, *madrina*?"

"I did it the way *every* manager does—I sold you like the second coming of the Spice Rack Girls, that's how," Dorothea brags. "You'll never say I don't work overtime for *my* artists."

"Mom, are you saying what I think you're saying?" Bubbles asks, smiling and putting her arm around Dorothea.

"Darling, one can never be too sure what you're thinking, but I'll tell you what I'm saying," Dorothea says, looking at all of us. "It's time for the Cheetah Girls to have *real* management—and you're looking at her."

We scream with delight, while Mom just looks on from the counter, amused. "I hope you know what you're doing, Dottie, because these girls will wear you out!"

"Oh, I know what I'm doing. I'm taking the Cheetah Girls right to the top, where they belong."

Angie can't contain her Southern charm any longer, and screams out, "Come on Mr. Sandman, show me your hook, 'cuz I'm ready for Freddy!"

Angie, of course, is referring to the famous bozo with the hook who runs bad acts off the stage if they get booed by the audience. The Sandman kinda looks like a brown clown, but his antics are no joke, for sure.

"All I can say is, I hope Freddy is ready for us at the world-famous Apollo," Bubbles adds.

All I can say is, *la dopa!*

"Come on, Cheetah Girls," Bubbles shouts. "Let's give the world a taste of our latest, greatest hit!"

We break into "Shop in the Name of Love," and the whole place is rockin', customers and all. We look at each other and smile, nodding our heads. Me most of all, 'cuz I'm so glad this all happened. It was all worth it, all the grief, all the tears—just to come out of it with a song like this one.

Yeah—it's just a matter of time. Look out, world—the Cheetah Girls are comin'—and we are large and in charge!

Shop in the Name of Love

Polo or solo
Gucci or Pucci
Prada or Nada
is the way I wanna live

Ma don't make me wait
or I'll gaspitate
till I get my own credit card
and sashay right to the bargain yard!

That's right, y'all
Honey may come from bees
but money don't grow on trees.
You may think you're large
'cuz you charge
But you're looking good
and sleeping on a barge!

When you shop in the Name Of Love
you gotta ask yourself
What are you dreamin' of?

What are you schemin' of?
What are you trippin' on, love?

That's right, y'all!
The Cheetah Girls are large
and in charge
but that don't mean
we charge up our cards

The Cheetah Girls are large
and in charge
but that don't mean
we charge up our cards

Polo or solo
Gucci for Pucci
Prada or nada
is the way I wanna live

Say what?

Polo or solo
Gucci for Pucci
Prada or nada
is the way I wanna live

You got that?
Yeah. I got that.
Excuse, Miss,
does that dress come in red or blue?
Well, that's all right
'cuz the cheetah print
will always do!

The Cheetah Girls are large
and in charge
but that don't mean
we charge up our cards
You got that?
Yeah. I got that!

That's right, y'all
Honey may come from bees
but money don't grow on trees.
You may think you're large
'cuz you charge
But you're looking good
and sleeping on a barge

When you shop in the Name of Love
you gotta ask yourself

What are you dreamin' of?
What are you schemin' of?
What are you trippin' on, love?

The Cheetah Girls are large
large and in charge
but that don't mean
we charge up our cards
You got that?
Yeah. I got that!

The Cheetah Girls Glossary

Abuela: Grandmother.

Adobo down: Mad flava.

Arroz con pollo: Rice and chicken.

Benjamins: Bucks, dollars.

Bruja: A good or bad witch.

Caliente mad: Really angry.

Confirmation: Catholic religion ceremony at the age of thirteen.

Cuatro yuks!: When something or someone is four times yucky.

Do me a flava: Do me a favor.

Duckets: Money, loot.

Down for the 'do: Ready to support.

Está bien: Awright.

Fib-eronis: Teeny-weeny fibs.

Flipping the flimflam: Acting or doing something shady.

Floss: Show off.

Frijoles: Beans.

Gracias gooseness: Thank goodness.

La dopa!: Fabulous.

La gran fantasía: Living in Happyville.

La wacka: Something that is wack.

Lonchando: Lunching.

Madrina: Godmother.

Majordomo: Legitimate.

Mentira: A not-so-little lie.

Muy coolio: Very cool.

Pinata-whacking mad: When someone is madder than *caliente* mad.

Poco paz: A little peace.

Qué broma!: What a joke!

Querida: Dear. Precious one.

Radickkio: Ridiculous!

Ready for Freddy: Ready to do your thing, no matter what happens.

Schemo: Idiot

Tan coolio: So cool.

Tú sabes que tú sabes: You know what you know.

Weakness for carats: Someone who is a lifetime member of the diamonds-are-a-girl's-best-friend club.

Wheel-a-deala: Making moves, both good or bad.

Winky dink: Blink and you'll miss it.

Yo tengo un coco: I have a crush!

Who's 'Bout to Bounce?

For my mother,
Ruth Gregory,
wherever you are

Chapter 1

When you put the *C* to the *H* to the *A* to the *N* to the *E* to the *L*, you've got one supa-fast Cheetah *señorita*! I mean, Chanel "Chuchie" Simmons is all legs, even though she is only five feet two—which is just a little taller than me. All right, Chanel is *four* inches taller, but that's not the point.

Right about now, after jogging all the way from Soho, where Chanel lives, up to Harlem, where I live (which is more miles than the Road Runner does in one cartoon episode) the rest of us Cheetah Girls feel like wobbly cubs. We're desperate for a little shade and some soda!

Chanel, on the other hand, looks like *she's* ready to do pirouettes or something. Now I can see why she used to take ballet lessons. She's got "gamma ray legs"!

"Wait up, Cheetah *Señorita*, yo!" I yell to Chanel, just to help her remember that she's not out here all by herself—that she is running with her crew. *Our* crew, that is. The Cheetah Girls.

Besides Chanel "Chuchie" Simmons, that would be: Galleria "Bubbles" Garibaldi, who is the leader of our pack; Aquanette and Anginette Walker, aka the "Huggy Bear twins"; and, of course, lucky me—Dorinda "Do' Re Mi" Rogers.

See, not too long ago, the five of us started a girl group, called the Cheetah Girls. You could pinch me every time I say it, 'cuz I still can't believe we got it like that.

Before I met my crew, I only sang for fun— you know, goofing around at home to entertain everybody. Bubbles and Chanel are the dopest friends I've ever had, and I'm so grateful that they got me to sing outside my bedroom.

I met them on our first day at Fashion Industries High School, where we are all freshmen, and it's the best thing that ever happened to me. Before, I was just plain old Dorinda Rogers. Now, I'm Do' Re Mi, which is the nickname my crew gave me. Do' Re Mi—one of the Cheetah Girls!

Bubbles and Chanel say we're gonna take over the world with our global groove. I hope they're right. For now though, we're just happy that Galleria's mom, Ms. Dorothea, has hooked us up with the famous Apollo Theatre Amateur Hour Contest! It's next Saturday—only a week and a half till we're up there, performing on that stage where the Supremes once sang. That is so *dope*!

See, Ms. Dorothea is not only Bubbles's mom—she has now officially become our manager. Our first manager was Mr. Jackal Johnson. We met him at the Cheetah-Rama Club, where we performed for the first time. He tried to manage us on the "okeydokey" tip. That means he was a crook.

When Ms. Dorothea found out Mr. Johnson was trying to get his hands on our duckets (not that we have any yet), she nearly threw him out the window! She doesn't play, you know what I'm sayin'?

Of course, Ms. Dorothea isn't out here

running with us today, because she is very busy with her boutique—Toto in New York . . . Fun in Diva Sizes—she runs the store, designs the clothes, and everything.

Aquanette says, "Dorothea's probably eating Godiva chocolates and laughing at us."

Word. She should talk! In fact, Aqua and Angie *both* like to eat a lot. If they keep it up, they're gonna be bigger than Dorothea by the time they're her age! (Dorothea used to be a model, but now she is "large and in charge," if you know what I mean!)

"Come on, Do' Re *Poor* Mi, move that matchstick butt!" heckles Chanel, poking out her tongue and "bugging" her eyes. Chanel is on a jelly roll, and she won't quit.

See, I can run almost as fast as her, but I don't wanna leave the rest of my crew behind.

I'm not flossin'. I can dance, skateboard, jump double Dutch, *and* I was the top tumbler in my gymnastics class last year in junior high, so what you know about that, huh?

Jackie Chan's got nothing on me, either. If I wanted to, I could do karate moves—well, if I had a black belt I could. At this point, I'd settle for a polka-dot belt, 'cuz you gotta watch your back in the jiggy jungle, especially in the part where I live, way up on 116th Street.

We've been running for a kazillion miles, and right about now Bubbles is at the end of her rope-a-dope.

"Chuchie, would you quit runnin' ahead of us? If you don't stop flossin', I'm gonna pull out one of your fake braids!" she snarls at the Cheetah *señorita*.

I start giggling. See, sometimes I'm scared to snap on Chanel or Bubbles, because I'm afraid if I do, then they won't let me be their friend.

Me, I'm just the new kid on the block. It's okay for them to snap on each other, though, 'cuz they've been friends forever—ever since Bubbles stole Chanel's Gerber Baby apple sauce—so they fight like sisters all the time.

They don't *look* like sisters, though. Bubbles is very light-skinned, and she has a really nice, full shape. About the only running she likes to do is to the dinner table, or to a party. I wish I had a shape like hers, instead of mine, which looks like a boy's.

Chanel is more tan and flat-chested, like me, and really skinny, too. But because she's taller, it looks really cute on her. She's kinda like a

Mexican jumping bean. She'll eat Chub Chub candies all day on the run, and keep jumpin'.

Anyhow, the reason why we're out here panting like puppies is not to lose weight. It's because Dorothea is putting us through this whole "divettes-in-training camp" thing, so we can become a legit girl group, like the Supremes or the Spice Rack Girls. That means we have to do what she says:

- We have to run five miles, at least once a week, to build up our endurance and lung power. This way, we'll be able to sing in big stadiums, and travel on the road without getting sore throats all the time.

- We have to take vocal lessons and dance classes.

- We have to watch old videos. Once a month, we have "Seventies Appreciation Night," which means we all get together over at Bubbles's house, and watch old videos of groups and movies with peeps in *mad* funny outfits.

☙ We have to develop other skills so we don't end up on the "chitlin' circuit." That's where singers go who don't even have a bucket to put their duckets in. They end up performing for no pay—they just pass a hat around for tips!

☙ We have to do our homework in school, read magazines, and dress dope, like divettes with duckets.

Chanel's mother, Juanita, has volunteered to run with us, but she is in better shape than we are and she just runs way ahead by herself. Since she's a grown-up, we don't mind. Because she is running ahead of us, she won't see us making faces, whining, giggling, and snapping on the peeps as we pass them by. Right now, though, we're too tired to even snap on a squirrel.

Juanita looks kinda funny from the back when she's running, because the bottom of her feet come up fast, like hooves on a horse, and her ponytail keeps bouncing up and down. She's kinda tall and skinny for a lady her age. See, she used to be a model, just like Dorothea (but *she* exercises like the Road Runner). Every now and then she looks back to ask us, "You girls all right?"

Poor Bubbles's mouth is hanging open, and she looks kinda mad, but she never gives up on anything. She just starts snapping. She sweats so much, though—there are droplets dripping down the side of her face, making her hair stick together like gooey sideburns!

The twins are kinda slow, too, but they don't complain a lot about running. Their minds are on other things.

"Do you really think the Sandman comes with a hook and pulls you off the stage if the audience boos you?" Anginette whines, running alongside me.

The Sandman at the Apollo Theatre is supposed to be this guy dressed like a scarecrow, with a big hook or something, who chases Amateur Hour contestants off the stage if they're wack.

"You sure he ain't like Jason from *Friday the 13th*?" Aquanette asks, chuckling nervously. Aqua and Angie are *Scream* queens. They love to watch horror movies with people getting their eyes poked out.

Who's 'Bout to Bounce?

"I don't know, Angie," I say, panting, "but if the audience even *looks* like they're gonna start booing, then I'm gonna bounce, *before* the Sandman tries to hook us!"

"Oh, no, that is too wack-a-doodle-do! And it's not gonna happen," Bubbles says, smiling again. "We're gonna be in there like swimwear."

Galleria always makes us feel better. That's why she's Cheetah number one. Anything goes wrong, and we all look to her, just naturally. She's not takin' any shorts.

We are running in Central Park now, and suddenly, a funny-looking guy with a silver thing on his head zooms by on his bicycle, and almost runs down Aquanette. "Dag on, he almost knocked me over," yells Aqua, looking back at him as he rides away.

The twins are not used to the ways of the Big Apple, or how fast everybody moves here. They say everybody moves a lot slower in Houston, which is where they grew up—in a big house with a porch and everything in the suburbs.

"Beam me up, Scottie, you wack-a-doodle helmet head!" Galleria yells back at the guy on the bike, then gasps for breath. She sticks up for us a lot, because she isn't afraid of anybody.

"Y'all, there are a lot of crazy people here," Anginette chimes in.

"Helmet Head probably woulda knocked her over if nobody was looking!" Bubbles says.

"I wonder if that was a strainer on his head," Chanel says, giggling.

"And what were those funny-looking antenna things sticking up?" I giggle back.

"Come on, you lazy *muchachas*!" Juanita yells back at us, waving for us to follow her.

I don't know how long we've been running, but I am so grateful when we finally reach the park exit at 110th Street.

"Thank *gooseness*," Galleria yelps, as we stop by the benches where Juanita is waiting for us impatiently, her hands on her hips. Bubbles bends over and is panting heavily, holding on to her knees. Her hair is so wild it's flopping all over the place like a mop.

This is where I get off, I think with a sad sigh. I wish I could invite my crew over to my house for some "Snapple and snaps." After all, I only live six blocks from here. But after seeing where *they* all live, I'm too embarrassed to let them see my home.

I live with my foster mother, Mrs. Bosco, her husband, Mr. Bosco, and about nine or ten foster brothers and sisters—depending on which day you ask me. We all share an apartment in the Cornwall Projects. We keep it clean, but still, it's real small and crowded. It needs some fixing up by the landlord, too—if you know what I'm sayin'.

It bothers me a lot to be a foster child but Mrs. Bosco is a pretty nice lady, even though she's not really my mom or anything—but now, I'm hanging with my new crew, and all of them have such nice houses, and real families. . . .

"Ms. Simmons, can't we at least *walk* to our house from here?" Angie asks, whining to Juanita.

Since I never invite anybody over, the next stop on this gravy train is the twins' house on 96th Street. Angie and Aqua live with their father in a nice apartment that faces Riverside Park. My apartment faces the stupid post office.

"Okay, lazy," Juanita huffs back.

"Well," I say, "bye, everybody."

Chanel puts her sweaty arms around me to kiss me good-bye.

"Ugh, Chanel!" I wince.

"Do' Re Mi, can't you see I love you!" she giggles back, kissing me on cheek and making silly noises. Then Chanel whispers in my ear, laying on the Spanish accent, "You know I was just playing *wichoo*. I know you can run as fast as me."

"Okay, *Señorita*, just get off me!" I giggle back. "Bye, Bubbles, and all you boo-boo heads!"

"Bye, Dorinda," Juanita says. Then she adds, "Don't stay up late, 'cuz *we're* going to bed *early*," giving me that look like "you better not be trying to hog the chat room on the Internet tonight."

See, Chanel's kinda grounded for life—until she pays back the money she charged on her mom's credit card last month. She's not supposed to be on the phone or the Internet, runnin' up more bills.

"See y'all tomorrow at school," I yell, then add, "not you two!" to Angie and Aqua. The twins don't go to Fashion Industries High, like me, Chanel, and Bubbles. They go to LaGuardia Performing Arts High School, which is even doper.

Maybe next year, me, Bubbles, and Chuchie can transfer to LaGuardia, so we can all be together. . . .

You know, you have to audition to get into LaGuardia. Chanel was too chicken to audition last year, coming out of junior high—even though Bubbles wanted to go to LaGuardia in the worst way. But Bubbles didn't want to audition without Chuchie, so they didn't go. That's why they both wound up at Fashion Industries, which is lucky for me!

But now, who knows? Sure, auditioning is kinda scary, but now that we're the Cheetah Girls, we've got each other, and we've had some experience performing—so I know we can do it.

Besides, Bubbles says if the Cheetah Girls really take off, and our lives get too hectic, we'll have to get private tutors anyway. Private tutors! Wouldn't that be the dopest?

That's Bubbles for you, always planning ahead to "destination: jiggy jungle." That's the place, she says, where dreams really do come true—*if* you go for *yours*.

Listening to Bubbles, we all feel like we really can do anything we set our minds to.

Chapter
2

I head uptown alone, on my way back to the apartment. Soon, my thoughts drift forward to next Saturday night.

What if the Sandman really does chase us off the stage? Or if somebody hits me on the head with a can of Burpy soda while I'm performing? Then I'll get a concussion . . . and I won't be able to take care of Mrs. Bosco and all my brothers and sisters. . . .

"Hey! Watch where you're goin', shorty!"

By the time I hear Can Man's warning, it's too late, 'cuz he's slammed his shopping cart filled with empty cans right into my back. I trip over a mound of rocks, and a thousand cans go flying everywhere.

"*You* watch where *you're* goin'!" I scream back at him. From my knees, I pick up a can and make like I'm gonna throw it at him.

Can Man is one of those people in New York who are out all day, collecting empty soda and beer cans, and returning them to places like the Piggly Wiggly supermarket around the corner for the deposit money.

In other words, he is a homeless man, but I think he is "sippin' more times than he is tippin'," because he screams a lot for no reason, and does wack things—like this.

"You better not take one of my cans, shorty!" Can Man yells. Now he is foaming at the mouth. His eyes are buggin', too.

I drop the can and run. I don't even listen to the people who ask me if they can help. No, they *can't* help me!

Why does everything happen to me? My real mother gave me away. My first foster mother, Mrs. Parkay, gave me up when I was little, for no reason. And now, Can Man runs into me with his stupid shopping cart!

My ankle really hurts, and I sit down on somebody's front stoop to massage it.

Sometimes I get scared that I'm just gonna

end up like a bag lady, and get married to Can Man or something. Who am I kidding? Maybe I'll never be anything! In fact, if it wasn't for my crew, I'd be just a wanna-be, I tell myself. Look at Bubbles and Chanel. You can tell they are born stars.

Me? Well, everybody says I can dance really good, and I guess I can sing okay. But I'm never gonna be famous. In fact, when I'm alone, and not with the group, I'm really scared of performing—and especially auditioning.

Now my legs *really* hurt from running all those miles, and I think Can Man might've broken my left ankle! I'm so mad, I wanna punch somebody. Let somebody—*anybody*—be stupid enough to get in my way now! Fuming like a fire engine, I hobble, step by step on my one good foot, to my apartment building.

"Hi, Dorinda! How come you limping?" asks Pookie, who is sitting in the courtyard. See, there are a lot of buildings in the Cornwall Projects, but only two of them have a courtyard, so all the kids hang out here.

Pookie is sitting with his mom, Ms. Keisha, and his sister, Walkie-talkie Tamela. We call her that because she never shuts up.

"Heh, Pookie," I respond, huffing and puffing. "Can Man hit me with his cart and knocked me over."

"You know he's crazy. You better stay out of his way, Dorinda, before he really hurts you," mumbles Ms. Keisha.

"I know, Ms. Keisha, but I didn't see him because he was behind me. Is Mrs. Bosco home?"

"Yep," she says, nodding her head at me. See, Ms. Keisha is nosy, and she knows that *we* know she's nosy. She sits outside all day, with a head full of pink hair rollers and even pinker bedroom slippers, talking about people's business like she's Miss Clucky on the gossip show.

Not that her motormouth doesn't come in "handy dandy," as Bubbles would say. See, if you're in trouble, and you wanna know if you're gonna get it when you get upstairs, you just ask Ms. Keisha. She knows if your mother is home—*and* if she's mad at you.

The courtyard isn't much of a playground for all the kids who live here, but it's better than hanging out in front with the "good-for-nothings," as Mrs. Bosco calls the knuckleheads who hang around all day and don't go to school or to work.

Some of the people who live here try to make it look nice, too. Once somebody tried to plant a tree right in the cement, but it was gone the next morning. So now there are no trees—just a few po' little brown shrubs that look like nubs. And there aren't any slides, swings, or jungle gym to play on, either—just some big old "X" marks scribbled with chalk on the ground, for playing jumping jacks.

I used to jump double Dutch rope out here all the time when I was little. I was the rope-a-dopest double Dutcher, too, even though Tawanna, who lives in Building C, thinks *she's* the bomb. She's such a big show-off, it just looks like she's got more moves than she *really* does.

It's getting dark out already. I know I've missed dinner, but Mrs. Bosco will still have something waiting for me. Hobbling on my good ankle, I open the door to the building, and get my keys out of my sweatpants. After dinner, I think, I'd better go see if Mrs. Gallstone down the hall is home. She's a nurse, and she'll know if my ankle is broken or not.

The Cheetah Girls

I hope little Arba is over her cold, too, I think, as I limp to the elevator. Arba is my new little sister. She's almost five years old—the same age I was when I came to live with Mrs. Bosco. She doesn't speak English very well, but we're teaching her.

Arba is Albanian by nationality, but her mother had her here, then died. Mrs. Bosco says a lot of people come to the Big Apple looking for the streets paved in gold, but instead they get "chewed up and spit out."

Most of the time, the caseworkers never say much about where foster kids come from, or what happened to them. They just drop them off, sometimes with bags of clothes and toys. Anyway, someone took Arba to the Child Welfare Department because she had no family, and they gave her to Mrs. Bosco to take care of until somebody adopts her—if anybody ever does.

You could say our house is kinda like the United Nations or something. My seven-year-old foster brother, Topwe, is African—real African, from Africa. He speaks English all funny, but it's his native language. They all talk like that over there!

Topwe gets the most attention, because he is

Who's 'Bout to Bounce?

HIV-positive, which means he was infected with the AIDS virus. His mother was a crack addict, Mrs. Bosco told me, but I'm not supposed to say anything to Topwe or the other kids. I'm the only one, she says, who can keep a secret. It's true, too. I really can.

Like I said, the United Nations. There's Arba for one, and Topwe for another. Then there's my four-year-old brother, Corky, who is part Mexican and part Bajin. (Bajin is what you call people from Barbados, which is in the British West Indies.)

Corky is really cute, and he has the most beautiful greenish-gray eyes you've ever seen. His father is fighting with Child Welfare, trying to get him back. I hope he doesn't. I don't want Corky to leave.

I know kids are supposed to live with their families, but I feel like Corky's *my* family, too— I mean, he's been here practically his whole life! What's his father know about him, anyway?

See, sometimes the kids in our house go back to their real parents. Once in a blue moon, they even get adopted by new families, who are looking for a child to love. Nobody has ever tried to adopt *me*, though.

Sometimes I cry about that—nobody wanting me. See, most parents who adopt want little kids, and by the time I got to Mrs. Bosco's, I was already too old—almost five. So yeah, it hurts when one of my brothers or sisters gets adopted and I don't. But I feel glad to have a place to live anyway. It could be worse—I could be out on the street, like a lot of other people. Like Can Man . . .

Besides, we may not have much, but life is pretty good here. We all stick up for each other when the chips are down. And Mrs. Bosco loves us all—she just doesn't let herself show it very often. I guess it's because that way, it won't hurt so much when the caseworkers take one of her kids away.

Even in the lobby, I can tell that somebody upstairs is cooking fried chicken. I *love* fried chicken—with collard greens, potato salad, and corn bread. That's the bomb meal.

We call where we live the "Corn Bread Projects" since, when you walk down the hallway, you can smell all the different kinds of food people are cooking in their apartments.

That's actually better than the elevators, which sometimes smell like *eau de pee pee*.

When the elevator door closes now, I get a whiff of some nasty smell. I hold my breath the whole ride up.

Everybody says the Cornwall Projects are dangerous, but nobody bothers us around here. That's because my foster father, Mr. Bosco, is *really* big, and he wears a uniform to work—plus he has a nightstick he says is for "clubbing knuckleheads."

He is a security guard who works the night shift, so he sleeps during the day. Most of us kids don't see him much, but he is really nice. He laughs like a big grizzly bear. Both times I got skipped in school, he gave me five dollars and said, "I'll give you five dollars every time you get skipped again!"

Chapter 3

As soon as I open the front door of the apartment, Twinkie jumps out from the corner. That's the game we play every day.

"Hey, Twinkie!" I say to my favorite sister, who is nine years old. Her real name is Rita, but we call her Twinkie, because she has blond fuzzy hair, and fat, yummy cheeks.

"Don't call me Twinkie anymore!" she announces to me, shuffling the deck of Pokémon cards she has in her hands. Twinkie grabs my hand, and pulls me down the hallway to the kitchen. Everybody else has eaten already, but Mrs. Bosco always puts my food in the oven, covered in a piece of tinfoil. All the kids know they'd better not touch it, either.

Who's 'Bout to Bounce?

"I have to whisper something in your ear," Twinkie says, pulling me down so she can reach.

"Okay," I say, hugging her real tight. Twinkie has lived with us for nineteen months, and we are really close—she will always be my sister forever, no matter what.

"You have to call me Butterfly now," Twinkie tells me, and her blue eyes get very big, like saucers.

"Okay, Cheetah Rita Butterfly!" I giggle, then tickle her stomach, which I know sends her into hysterics.

"Stop!" she screams. "You big Cheetah monkey!"

"What's a Cheetah monkey, Cheetah Rita Butterfly?" I ask, poking her stomach some more. "Tell me, tell me, or I'm not gonna stop!"

"I don't know, but *you* are!" she screams, and giggles even more hysterically.

"Okay, I'll call you Cheetah Rita Butterfly, if you promise that we are gonna be sisters forever. You're never gonna get away from me!"

"Okay, okay!" she screeches, and I stop tickling her. After a minute, she stops laughing. "We're not really sisters though, are we?"

Twinkie asks me with that cute little face.

"Yes, we are," I say.

"Then how come we have different last names?" Twinkie asks, suddenly all serious. She is so smart.

"That doesn't mean we're not sisters, Cheetah Rita."

"Okay, then, I promise," Twinkie says, teasing me, then she runs off, daring me to chase her. "I'm Cheetah Rita Butterfly! Watch me fly so high!"

Putting one of the Pokémon cards from the jungle deck over one eye, Twinkie turns, then squinches up her face and yells, "Dorinda!"

"What?" I turn to answer her back.

"You can call me Twinkie again!" She giggles up a storm as I chase her down the hallway into her room, yelling, "You little troublemaker!"

Twinkie shares her bedroom with Arba, who I already told you about, and my sister Kenya.

Kenya is six, and she is a "special needs child," because she is always getting into trouble at school, or fighting with the other kids. But I don't think she is "emotionally disturbed" like they say. She is just selfish, and doesn't like to share anything, or listen to anybody. Twinkie and Arba don't seem to like sharing a room with Kenya. Can't say I blame them.

I share a bedroom—a tiny one—with my two *other* sisters, Chantelle and "Monie the Meanie." Monie is the oldest out of all of us. She is seventeen, and has a major attitude problem. I'm so glad she has a boyfriend now—Hector—and she's over at his house a lot. She doesn't like to help clean or anything, and she likes to boss me around. I wish she would just go stay with Hector. It would make more room for me and Chantelle.

Chantelle is eleven, but tries to act like she's grown already, sitting around reading *Sistarella* magazine, and hogging my computer.

Mr. Hammer gave *me* the computer last year. He's our super, and he knows how to fix everything—and who throws out what. He told me that a tenant from one of the other buildings was gonna throw out her computer, and he got her to give it to me. I call Mr. Hammer "Inspector Gadget," 'cuz he's got the hookup, if you know what I'm saying.

The boys all share the biggest bedroom. That would be Topwe and Corky, along with Khalil (who has only lived here two months), Nestor (who we nicknamed Nestlé's Quik because he eats really fast), and "Shawn the Fawn" (we call him that because he's really shy, and always runs away from people). Four of the boys sleep in bunk beds to make more space.

Mr. and Mrs. Bosco's bedroom used to be the pantry—that's how small it is. But since Mrs. Bosco is up all day with us kids, and Mr. Bosco works all night, usually only one of them sleeps at a time—so I guess it doesn't seem as small to them as it does to us.

Every time one of us leaves for good, I always think the Boscos will switch bedrooms around. But they never do. They always go and get another foster child to fill the empty bed. That's the way they are. Lucky for all of us . . .

I have followed Twinkie into her bedroom. Arba is sitting there on the floor, drawing with crayons, and Kenya has her mouth poked out, staring at a page in her school notebook. She's always mad about something. I feel bad for her. But I know if I ignore her, then she will at least act nice for five minutes, trying to get my attention.

I pretend Kenya isn't even there. "There's Arba!" I exclaim, kissing her dirty face. Then I sit on the floor to take off my smelly sneakers and socks.

That gets Kenya. "Abba!" she yells, taking a crayon from Arba's hand. Kenya never pronounces anybody's name right. "Don't eat that!"

"She wasn't gonna eat it, Kenya," I say, forgetting that I'm trying to ignore her.

Kenya sticks out her tongue at me, happy to have gotten my attention.

"Abba-cadabra," chants Twinkie, suddenly taking off her shorts. "I'm smelly. I'm gonna take my bath first, okay?"

"I'm smelly, too." I giggle. "You feel better, Arba?"

"Bubba bath! Bubba bath!" she says, smiling.

Then I hear Mrs. Bosco coughing in the living room. "You take your bath first, Twinkie," I say. "I'll be right back."

Mrs. Bosco just got out of the hospital last week. She was real sick, and she still has to rest a lot. When I go in the living room, I see her lying on the plastic-covered couch, with a blanket pulled over her. The lights are off in here, so that's why I didn't see her when I first came in.

"Hi, Mrs. Bosco. What's the matter?" I ask

her. She doesn't really like to kiss or hug much, and she says I don't have to call her Mom. I guess that's good, because I called my last foster mother Mom, and she gave me away. Still, I sure wish I had *somebody* I could call Mom.

"My arthritis is acting up again." Mrs. Bosco moans.

"Lemme rub your arms," I tell her. She likes when I give her massages, and I think it helps her arthritis too.

"No, baby—or . . . what your friends call you now?"

"Do' Re Mi," I tell her with a giggle.

"That's right. You go and get your Do' Re Mi self some dinner. I'll be awright," Mrs. Bosco says, chuckling and waving her hand.

Then she gets serious. "Oh, Dorinda— Kenya's teacher called today, and said she's having trouble with that child. Seems she's stealing things from the other kids. Can you talk to her? She'll listen to you."

"Okay," I yell back.

"And when you get a chance, look at that letter from the electric company. I don't have my glasses on. Tell me what it says." Mrs. Bosco sighs, and lies down again.

Who's 'Bout to Bounce?

Mrs. Bosco can't read or write. We're not supposed to know this, but I don't mind taking care of the bills for her, because if the social workers find out, she won't be able to have any more foster kids.

"Is something wrong with your leg?" Mrs. Bosco asks me as I hobble to the kitchen.

"Yeah, I think my ankle is broken," I whine.

"If it was broken, you wouldn't be able to walk on it, but you'd better let Mrs. Gallstone look at it. Oh, I almost forgot. What's the name of that lady where you take them classes?"

"You mean Drinka Champagne?"

"No, I remember her. You know, I was young once, too—'tippin' and sippin',' like her song says. No, I mean the other lady you talk about—at the YMCA."

"Oh, Ms. Darlene Truly?" I ask, squinching up my nose.

"What's that child's name?" is another "game" we play, because Mrs. Bosco can't write down the messages, so she tries to remember who called, and sometimes she forgets.

"Yeah, that's her. She said it's very important for you to call her if you ain't coming to class tomorrow, because she needs to talk to you—

and it's very important," Mrs. Bosco repeats herself. Then she adds, rubbing her forehead, "Lord, now I got a headache, too."

I want to tell Mrs. Bosco to take off her wig, and maybe that would help her headache, but Mrs. Bosco doesn't take off her wigs until she goes to bed at night. She is wearing this new one that we ordered from It's a Wig!, but it looks terrible. It's kinda like the color silver gets when it's rusted, even though the color was listed as "salt and pepper" in the catalog.

Why is Ms. Truly calling me? I wonder. I can feel a knot in my stomach. She's never called me at home before, and I don't like people bothering Mrs. Bosco. I must have done something wrong!

"I don't know what Ms. Truly wants," I say, "but I'll probably see her before class, since I'm working at the YMCA concession stand after school tomorrow."

I don't want Mrs. Bosco to worry about anything, or think I'm in trouble for some reason. She has enough to worry about.

"How'd you hurt your leg, Dorinda?"

"I fell," I say. "Can Man hit me with his cart.

Maybe it was my fault, anyway. I'm just gonna put ice on it and go to bed."

Luckily, Mrs. Gallstone said my ankle isn't broken. It's just strained. I hate going over to her apartment, because the kitty litter box really stinks. I made it a really quick visit, telling her I had to get back home and go to bed early.

It's only nine o'clock, but it's been a long, hard day. Once I lie down on my bed, I'm too tired to get up and put ice on my ankle after all. Chantelle is popping her gum so loud—but if I say anything, she'll get an attitude, so I just ignore her.

On a table in between her bed and mine is my Singer sewing machine. I'm trying to design a new costume for the Cheetah Girls, but I haven't figured out what to do on the bodice.

Oh, well. I'm too tired to work on it tonight. Instead, I turn my face to the wall. I'm even too beat to take off my shorts and take a shower!

As usual, whenever I'm lying awake in bed, things start bothering me.

What if I'm really not a good singer after all? If

the Cheetah Girls find out, then they are gonna kick me out of the group. They probably only let me stay in the group because they feel sorry for me, anyway.

"How come you wuz limping?" Chantelle asks me, popping her gum extra loud.

"Can Man hit me from behind with his shopping cart," I moan, hoping Chantelle will stop bothering me.

What does Ms. Truly want? I wonder. Please tell me, crystal ball. I wish I knew a psychic like Princess Pamela—she's Chanel's father's girlfriend, and she can read the future. But I'm not close enough to her to get her to read mine for free, and I don't have any money to pay her.

I get real quiet, thinking again. I'll bet Ms. Truly doesn't want me to take dance classes anymore, because there are other kids who need them more than I do. Or maybe the YMCA found out that I'm not really fourteen! That's it—they're gonna kick me out of the Junior Youth Entrepreneurship Program!

I know if I keep this up, I'll be awake all night. So I make myself go to sleep by thinking about my favorite dream. In my dream, I am dancing across the sky, and I see my real mother in the clouds, smiling at me. I can dance so high that she starts clapping.

Dozing off, I whisper to myself so that Chantelle doesn't hear me, "Dancing in the clouds, that's me—I'm not just another wanna-be. . . ."

Chapter 4

Two days a week after school, I work the concession stand at the YMCA on 135th Street as part of the Junior Youth Entrepreneurship Program, which teaches peeps like me skills to pay the bills—marketing, salesmanship, motivational training, and stuff like that.

It's almost six o'clock, and I'm kinda nervous because I haven't seen Ms. Truly walk by yet. She teaches a dance class here—earlier than the one I take—so I thought I would see her going to the cafeteria for a soda or something between classes. Sucking my teeth, I realize I must have missed her, because I was too busy folding these boring T-shirts!

Abiola Adams works the stand with me.

Who's 'Bout to Bounce?

She's a freshman at Stuyvesant High School, and studies ballet at the American Ballet Theater School in Lincoln Center. In other words, she's smart *and* she's got mad moves.

I call her "Miss Nutcracker"—and she's really cool, 'cuz she's into flava like me. She has on this dope vest with red embroidery like paisley flowers, and baggy jeans. We are both wearing the same black Madd Monster stomp shoes.

"You know why nobody is buying these T-shirts?" I turn to Abiola with a mischievous smile on my face.

Abiola is sitting like a high priestess of price tags on a high chair, tagging baseball caps stamped with the YMCA moniker in big, ugly white letters. "Why?" she says, trying to stuff a yawn.

"'Cuz they're having a wack attack, that's why," I say with a frown. "See, if they would let me design the shirts, they'd be flying off the rack."

"Well then, why don't you ask them if you can? You could put, 'Cheetah Girl is in the house at the YMCA, yo!'" Abi says sarcastically.

"I'm not trying to floss. I'm serious, Abbacadabra," I say, smiling, 'cuz I'm imitating my sister Twinkie. "This lettering could put a hurtin' on a blind man's eyesight. Who's gonna pay fifteen dollars for these T-shirts, anyway, when they can go to Chirpy Cheapies and get one for $5, with their *own* name stamped on it?"

"They don't charge extra for that?" Abiola asks me, like she's a news reporter or something.

"I don't know, but you know what I'm sayin'. I'm not playin'. Next semester, I get to take an embossing class, so I'll learn how to do some dope lettering. You watch."

"I will," Abiola says, shaking her head at me. What I like best about her is she can keep a secret. See, she's the only one here at the YMCA program who knows that I'm only twelve.

Sometimes I feel bad because I haven't even told my crew yet—but I don't want them treating me like a baby or something. I didn't mean to tell Abiola, but it just kinda slipped out one day.

See, she was telling me about the trick candles her mother put on her birthday cake. No matter how hard she blew, they wouldn't blow out. So I slipped, and told her how on my last birthday, Mrs. Bosco only put eleven candles on my cake instead of twelve. I thought it was so funny that she forgot how old I was.

See, when I was in elementary school and junior high, I hated how all the kids used to make fun of me, just because I was in the "SP" programs—that means Special Program for kids who are smart. But Abiola is real cool—she won't say anything, because I could lose my spot in the Junior Youth Program.

Okay, so you're supposed to be fourteen to be in the program. But on the other hand, it's for high school students—and that's what I am, right?

"Guess where I hear they're hiring?" Abiola says, all confidential like a secret agent.

"Where?" I ask, my eyes opening wide like flying saucers.

"At the Project Wise program at University Settlement, down on Eldridge Street on the Lower East Side," she whispers.

"Word?"

"Mmm-hmm. I hear they're paying the same as here—minimum wage, two nights a week. But in the summer, you can put in twenty-four hours a week, and they got all kinds of programs."

"Yeah?"

"Uh-huh. They got this dope dance program, I hear," Abiola says, nodding her head, then turning to see if anyone is looking. "You sit around and tell stories about your culture, then you interpret it into dance, and at the end of the year, you put on a big show called the Roots Celebration."

"Word? You think I could go down there?" I ask aloud.

"Try. They may not ask for your birth certificate or anything—just a letter from one of your teachers at school, so they won't know you're only twelve."

"Shhh," I smirk, putting my finger over my mouth.

"Nobody heard me," Abiola says, giggling, then putting some more of the ugly T-shirts in a stack on the concession stand.

"Look at the new leotard I got," I say, pulling my cheetah all-in-one out of my backpack to show to Abiola. "Mrs. Bosco bought it for me out of the money I gave her from the Cheetah Girls show at the Cheetah-Rama on Halloween.

Four hundred duckets! I couldn't believe it. But I didn't keep the loot, because I knew Mrs. Bosco needed the money for her hospital bills."

"She sick?"

"Uh-huh. She coughs all the time."

"Where'd she find a cheetah leotard like that?" Abiola asks, smiling. She thinks it's cute that I'm a Cheetah Girl now.

"I think at Daffy's, or Chirpy's," I say, then let out a sigh. "I wonder why Ms. Truly wants to see me."

"Don't know, but you'll find out soon enough, 'cuz it's time to go with the flow," Abiola says, then grabs her bag to leave. She goes upstairs to the computer room, to work on the youth program's newsletter, *Mad Flava*.

Sometimes Abiola acts like she's a newscaster or something, like Starbaby Belle on television—but she's learning mad skills. So I guess she's got a right to floss a little.

The butterflies in my stomach start flapping their wings again as I change into my leotard. Then they flap some more when I walk into the gymnasium where I take Ms. Truly's hip-hop dance class.

That's the only thing I really like about working here—taking free dance classes. And now I may even lose that? It's not fair!

Pouting, I think of something Mrs. Bosco always says. "You can get mad, till you get glad!" It makes me laugh. She used to always say it to Jimmy, one of my used-to-be foster brothers. He used to walk around with his mouth poked out so far, you'd think someone had stuffed them with platters. Then one day, his real mother decided she wanted him back, so they came and took him away from us. I haven't seen or heard from him since.

I wonder where Jimmy is now? I'm gonna ask my caseworker, Mrs. Tattle, when I see her. That's *if* I see her. Lately, the caseworkers have been coming and going, quittin' their jobs so fast it could make your head spin. Mrs. Bosco says, "For the little money they get paid, it's a miracle they show up at all."

"Dorinda! There you are. Why didn't you return my phone call?" Ms. Truly asks me sternly, as I take my place on the gym floor. She doesn't smile much, and it makes me kinda nervous.

"I thought you said to call you if I *wasn't* coming to class," I say, getting nervous again.

"No. I spoke to your mother, and I distinctly told her to have you call me *before* you came to class today," Ms. Truly insists.

"Oh, I'm sorry, Ms. Truly. Sometimes Mrs. Bosco, um, writes down the messages wrong because she's so busy," I say, trying to cover up for my foster mother. I wish Mrs. Bosco could read and write, but she never finished school.

"Well, that's all right, but don't leave without seeing me after class," Ms. Truly says.

I *hate* when grown-ups do that. Why don't they just blurt out whatever it is they want to say, and get it over with!

Usually, I stay near the front of the class, but today I'm so nervous that I go to the back, where Paprika is standing. Maybe *she* knows something, because she is one of Ms. Truly's "pets."

Ms. Truly always starts the class with warm-up *pliés*. So while we're doing them, going up and down, up and down, I turn to Paprika and whisper, "Did Ms. Truly talk to you about anything?"

"No, why?" Paprika asks, extending her arms out in second position.

"'Cuz she called my house and said she

wanted to see me after class today," I say nervously. I'm sweating already, and we haven't even started dancing yet.

"I don't know anything," Paprika says, giving me this serious look, like, "You must be in trouble, so get away from me!"

Bending my body over my feet, I feel like a croaked Cheetah.

Some hyena is coming in for the kill. I can *feel* it.

Usually, class is over much too soon, but today, I thought it would go on and on till the break of dawn! I guess that's good, though, since this will probably be the last class I take with Ms. Truly.

Sighing out loud, I pick up my towel and walk to the front of the gymnasium to wait for her. She's not even finished talking to the other students, before I start apologizing again for not calling her back.

"That's all right, Dorinda," Ms. Truly says sternly, "it's just that you won't have much time to practice."

"Practice?" I say, squinching up my nose because now I'm really confused. "Practice for what?"

"Come inside my office for a second," Ms. Truly says, taking me by my arm and leading me outside the gym to her office.

I can feel my heart pounding right through my cheetah leotard. I think it's gonna pop out of my chest like in *Alien* and start doing pirouettes or something!

Ms. Truly's perfume is strong. I know this smell. It's Fetch by Ruff Lauren, the perfume Bubbles likes.

"Sit down," Ms. Truly says, then closes the door.

I flop down in the chair like I have spaghetti legs. I must *really* be in trouble, 'cuz Ms. Truly is being super-nice to me. That's not like her.

Suddenly, a lightbulb goes off in my dim head. Ms. Truly probably wants to hook me up with an audition at *another* school or something, so she can get *rid* of me! I am getting so upset, I have to fight back the tears.

Ms. Truly pulls out a folder, looks at a piece of paper, then mutters, "There's still time. Can you stay after class tonight?"

"Yes." I croak like a frog, because the word got stuck somewhere down my throat. I wish Bubbles were here. She'd stand up and fight for me. So what you know about that, Ms. Truly? What a phony-baloney. Always acting like she likes me, but she doesn't!

"Okay," Ms. Truly says. Then she sighs, like she's Judge Fudge on television and she's gonna read me the verdict for a death penalty or something. "A friend of mine just got hired as the choreographer for the upcoming Mo' Money Monique tour, 'The Toyz Is Mine.' It's a one-year tour around the world, and they're looking for backup dancers, with hip-hop and some jazz training." She gives me a look. "I think you should audition for it."

All of a sudden, I feel like the scarecrow in *The Wizard of Oz* when he got cut down off his post. I just wanna flop to the floor in relief. *Ms. Truly thinks I can audition for Mo' Money Monique!*

"The only thing is, the audition is tomorrow morning. But if you stay after class tonight, we can practice for about half an hour. That way you'll go in there with full confidence, and be able to work your magic," Ms. Truly says, all smiley-faced.

I am so stunned, I must be acting like a zombie, because Ms. Truly looks at me and says,

"Dorinda, are you with me?"

"Yes, Ms. Truly. I'll, um, stay after class and go to the audition," I say, stuttering with excitement.

"Here, take the name of my friend, and the address where you have to go for the audition." Ms. Truly hands me a piece of paper.

"Dorka Por-i-," I read, but I'm having trouble pronouncing the lady's last name.

Ms. Truly helps me. "Por-i-skova," she says with a smile.

"Poriskova," I say, this time pronouncing it correctly. "What kind of name is that?"

"It's Czech."

"Oh," I say.

"The Czech Republic is a country in eastern Europe," Ms. Truly says.

"I know that," I tell her. I do, too. Geography is one of my best subjects in school. "It's near Albania, where my new sister Arba is from."

"I'm impressed!" Ms. Truly beams at me. "Anyway, you're gonna like Dorka. She's a fierce choreographer, and she's got 'mad moves,' as you would say. We studied at Joffrey Ballet together, back in the day."

"I didn't know you took ballet, Ms. Truly!" I

say, getting more excited. "My best friend, Chanel, used to take ballet. It's really hard, right?"

"Sure is," she agrees. "I wouldn't trade anything now for hip-hop, though. It gives you the cultural freedom to express yourself—and that's more important than any perfect *plee-ay*," she says, stretching out the word.

"I always had this secret fantasy about being a ballerina," I confide in Ms. Truly. "I wish I could have taken classes when I was little."

"Well, that's what daydreams are for," Ms. Truly says, chuckling like she knows. "You've got a feel for hip-hop though, Dorinda, and if you stick with it, you'll probably be able to write your own ticket."

I'm not sure what kind of ticket Ms. Truly is talking about, and I'm afraid to tell her how much I like being a Cheetah Girl. I don't want her to think I'm not grateful for the chance to audition for the Mo' Money Monique tour.

As if reading my mind, Ms. Truly says, "You're thinking about that group of yours, aren't you? I see you girls together all the time. It must be very exciting for you."

"Yes, Ms. Truly," I admit.

Who's 'Bout to Bounce?

She sighs, gives me a sad smile. "I tried to be a singer once," she says. "But it just wasn't happening. I couldn't play the games you have to play to get a record deal."

She gives me a big smile now. "You'll have more control over your career as a dancer, Dorinda. The worst that could happen is, you'll end up a teacher, like me—and that's not so bad, is it?"

"No, Ms. Truly. You're the *best* teacher. You're dope," I say, hoping I haven't hurt her feelings.

"And you're the best dancer, Dorinda. It's a joy to teach you," Ms. Truly says, then comes around the desk to put her arms around me. Her hug makes me feel like a grilled shrimp, because she is so tall. *Everybody* is taller than me.

"I just hope one day you'll know what a great dancer you are," she says.

I can barely believe it's true—that Ms. Truly thinks I'm such a great dancer. But what about the Cheetah Girls? How can I leave them and my family, and go off around the world for a whole year?

All of a sudden, I feel like a total crybaby. I'm so exhausted from being nervous, I just let the tears come, one by one.

The Cheetah Girls

Ms. Truly holds me, and whispers, "Just give it all you've got tomorrow at the audition. God will take care of the rest." She lifts my chin in her hand and gives me a wink. "And make sure to wear this leotard," she adds. "It's *fierce*."

Chapter 5

I smile all the way home, thinking about Ms. Truly and my audition. That is, until I have to hold the stupid ice pack on my ankle for a whole hour so that the swelling will go down. I shouldn't have taken class, I tell myself.

But how was I to know it wasn't going to be my last class? How was I supposed to know there was a big audition in my future? What do I have, a crystal ball?

I ask God to please make the swelling go down tomorrow for my big audition. I also wonder if God could get Chantelle to stop popping her gum like a moo-moo.

Since I'm too nervous to go to sleep, I hobble quietly into the kitchen to call Bubbles's and

Chanel's pagers. When one of us wants to talk in the chat room on the Internet, but it's too late to talk on the phone, we page each other. Whoever gets the page first is supposed to call Angie and Aqua, then all five of us assemble in the chat room. I wish I had a telephone in my room, but then Monie would probably hog it anyway, talking to her knucklehead boyfriend.

When I was little, she used to wake me up when I was sleeping, because she said I snored. That was before I got my tonsils out, but I don't think I really snored. She just hated me because, even then, I was Mrs. Bosco's favorite.

As I log on to the Internet, it hits me—*I can't tell my crew about the audition!* That really makes me feel like a Wonder Bread heel. What was I thinking, agreeing to audition as a backup dancer, when I'm already a part of a superhot group?

Well, it's too late now. I already said I'd go. Besides, it won't be the first secret I've kept from my crew. They still don't know how I live, really. Or how old I am.

Besides, I'm not gonna get this gig anyway. I don't care how good a dancer Ms. Truly thinks I am. I mean, we're talking about Mo' Money

Monique, you know what I'm saying? I bet Ms. Truly is sending a lot of girls to audition for the Dorky lady. I'll probably run into Paprika there.

As it turns out, I don't have to worry about telling my crew anything, because Bubbles needs to blab tonight. So I'm safe—for now.

"What makes you think your mom has hired some Bobo Baboso private detective?" Chanel types on the screen. That makes me laugh, 'cuz Chanel is making a snap on this television show on the Spanish channel, about a bumbling detective, Bobo Baboso, who fumbles cases.

"I'm telling you, my mom's hired a private detective, Miss Cuchifrita, so don't get 'chuchie' with me!" Bubbles types in.

"Why would she need to hire a private detective, Bubbles, can you tell us that?" Chuchie asks.

"NO! If I knew the answer to that, I wouldn't be asking all of you!" Bubbles is mad—she's reading Chanel.

"Why don't you just ask your mom what's going on—maybe she'll tell you," I type on the screen.

Then I feel sad, because I wish I could take my own advice and just be *honest*. Now that would *really* be dope.

My fingernails look like stub-a-nubs. I've bitten them off because I'm *mad* nervous. I'm so glad Bubbles isn't here, because she would be readin' me, but I couldn't help myself!

I feel *really* guilty that I didn't tell my crew last night about the audition, but I don't want them to think I'm not mad serious about being a Cheetah Girl. On the other hand, sometimes you gotta flex, you know what I'm saying?

Not that I'm flexing now. There are so many tall girls at the Mo' Money Monique audition that I feel like a grilled shrimp, as usual. I think maybe Ms. Truly made a mistake, because most of the girls here look older than me. *None* of them looks my age. My *real* age, you know what I'm saying?

I've got to chill. Maybe they'll never get to my number. After all, just by looking at these dancers' "penguin feet," I can tell they've got *mad* moves. They'll just send the rest of us home long before they get to my piddly place.

Who's 'Bout to Bounce?

I have never seen so many people waiting in line before. Not one, but *two* lines. Not even at the MC Rabbit concert last summer. Both lines are trailing like an out-of-control choo-choo train, all the way down the endless hallway outside of Rehearsal Studio A, where the audition is.

I'm so far back in line, I can't even hear what music they're playing inside the studio. I can only feel the vibration from the bass, thumping through the wall. They're probably using one of Mo' Money Monique's tracks. I really like her songs, so that's cool.

Right now, she has two of the dopiest dope hits out: "Don't Dis Me Like I'm a Doll" and "This Time It's Personal." They play them a kazillion times a day on the radio. I like the second one better, because it has more of the rap flava that I savor.

I wonder if I'm in the right line. . . . One line is for even numbers, and the other is for odd numbers. I'm number 357. Since I don't have any nails left to bite, I start yanking and twirling the curls on the side of my face. I'd better ask somebody if I'm on the right line, I think—just to make sure.

"What number are you?" I nervously ask the girl in front of me, who is wearing a red crop top and a baseball cap turned backward. I don't think she heard me, because she doesn't answer me, so I ask her again.

"Three hundred and *fifty-five*," she turns and snarls at me, giving me a nasty look, like, "I heard you the first time, shorty."

That's awright, Miss Pigeon. At least I'm not wearing wack contact lenses that make me look like the girl in *The Exorcist*!

"Girls, keep the aisles clear, please," yells a *really really* tall guy wearing a black leotard and tights. He is the one who wrote my name down and gave me a number, like we're in the bakery or something. All I can see of him now is the top of his really bald head, until he comes closer a few minutes later, with his clipboard in his hand like he's a high school principal.

"Everyone is going to get seen," says the exasperated giant, "and crowding the front, or hanging out in the middle of the hallway, isn't going to help the lines move any faster!"

All of a sudden, he adjusts his headset, then barks into it, "They're coming out? Okay, copy that. I'll send the next group in." Then he prances away like a gazelle. You can always tell a dancer, because they don't run like normal people. Except for me, 'cuz I don't floss like that.

Another hour goes by, which means I've been waiting in line for *two* hours now, and my throat is so dry it feels like it's gonna start croaking up frogs any minute.

I shoulda brought a Snapple and an apple, I chuckle to myself. But it's no joke, how sore my ankle is getting from standing around here so long. What if I can't dance because my ankle stiffens up or something?

The girl in front of me must be getting nervous too, because all of a sudden, she starts acting nice. "I need to stretch my legs," she says, sucking her teeth, then takes off her cap and pulls out a mirror to fix her hair. "I'm gonna be mad late for class. Do you think I should wear the cap, or keep it off?"

"I think you should keep it off—and maybe put your hair up, or something," I advise Miss Pigeon. She's dark brown, like Aqua and Angie, and her long blond extensions are so thick and straight, it looks like somebody played pin the donkey on her head. I think she should take off her big gold earrings, too, but I'm not gonna tell her that.

"You know how many dancers they're gonna pick?" Miss Pigeon asks me, pulling down her red crop top.

"No, but it must be a lot, 'cuz they're seeing a lot of dancers," I say, trying to act like I know something.

"No, I don't think Mo' Money Monique likes a lot of dancers onstage with her. It wrecks her flow. I bet you they're gonna pick about five—at the most," Miss Pigeon says, looking at me with those scary green *Exorcist* eyes.

"Where do you, um, go to school?" I ask, trying to be nice back. She must be a senior, I'm guessing.

"LaGuardia," she says nonchalantly. Folding her arms in front of her, she leans on the wall, like she is *really* bored.

I get so excited, I almost tell her that part of my crew goes to LaGuardia too. Then I realize—*What if she knows Aqua and Angie?* Then she'll tell them she met me at an audition for backup dancers!

Probably everybody at LaGuardia knows Aqua and Angie because they're twins—who can sing. I get so scared thinking about what I almost just did, I don't even hear Miss Pigeon asking me a question.

"I'm sorry, what'choo say?"

"Where do *you* go to school?"

For a second, I think about lying, but then I'll be frying, so I decide to tell the truth. "Fashion Industries."

"Oh," she says, like I don't have skills.

I am so grateful when the not-so-jolly giant calls our numbers, so I don't have to talk anymore to Miss Pigeon. My own thoughts come flooding back at me—mainly, "How could you go on an audition without telling your crew?"

"Okay, you girls can go inside now," Mr. Giant with the clipboard says, pointing to five girls, including me and Miss Pigeon. This is it—time to do or die.

When I get inside, I nervously look around and see one, two, *five* people sitting at a long table with a pitcher of water on it and some paper cups. I'd audition with that pitcher on my head, just to get a sip of what's inside!

I don't see Mo' Money Monique anywhere. At least I won't make a fool of myself in front of her.

The Cheetah Girls

A tall lady with a long ponytail and a bump on her nose motions for us to stand in a single line in front of her. She is really pretty, and I can tell that she used to be a ballerina, just by the way she is standing.

"Hell-o, lade-eez, I'm Dorka Poriskova, the choreographer. First I want you to introduce yourselves one by one, then I'll give you the combee-nay-shuns for the dance sequence to follow."

"I'm Dorinda Rogers," I say, speaking up loudly when it's my turn. Dorka has a really heavy accent, and I want to make sure she understands me.

"A-h-h," says Dorka with a smile. "We have the same name."

"I said *Dorinda Rogers*," I repeat, louder, 'cuz she obviously didn't understand me the first time.

"I know what you *said*, Dor-een-da," Dorka says, stretching my name out.

Omigosh! Now I've made her mad at me! Why did I have to open my big fat trap—my *boca grande*, as Chanel would say. I'm finished even before I get started!

"Each of our names means 'God's gift,'"

Dorka explains patiently. "Yours is the Spanish, um, var-ee-ay-shun, and mine is Czech."

"Oh," I say with a smile, but I'm so embarrassed, I want to shrivel right down to the size of a pebble and roll away! I act like I'm so smart, but I didn't even know what my own name meant!

"That's okay—you are too young to know ever-r-r-ything," Dorka says, smiling.

"Word, that's true, because nobody ever told me what my name means before," I say with a relieved laugh. In fact, everyone in the room laughs at my joke. Whew! Now I hope I can dance. Please, feet, don't fail me now.

While Dorka calls out the other girls' names, I start to think again about my name: Dorinda. God's gift. I wonder who named me that. Was it my real mother? If I was God's gift to her, then how come she gave me up?

I asked Mrs. Bosco once about her. Mrs. Bosco told me my "birth mother" was on a trip around the world. She must've gone around the world more than once, if you know what I'm saying, because that was seven years ago, and I'm *still* living at Mrs. Bosco's.

Flexing my ankle so it doesn't stiffen up on me now, I decide to go to the library after the audition and read some name books. I'm so nervous, I don't even hear what the other girls say about themselves, but like a zombie, I snap out of it when Dorka begins to give us the combinations to follow.

"Let's start in fifth position, right foot front. Move your foot to the side on *two*, then back on *three*, and close in first position on *four*," Dorka instructs us.

It's basically hip-hop style with jazz movements. I've got this covered on the easy-breezy tip.

But wait a minute . . . did she say back on two or three?

"Are you ready, girls?"

"Yes!" we answer in unison, and I quickly figure out that she had to have said "on three." The whole combination wouldn't make sense otherwise.

They're playing the MC Rabbit song "Can I Get a Nibble?"—which is straight-up hip-hop. I'm groovin' so hard, I don't even feel nervous anymore—until we're finished a few minutes later, and Dorka says, "Thank you, girls. If you've been chosen, you will receive a phone call. You were gr-e-a-t."

As I'm leaving, I say thank you to Dorka, since she knows Ms. Truly.

She smiles at me and says, "Good-bye, Dor-i-n-d-a!" That makes me feel like, well, "God's gift," if you know what I'm sayin'. She's so nice!

Chapter 6

As we are led back out by the giant in tights, I'm feeling dope about how the audition went. I worked it, Dorka liked me, and they all laughed at my joke. They won't forget my name, either.

Then, just like that, I feel like a wanna-be. I wonder why that is . . . Galleria and Chanel aren't like that at all—they never think of themselves that way. Even Aqua and Angie aren't exactly shy. A lot of times, I feel like I don't really belong with them at all. Like, with all my skills, I still don't feel like I got it like that.

Sometimes, I dream how they'll find out I'm twelve, and they'll think I'm wack, and a liar, and a fake, and they'll kick me out of the Cheetah Girls, and not be my crew anymore. . . .

As I come back out into the hallway, I can't believe there is still a long line of girls waiting to audition. They'll be here till the break of dawn.

Who am I kidding? There is no way I'll get picked for the Mo' Money Monique tour—no matter how dope I think my moves were. I'm only twelve. Look at how gorgeous these girls all are! Why did I even come here?

And then, I answer my own question. "I came here to prove to myself I could do it," I say. "And I did. I'm not a wanna-be—I'm a really good dancer, just like Ms. Truly said. Even though I have no chance at this job, I was great in there. And I'm as good a dancer as any of those other girls. *Better.*"

I take a deep breath and exhale, smiling. All of a sudden, it doesn't matter anymore whether I get the job as a backup dancer, because right now, I feel like dancing till the break of dawn.

"Float like a butterfly and sting like a bee, all the way to the library," I hum to myself as I step outside onto Lafayette Street.

Maybe Ms. Truly is right. Maybe I should give up singing, which I'm just okay at, and stick to dancing. I do like singing though, even if I'm not that good. And I am getting better at it, thanks to Drinka Champagne's lessons.

Sitting down at a library desk, I settle down with the fattest name book I can find—*Boo-Boos to Babies Name Book*. Word. They have so many names in it from all around the world—and most of them I've never seen before.

Starting with the "A's," I decide to look up Arba's name, but I don't see it listed. Then I think, What about Topwe's name? I look it up . . . Here it is: "In southern Rhodesia, the topwe is a vegetable." I'd better not tell Twinkie, I think, 'cuz then she'll tease Topwe, and call him "Hedda Lettuce" or something. She is smart like that.

Then I see my name. Ms. Dorka is right. "Dorinda" means "God's gift." Ooh, look—the English variation of the name is "Dorothea." That's Bubbles's mom's name! Wait till I tell Bubbles that I have the same name as her mom!

Suddenly I get a pang in my chest. I *can't* tell Bubbles, because then she'll ask me how I met Dorka! It hits me full force that I'll never be able to tell my crew anything about my big audition! I'll never be able to say how Ms. Truly praised my dancing, or how I was brave enough to show up, and how I came through when it counted most. They'll never hear about Dorka.

It's a good thing I haven't got a chance at this job, I think with a laugh, 'cuz what would I tell them then? "Hey, y'all, I'm going on a 'round the world tour with Mo' Money Monique. See you later, cheetah-gators!"

I laugh at the thought of it. "Fat chance," I say, thinking of the hundreds of girls trying out for the job.

Hmmm . . . but there *is* a job I *can* possibly get, I think, remembering what Abiola told me.

Walking out of the library, I decide not to go home just yet. If I could get up the courage to go on the audition, then I can go downtown to see if I can get a job in the University Settlement's after-school program.

Being a Cheetah Girl is dope, but since our first gig, we haven't made any money at it, and the Apollo Amateur Night, while it's good exposure for us, doesn't pay either. Meanwhile, I need to start making *serious* loot.

The Cheetah Girls

Sure, we make a lot of our own outfits, but there are some things a Cheetah Girl just has to go out and buy. That's no problem for the rest of my crew. But as for me, my job at the YMCA concession stand doesn't pay enough, and I hate asking Mrs. Bosco for *anything*, because I know she can't afford it.

On the subway, I wonder again why my name is Dorinda. Did my real mom name me after someone? Why do I have a Spanish name? Nah, I can't be Spanish!

One thing is for sure—the receptionist at the University Settlement is *definitely* Spanish. "May I help you?" she asks, pushing her long, wavy black hair behind her ear.

"Um, I'm a freshman at Fashion Industries High School, and I want to apply for the after-school work program," I say, feeling large and in charge now that I've been to a big audition for a job that pays a zillion times what this one does.

The pretty *señorita* hands me an application form and says, "You'll have to fill this form out, then someone will be right with you."

Word. I knew this would be on the easy-breezy tip. I'm in there like swimwear! Smiling from ear to ear, I sit down on the marble bench across from the receptionist to fill out my form.

"Excuse me, miss," the receptionist says to me.

I jump right up and go back to her window so she doesn't have to talk loud. Drinka says it's very bad for your vocal cords.

"You're going to need three pieces of identification. Do you have your birth certificate with you?" she asks me.

"No, I . . . didn't know I was supposed to bring it," I mutter, my face falling flat as a pancake.

"That's okay. You can fill out the form and leave it here, then come back with your ID when you have it," she says nicely. "You can see a job placement counselor any time from nine to five, Monday through Friday."

Where's the trapdoor in the floor when you need it? How am I gonna get out of this one?

"You know, I have to go home now anyway, because I have to baby-sit," I fib, but I'm so embarrassed because I know the receptionist *knows* I'm fibbing. She's probably wondering where my bib is!

Not batting an eyelash, the receptionist says,

"Sure, just come back another time, and bring your birth certificate, social security card, and a letter from one of your teachers. We just need proof that you're fourteen years old and attending school. You understand."

She knows I'm not fourteen! I walk out the door with my Cheetah tail between my legs. I walk past a big hole in the middle of Eldridge Street, where they're doing construction work. I wish I could just fall into that hole and disappear, and save everybody the trouble of having to put up with me!

Chapter 7

Mornings are always madness in my house, because all the kids try to get their breakfast at the same time, and "make some noise," like they're at a concert or something. Kenya is banging her spoon on the table. Topwe is playing his mouth like a boom box, and Twinkie is jumping up and down, trying to reach the knob on the cupboard over the sink.

"Twinkie, sit down, baby. I'm gonna get your cereal," Mrs. Bosco says, yawning and opening the cupboard. "Which box you want?"

"Oatmeal," Twinkie announces. In our house, there are no brand names with cute pictures of leprechauns or elves—just "no name," Piggly Wiggly supermarket stuff, with big black letters that say Corn Flakes, Rice, Beans and on and on till you could yawn.

"I want toast! I want toast!" Kenya yells, then thumps her elbow down on the counter.

"Kenya! *Can ya* please hush up!" Twinkie says, exasperated, causing all the kids to burst into a chorus of giggles.

"What's so funny?" Mrs. Bosco says, turning around to look at us, and pushing her bifocal glasses farther up her nose.

"Kenya, *can ya*, please hush up. Get it?" I volunteer.

"Oh." Mrs. Bosco chuckles, pouring the milk into Twinkie's cereal. "I'm sorry, Kenya, but you gonna have to have cereal today—so *can ya* please eat it before my nerves leave town?"

That's good for another round of hysterical giggles. Mrs. Bosco just smiles, and wipes her hands on a dish towel. "And y'all better hurry up, because we ain't got all day to get to school."

Kenya sticks her lip out as far as she can, then gets up from the table and storms out of the kitchen.

"I'll go get some bread. I'll be right back," I moan, then tell Kenya to come back to the table. I don't have time to fight with her today, even though she can be such a pain.

She doesn't say anything, but she does act like she feels a little guilty, so I can see that the little talk I had with her before bed last night must have made a difference. I explained to her how lucky we are to live here, and how sick Mrs. Bosco is, and how stealing kids' stuff at school isn't going to make her *any* friends.

I guess Mrs. Bosco was right, asking me to talk to her. The littler kids all listen to me— kinda like I was their mother or something. I don't think Mrs. Bosco would have wanted me to say anything about her being sick, but I said it anyway, and I'm not sorry. She needs us all to help her, not to get in her way. And whatever it takes to keep Kenya behaving, I'm going to do it.

As I'm slipping on my windbreaker hood, the phone on the kitchen wall rings. Mrs. Bosco answers it, then says, "Hold on a minute," before passing me the receiver.

"Who is it?" I ask, afraid.

"It sounded like she said 'Dokie Po' something," Mrs. Bosco says. She wrinkles her forehead with a puzzled frown, causing Topwe to burst out laughing.

"Oh, I know who it is," I say, because I don't want to embarrass Mrs. Bosco.

"Hello?" I say nervously into the receiver.

"Dor-e-e-nda?" asks a strange voice with a heavy accent.

"Yes," I answer cautiously, because I still don't know who it is.

"It's Dorka Poriskova, the choreographer. Dor-e-e-nda, I have good news for you."

Suddenly, I feel like someone could blow me over with a peacock feather or something. "Yes?" I ask in a squeaky voice.

"We want you for the Mo' Money Monique tour. Rehearsal starts on Sunday morning at ten o'clock. Can you make it?"

"I—I have to ask my mom," I stammer. What I really want to do is scream for joy!

"Okay, but let us know today, because we haven't much time to prepare before the tour begins," Dorka says excitedly.

I am so numb when I put down the receiver, for a second I don't hear Kenya's piercing voice yelling at me to get her some toast.

I'm in such a daze, I just turn to Mrs. Bosco

and say, "They want me to tour with Mo' Money Monique as a backup dancer. . . . "

"Is that right?" Mrs. Bosco says, surprised, then wipes Topwe's crumb-infested mouth with a napkin. "Ain't that somethin', now!"

Stuffing my hands in my pockets, I stand motionless for a minute. How could they have picked *me*, out of all those dope dancers? There must be some kind of mistake, I tell myself, and they'll realize it as soon as they see me again. . . .

I start to feel a wave of panic creeping over me. I don't have time right now to even *think* about this. About leaving my family . . . my *crew* . . .

"You awright, baby? That's good news, right?" Ms. Bosco asks—'cuz she can see I'm not happy. She spills the orange juice in Topwe's cup, because she's so busy looking at me.

"Yeah," I say, my throat getting tight, like it does whenever I get nervous. "But I don't know if I wanna go."

What I *wanna* do is go back to bed and hide under the covers! I can't go to school and tell my crew *more* fib-eronis. So what *am* I gonna tell them?

I'd better bounce, I tell myself, so I can get to

school early and see Mrs. LaPuma, the freshman guidance counselor. I met with her when I first registered, and she was really nice. She told me if I ever had a problem, or needed career guidance, to come to her. Well, I guess I sure need it now!

I know I'm supposed to be happy, but all I feel is scared and confused, like that time my polka-dot dress came apart in school in sixth grade. It was the first dress I ever made, and I stayed up all night sewing it—by hand, since I didn't have a sewing machine yet.

I was so excited to wear it to school, but the seams started popping open by first period! I waited until everybody left the classroom before I got up and ran home. Everybody was laughing at me in the hallway.

I didn't go to school the next day, either. I was too embarrassed. Mrs. Bosco had to walk me to school herself the day after that, or I wouldn't have gone back even then!

"Can I help you?" asks the girl sitting at the front desk outside Mrs. LaPuma's office.

"Do you think Mrs. LaPuma could see me for a few minutes?" I ask her really nicely.

The girl's gold chains clank as she goes in to

ask Mrs. LaPuma, then they clank again as she walks back to her desk. "Mrs. LaPuma has a few minutes," she says. "Go on in."

I go inside, sit down by Mrs. LaPuma's desk, and tell her the whole drama.

"Well, Dorinda," she says when I am finished, "I think it would be good for you to go on the Mo'—what is her name?" Mrs. LaPuma asks, arching her high eyebrows even higher. I wonder how she draws them so perfect, 'cuz they both look exactly the same—like two smiley faces turned upside down and smiling at me.

"Mo' Money Monique. She's a *really* big singer right now," I explain, trying to impress Mrs. LaPuma so she won't think *M* to the *M* to the *M* sang at The Winky Dinky Lizard or something. "She has two songs on the chart right—"

"Yes, my daughter listens to rap music," Mrs. LaPuma says, cutting me off. She takes a sip of her iced coffee through a straw, leaving behind a red lipstick stain.

"Dorinda, I know how attached you feel to your friends, and your foster family. But this is a great opportunity for you. You deserve to try new experiences, dear, even at your young age.

Besides, if I may say so, it seems like you have your hands full at home. I know you may think you're not ready, but getting a break from your everyday life might be the best thing you ever did."

Mrs. LaPuma folds her hands on the desk, and looks at me for an answer. I sit there frozen, not knowing what to say. Why is Mrs. LaPuma trying to make it sound like I should run away from home?

"I'm not unhappy at home, Mrs. LaPuma," I try to explain, and I can feel my cheeks getting red because I'm getting upset. I don't want Mrs. LaPuma to tell Mrs. Tattle, my caseworker, that I was complaining or anything. See, I know that my teachers send reports about me to my caseworkers, since I'm legally a ward of the state.

"I'm not saying you are unhappy at Mrs. Bosco's, Dorinda," Mrs. LaPuma says sternly.

If there is one thing I hate, it's when grownups get that tone of voice like they know everything—and they don't!

"But what I *am* saying is, I don't think you realize what kind of daily strain you're under," Mrs. LaPuma goes on. "Being in a whole new environment, especially a creative one, may open up a whole world of new possibilities for you."

"I'm not trying to be funny, Mrs. LaPuma, but what strain am I under, washing dishes every night? It makes me feel good to help Mrs. Bosco. She's my *mother*. And the Cheetah Girls help me with *lots* of stuff."

"Dorinda, don't get so defensive," Mrs. LaPuma says, frowning. "The Cheetah Girls are wonderful, I'm sure—but you have to think about your *own* future. Being part of a major artist's tour, traveling around the world at your tender age . . ."

She sighs and leans forward, giving me a searching look. "I know that you're exceptionally bright, because I've looked at your junior high school records, but if it is your calling to be a dancer, then—"

At that moment, the girl with the musical jewelry comes in and interrupts us. "Mrs. LaPuma, may I speak to you a moment?" she asks, giving the guidance counselor a look.

"Excuse me for a moment, Dorinda," Mrs. LaPuma says, agitated. "Yes, what is it, Chloe?"

She follows the secretary into the outer office, and is gone for half a minute or so.

When she comes back in, she says hurriedly, "Dorinda, there's an emergency I have to attend to. We're a little short-staffed right, now so there is never a moment's peace around here. Good luck with your decision, and come back and see me if I can be of any further assistance."

"Oh, okay, bye, Mrs. LaPuma, thanks a lot," I say, getting up quickly in case she needs the chair. Emergency—yeah, right. I'll bet. The coffee machine is probably broken or something. Oh, well. I already got her point of view, and I know she's right—but I still feel really really bad.

Like it or not, it's show time. Time to see Bubbles and Chuchie before homeroom period. The three of us meet every morning, by the girls' lockers on the first floor. I hesitate now. How am I gonna tell them I got this job? They're gonna yell at me for not telling them sooner, and then—then, they're gonna talk me into *turning it down*! They're going to *hate* me!

Without even thinking, I walk over to the pay phone on the wall and deposit some change. I dial Ms. "Dokie Po," as my foster mother called her.

"Hi, Ms. Dorka, it's Dorinda Rogers. Yes. I just wanted to let you know that I'll be at rehearsal on Sunday. Yes. Ten o'clock. Thank you so much! Bye!"

Hanging up the phone, I feel instantly relieved. For better or worse, I've made my decision. There's no way for my crew to talk me out of it now.

I know Mrs. LaPuma is right. It'd be better for everybody if I just go away somewhere. Better for Mrs. Bosco. Better for the Cheetah Girls . . .

I mean, they don't need me, I tell myself. After all, Chuchie and Bubbles have each other, and Angie and Aqua have each other. Who do *I* have?

Besides, if this tour leads to more jobs, Mrs. Bosco can make room for some other foster child who needs a home. That's probably what Mrs. LaPuma was trying to say, but she was trying to be nice about it.

As I walk toward the lockers, I can see Chanel standing with her back turned, talking with Bubbles. Actually, I see Chanel's cheetah

backpack first, and suddenly I feel the butterflies fluttering in my stomach again. They are
the dopest friends I've ever had. How can I
leave them?

When Chanel turns around, I see she has red
scratches on her nose. I wonder if she and her
mother have been fighting or something. I
know Ms. Simmons is still upset with Chanel
for charging up her credit card.

"Where'd you get the scratches, Cheetah
Señorita?" I ask Chanel, trying to act normal.

"Kahlua's stupid dog Spawn did it," Chanel
sighs, then starts twirling one of her braids, like
she does whenever she gets nervous.

Kahlua is one of Chanel's neighbors. Chanel
doesn't like her, because she says she's stuck-
up, but since Kahlua has a dog and Chanel
doesn't, she visits her anyway. Chanel loves
dogs.

I ask, "What happened? Spawn caught you
drinking out of her bowl?"

"It's a *he*, Do' Re Mi," Chanel smirks. "And
where have you been?"

"Wh-what do you mean?" I stutter.
Suddenly, I can feel my cheeks turning red for
the second time today.

Who's 'Bout to Bounce?

"I called you *twice* last night, and spoke to Mrs. Bosco for a long time," Chanel says, looking at me like I was a sneaky Cheetah.

"Word. She didn't tell me," I say, getting *really* nervous. I wonder what they talked about. And why didn't Mrs. Bosco tell me? Maybe she didn't *forget* to tell me. Maybe she didn't tell me for a reason!

"I talked to her, too," Bubbles says nonchalantly.

"You called, too?" I ask, squinching up my nose like I do when I'm confused. Sometimes the dynamic duo act like they are detectives or something.

"No, silly willy, we just did a three-way conference call," Bubbles says, flossing about her phone hookup.

Right now, I can feel something is happening on the sneaky-deaky tip, but I'm feeling too guilty to ask them what it is. These two are definitely up to *something*. If I'm lying, I'm frying!

"We have a surprise for you," Chanel says, then Bubbles pokes her.

"You're always blabbing your *boca grande*, Chuchie!"

"What kind of surprise?" I ask. I get the feeling

I'm being played like one of the contestants on "It's a Wacky World" who finds out they've won the wack booby prize.

"We'll tell you after school," Bubbles says, winking like a secret agent. Then she pulls out her furry Kitty Kat notebook, the one that she writes songs in, and scribbles something.

"Why don't you tell me at lunch?" I ask, trying to peep the situation.

That's when Bubbles and Chuchie give each other a look, and I *know* something is jumping off!

"Bubbles is gonna help me study for my Italian test. You know I'm not good at it, and I'm gonna fail if I don't study! So we can't meet you today at lunch, okay, *Señorita*?" Chuchie gives me a hug. "Don't be upset. We'll see you at three o'clock."

"I'm not trying to hear that, Chanel," I say— with an attitude, 'cuz now I am getting a little upset. "I know you two. You're up to something."

"You never answered our question," Bubbles says, butting in. "Where *were* you last night? How come you got home so late?"

"I, um, went to the library to study and I

couldn't take the books out 'cuz I owe too many," I say, trying to act on the easy-breezy tip.

"Yeah, right. What were you studying?" Chanel asks me, trying to act like Bobo Baboso again.

"Shoe design books and, um, I was reading this book about names and stuff," I volunteer.

"Names?" Bubbles asks, curious.

"Yeah," I say, exasperated, *"Boo-Boos to Babies Name Book."*

Chuchie and Bubbles fall over each other giggling, then Bubbles stops laughing on a dime, and asks, all serious, "Do' Re Mi, is there something *you're* not telling us?"

All of a sudden, I feel like a frozen Popsicle got stuck to my tongue. They're just playing with me, 'cuz they already *know* about the Mo' Money Monique tour! Or even worse—they know I'm only twelve! Mrs. Bosco must have slipped and told them!

When Chuchie pats my tummy and bursts out laughing, I suddenly realize what they *really* mean. They *are* playing with me.

"I'm not picking out baby names, silly!" I blurt out. If they only knew that I'm twelve, and haven't even gotten my stupid period yet like they have, maybe they would stop laughing at me!

"Okay, Do' Re Mi, but a little fishy told me that you were playing 'hooky' with Red Snapper or Mackerel," Bubbles says, cackling just like a jackal!

Red Snapper and Mackerel are these two bozos who go to school with us, and seem to like Cheetahs, if you know what I'm saying. Their names are Derek Hambone and Mackerel Johnson, and they are ga-ga for Bubbles and Chanel.

They don't pay too much attention to me, which is good, 'cuz I'm not interested in them either. But that doesn't stop Bubbles and Chanel from teasing me about it.

"Yeah, well those fish had better keep swimming upstream, if you know what I mean," I say, playing back with Bubbles.

"Now *that's* the flava that I savor," Bubbles says, winking at me.

The three of us do the Cheetah Girls handshake. Then Bubbles and Chanel run off, screaming, "See ya at three, Do' Re Mi!"

I wave after them, my secret still a secret. But for how much longer?

Chapter 8

It's "five after three" and I'm trying not to "see what I see." My foster mother is standing right outside my school, right next to troublemaker Teqwila Johnson and her posse! What is Mrs. Bosco doing here, anyway? Something *must* be wrong.

I'm 'bout to bounce, but Mrs. Bosco sees me before I can make my move. "Hi, Mrs. Bosco," I say with a smile, trying to act normal.

I always call her Mrs. Bosco, even when we're in public, so kids don't make fun of how she looks. The first time she came to my school, I was in the first grade, and kids teased me the whole year, saying, "That's not *really* your mother! She's ugly!"

The Cheetah Girls

"What you are doing here?" I ask my foster mother nicely. Mrs. Bosco doesn't really like huggy, kissy stuff, especially in public, but I would really like to smooth the wrinkles down on her hot pink dress, which is shaped just like a tent.

"I just wanted to surprise you," Mrs. Bosco says, grinning from ear to ear.

Suddenly I feel sick to my stomach. I remember the day when I was almost five years old, and Mrs. Parkay was *really* nice to me for the first time. That was the very day the caseworker, Mrs. Domino, came to take me away.

"You're going to live with really nice people," she had said, as she held my hand and we crossed the street together. *Is that what Mrs. Bosco is gonna tell me now*? That I'm going to live somewhere else, with *"really* nice people"?

Well, I'm going away on tour with Mo' Money Monique, anyway, I remind myself. And I'll be gone a whole year. So it doesn't really matter whether she wants me or not. So there!

All of a sudden, I start to notice all the things about my foster mother that really bother me.

Who's 'Bout to Bounce?

Like her false teeth, which she takes out at night, and puts in a glass of water on her dressing room table. And her thick mustache! Why can't she wax it off like most ladies do? And her really thick bifocal glasses!

And why didn't she wear the dope brown dress I made for her, with the big, oversized patch pockets in the front? Why couldn't she wear it to school if she really loves me?

I decide that I can't let Bubbles and Chanel see her—not looking like this. "I'm not gonna wait for Galleria and Chanel today, so we can leave now," I say to Mrs. Bosco, praying we can make it to the subway station before the dynamic duo come breaking out of school, which will happen any minute now.

"No, baby. I wanna see—I mean, meet your friends. You never bring them over to the house," Mrs. Bosco says, still smiling.

"I heard that!" Teqwila Johnson says loudly, letting out a big laugh like the stupid hyena she is. She whispers something to her friend Sheila Grand, whose last name fits her, because she's always acting like she's large and in charge.

Both of them are in my Draping 101 class,

and they never even talk to me. Now they must be making fun of me! I throw a cutting glance in their direction, but they pretend they're not looking at me.

All the people from my school are standing on the sidewalk, trying to act like they've got it going on. Fashion Industries is like that. We style and floss a lot.

All of a sudden I feel sad, like a wave washing over me. Suddenly, it doesn't matter that Mrs. Bosco isn't nice-looking, or that she dresses all frumpy. She's *real*—she never styles or flosses about anything. I don't wanna leave Mrs. Bosco, or Twinkie, or Arba.

And I don't wanna leave my crew, either. They're the dopest friends I've ever had in my whole life!

Just as I'm thinking all this, I hear, "Hi, Mrs. Bosco!" coming from my left side. It's Chanel, hiking up the waist on her pink plaid baggy jeans.

Wait a minute! How did she know this was my foster mother?

"Hi, Chanel. How you doin'?" Mrs. Bosco asks Chanel, like they've known each other their whole lives or something.

"Good. I just took a quiz in Italian class. I hope I pass it." Chanel giggles.

"Is that right?" Mrs. Bosco asks, acting all interested.

"Galleria made me switch from Spanish to Italian—but it's a lot harder," Chanel tells her.

"Y'all are matching," I say, pointing to Chanel's pants and Mrs. Bosco's dress.

"I know," Chanel says, smiling at Mrs. Bosco, then she even gives her a hug!

I can't believe it when Bubbles walks up and does the exact same thing to Mrs. Bosco! What's up with this situation?

Now *everybody* is looking at us. See, where there is Chanel and Bubbles, there is *mad* attention. Everybody is kinda jealous of them, because they're so pretty, and have the dopest style. Everybody knows we're in a group together, too, but I don't think anybody is jealous of me.

So what if they are, anyway? I don't care about that. All I wanna know is, what is this big surprise Chanel and Bubbles were flossin' about earlier? And how do they know Mrs. Bosco?

Picking up on my confusion, Chanel pipes

right in. "Do' Re Mi, *mamacita*, you are not gonna believe what we hooked up for you."

"That's the truth, Ruth," I say, squinting my eyes. This better be a good one.

"Princess Pamela has given the Cheetah Girls an all-day Pampering Pass at her Pampering Palace! Facials, pedicures, manicures, seaweed body wraps—the works, *mamacita*! We'll be so hooked up for the show at the Apollo, we'll win just because we look and feel so good, *está bien?*"

"Word!" I say in total surprise. So *this* is the big surprise the dynamic duo have been concocting! Mrs. Bosco was probably in on it, too— that's probably how she got hooked up with Bubbles and Chuchie. Now I feel stupid for being so worried.

"Can my mom come, too?" I ask my crew, calling her "mom" in front of everybody. I mean, Mrs. Bosco is always being nice to me, and here I've been acting like a spoiled brat, thinking about everything that's wrong with her. *She* deserves to go to Princess Pamela's— not me.

But my foster mom is not having it. "No, baby, I got too much to do around the house to be sitting up in some beauty parlor, like you girls. The only show I got to get ready for is the one I watch on TV," she says, chuckling. Then she suddenly starts coughing again. She doubles over, one hand over her mouth, the other on her chest.

It sounds like she's getting sick again. Please, I ask God, don't let her have to go back to the hospital! If she got sick again before I left on tour, I wouldn't go. I'd stay here and take care of her, I say, still praying.

And I guess my prayer is answered, 'cuz Mrs. Bosco stops coughing as fast as she started. She takes a deep breath. "Whoo," she says. "That's over. I feel better now. Uh, what were you tellin' me again?"

"Mrs. Bosco, I wuz sayin' that it's Princess Pamela's Pampering Palace—not just any beauty parlor, *está bien?*" Chanel says, giggling.

"Who is this Princess Pamela? She some kind of royalty?" Mrs. Bosco asks, amused.

"She's a gypsy," Bubbles chimes in.

"She's a psychic," Chanel continues.

"Well, she's a gypsy psychic gettin' paid," Bubbles adds. "I mean, she's got businesses all over the Big Apple. Princess Pamela's got growl power, and she doesn't even know it!"

"*And*, to top it all off, she's my father's girl-friend," Chanel flosses. She really loves Princess Pamela.

"What is growl power?" Mrs. Bosco asks, 'cuz now she is really finding my friends funny.

"That's when you really got it goin' on, and you got the brains, courage, heart—and busi-nesses—to prove it," Bubbles says. She loves to explain our whole vibe to anybody who asks—and everybody who doesn't.

"We'll get you to Princess Pamela's one day, Mrs. Bosco, you wait and see," Chanel says, laughing. "'Cuz you haven't lived until you've had a Fango Dango Mud Mask, *está bien?*"

"The passes are for a full day treatment, plus a free touch-up the week after. So if we go with the flow this Saturday right after Drinka's, we can get our touch-ups next Saturday afternoon, right before our show at the Apollo. We'll be lookin' so phat, we're bound to make people sit up and take notice," Bubbles finishes, flossing for Mrs. Bosco's sake.

That makes me a little uncomfortable. I mean, getting to perform one song in the Apollo Amateur Hour isn't exactly a show, if you know what I'm saying—not like doin' a whole world tour with Mo' Money Monique.

I give Mrs. Bosco a quick look. Did I warn her not to say anything about the tour to my friends? I can't remember! I've got to get her out of here, quick, before she starts blabbing about it. I know I'm going to have to tell my crew eventually, but not yet—not now! I'm not ready to face their reaction. No way!

"Why you calling yourself fat, baby?" Mrs. Bosco says to Bubbles, misunderstanding. "You so pretty, and there ain't nothing wrong with a little meat and potatoes."

We all start laughing so hard, *everybody* is looking at us—including Derek Hambone and Mackerel Johnson.

"Mrs. Bosco, *phat* doesn't mean fat—it means *dope*," Chanel tries to explain, confusing my foster mother even more. This sends us all into fits of giggles again.

"It means, like, fabulous," Bubbles adds, sounding like her mom, Dorothea—my namesake.

Now the Mackerel and the Red Snapper have worked their way over to us, and are standing behind Bubbles, listening to our conversation!

I'm trying to get Bubbles's or Chanel's attention, but they aren't looking at me.

"Oh, I understand, baby. You girls are so smart, with all your words. Dorinda is always telling me some new words y'all made up," Mrs. Bosco says, fixing her bifocal glasses again.

"Hey, Cheetah Girls, what's the word for the day?" Derek busts in, trying to cash in his two cents.

"Cute but no loot, Red Snapper," Bubbles says, but nicer than she usually talks to Derek-probably because my foster mother is standing right there.

"Come on with it, Kitty Kat, and show me where the money's at!" Derek says, slapping his boy Mackerel a high five, like he's saying something.

"See ya, *schemo*, we gotta bounce," Bubbles says, then motions for Chanel to walk with her.

Mackerel and the Red Snapper follow them for a while, then give up and walk away. I'm so relieved that I didn't have to introduce them to Mrs. Bosco.

Not that I'm ashamed of her—I'm not. But

still, I don't want everybody at school to know my business. My private life is private, you know what I'm sayin'? Why should they even know I have a foster family, not a real one? I mean, not even my crew knows everything about me, right?

Bubbles and Chanel are off to Toto in New York. I'm alone with my foster mother now, and she's being really quiet. Unusually quiet. I wonder what's up with her. "Are you okay?" I ask, scared. "You're not getting sick again, are you?"

"No, baby, I'll be all right. Doctor says all's I need is rest."

"Rest? You never rest," I say, worried.

"Don't worry 'bout me," she says. "I'll be all right. Long's I have my nap every afternoon . . . "

"But how will you do that when I'm on tour?" I ask. "Who's gonna look after Kenya and all them?"

"Monie will have to help out. She's been spending too much time with that Hector anyway. Don't you worry, baby, like I said. You go off on your tour and don't even think about us."

Yeah, right. "Here. Let me hold that bag."

"Awright, child." Mrs. Bosco hands me the Piggy Wiggly shopping bag, but it's really heavy.

"What's in here?" I ask.

"Q-Tips," Mrs. Bosco says, chuckling at her little joke. See, she uses Q-Tips dipped in peroxide to clean Corky's ears, 'cuz she says he must be hard of hearing. She always yells at him, "Why else do I have to tell you to pick up your socks and pants fifty times and you *still* don't do it?"

We're almost to the subway entrance now, and I start thinking again about why Mrs. Bosco is being so quiet. And how my friends all acted like they knew her, when I know I made sure they never got to come to my house.

Something is definitely going on, I can feel it. And if it isn't about Mrs. Bosco's health, then what is it?

As if she can hear my thoughts, Mrs. Bosco stops at the bottom of the subway steps and turns to face me. "How would you feel about me and Mr. Bosco adopting you?" she asks all of a sudden.

We've never talked about this before. Never. When I first got to her house, she told me that my birth mother might come back to get me at any time, so I shouldn't get too attached to her or Mr. Bosco—but that she would always be my second mom.

I wonder why she's asking me this now? "I don't know how I feel about it," I say. This is making me really nervous. "What about my, um, *real* mother?" I ask her, but I'm looking down at my shoes. I can feel my whole body shaking.

"Well, I'm just asking you a question. If I could adopt you, would you want me to?" Mrs. Bosco repeats, coughing into a tissue. She always loses her breath when we have to go up or down subway stairs.

"But what about the money you get from foster care for taking care of me?" I ask nervously. I don't want Mrs. Bosco to have to stop getting her foster care checks, just to adopt me. I know she loves me anyway. I wouldn't want to cost her that money.

"Don't worry about that," Mrs. Bosco says. Then she puts her arm around my shoulder and leans in toward me. She always used to do this when I was little, and I know exactly what she is going to say.

"I know when you grow up, we gonna go live in a big ole fancy house together, with a whole lot of bedrooms—'cuz you always had the smartest head on your shoulders."

Now I *do* smooth down the crease that's riding up in the front of dress, and she lets me, too. "Yeah," I say.

"Yeah, what," Mrs. Bosco asks.

"Yes! Yes, I want to be adopted!"

"Awright, baby," she says with a sweet smile. "I'll see what I can do, but I can't promise you anything—'cuz you know how trifling those people can be."

"Those people" are what my foster mother calls everyone who works at the Department of Child Welfare, Division of Foster Care Services, which is a big, dingy office in downtown Manhattan. I go once a year for psychological testing, and to visit my social worker, Mrs. Carter. She is in charge of all the caseworkers who make visits in the field.

"Do you really want me to go on tour with Mo' Money Monique?" I ask my foster mother.

"If that's what you want to do, that's fine with me, Dorinda. You always was dancing around the house, even when you wuz little. I know you got your new friends, and you don't wanna leave them—but you got to do what's right for you. You know I always say, ain't nuthin' wrong with Mo' Money!"

Mrs. Bosco puts her arm through mine, and leads me onto the subway platform. "But if you're not ready to go off around the world and be a working girl, don't worry 'bout that, either," she says. "After all, we got plenty of time to go live in that big ole mansion some-where."

Suddenly, I feel like crying. It's almost too good to be true. Me—adopted after all these years, with Mr. and Mrs. Bosco as my real parents. And going on tour with Mo' Money Monique!

I guess Monie the meanie will have to finally help out for a change. And I guess the Cheetah Girls will have to carry on without me.

I wonder if I'll still be around for the Apollo Amateur Night. I mean, the tour probably won't leave town that soon, right? Maybe I can get away with not telling my crew about the tour until after we perform at the Apollo. That way, I can still be a Cheetah Girl for just a little longer.

The Cheetah Girls

I like this new plan of mine. Sure, it means I have to keep my secret for a whole 'nother week. But it's worth the stress. I mean, what if I go to rehearsal tomorrow, and it turns out there was a big mistake, and I didn't really get the job after all? You know what I'm sayin'? Or what if I mess up so bad at the rehearsal that they fire me? I'd be so embarrassed if I'd already told my crew about my big new job!

Besides, I figure, the longer I don't tell them, the better. 'Cuz once I do, the Cheetah Girls are really gonna pounce. They'll probably never even speak to me again!

Chapter 9

When you're standing on the corner of 210th Street and Broadway, you'd think that Princess Pamela owns the whole block or something. Both of her businesses—Princess Pamela's Pampering Palace, and Princess Pamela's Poundcake Palace—take up several doorways on each side.

The Pampering Palace is really the bomb. It's got a glittery ruby red sign outside, with stars, balls, and moon shapes hanging in the window.

"The stars, moon, and planets are supposed to symbolize another galaxy—'cuz that's where you are when you step inside the Palace," Chanel explains to us proudly.

When you walk in the Palace, you feel like

The Cheetah Girls

you're taking a magic carpet ride, because everything is covered in red velvet, and the floor is covered with red carpet! When I look up at the ceiling, there are all these chandeliers that look like crystal drops falling from the sky! It's the dopiest dope place I've ever been—besides Bubbles's mom's store, Toto in New York.

"Close your mouth!" Bubbles instructs Angie, who is as awestruck as I am by the Princess's Palace. It's a diggable planet look, all right.

"Ah, my boot-i-full Chanel and her friends!" Princess Pamela says, rushing to greet us with open arms. She goes over to Chanel and starts crushing her to death. I wish my foster mother would hug me like that. Maybe once she really adopts me, she will. . . .

When you put the *P* to the *P*, Princess Pamela looks just like a gypsy psychic lady is supposed to. She is really pretty, and she has dark, curly hair streaked with white in the front. Her eyebrows are dark and thick, and she has a red, red mouth. She probably doesn't eat bologna and cheese sandwiches like I do, because she has to keep her lipstick looking so dope.

366

Who's 'Bout to Bounce?

"Is that rayon crushed velvet?" I ask Princess Pamela, goggling at all the yards it must have taken to make her dress, which is sweeping to the floor like Cinderella's gown.

"Yes, dahling. You like?" Princess Pamela asks me, her big brown eyes twinkling. "I know where you can get an *excellent* price on velvet. Let me know if you want to go, dahling."

"Awright, 'cuz I'd be hooked up if I had a dress like that," I tell her.

"You, dahling, are so boot-i-full, like my little Chanel, that you could wear nothing but a leaf, and e-v-e-r-y-o-n-e would be *green* with Gucci Envy!" she says, pinching my cheeks. Usually I hate when grown-ups do that, but she's so cool, I don't mind.

You can tell Chanel is proud of Princess Pamela by the way she beams with pride at the Princess's jokes.

The receptionist, who has a hairstyle that looks more like a "boo-boo" than a bouffant, tells us in this heavy British accent to "go back and change into your robes and slippers in the dressing room, and someone will be with you in a jiffy." Then she starts sneezing into a tissue, and her eyes are watering like she's crying.

"Is the English lady sick?" I ask Princess Pamela. I don't know the lady's name, but I don't want to call her a receptionist, in case she turns out to be royalty, or something.

"No, she has allergies, dahling, and she's not from England. She's from Idaho," Princess Pamela whispers, putting her arm around me.

"Then why does she talk like that—with an accent?" I ask, puzzled.

"When you're from a place named after a potato, you have to do something to make yourself interesting, no?" Princess Pamela says, smiling mischievously. Now I see why Chanel loves her. Princess Pamela's got mad flava.

"Okay, Mademoiselle Do' Re Mi, what will it be?" Bubbles asks, whipping out the beauty menu like she's a French waiter. "Le lavender mousse conditioning body scrub, or le peppermint pedicure?"

"Gee, Bubbles, I never really thought about it," I quip. "But now that you mention it, I would like a cherry sundae back rub!"

"You're a mess, Dorinda!" Aqua heckles me. Then she turns to Galleria and asks, "You think they got anything for athlete's foot? All these dance classes are giving me fungus right in between my toes. See right there." Aqua holds up her foot so Bubbles can get a good view.

"If I were you, I wouldn't be worried about fungus 'till I took care of those *Boomerang* toes, Aqua," Bubbles says, holding her nose closed like something stinks. "I mean, you got any hot dogs to go with those corn fritters?"

"That's all right, I'm not mad at you," Aqua says. "But I sure hope they got something for them."

Seriously studying the beauty menu, Bubbles exclaims, "Aqua, look, it says here that a tea tree oil bath is such a powerful antiseptic, it will even get rid of the cock-a-roaches between your toes!"

"Lemme see that menu, 'cuz I know it does not say that," Angie says, coming to the defense of her twin sister.

Angie is the more "chill" of the two, but sometimes the Walker twins are so much alike I can't tell them apart—especially now that they are wearing matching red velvet robes and slippers.

I wish I had a twin sister like that. A *real* sister, anyway. Someone who'd stick up for me. When I turn around from putting my robe on, I catch Bubbles, Chanel, and the twins whispering together.

"Don't be making fun of me!" I say, wincing. "So what if the robe *is* really big on me!"

My crew looks at me all serious, and Aqua says, "What makes you think we wuz talking about you anyway, Dorinda?"

"'Cuz I know you four. You'll read me through the floor," I say. Aqua never calls me by my nickname, Do' Re Mi, but I like the way she says Dorinda, because it sounds cute with her southern drawl.

"Well, we have a special treat for you, Miss Dorinda," Bubbles says.

All of a sudden, an attendant appears, in a white uniform and white shoes, with a white towel draped around her arm. She looks like a nurse in a cuckoo hospital, and I'm beginning to feel like a cuckoo patient.

"Could you come with me, *mademoiselle*?" she says, looking at me.

Princess Pamela's place is like the United Nations, I think to myself. Kinda like my house. But I think the French nurse's accent is real, and I'm not sure I wanna go anywhere with her.

"Not having it," I moan, looking right at Bubbles, who is probably the ringleader behind this whole situation.

"Come on, Dorinda, we're going with you, too," Aqua volunteers. They all escort me to a room with red velvet walls, and a long, pod-shaped tub that looks really weird.

"What's this for?" I ask the French nurse lady.

"It is for *ze cell-yoo-lete* treatment, *mademoiselle*," she explains to me.

"*Mademoiselle* doesn't want any treatment," I say, looking at Angie and Aqua, and not even trying to pronounce whatever that word was she said.

"Dorinda, that's the whole idea. This is so you won't get any cellulite," Aqua pipes in.

"How am I gonna get something that I don't even know what it is?" I exclaim, sucking my teeth. How did Aqua know what it is, anyway? She's such a show-off.

"Cellulite is that lumpy cottage-cheese-looking stuff that girls get on the back of their thighs," Aqua says, pointing to her butt.

If I didn't know any better, I'd swear Aqua and Angie are making this stuff up as they go along. "Where's Bubbles and Chanel?"

"They're in the, um, other—" Angie hems and haws.

"Super cellulite treatment room," Aqua joins in.

"Please try, *mademoiselle*," the attendant begs me.

"Okay, but *mademoiselle* doesn't like this one bit," I moan, giving in to what I have a feeling is somebody's idea of a Cheetah Girl joke.

"You have to stop talking now, *mademoiselle*," the French lady whispers in my ear. "For all of the impurities to leave your body, it requires absolute silence."

She wraps this Saran Wrap stuff around me—so, so tight that I swear *I'll* be leaving my body soon. Then she seals me in the pod, and turns on a dial. Just what I need. Some science project experiment gone wrong!

I lie there, wrapped in plastic like a sandwich in the fridge. Suddenly, I feel real sleepy, like my body is being deprived of oxygen or something. As I doze off, I swear to myself, if I grow up and have cellulite after this, I'm gonna sue—guess who!

When I wake up, I'm the only one in the room

with the French nurse lady, who peers up her nose at me over her little glasses. When I get some more duckets, I'm gonna buy Mrs. Bosco nice little glasses like that.

Yawning, I wonder how long I've been in this "invasion of the body snatcher" pod, but I'm definitely ready to bust out.

"*C'est bien, mademoiselle?*"

"No, *mademoiselle* is not all right." I moan. At least that gets her hopping like a hare, and soon, I'm out of the Baggie. I'm so happy to be back in a robe, just chilling.

But before I know it, the nurse has covered my face with a gucky banana-cream facial mask, and my eyes are covered with cucumber slices! I'm beginning to feel like an appetizer, if you know what I'm saying!

"Now what?"

As I try to recline in the chair and relax, I wonder—why am I always in a room by myself? I thought this was supposed to be fun. You know, the Cheetah Girls sitting around in some big bubble bath all day, talking and giggling.

Why do ladies do all this stuff, anyway? It's *boring*. I don't know how long I'm leaning back in the reclining chair, looking like a moonpie, before I finally hear the voice of the mischievous one.

"Do' Re Mi, can't you see how boot-i-full you look?" says Galleria. The nurse removes the cucumber slices, and I see Bubbles, Chanel, Aqua, and Angie standing over me, giggling.

"Was I sleeping again?" I ask them. I'm so annoyed, I don't think I'm ever gonna get a facial, or even wash my hair, ever again.

"Like Sleeping Beauty," Chanel says.

"It's time to bounce," Bubbles says, standing by while the French lady helps me off the table and hands me a glass filled with bubbles.

"This will help replenish your epee-dermis," advises the French lady.

"What's an epee-dermis?" Angie asks.

"It's the top layer of your chocolate skin, missy," Bubbles explains.

"Ooh, epidermis," Angie says, sucking her teeth. "We don't just sit around and sing all day at school, Galleria. Sometimes we have classes, and study things like *biology*."

"Let's all go over Dorinda's house, and eat popcorn, and watch *Scream*," Aqua says, interrupting her sister—and looking straight at *moi*.

Who's 'Bout to Bounce?

"Are you crazy? The only 'scream' you two are gonna see at my house is all my brothers and sisters doing it for real," I say, rolling my eyes.

"Well, we already called your—um, Mrs. Bosco, and she says it's okay if we come over," Angie volunteers.

"No way," I say, looking at all four of them like I'm gonna pounce. "We're not going over my house."

"*Sí, sí,* Do' Re Mi," quips Chanel. "We're there, baby!"

"Word, I don't know what y'all have been drinking, but I'm not having it, okay?" I say, changing back into my clothes—*finally*!

Chapter 10

When we finally get outside on Broadway, Bubbles announces that we're taking a taxi, because we're late.

"Late for what?" I ask.

"Um . . . you know that show we watch on television?" Aqua chimes in. "Aqua—what's the name of that show we watch on Saturdays?"

"Dag on, don't *poke* me," Angie whines, rubbing her arm. "I can't remember."

"Taxi!" Bubbles yells loudly. She runs to the curb, and waves her hand in the air.

In the Big Apple, the yellow taxis fly by faster than Can Man with his shopping cart. I've been practically run over by them more than once. But Bubbles knows what she's doing. She stands on the edge of the curb, waving and tilting way forward. Then she quickly leans back whenever a car zips by. A real native New Yorker.

"Let's take a 'gypsy' cab!" Chanel giggles, making a joke on Princess Pamela, but Aqua and Angie don't get it.

"What's a gypsy cab?" asks Aqua, squinching up her nose. We all heckle. We love to tease Aqua and Angie because they're kinda, well, Southern. They've only been in New York since last summer, and they don't know the ways of the Big Apple.

Chanel explains the gypsy snap to her, and then Bubbles explains what a gypsy cab *really* is: "The seats are always dirty in the back, and they always have some smelly pine freshener stinking up the whole car. You only take 'em when you're desperate, or when your hairdo is gonna flop from the sopping rain."

"Oh," Aqua says, nodding her head, then laughs, "How you know 'Freddy' or 'Jason' ain't driving the cab, though?"

"'Cuz they wouldn't pick *you* up!" I throw in. "They'd be too scared of you, the way you two scream!"

We all start screaming—"Aaahhh!"—imitating Aqua and Angie last Halloween, when they screamed so loud, all the kids were scared of *them*.

"We're in!" Bubbles says, motioning us to hop in a yellow taxi. Since we're heading downtown from 210th Street, the first stop is gonna be my house on 116th Street. Then the taxi can keep going downtown and drop off the twins at 96th Street before taking Bubbles and Chuchie home.

When the taxi pulls up in front of the Cornwall Projects, though, Bubbles, Chanel, Aqua, *and* Angie jump out, and hightail it to the entrance of Building A, where I live.

"Come on, y'all, I already told you—you can't come to my house," I whine, slamming the taxi door. How'd they know which building I lived in, anyway?

"Oh yes we can, *Señorita*, 'cuz Mrs. Bosco invited us. *Está bien?*" Chanel says, leaping along like a ballerina.

Suddenly I realize the danger I'm in. Never mind that my house is small and crowded. What if my foster mother slips, and says something about the Mo' Money Monique tour?

Mrs. Bosco probably thinks I've already told my crew about it.

Panicking, I run as fast as I can to warn her, but Chanel is hanging on to my jacket for some reason. I pull at it, trying to get free. I can't have my secret come out. Not yet!

"Do' Re Mi, we don't care if you don't live in a palace. Leave that to Princess Pamela!" Chanel says. Then she gives me a *really* tight hug, while ringing my bell with her free hand.

"Chanel! Let go of me!" I giggle. "Why are you ringing my doorbell when I have keys?"

Mrs. Bosco opens the door, and me and Chanel fall on top of her. Except, I'm not so sure it's my foster mother. It doesn't really *look* like her. She looks . . . *better*, if you know what I'm saying.

"Hi, baby, we've been waiting for you."

I would know that voice in a tunnel. It's my foster mother, all right—and if I still had any doubts, she starts coughing into a tissue.

But look at the pretty flowered dress she's wearing. And I like her new wig—it's nothing fancy, just a nice soft brown, with curls.

And she's wearing *makeup*! My foster mother *never* wears makeup.

Now I know why she looks so different. She doesn't have a mustache anymore!

"Mrs. Bosco, you look *really* nice," I say.

Bubbles starts heckling. "You should have seen what we had to go through to wax her mustache!"

This sends everyone into a fit of giggles. "We told her we had a surprise for her, *está bien?*" exclaims Chanel. "Then we blindfolded her, and Bubbles put the wax on her upper lip—then pulled it off while me, Angie, and Aqua held her down!"

"When did you do all that?" I ask, surprised.

"While you wuz getting cell-yoo-leeted!" Angie says, beside herself with laughter.

Then I look around at the crowd of people in the living room. I hadn't noticed them all at first—and they start yelling, "Surprise!"

I mean, all of my brothers and sisters—including Monie the Meanie—Dorothea and her husband, Mr. Garibaldi, Ms. Simmons, and even some people I don't know! Everyone is standing around like they're at a party. Even Mrs. Gallstone from down the hall is here.

I *really* don't get whazzup with this situation. I mean, it's not my birthday. And then it hits me. Oh, no! *They already know my secret!*

If I wasn't so young, I think I would have a heart attack. My heart is beating so fast, I'm still not sure I won't be the first twelve-year-old to have one—and get written up in the *Guinness Book of World Records*. I'm not lying.

Mrs. Bosco must have told everybody that I'm going on the Mo' Money Monique tour! That's what this party is all about! I could just scream. How could she do this without asking me? I'd like to read her right now!

But instead of saying what I want to say, I hear myself blurting out, "Look at all the pretty flowers."

Then my eyes feast on the long banquet table that Mrs. Bosco always borrows from Mrs. Gallstone when we have a party. It's filled with all my *favorite* foods—fried chicken, potato salad, collard greens, rice and beans, black-eyed peas, corn bread, and one, two, *seven* sweet potato pies! Too bad I'm not the least bit hungry.

But wait a minute. If everybody knows I'm going on tour, how come they're not all upset? They're being so nice, even though I'm leaving them.

I feel so sad. Look at all the trouble they went

to for me! And I was about to yell at them! I flop down in a kitchen chair, like a scarecrow stuffed with straw. I don't deserve all of this. I feel so stupid—like Chanel did when she got caught using her mother's credit card.

"You and my mom did all this?" I ask, looking at Bubbles, Chanel, Aqua, and Angie.

"Yep. The body snatcher contraption was Princess Pamela's idea. We got you *good*," Aqua says proudly. "And me and Angie helped Mrs. Bosco cook all this dee-licious food just for you."

"Oh, no, honey—it's for us, too," Angie counters, "'cuz you know I'm hungry after all that tea tree oil!"

"Ah, ah, ah, don't forget about my Italian pastries," Mr. Garibaldi adds, waving his hand.

"Yeah, that's right. Dad made Chuchie's favorite—chocolate-covered cannolis!" Bubbles says, beside herself.

I heave a huge sigh. All this beautiful food. Too bad I'm not the least bit hungry. In fact, I feel sick about everything.

I look around the room, and I see people I don't even know. Who is this tall man with a mustache? Who is the tall woman with the

African fabric draped around her, and a turban that almost touches the ceiling?

The man catches my look. "Dorinda, I've heard so much about you from my daughters, and I'm quite honored to be here. I'm Mr. Walker," he says, extending his hand to me.

"Oh," I say smiling. It's Aqua and Angie's father. He looks like a successful businessman, all right.

"And this is my girlfriend, Alaba."

She looks like a model from some African tribe or something. I wonder what her name means? I'll have to look it up in the *Boo-Boo* name book. Aqua is behind her, making a face.

Galleria isn't finished talking. She puts a hand on my shoulder, and points the other one at my foster mom. "I want you to know that, even though we helped put it together, throwing the adoption party was always Mrs. Bosco's idea."

Adoption party? Did Bubbles say adoption party?

Now I need *my* ears poked with a Q-Tip dipped in peroxide, 'cuz I must be hard of hearing, like Corky. "Did you say, 'my adoption party'?"

"Mrs. Bosco has adopted you, silly willy Do' Re Mi!" Bubbles blurts out.

So *that's* why Mrs. Bosco was asking me all that stuff by the subway the other day. And that's how they all knew each other—they were planning this whole party together, complete with the visit to Princess Pamela's to get me out of the way!

I burst into a round of tears that would make the Tin Man in *The Wizard of Oz* squeak. Mrs. Bosco has *already* adopted me! I have a *real mom*!

"Dorinda, look at you, you're going to ruin all the effects of that delicious banana cream pie facial mask!" Dorothea says. Coming over to hug me, she pulls a leopard-print tissue out of her pocketbook. I notice that she's crying, too. "You don't know how happy I am for you," she says.

"Thank you, Ms. Dorothea," I say through my tears. I look across the room at my crew, who are all beaming at me. They all love me, I can see that. Look at the trouble they went to for my sake. How can I keep on lying to them?

I can't.

"I'm so sorry to be leaving all of you," I say.

"Huh?" Ms. Dorothea says. "What's this about leaving?"

"It won't be forever," I say. "Just for a year. As soon as the tour is over, I'll be back, and we'll be better than ever, I promise."

"Tour? What tour?" Galleria asks, looking at me, puzzled.

That *really* makes me start bawling like a crawling baby.

"Dorinda is a crybaby! Dorinda is a crybaby!" Kenya says, sucking her teeth.

"Kenya, *can ya* please hush up for a second," Mrs. Bosco says, putting her finger to her mouth.

"What tour?" my crew says in unison.

I just blurt out my whole confession, all at once. I tell them about the trail of lies I told to cover up my big audition, and about the rehearsal tomorrow.

Suddenly I feel everybody's eyes staring at me. Behind Alaba, I see Angie and Aqua looking stunned. And Chanel looks like she just got hit on the head with a brick.

They all turn to Galleria, waiting to see how she's gonna react. I look at her, too. She's our leader. Whatever she says, goes. If she says I'm out, then that's it. I lower my eyes, waiting for the verdict.

"Don't let us stop you from making 'Mo' Money,' Do' Re Mi. If you want to go on tour, you *go*," Bubbles says proudly. She looks at the rest of our crew as if she's answering for all of them. "We're proud of you for getting such a big gig. And don't worry—we'll always take you back as a Cheetah Girl, even if you come back when you're a hundred! Ain't that right, girls?"

"Right!" they all shout, gathering around me.

That gets me crying again, and I feel *really* bad, because now I don't know what to do about anything! I love my family and my crew so much—how can I bear to leave them?

"Are you happy about it?" Bubbles says, kneeling down next to me and holding my hand.

"I don't know. I don't wanna leave y'all now," I mumble.

"No, I mean about being adopted. You said you always dreamed about being adopted, and now it's happening. Dorinda, it's your dream come true."

Before I can answer Galleria, Ms. Dorothea suddenly bursts into tears! She runs out of the living room, her peacock boa dropping feathers behind her.

"Mom, what's wrong?" Bubbles turns around to look, but all she sees is the flurry of feathers falling to the floor, like snowflakes.

Dorothea locks herself in the bathroom, and she won't come out. After what seems like—well, forever, me and my crew and Ms. Simmons put our ears to the bathroom door.

"Ms. Dorothea is still crying," Angie whispers.

I feel terrible. "Do you think it's something I said?"

"No, Dorinda, I think Dorothea has always been a little dramatic," Ms. Simmons says.

She should talk. That "off-Broadway performance," as Bubbles called it, that Ms. Simmons pulled when Chanel got caught charging on her card would have sent the Wicked Witch of the West flying away on her broomstick!

"Ms. Dorothea, can I come in?" I yell through the keyhole.

"Only if you come in by yourself," Dorothea says, sniffling, then bawling again.

Bubbles looks at me like, "Whazzup with that?" But she has to understand that she can't always take care of everything.

"I'll handle this," I whisper, then knock softly on the door.

"Dorinda, I'm so glad we can talk by ourselves," Dorothea says, sniffling and laughing after she's closed the door behind us. "Sorry we have to meet like this," she says, balancing herself on the edge of the bathtub.

I feel embarrassed because the paint has chipped off, but Mr. Hammer, the super, keeps saying he's going to repaint it soon. I wish my apartment was dope like hers, with cheetah stuff everywhere.

"You know, Dorinda," she says, sniffling into her tissue, "from the first time I met you, I felt close to you."

"I know, Ms. Dorothea. I feel close to you, too," I reply.

"Now I know why," she says, pausing, then pulling down her leopard skirt over her knees. "I, um, I, um, always wanted to be adopted, too." Then she starts bawling again.

"You were a foster child?" I ask, amazed. "Bubbles never told me that."

"Bubbles doesn't know," Ms. Dorothea says, smiling at her daughter's nickname. "I never told her."

"Oh," I say, then we both hug. I would never have known Ms. Dorothea was a foster child. She is so beautiful and everything.

"I've hired a private detective to help find my mother, but I'm not having much luck," she says, sobbing some more.

So that's why she hired a detective! I think, remembering Bubbles and Chuchie's conversation in the chat room that night. "Oh, I'm sorry, Ms. Dorothea," I say, comforting her. "Don't give up, you'll find her."

"Maybe, maybe not," Dorothea says, then pauses. "Do you know what happened to your birth mother?"

"No. Um, Mrs. Bosco says she went on a trip around the world or something, but I don't know." I'm whispering, because I don't want anyone to hear me through the door. "I never told anybody that. Not even them."

Pointing outside the door, Ms. Dorothea smiles. "Well, let's just keep this our little secret, okay?"

"Okay. I won't say anything."

"I'm not ready to tell Galleria about my childhood. I never told her, because I've always wanted her to have a perfect life. But watching you just now, telling the truth, I felt so proud, like you were *my* daughter. One of these days, I'm gonna tell Galleria the truth—she deserves to hear it."

"Yes, she does," I agree.

"And you, Dorinda—now you have two mothers, whether you like it or not, okay? Mrs. Bosco—and me."

"Yes, Ms. Dorothea," I say. Now I'm crying harder than ever, and she holds me for what seems like hours. Then I remember about our names.

"Did you know that Dorothea and Dorinda are both variations of the same name—meaning 'God's gift'?"

"No, I didn't know that," Dorothea says, wiping her eyes with what's left of her tissue. Then she starts laughing uncontrollably. "God's gift—wait till Ms. Juanita hears that one!"

We're still laughing when I open the bathroom door, but Dorothea wants to stay in there for a while longer, so I go out by myself. Of course, Bubbles, the rest of my crew, and Ms. Juanita are still standing outside the door—being nosy posy, no doubt.

"What were y'all laughing about?" Bubbles says.

"I told her that my name and her name both mean 'God's gift.'"

"Really?" Bubbles exclaims.

"No wonder she's so conceited!" Juanita says, huffing.

"I wonder what *your* name means!" I heckle, then the six of us huddle outside the bathroom door, hugging and giggling together.

"We should leave her alone in the bathroom for a while," I say, pushing everyone toward the living room.

"That's for sure, 'cuz she wouldn't be caught dead crying and then not fixing her makeup!" Juanita chimes in.

Bubbles gives us a look behind Juanita's back, then blurts out, "Neither would *you*, Auntie Juanita!"

Chapter 11

Yesterday I may have been adopted, but today, nothing has changed in my house. Mrs. Bosco is washing dishes. Topwe is fighting with Kenya over the last slice of sweet potato pie, and Monie the Meanie is still here, talking on the phone with her boyfriend Hector. "Shut up!" she screams at the other kids. "Can't you see I'm talking?"

I don't pay much attention, though. I've got bigger things on my mind. Today is do-or-die day. I'm going to my first rehearsal for the Mo' Money Monique tour. Not only are the butterflies fluttering in my stomach, but I actually feel *nauseous*. That must be from the three slices of sweet potato pie I ate last night—I think two must be my limit.

I'm too sick to eat anything, but luckily my ankle feels a whole lot better. Drinking a glass of orange juice, I wonder who helped Mrs. Bosco with all the papers she must have signed for my adoption? If there is one thing I know about the Child Welfare Department, there are more forms to fill out than at the CIA, ABC, or FBI, if you know what I'm sayin'. And normally, I'm the one who helps her fill out forms.

After the kids finish breakfast, I help Mrs. Bosco clear away the plates, then get ready to leave.

"Dorinda, baby, I gotta tell you something," Mrs. Bosco says, walking over to a kitchen chair and sitting down real slow. Pulling out some papers from the knickknack ledge, she coughs, then says slowly, "When I got these papers and signed them, I didn't have my glasses on, so I guess I didn't realize what they were saying."

Mrs. Bosco pauses for a long time, which makes me feel uncomfortable, so I say something to fill up the empty space. "Yeah?"

"Well, Dorinda, I guess the adoption didn't go through," Mrs. Bosco says, letting out a sad sigh. "I found out on Friday, but I didn't want to say anything to your friends, since they were so excited setting up the party and everything,"

I sit there, too stunned to move. "So, I'm not legally adopted or anything?" I ask—but I already know the answer.

"I guess not, baby—but I'm gonna keep trying, you hear," she says, looking at me so sad. "You know how trifling those people downtown can be. They can't do nuttin' right but mess up kids' lives. That's the only thing they seem to do good."

"It doesn't matter," I say, although of course it does. I guess Mrs. Bosco will straighten it out with "those people" eventually. One of these days, I really will get adopted. Still, after all the celebration, it feels pretty empty to know it isn't really true.

I get a sudden urge to ask Mrs. Bosco where my real mother is. Or if it's true she's really around the world on a trip—but I think I already know the answer to that. Besides, looking at how sad Mrs. Bosco is, I don't think it's a good time to talk about it now.

Who's 'Bout to Bounce?

"I don't mind being a foster child," I say, "as long as *you* are my foster mother."

She lets out another sigh. "You always were the smartest child I ever had. Nuttin' you can't do if you put your mind to it. That's what I always said."

At least I can be sure of one thing—if Mrs. Bosco went to all that trouble to adopt me, then no matter what happens, at least I don't have to worry about her giving me away, right?

I decide this is as good a time as any to ask her for the one thing I *really* want. "Can I call you Mom now, instead of Mrs. Bosco?"

"Yes, baby. I guess after all these years we've been together, you can call me anything you want!" Mrs. Bosco beams at me, then pulls out a tissue to cough.

I know it would be pushing too much if I started hugging her, so I don't. And I don't wanna start crying again like a crybaby, as Kenya says, so I tie my jacket around my waist and get up to go. "See ya later, Mom."

"See ya, baby," my foster mom says.

It's a good thing I'm early for rehearsal, because my stomach starts acting up again, and this gives me a chance to sit on the studio floor and calm down.

Pigeon girl from the audition was right. So far, there seem to be exactly five dancers. There are two guys and three girls, including me. They are all definitely older than I am, but they are all kinda small, like me—okay, they're taller, but not *that* much taller.

I smile at the dancer with long black hair down to her waist. She is so pretty. I don't remember seeing her at the audition. She musta been near the front or something.

She smiles back and introduces herself. "Hi, I'm Ling Oh."

"Hi, I'm Dorinda," I say, because I'm not sure if she just told me her first name, or her first and last name—so I wanna be on the safe side. Now I feel sorta self-conscious, because all the dancers are wearing black leotards, and I'm wearing my cheetah all-in-one. It makes me feel like a spotted mistake in the jiggy jungle!

Rubbing my ankle, I hear cackling in the hallway, and a whole group of people comes in, bringing in the noise.

Omigod, I can't believe my eyes. It really is Mo' Money Monique herself!

Who's 'Bout to Bounce?

She is *really* pretty. Her hair is really straight, and her skin is a pretty tan color, and she isn't even wearing any makeup. I read in *Sistarella* magazine that she is sixteen now, but she still lives with her mom in Atlanta.

Mo' Money Monique adjusts her black leotard, and stands next to Dorka, the choreographer.

"Hi, Ms. Dorka," I say, because I can't pronounce her last name, and I don't want to embarrass myself by trying.

"Hello, Dor-een-da. I'm so glad to see you."

Mo' Money Monique comes over and introduces herself to us. We introduce ourselves back, and then she says to me, "I love your leotard, it's dope."

Word, she's *really* nice!

Dorka then takes over, and tells us that we are going to be practicing the moves without music first, just to get the combinations down.

The moves in hip-hop dancing are all about attitude. You have to move quick, sharp, *and* give attitude, as opposed to being graceful, like with jazz. For me, that's what makes it so dope.

Suddenly, it hits me that I'm doing what I've always dreamed of doing—dancing in real life, instead of in the clouds—and yet, I don't feel happy at all. I don't even feel nervous anymore. I just feel, well, *sad*.

At the end of rehearsal, the not-so-jolly giant from the audition, who it turns out is also the principal dancer, tells us to fill out a form.

That's when it hits me. I don't want to fill out any form. I don't want to be a backup dancer. I wanna be like Mo' Money Monique—the star. And if I can't be with my crew, then I don't want to be here, 'cuz I really am a Cheetah Girl.

Now my legs are shaking, as I go over to Dorka to break the news. "I can't do this, Ms. Dorka," I say, even though I'm so nervous, my throat feels like it's shaking.

"You can't do what?" she responds.

"I, um, can't go on the tour—because I'm already in a group," I say, proud of myself that I'm acting like a Cheetah instead of a scaredy cat.

"What kind of group, Dor-een-da?" Dorka asks, genuinely interested in what I have to say.

"We're the Cheetah Girls. It's five of us, and we sing and dance, and we're gonna travel all over the world one day too."

Now Dorka seems amused. "I remember when I left my country to come to America. I got accepted to ballet school here, and I was so scared that I told my mother, 'I don't want to go.' Do-reen-da, I hope you're not doing the same thing, are you?" She gives me a searching look.

"No. I'm not scared anymore. I'm just sad," I reply. "Sad that I could let myself forget so quickly how happy I was that the Cheetah Girls wanted *me* in their group."

"Okay, Dor-een-da. It's up to you. We would like you to tour with us, but remember, there are hundreds of girls who would be very happy to be in your place."

"I know, Ms. Dorka, and I'm sorry, but right now, I'm not one of those girls. I'm a Cheetah Girl."

"Good-bye then—Cheetah Girl," Ms. Dorka says, smiling. "God's gift is a good name for you. You are very brave, and also very talented. And so young, too . . . only twelve years old."

I gasp. How did she know? Of course—Mrs. Bosco must've told her.

"We would have gotten a tutor for you and everything," Dorka says. "Of course, it will be less expensive to hire someone older than you—but you are very special. I'm sure you and your Cheetah Girls will be touring the world someday, just as you say."

"Thanks, Ms. Dorka," I say. "Bye, now. Bye, everyone."

"Good-bye, Dorinda!" they all say, waving to me as I walk out the door, and close it behind me forever.

When I walk outside onto Lafayette Street, I practically run all the way to Chanel's house, which is only a few blocks away. I am so mad at myself for missing rehearsal with my crew! I should have made up my mind yesterday, but I guess I really wanted to know if I got the job for the Mo' Money Monique tour—*for real*, if you know what I'm sayin'.

"Well, looky, looky," says Aqua, when I walk into the exercise studio in Chanel's loft, where my crew have just finished rehearsing.

"We didn't think you were coming," Bubbles says, her eyes twinkling. Her hair looks nice. She's put it up with one of those cheetah squingee hair things.

"I didn't think I was, either, but I missed y'all too much—so I'm not going on that tour," I blurt out. "I'd rather be 'po' up from the floor up,' and a broke Cheetah Girl, than some back-up dancer."

All four of them jump up and down, and start yelling and screaming.

"Chanel, what's going on in there?" Juanita yells from the kitchen.

"*Nada, Mamí!*" Chanel yells back. "We're just happy!"

"We knew you'd be back," Bubbles says, poking out her mouth at me. "Now, listen. We only got a week left before we perform at the Apollo Amateur Hour contest. But we're gonna sing 'Wanna-be Stars in the Jiggy Jungle,' okay? I mean, we rocked the house at the Kats and Kittys Klub Halloween bash with that number, remember?"

"Yeah, that was a dope night," I say. Then I realize something. "Hey, how come you didn't write a song about *me*?"

Bubbles gives me that cheetah-licious look of hers, and says, "Who said I didn't? I just didn't finish it yet."

"What's it called?" I ask, excited.

"Guess."

"Do' Re Mi, Can't You See?"

All four of them heckle me, and Aqua says,

The Cheetah Girls

"We'd be po' for sho' if you wuz writing the songs!"

Bubbles stops laughing long enough to say, "The song's called, 'Who's 'Bout to Bounce, Baby?'"

"Word. That's dope."

Juanita walks into the studio, huffing. She's wearing her running sweats and shoes, and she's got a towel around her neck. "Let's hit the road, girls. Running your mouth isn't the same thing as running, *está bien?*"

"What? You mean we're running *again?*" Angie moans.

"That's right," Juanita says sharply. "Any complaints?"

"Dag on," Angie says. "We sure do run a lot."

"Yeah, well, I'm ready for Freddy today, baby," Bubbles says, giving me a little squeeze of affection.

Without any further delay, we hightail it down to the East River and start running uptown. One week until show time, I tell myself as we go. That is really, really dope.

Bubbles is right. We are "ready for Freddy." We're gonna rock the Apollo, so what you know about that, huh?

Who's 'Bout to Bounce?

I look around at my crew—Chanel up front as usual, the rest of us lagging behind—and I realize something. In spite of everything that's gone down, they still don't know the *whole* truth about me.

Telling them I'm really twelve years old right now might push my crew right over the edge. I mean, they put up with me lying to them about the Mo' Money Monique tour, but I'd better not rock the boat again—at least not for a while.

While I'm at it, I decide I'm not going to tell my crew that I'm not legally adopted, either. If I do, then I'll have to tell them what happened, and I don't wanna embarrass my mom.

"My mom . . ." I like the way that sounds. Besides, I know they want me to be happy, so I wanna pretend that I'm adopted for a while longer. Who knows? Maybe by the time I decide to tell them, Mrs. Bosco will have adopted me for real.

Anyway, the deal is, I can be a good friend to my crew, and still keep one or two little secrets to myself, you know what I'm sayin'?

By the time we get to 23rd Street, I notice something very strange. I've been so busy thinking about stuff that I suddenly realize I'm running by myself. Even Angie, Aqua, and Bubbles are running faster than me!

I can't believe that—*Bubbles*, running faster than *me*! She should eat sweet potato pie *every* day! Trying to catch up, I yell, "Hey, Bubbles, wait up!"

She pays me no mind, and yells back, without looking, "Yo, God's gift to the world—*catch up if you can!*" That sends them all into Cheetah heckles.

Yeah, I'm back, all right. Back where I belong. I'm not a wanna-be—not when I'm with my crew. That's what the world needs now and they're gonna get some at the Apollo Theatre, on Saturday night!

Wanna-be Stars in the Jiggy Jungle

Some people walk with a panther
or strike a buffalo stance
that makes you wanna dance.

Other people flip the script
on the day of the jackal
that'll make you cackle.

But peeps like me
got the Cheetah Girl groove
that makes your body move
like wanna-be stars in the jiggy jungle.

The jiggy jiggy jungle!
The jiggy jiggy jungle!

So don't make me bungle
my chance to rise for the prize
and show you who we are
in the jiggy jiggy jungle!
The jiggy jiggy jungle!

Some people move like snakes in the grass
or gorillas in the mist
who wanna get dissed.

Some people dance with the wolves
or trot with the fox
right out of the box.

But peeps like me
got the Cheetah Girl groove
that makes your body move
like wanna-be stars in the jiggy jungle.

The jiggy jiggy jungle!
The jiggy jiggy jungle!

So don't make me bungle
my chance to rise for the prize
and show you who we are
in the jiggy jiggy jungle!
The jiggy jiggy jungle!

Some people lounge with the Lion King
or hunt like a hyena
because they're large and in charge.

Some people hop to it like a hare
because they wanna get snared
or bite like baboons and jump too soon.

But peeps like me
got the Cheetah Girl groove
that makes your body move
like wanna-be stars in the jiggy jungle.

The jiggy jiggy jungle.
The jiggy jiggy jungle.

So don't make me bungle
my chance to rise for the prize
and show you who we are
in the jiggy jiggy jungle!

The jiggy jiggy jungle.
The jiggy jiggy jungle.

Some people float like a butterfly
or sting like a bee
'cuz they wanna be like posse.

Some people act tough like a tiger
to scare away the lynx
but all they do is double jinx.

But peeps like me
got the Cheetah Girl groove
that makes your body move
like wanna-be stars in the jiggy jungle.

The jiggy jiggy jungle.
The jiggy jiggy jungle.

So don't make me bungle
my chance to rise to the prize
and show you who we are
in the jiggy jiggy jungle.

The jiggy jiggy jungle!
The jiggy jiggy jungle!

The Cheetah Girls Glossary

At the end of her rope-a-dope: To run out of moves. When you wanna give up.

Boo-boo: A mistake. A cuddly dog like Toto.

Boomerang toes: Feet that have corns, bunions, or critter-looking toenails.

Bouffant: A puffed-up hairdo.

Bounce: To leave. To jet. To go away and come back another day.

Cellulite: Lumpy fat that looks like cottage cheese and makes grown-up ladies go to beauty parlors and throw duckets out the bucket trying to get rid of it.

Chitlin' circuit: Wack clubs that don't pay singers well.

Diggable planet: A cool place.

Dopiest dope: The coolest of them all.

Easy-breezy tip: When something doesn't take a lot of effort. When you're not sweatin' it.

Knuckleheads: Bozos who don't have jobs and hang out all day doing nothing.

Large and in charge: Successful.

Mad moves: To dance really well.

My face is cracked: I'm embarrassed.

Not having it: When you don't like something.

Penguin feet: Dancer's feet that are slightly pointed outward.

Pigeons: Girls with fake eyeballs and tick-tacky weaves.

Rope-a-dope: When you're doing something *really* well—like double-Dutch jump rope, freestyle moves.

She's on a jelly roll: When someone is jammin' with snaps, knowledge, or moves.

Something is jumping off: When something is about to happen.

Stub-a-nubs: Fingernails that have been chomp-a-roni'd to the max.

Whazzup: A popular salutation for greeting members of your crew.

Word: Right. I hear that. Is that right? I know that's right.

Hey, Ho, Hollywood!

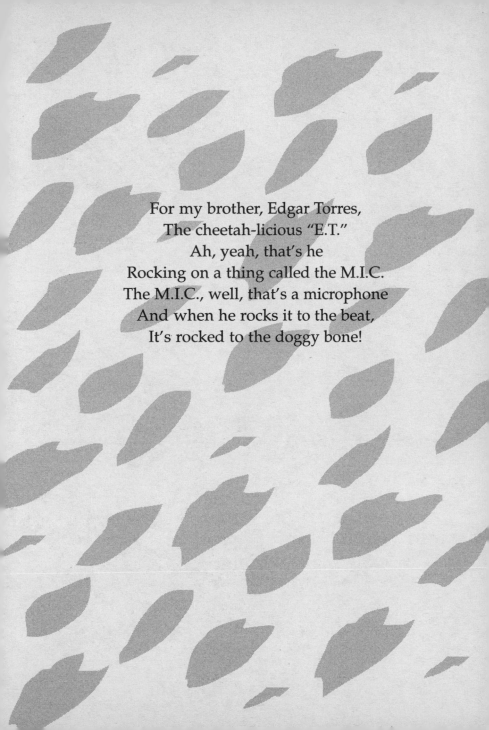

For my brother, Edgar Torres,
The cheetah-licious "E.T."
Ah, yeah, that's he
Rocking on a thing called the M.I.C.
The M.I.C., well, that's a microphone
And when he rocks it to the beat,
It's rocked to the doggy bone!

Chapter 1

The plastic slipcover on the couch makes a real loud *crunch* sound when Galleria sits down. Me and Angie are used to the funny noise so we pay it no mind, but Galleria looks kinda embarrassed like she farted an "Alien egg," or something strange like that. Me and Angie just look at each other and smile because we're probably thinking the same thing. That's how it is when you're twins—you can read each other's mind, finish each other's sentences, *and* know when each other is "lying, crying, or testifying," even when you're not in the same room.

My sister Angie and I are as much alike as any identical twins you're ever gonna meet.

When we stand together looking in the mirror, it's almost like we're two of those alien clones in horror movies (which we *love*).

I remember way back in sixth grade we fooled *both* our homeroom teachers by switching places on April Fools' Day. We didn't get into trouble, but we did get called to the principal's office. Still, "the Fabulous Walker Twins" pulled the best April Fools' Day joke that school ever saw! We go to high school in New York City nowadays, but we have not been forgotten. I guess you can't blame them for never putting identical twins in the same class again after that!

Now that we have turned thirteen (our birthday is September 9, which makes us practical-minded Virgos), Angie and I don't always dress alike anymore—which makes it easier to tell us apart. But even when we do put on the same outfit, you can tell I'm Aquanette. I'm the one who's always running my mouth. Anginette is more the quiet type. But as Big Momma says, "She doesn't miss a trick."

Big Momma is our maternal grandmother, and she loves to brag about us—even to ladies in the supermarket! "I can't tell which one of them is smarter or cuter sometimes," she'll say. Or, "You know they've been singing like angels since they were cooing in the cradle."

That's not exactly true. I think we started singing when we were about three years old. Anyway, Big Momma says, "Singing is a gift from the Lord." Well, nobody else in our family can even hold a note, so it must be true.

And I *guess* we're kinda cute: Angie and I are both brown-skinned, with nice "juicy" lips and big brown eyes. Still, we're not *real* pretty, like the rest of the Cheetah Girls—that would be Galleria "Bubbles" Garibaldi, Chanel "Chuchie" Simmons, and Dorinda "Do' Re Mi" Rogers. That's right—Angie and I have only just moved to New York, and here we are, already in a singing group!

Angie and I met Galleria and Chanel at the Kats and Kittys Klub Fourth of July Bash last summer. It was right after we moved to New York from Houston, leaving Ma, Big Momma, and all our cousins behind. We woulda been real lost if it hadn't been for our fellow Kats and Kittys.

In case you've never heard of it, the Kats and Kittys Klub is this national organization for young, up-and-coming African Americans. They do lots of things for the community, and we used to go all the time back home. So we were real happy to join the metropolitan chapter in New York City, and that they were havin' a Fourth of July bar-b-que. It was our first chance to meet kids our own age in the Big Apple.

So there we were, singing up a storm by the barbecue grill, when Chanel and Galleria started looking at us *real* funny. I guess we were kinda showing off. They were the prettiest girls we had seen in New York, even though Galleria wasn't very friendly to us at first. Luckily, Chanel was, and now we're all *real* good friends and singing together.

We can't wait till Ma meets Galleria and the rest of the Cheetah Girls—which may not be anytime soon. See, she and Daddy are getting a dee-vorce, and Ma remained in Houston, while Daddy moved up here to New York.

Of course, Daddy sent for us to come live with him, so he could keep an eye on us. He feels that Ma can't properly supervise us. See, she's a regional district sales manager for Avon, and travels quite a bit for her job. Daddy used to be her boss, but you knew that wasn't gonna last long, because he can be *real* hard on people.

Even though he's *real* hard on us, too—making us do our vocal exercises and clean our rooms *every* night—we know he loves us. And we are real glad he let us invite our friends over here tonight.

That's right—he told us we could invite the Cheetah Girls over! This is the first time we've had company in New York. And the only reason Daddy said okay is because his new girlfriend came over, too.

Her name is High Priestess Abala Shaballa Bogo Hexagone, and believe it or not, she really is some kind of priestess from some far-away place we never even heard of (even though we don't really know what a High Priestess is for sure). Angie and I don't like her much, but Daddy sure does. She's real tall and pretty, so I guess I can understand why.

Anyway, she came over today with her . . . well . . . friends, if that's what you want to call them. If you ask me, they are some of the strangest people you'd ever want to meet. And tonight, they're cookin' up some kind of spooky ritual for the Cheetah Girls!

The Cheetah Girls

I told my friends all about this at our last Cheetah Girls council meeting. But they thought I was just joking! Well, I wasn't, and they're about to find that out!

See, as a singing group, we've only performed together once—at the Cheetah-Rama club last Halloween night. It was a lot of fun! I think the Kats and Kittys liked us, and we got paid, too! We even got a manager out of it—but Mr. Jackal Johnson turned out to be a crook.

Still, even though we haven't performed much, we've got the biggest night of our lives coming up. Tomorrow night, the Cheetah Girls are performing at the world-famous Apollo Thee-ay-ter! Angie and I have never been there before, but we've seen it on television, so we know it's *real* big, with a lot of seats and bright lights and everything.

Don't get me wrong. We're just performing in the Apollo Theatre Amateur Hour contest—but we're still real nervous about it. Most of all, we're *real* scared about the Apollo Sandman. He is this kooky guy in a clown outfit who pulls you off the stage if people start booing at you!

Hey, Ho, Hollywood!

So High Priestess Abala invited her friends over here to conduct this ritual to give the Cheetah Girls more "Growl Power." That's what she said. It sounds okay, till you get a good look at what they're doing back there in the kitchen. They're all standing around this table preparing stuff and jabbering something or other. And believe me, they are a weird collection of folks. I'll tell you, I don't know who I'm more scared of—the Sandman, or High Priestess Abala and her friends.

While they're all back there makin' their "witches' brew," Galleria is putting on a show in our living room. (Chanel and Dorinda are on their way over, too. They're just late.)

"Well, Miss *Aquanette* and *Anginette* Walker, that's downright plummy that you *finally* invited me to your house. Well, you Southern belles are just so swell!" Galleria says, fluttering her pretty eyelashes, and mocking Angie and me.

She loves to do that, and we think it's kinda funny, how she can find a way to rhyme almost anything. We know she's just playing with us, though, because we have a lot of fun together. There is nobody back home in Houston like Galleria Garibaldi. As Big Momma would say,

"They threw away the mold after they made her."

Next year, we hope Galleria and the rest of the Cheetah Girls are gonna transfer to *our* high school. See, they're freshmen at Fashion Industries High, but Angie and I go to LaGuardia High School of Performing Arts. It's very prestigious and all, so we're *real* lucky to be going there. We had to come to New York just for an audition, then go back home, all the way to Houston, and wait to see if we got accepted!

Angie and I just can't wait till the kids in our school see the Cheetah Girls singing together. They're gonna be so jealous—especially JuJu Beans Gonzalez, who's in our vocal and drama classes, and thinks she's the next Mo' Money Monique, just because she can rap and wiggle her shimmyshaker.

Angie and I don't dance *that* good, but still, we've got the shimmyshakers to do it, if we try real hard. That's all I'm saying. And we sing better than JuJu Beans does, even when we have colds (Angie and I always get sick together, too).

JuJu treats me and Angie like corn bread

bakers, or something "country" like that, just because she has never been to Houston. Houston is beautiful—even Galleria's mom, Ms. Dorothea, says so.

Anyway, we've got all year to convince our teachers to let us perform together as the Cheetah Girls for LaGuardia's big June talent showcase. We've been praying on it, and God always gives us an answer (even though most of the time it's not near as quick as we'd like!).

Galleria is acting like company. She sips her lemonade all dainty, then places the glass on its coaster on the coffee table—like it's Aladdin's lamp or something, and she's afraid all the wishes are gonna fly out of it!

Then she sits back on the couch with her legs tight together and her hands on her knees—just like some of the New York ladies sit in church (like they don't belong in the house of the Lord, or they don't know how they're supposed to sit in the pew).

"Dag on, Galleria, you don't have to be so proper. You can just be yourself," I heckle her, then throw Angie another glance. After all, we have seen the real Miss Galleria, and believe us, she does *just* as she pleases.

The Cheetah Girls

Now Galleria's eyes are moving around the living room like a pair of Ping-Pong balls. "Those drapes look like they belong in the Taj Mahal," she says, like she's amusing herself at a porch party down South, or something fancy like that.

The drapes *are* kinda nice, though. They're ivory chiffon, with a scarf valance that has fringes, just like the panels.

Daddy decorated the living room himself, right down to the plastic slipcovers—and he's real proud of it. The big glass coffee table has a brass lion base, and the only thing we're allowed to keep on top of the glass is a big white leather-bound Holy Bible. Then there's a big white shag rug shaped like a bear, lying in the center of the floor. The head has real ivory-looking fang teeth—we checked his mouth with a flashlight!

Daddy keeps his new snow globe collection in a big white wooden case with glass partitions. The snow globes are on the top shelves, and the bottom shelves are lined with his *precious* collection of LP albums—not CDs, but real records of people like Marvin Gaye, the Supremes, the Temptations. Daddy says he's

invested too much in his record collection to
start buying CDs now. When we were little, if
we ever messed with Daddy's records, or broke
one, he would get *real* mad at us.

"Holy cannoli, we got records like this
too—but Momsy keeps them in storage, where
they're just collecting dust!" Galleria says,
laughing. "We could play Frisbee with one
of these!"

She pretends to toss the vinyl record at me,
but she knows better, because she's *real* careful
putting it back into its jacket. Even *she* can tell
Daddy is real particular about things. That's
why he keeps the sofa and sectionals covered in
plastic—"because the fabric is a very delicate
imported ivory silk," he says. So nobody ends
up sittin' on the couch but company.

Even Daddy, when he sits in the living room,
sits in the big brown leather reclining chair—
so he can watch the big television, which is
behind a set of wooden panels. The couch just
sits there, showin' off, "no use to nobody," as
Big Momma used to say. But this is Daddy's
house now, and he decorates it like he pleases.

One thing is for sure—our house in New
York (we call it a house even though it's just a

two-bedroom duplex apartment) is decorated *real* different from the way Ma decorated our house in Houston. Daddy likes everything to be white, ivory, or brown, which are *his* favorite colors. Ma liked peach, and green, and blue colors.

Before I start making myself jittery again—about tonight *and* tomorrow night—the doorbell rings. Thank God, it's finally Chanel and Dorinda. After quick kisses and hugs, Chanel becomes fascinated with our house too.

"Ooh, *qué bonita*! My abuela Florita would love these," she coos, pointing to Daddy's prized collection of snow globes. (That's her grandma she's talkin' about. That's how they say it in Spanish.)

"Abuela just loves the snow here. She'll go outside on her stoop and sit there all day, waiting for snowflakes to hit her on the nose!" Chanel takes the castle snow globe and shakes it up and down, to see the snow fall.

"Daddy just started collecting those. It's really kinda strange," I explain, my voice trailing off as I start to think how much Daddy has changed since he moved up here to New York.

"Aqua, what's wrong with collecting snow globes?" Dorinda asks.

Galleria has finally jumped up from the couch, now that Chanel and Dorinda are here. "Your *daddy's* probably fascinated by the snow we have here in 'New Yawk,'" she says with a laugh. "Wait till he experiences his first snowstorm—he'll be throwing those things out the window!

"My dad used to love the snow," she goes on. "When I was little, he would get more upset than I did if it didn't snow before Christmas. Then we had that majordomo snowstorm a few years ago, and it completely covered my Dad's van. He sat at the window for three days, cursing in Italian till he could shovel his van out!"

"It's not just the snow globes, *Galleria*," I say, exasperated. "That was only the beginning. Then he bought a blender—"

"What's wrong with a blender?" Chanel asks.

"Now everything he eats comes outta that thing!" I say, exasperated.

Chanel bursts out laughing, which makes Galleria and even Dorinda smirk.

"I wish *I* had a blender," Dorinda says,

narrowing her eyes at me, which almost makes her look like a real cheetah. "Where I live, I've got to chop up all the vegetables by hand." Dorinda lives in an apartment with about ten foster brothers and sisters. Bless her heart. I wouldn't trade with her for nothing in the world. Lucky for her, her foster mother just adopted her—so at least she knows she can keep on living where she is, instead of going to another foster home.

Galleria is still riffing about Daddy's blender. "Oh, snapples, he blended apples, and now Aqua thinks he's gonna turn into Freddy!" Galleria snaps, doing the Cheetah Girl handshake with Chanel.

"What Aqua means, is—" Angie says, coming to my defense, "he used to love to cook, you know? Cajun crawfish—"

"—Steaks smothered in onions and gravy," I chime in, so they understand that our Daddy used to like to *eat*. "Now he's blending strange vegetables and fruits, and he sits there and drinks it, like it's supposed to be dee-licious."

"And he expects *us* to drink those dees-gusting shakes too!" Angie cuts in.

"I mean, celery and turnip shakes—please, where's Mikki D's?" I say, rolling my eyes. My friends start laughing again, because they know *we* love to eat, too.

"Snow globes, a stupid blender, and now *this*," I say, pointing to the kitchen, where Daddy is standing with his new girlfriend and those other strange ladies she brought with her.

"What's her name again?" Chanel asks, pulling on one of her braids.

"High Priestess Abala Shaballa Bogo Hexagone," I tell her. "She says she is a Hexagone High Priestess, and her ancestors reigned in Ancient Hexagonia." I roll my eyes like I can't believe it myself.

"Is a Hexagone High Priestess supposed to be like Nefertiti or someone like that?" Dorinda asks, narrowing her eyes again. She knows about all kinds of stuff, because she reads a whole lot of books.

"I don't think so, 'cuz this 'High Priestess' has definitely got a broomstick parked around the corner! Right, Angie?"

"I think High Priestess is just a fancy name for *witch*!" Angie answers.

"*Parate*, Aqua," Chanel says, bursting into giggles. "Help, you're killing me—maybe she's a good witch, *mija*?"

"Well, I don't know, but I'm glad y'all are here, because the show is about to begin! Right before Galleria came, they went to the Piggly Wiggly Supermarket to buy ingredients—'for the ritual!' they said!"

Finally, Galleria and Chanel aren't laughing anymore. Now they're sitting on the edge of their seats, like they're about to see a horror movie. And, believe me, I think we are!

Chapter 2

Suddenly, we hear a loud, grinding noise coming from the kitchen.

"You hear that?" I ask, my eyes popping open.

"*Sí*," Chanel responds.

"That's the blender going—see?" Angie says, her eyes getting wide.

"You know, you and Angie do the same things with your eyes," Chanel says to me, bugging her eyes wide and imitating us.

"I'll bet you they're blending the witches' brew for us to drink!" I whisper.

"That's it—I'm outtie like Snouty," Dorinda says, crossing her arms and looking at Chanel.

"What's that you said, Dorinda?" I ask

politely. Sometimes, when Galleria, Dorinda, and Chanel talk, Angie and I don't understand them. I mean, everybody in New York talks so fast—but our friends just have their *own* way of talking.

Angie says we shouldn't ask when we don't understand what they say, because it makes us look stupid. But as Big Momma always says, "If you don't ask, you gonna miss a whole lot of conversation!"

"It means, Aqua, that I'd rather go get a soda and some chips at the Piggy Wiggly Supermarket than sit here and wait to get hit over the head with a broomstick!" Dorinda grunts, then sits up straight on the couch and folds her arms across her little chest.

Oh, *I* get what she means. She's talking about the snout on the plastic pig outside of Piggly Wiggly. That Dorinda is so cute. She sure can eat, for someone so little. She must have had three slices of our sweet potato pie at her surprise adoption party. (We made it from scratch, too. Not like those store-bought winky-dinky pies and cakes that people serve their families here. Shame on them!)

"Do' Re Mi, why you trying to flounce, when

we know you wuz 'bout to bounce?" Galleria says in her singing voice. "That's why I'm writing my new song about you. You're always trying to bounce!"

Dorinda just sits with her arms folded, looking *real* sheepish, but Galleria lets her off the hook. See, Galleria wrote a new song about Dorinda, because she almost left the group when she got offered a job as a backup dancer for the Mo' Money Monique tour. Do' Re Mi turned the job down in the end, 'cuz she wanted to stay with all of us. But I guess Galleria and Chanel are still sore about it, since they were the ones who made Dorinda a Cheetah Girl in the first place.

"It's time to 'winter squash' this situation, if you know what I'm saying," Galleria says, laughing. "Let's go in the kitchen and blend us a High Priestess Abala shake!" She jumps up, like she's gonna march into the kitchen herself. We all start giggling.

"Dorinda's 'bout to bounce!" Chanel sings, and we all sing a call-and-response verse:

"Who's trying to flounce?"

"Dorinda! Dorinda!"

When we finish singing, I ask, kinda

nervous, "Do you all understand *why* we're waiting for Abala and her friends?" I'm not quite sure how to get through to them.

"No, why?" Chanel asks, sipping her lemonade. One of her braids accidentally dips in the glass, and she starts to giggle nervously. "Oops, *Lo siento*. I didn't see the glass coming!"

"Y'all better listen to what I'm sayin', Chanel," I continue, "and all the rest of you, too! The High Priestess Abala Shaballa says she wants to put a 'Vampire Spell' on us—so we'll captivate the audience at the Apollo Theatre tomorrow night."

The living room gets *real* quiet. It's so quiet, if you listen real close, you can probably hear the fake confetti snowflakes swirling around in Daddy's snow globes in the showcase.

"A 'Vampire Spell'?" Dorinda repeats, narrowing her eyes like a cheetah cub ready to pounce on its prey. "How do you spell, 'I'm outtie like Snouty'?"

She jumps up, but Galleria pushes her down. "Aqua, how could you have us come over here? This is not just some guy jumping out of his coffin and chasing us with his fake rubber arm, like at the haunted house in Madison 'Scare' Garden. This is *for real!*"

"Dag on!" I say. "I told you all during the Cheetah Girl council meeting this was *serious*." Looking at my hands in my lap, I try to figure out what to say to get the Cheetah Girls to help me and Angie. *God, give me the words.*

"What do you expect us to do? Stay here by ourselves, and let these people turn us into frogs instead of Cheetah Girls?"

"Aqua is right," Angie says, speaking up for me. "Then what are y'all gonna do without us? Aqua and I can't exactly go on stage hopping around and croaking, can we?" Angie folds her arms, like that's supposed to really make them help us, but all they do is start laughing.

I'm thinking this whole thing is a lost cause, but when they finish their latest round of giggles, Galleria quips, "Okay, we'll stay. But after this, you owe us, so don't snow us, Aqua." She turns, and looks at Chanel and Dorinda for backup.

"Dag on, all right, we owe y'all, Galleria," I say, giving in. "We're crew now, like you said, right?"

"Yeah," Galleria says, looking at me like, *what's your point?*

"Well then, we have to help each other out no matter what, right?" I continue.

"Yeah, but like I said before, after this you owe us, so don't snow us." When Galleria gets that tone in her voice, we know that's the final word—like she's Reverend Butter at church!

Angie cuts us a quick look, to tell us that Daddy is coming this way. We just sit *real* tight and wait for the fright show to begin.

"Hello, ladies," Daddy greets my friends. Right behind him are High Priestess Abala Shaballa and her coven of witches pretending to be normal ladies.

Abala is real dark—darker than *us*—and it makes her teeth look real white. She is real pretty, though, and she wears African fabric draped around her body and head.

Her friends, on the other hand, are real strange-looking. They trail into the living room, with their long gowns sweeping the floor, and their arms full of all kinds of what look to be witchcraft things. One of them is this dwarf lady, carrying the little folding table Daddy uses when he eats in front of the television.

"Good evening, ladies," High Priestess Abala Shaballa Bogo Hexagone says in a booming voice. "All blessings to Great Hexagone, and the bounty she has prepared for us this evening." Abala Shaballa stretches out her arms to us.

I give Daddy a look, like, I hope you know what you're doing. But what I'm really thinking is, How could you do this to us?

"The Piggly Wiggly Supermarket here is *divine*," says the dwarf lady, in a squeaky voice that sounds like the Tin Man in a rainstorm! "Ah, I see your friends have arrived. I'm Rasputina Twia."

"I'm Hecate Sukoji," says a woman with long black hair and no eyebrows. I wonder, did she shave off her eyebrows, or was she born that way?

"I'm Bast Bojo," says the third lady. She has a bald head, and is looking at us with beady eyes that are so dark and slanty, she looks like a spooky black cat!

"Let us begin," High Priestess Abala Shaballa says.

Rasputina puts down the folding table. On top of it, High Priestess Abala and her three friends put a goose, some tomatoes, beets, Tabasco sauce—

Now, wait a minute! I know Daddy is not

gonna let us use *that*. He always says hot sauce is bad for our vocal cords! But he's just smiling proudly, looking on.

I know—she probably already put a spell on Daddy! *And now we're next!*

Bast pulls some strange-looking fruits out of her pockets. "These are kumquats," she says, as if reading our minds. Then she pulls out a head of lettuce and a teddy bear from the basket she's carrying. Well, at least our pet guinea pigs Porgy and Bess will have something to eat for later—the lettuce, that is.

"You got that at Piggly Wiggly?" I ask in disbelief, looking at the raggedy teddy bear. *What on earth are they gonna do with a teddy bear, anyway?*

"Yes. Apparently it was left over from last Christmas," Rasputina says, all proud of herself.

High Priestess Abala kisses the garlic necklace around her neck. Then she pours some Tabasco sauce into the witches' brew in the blender, shakes it a little, and pours it out into five big glasses!

"Now, let us stand in a circle and drink up, Cheetah Girls, so that tomorrow night, when you're out for blood on the stage, you'll be able to hold your ground!" The High Priestess gives us a big, scary smile.

"What's in this, um, brew?" Dorinda asks, kinda nervous. Good for her. At least she has the nerve to speak up! Daddy must be in a trance or something!

"Raw steak, beets, tomatoes . . . I added pimientos, Tabasco, and, um . . . other things, to prepare you for battle!" High Priestess Abala smiles again, revealing her big, white teeth.

Sniffing at my glass, I think, I'll bet she put blood in it, too!

"Drink up," Abala commands, watching me closely. I drink the dag on thing—which to my surprise, actually tastes kinda good.

"Excellent! And now the rest of you! Come, drink up, girls!" Abala commands.

After we all drink the brew, we hold hands. "We must finish the ritual by paying homage to the sylphs of the east, the salamanders of the south, the bats of the west, and the gnomes of the north," Abala says, her voice sounding stranger and stranger.

At the end of the ritual, Abala gives each of us a shoe box. "You must not open these," she tells us. "Just put them in your closets, and close the door."

"What's in here?" Galleria asks, trying to hide a smirk.

"Parts from stuffed animals—teddy bear eyes and noses, poodle tails, rabbit whiskers . . ."

The High Priestess looks Galleria right in the eye, and Bubbles seems to shrink. "After midnight, the teddy bear, poodle, and rabbit will merge with you, and give you the strength of a true Cheetah Girl!"

"Oh," says Galleria, still smirking. "Well, I guess I'd better let my dog Toto know we'll be having company later—I wouldn't want 'Mr. Teddy Poodly' to get his nose bitten off when he comes out to play."

We all start laughing. High Priestess Abala just looks at us, amused. I wonder what's going through her mind. I don't like all this one bit, I'll tell you that!

Angie and I are gonna do some real praying tonight—and I'm gonna Scotch-tape our shoe boxes so tight, even the Mummy himself wouldn't be able to get out of them!

That High Priestess may have Daddy under a spell, but she doesn't fool me. Tonight, I'm gonna ask *God* to please help us win the Apollo Theatre Amateur Hour Contest—and not to let High Priestess Abala Shaballa turn Daddy into a salamander!

Chapter 3

Mr. Garibaldi wanted to drive us Cheetah Girls to the Apollo Theatre tonight, but Daddy insisted that *he* drive us. It made us feel *real* important to have everybody fussing over us, like we're a big singing group already, with cheetah-licious ways.

Daddy has two cars—a white Cadillac with a convertible top, and a white Bronco—and, can you believe this? He has to *pay* to keep them in a garage near our house!

He's always fussin' about that. Back home we had three cars—including the blue Katmobile, which is now Ma's—*and* our own four-car garage in the back of the house. And we didn't have to pay a dime extra for all that parking space! I'll tell you, New York City sure is strange—and expensive. I'm surprised they don't charge for breathing air here!

Anyway, Daddy *insisted* that Mr. Garibaldi and Ms. Dorothea drive with us to the Apollo. (Chanel's mom is out on a big date with her boyfriend, Mr. Tycoon, so she can't come see us tonight. She's tryin' to get Mr. Tycoon to marry her, but he's playin' hard to get, so *she's* taking belly dancing lessons to "get" *him*!)

Ms. Dorothea doesn't like us to call her Mrs. Garibaldi, because she isn't a "prim and proper" kind of person. If you met her, you would understand where Galleria gets all her personality. I mean, Galleria is tame compared to her mother—Ms. Dorothea even eats Godiva chocolates for breakfast, and hits people over the head with her Cheetah pocketbook when they're acting up. We just love her! By putting up the two extra seats in the back of Daddy's Bronco, we're all able to fit. Since Dorinda and Chanel are the smallest, they sit on the two little seats way in the back. Galleria sits next to her mom and dad.

We're *so* glad High Priestess Abala Shaballa couldn't come with us tonight to the Apollo

Theatre, even though she says she is "with us in the spirit." Well, I keep looking out the car window to make sure I don't see her in the *flesh*, flying by on her broomstick with her flock of kooky friends! (So far, the coast is clear.) I'm sorry, but Angie and I decided last night that we don't trust "High Priestess Hocus Pocus," as Galleria calls her.

"Angie, would you look at all these people?" I say, as we drive across 125th Street. It seems like there are millions of people in New York, and they are *all* walking around up here in Harlem. I mean, the sidewalks are so crowded, it looks like they're having a fair or something!

"*Mira*, look at their outfits. Some of them look like they're dressed for church!" Chanel exclaims.

"What church is *she* going to in a yellow satin cape?" Dorinda chides Chanel, pointing to a lady whose earrings are so big, they look like plates hanging from her ears. Girls in New York just *love* their jewelry.

"Well, you never know—this is the Big Apple," Angie chimes in.

"I know. I've never seen so many neon signs before in my life!" I say.

Dorinda points to a hair-supply place with a giant neon sign that says RAPUNZEL. "Word, that's the hair place Abiola at the YMCA told me about!"

Dorinda has a *real* after-school job—through the youth entrepreneurship program at the YMCA—even though it doesn't pay that much. "That's where we should buy hair, so we don't look like wefties!" she adds, chuckling. Wefties are girls with weaves that are so tick-tacky the tracks are showing, as Galleria says.

"*Mamacitas*, they've got some hefty wefties up here," Chanel says, looking at more girls walking by in their fancy outfits. "They must be going to some kinda club around here."

"Yeah—a club for vampires!" exclaims Galleria, as we pass the Black Magic movie-theater complex. "Ooo, look, Aqua and Angie, they're having a Fang-oria Festival there!"

From what I can see, the Black Magic looks big enough to fit all the people in New York *and* Houston. "Let's go see Freddy before we get ready!" I say excitedly.

"Hmmph—then Freddy will have to deal with me, because no ghoul is gonna stop this show!" Ms. Dorothea quips, then yawns into her leopard-gloved hand.

"Gee, Momsy poo, I think the Sandman has already sprinkled you with some poppy dust or something," Galleria giggles.

"I'm fading *pronto*, too," says Mr. Garibaldi, who is also yawning. "I get up every day at five o'clock, you know."

"Before the rooster can say cock-a-doodle-do!" Galleria chides her father.

Ms. Dorothea is getting up early too these days. She's working *real* hard now that she is our manager, and she still runs her fancy boutique—Toto in New York . . . Fun in Diva Sizes—which is the most beautiful store I've ever seen.

"Ooh, they got *Blacula* there! We've never seen that one!" Angie says to me, getting real excited. We just love horror movies—especially the old ones, because they show more gory stuff up close, like eyeballs hanging out of the eye sockets, or brains popping out of the skull.

The only thing I love more than singing is looking at dead bodies, and figuring out how they died, and wondering if they'll tell any secrets. I guess that's because our Granddaddy

Walker is a mortician and owns Rest in Peace, the biggest funeral parlor in Houston.

Over the last forty years, Granddaddy Walker has buried half of the dead people in Houston. That's what Big Momma says.

When our singing career is over, I'm going to become a forensic scientist, like that guy on the old TV show—you know, the one who solves crimes by examining the victims. Angie wants to be a neurosurgeon, so she can operate on people's brains and stuff.

I'm so scared, I wish we could see a horror movie right now. When Daddy gets out of the car to find out where he should park, we all start cackling about last night's strange events.

"Did any of y'all dance with a teddy bear or a poodle last night?" I ask. Then I wonder, What on earth did Abala mean by giving us stuffed teddy bear heads in a shoe box? How was that supposed to help us win this competition?

"I couldn't believe Aqua got up in the morning and checked our shoe boxes in the closet, just to make sure they were still taped," Angie says, acting all grown.

"Angie, don't act like *you* didn't look at your box, too," I shoot back.

"Can you believe Abala says Galleria was probably Egyptian royalty in her past life?" Dorinda remarks, still in disbelief about last night.

"Well, she's definitely not psychic, or she would know that we don't like her!" I say, huffing and puffing. Angie and I are squeezed into the front seat, and we're trying not to breathe, so we don't bust out of our Cheetah Girls costumes.

"I'm gonna ask Princess Pamela about her, *para seguro*," Chanel says. "Just to be safe. You can count on that, *está bien?*"

Like I said before, Princess Pamela is Chanel's father's girlfriend. Chuchie's parents have been divorced for a while, and she just loves Pamela. The Princess owns a whole lot of businesses— she does hair and nails, bakes the best pound-cake in New York, and tells people's fortunes. Princess Pamela is a psychic. She may not be a High Priestess like Abala, but I like Pamela a lot better. *She* can tell *my* fortune any time.

"I think my jumpsuit is tighter than it was the last time," I say.

"Those sweet potato pies you made for Dorinda's surprise adoption party were dope-a-licious, but did you have to eat five of them all by yourself, Miz Aquanette?" Galleria asks, laying on that syrupy Southern accent again.

"No, I guess not, Miz Galleria," I sigh back, playing along with her. "And I guess it didn't help that I ate all of your father's chocolate cannolis at the same time!"

"Aah, *mama mia*, I wondered who ate them all!" Mr. Garibaldi says, waving his hand.

I take another deep breath. I'm scared I'm gonna pop out of my costume right on stage, and the Sandman is gonna tear the rest of my costume with his big ol' hook!

Now I feel like poor Dorinda did when she tore her costume onstage at the Cheetah-Rama. You should have seen her face when she ripped her jumpsuit. That's right—there we were, in the middle of a song—and Dorinda did a lickety-split, right there on stage!

"Don't worry, Aqua. You won't be a witch without a stitch," says Galleria, leaning from the back of the car and whispering in my ear. "And it's just a matter of time before we pull the curtain on the High Priestess of Hocus Pocus. The Wizard of Oz she ain't, or I'll faint!"

"What does she do when she isn't concocting Vampire Spells?" Dorinda asks.

"Daddy says she teaches this, well . . . witchcraft stuff to people. And she has a store called Enchantrixx up here somewhere."

Then I see Daddy on his way back to the car. "Shh, he's coming," I whisper, then announce loudly as he opens the door, "Well! Here we are at the world-famous Apollo Theatre."

Mentioning the Apollo reminds me of why we're here tonight, and how much is at stake. It makes me start feeling nervous, and when I get nervous, my stomach starts churning like it's mashing potatoes or something.

"Y'all feeling scared like I am?" I ask, this time turning around so I can look at Galleria.

"*Sí, mamacita*," admits Chanel.

"I guess that's natural, right?" Dorinda asks Ms. Dorothea. Ever since the adoption party, the two of them seem like two peas in a pod—which we're all *real* happy about.

Dorinda needs all the love she can get. She's been a foster child all her life—till now, that is. The day her foster mother, Mrs. Bosco, adopted her was the best day of Dorinda's whole life. It sure made Ms. Dorothea cry a lot, though. I wonder what that was all about. She seemed *so* sad about something.

"Darling, when the day comes that you're not afraid as you walk on that stage—cancel the show immediately!" Dorothea says, reaching for the door handle to get out.

But Mr. Garibaldi quickly says, "*Cara*, no, let me get the door for you!"

Mr. Garibaldi is such a gentleman. Galleria says he's very "old school," because he grew up in Italy and not here in the States.

That's probably true. When we were at Ms. Dorothea's store, Galleria showed us the personals ad from *New York* magazine that Ms. Dorothea answered to meet Mr. Garibaldi. We almost died right there on the spot! He called himself a "lonely oyster on the half shell" in the ad. I can't imagine him like that. He seems like the happiest man we've ever seen. We wish Daddy was more like that—just a lot of fun, that's all I'm saying.

After Mr. Garibaldi helps all of us out of the car, we take a look up at the sign for the Apollo Theatre. "Look at all the lights up there!" I exclaim.

"They should have *our* name up there in bright lights, taking up the whole marquee!" Galleria says, giggling.

"Darling, one day they *will*," Ms. Dorothea says, then flings her fur boa around her neck, which hits Mr. Garibaldi in the face.

"Don't knock me out with your love, *cara*!" he quips, then puts the boa back on her shoulder.

We are giggling up a storm, because we are just so happy to be here. People are looking at us as we walk in, and Ms. Dorothea tells the usher that we're The Cheetah Girls and we're here to *perform*.

"Go right in, ladies," the usher says, smiling at us. He looks so nice in his uniform. He's wearing a red jacket, black pants and white gloves—and his teeth are almost as bright as the neon lights in the sign!

As we're walking by all the people waiting to buy popcorn and stuff at the concession stand, these two tall, skinny guys with baseball caps and real baggy pants start calling to us. "You're grrrr-eat! Yo, check it, D, there's Tony the Tiger with his girlfriends!" They stand there stuffing popcorn in their mouths, and heckling up a storm. They are so loud that everybody turns and looks at us.

"Well if it isn't the baggy, bumbling Bozo brothers, trying to get full at the concession stand!" Galleria hisses back.

"Shhh, darling, never let them see you sweat," Ms. Dorothea tells her. "Besides, those children look like they could use a home-cooked meal."

It's still so hard for me and Angie to believe how rude people in New York can be. I mean, we have *some* "bozos" in Houston, but not like this. People will just walk up to you anywhere and get in your face, for no reason!

"Dag on, I hope everybody ain't like him, or this is gonna turn into a 'Nightmare on 125th Street,'" I turn and say to Galleria. (One of my favorite horror movies is *Nightmare on Elm Street*, 'cuz that scar-faced Freddy Krueger always finds a way to get in your dreams and scare you to death!)

"Not to worry, Aqua. There is always one sour bozo in a bunch of grapes!" Galleria mutters.

"Let's find our dressing room," quips Ms. Dorothea, acting now like our manager—which is what she *has* been, ever since she helped us get rid of that no-good Mr. Jackal Johnson.

"Darling, I'll see you later," Mr. Garibaldi says, kissing Ms. Dorothea on the cheek. Then he says good-bye to us, so he can find some seats up front for himself and Daddy.

"Try to sit in the first row, Daddy!" Galleria yells back to him, as we walk toward the back.

Ms. Dorothea speaks to another usher in a red jacket who points straight ahead of us. "Right that way, ladies."

"Look at all the people!" Chanel says excitedly. Lots of them are already filing into the theater and finding their seats.

"It *is* as big as it looks on TV!" I whisper to Angie.

"You think it'll get filled up?" Dorinda asks, kinda nervous.

"*Sí, sí, Do' Re Mi,*" says Chanel, giggling. "As soon as they find out *we're* here, *está bien?*"

At the base of the stairs, there is a woman with a walkie-talkie and earphones. Before Ms. Dorothea says anything to her, the woman tells us in a brisk voice to "go up the stairs."

Dag on! She could be a little friendlier, I think to myself, as we all climb up a real tiny staircase. It seems like the longest time before we get to the stairwell landing for dressing room "B."

When we open the stairwell door, there are a lot of people crowded in the hallway! *Are we supposed to share a dressing room with all these people*? I wonder.

"Excuse me, darlings," Ms. Dorothea says firmly, pushing her way through the throng of people.

"You'd think we were at the mall or something, and they were giving things away!" Angie exclaims.

As we pour into the dressing room, just to plop down our things, Ms. Dorothea quips, "They said the dressing room would be small, but this looks like a *prison cell*!"

"I guess it's a good thing we already have our costumes on," I say nervously, looking around at the other people. They are in costumes too, but not like ours. One man looks just like The Cat In the Hat or something, his hat is so high up on his head. He has striped kneesocks, too, and shorts, and big cartoon-looking glasses!

Galleria whispers, "If all we've got to deal

with is The Cat In the Hat, then we've got it made, like green eggs and ham!"

I sure hope so, I think nervously—because between my too tight costume, this too tight dressing room, and High Priestess Abala's too spooky Vampire Spell, this whole thing is turning into a New York frightmare!

Chapter 4

"I bet Dressing Room 'A' is for the stars," Dorinda says, looking kinda sad, then puts her cheetah backpack down on the floor.

"What *stars*, darling?" Ms. Dorothea says. "In my humble opinion, you girls are the most cheetah-licious thing the Apollo Theatre has ever seen—or will ever see!"

We may not exactly believe her, but at least her words make us feel less nervous. Now we have to push through the people again, and climb all the way back down those steep little stairs until we get backstage. *Then* we have to wait backstage for our number to be called.

"I'm exhausted already!" I moan to Dorinda, who is scratching herself through her costume.

Oh, no, not again. She can't be busting out of her costume, after Ms. Dorothea took all that time to fix it!

As if reading my mind, Dorinda squints her eyes and says, "Don't worry, Aqua, my costume is not gonna rip again. I must have got bitten by mosquitoes or *something* last night. Our screens at the house have holes in them."

"Maybe it was the little teddy bear vampire from your shoe box!" Galleria says, her eyes lighting up.

"Lemme see," Chanel says to Do' Re Mi, who rolls up the left leg on her cheetah jumpsuit. "*Ay, Dios!* Look how red they are. *Mamacita*, it sure looks like mosquito bites to me."

"Maybe you got bitten by those mosquitoes carrying the killer virus!" Galleria says, concerned.

"Maybe it was one of those six-foot bloodsucking mosquitoes like in the movie me and Aqua saw," my twin blurts out.

"I'm not trying to hear this," Dorinda says, getting upset.

"Don't worry, Dorinda. I know how to stop the itching," I say.

Hey, Ho, Hollywood!

"How, brown cow?" Bubbles asks, giggling.

"Darling, that's not funny," Ms. Dorothea says suddenly.

"What, Mom? I'm just riffing off a *nursery* rhyme!" Galleria protests.

"Even so, darling, sometimes you have to give your 'riff' the 'sniff test' before you 'flap your lips'—if you 'get my drift,'" Ms. Dorothea says, looking at Galleria like she's not the only one with rhyme power.

Galleria gets real sheepish. Ms. Dorothea is real nice, but she doesn't play.

"That's all right, Ms. Dorothea, I know Galleria didn't mean anything bad. She's just being, well, herself," I offer as an explanation.

"Well, she can stir that saying with some jam, and make *flimflam*," Ms. Dorothea says, closing her cheetah purse with a loud snap.

We all get quiet, but I don't want Galleria to feel bad, so I say, "I can go upstairs and get the deodorant out of my backpack."

"For what, *mamacita*? You trying to say we smell now?" Chanel asks me.

"No, Chanel! It's an old Southern remedy. If you rub deodorant on a mosquito bite, it stops the itching!"

"Word?" Dorinda asks hopefully.

"Well then, go get it, Aqua, 'cuz we don't want Dorinda wiggling around like Mr. Teddy Poodly onstage," Galleria says, making a joke about the stuffed teddy bear head and poodle tail in the shoe boxes Abala gave us.

"Dag on, I hope that thing doesn't try on any of my clothes while I'm gone!" I retort. That gets everyone laughing, which is good, because we don't want to get a bad case of nerves before we perform.

"I'll go with you, Aqua," Ms. Dorothea says. "You girls stay here, so nobody takes our spot." She looks annoyed. "Of course, at the rate they're going, we'll be here until the Cock-a-doodle Donut truck pulls up to make a morning delivery!"

When we get back upstairs, I can't believe that those bozo boys we met when we came in are hanging out near our dressing room. They're putting on yellow satin jackets, with the words "Stak Chedda" written on the back in blue letters. That must be the name of their group, I figure.

I grab the deodorant for Dorinda and we head back downstairs. "I bet they're probably rappers," I say to Ms. Dorothea, once we're safely out of hearing range.

"Like I said, darling, that is still no excuse for bad manners!" Dorothea quips.

When we get backstage and rejoin the others, I give Do' Re Mi the deodorant for her legs, and she starts working on herself.

"Guess who's performing!" I moan. "Those bozos we met outsi—"

Galleria jabs me before I can finish, so I turn around. Can you believe it? Those rude boys are coming our way!

"Whazzup, ladies?" the one with the Popeye eye sockets says to us, chuckling under his breath.

"Are you performing too?" Dorinda asks. Galleria is propping her up while Angie puts the deodorant on the mosquito bites on her leg.

"Yeah. We're rappers—'Stak Chedda.' I'm Stak Jackson and this is my brother Chedda Jackson," Popeye says to us.

"Who are you lovely ladies?" Chedda asks. His head is bigger than his brother's, but the rest of his body still looks like he could use a home-cooked meal—just like Ms. Dorothea said.

"We're the Cheetah Girls," Galleria answers for us, then gives them a smirk, like, "don't try it."

"See? I knew y'all were related to Tony the Tiger!" Popeye riffs. "Those costumes you're wearing are fierce, though."

"They're not costumes—it's our survival gear for becoming stars in the jiggy jungle—not wanna-be's like you." Galleria sniffs, then adds, "And you two must be related to Dr. Jekyll and Mr. Hyde?"

"Oooops," Chedda says, then slaps his baseball cap at the crown.

"I mean the rappers, not the loony doctors," Galleria assures them. "But maybe . . ."

"We could have it like that. You never know, with how we flow," Popeye says, then slaps his brother a high five.

"It's show time at the Apollo!" booms the announcer's voice from the front of the stage. Then we hear loud applause.

"It's crowded out there, right?" says one of the girls in back of us, really loudly.

"Quiet, please, and keep your places, so you can be called on," says an attendant with a walkie-talkie.

When the girls in back of us keep yapping, Ms. Dorothea gives them a look, then says, "Shhh!" Then she huddles the five of us together in a circle. "It's time to do your Cheetah Girls prayer."

Even though the area backstage is small and crowded with all the contestants, we try to ignore everybody and do our Cheetah Girls prayer. We have plenty of time, because we're the fourth contestants—even though I wish we were the last, because I'm starting to feel real nervous. The hamburger I ate for dinner is churning around in my stomach.

Ms. Dorothea instructs us to join hands, bow our heads, and close our eyes. Galleria starts the prayer; then we join in, keeping our voices low, so the other people around us don't start looking at us.

"Dear Head Cheetah in Charge, please give us the growl power to perform our cheetah-licious best, and make you proud of all the gifts you've bestowed on us . . ." We end the prayer by doing the Cheetah Girl handshake together and chanting, "Whatever makes us clever—forever!"

The other people backstage cheer us on

quietly. But they don't have to worry—there is so much noise coming from the stage and the audience, you can't even hear us back here.

"Bacon, Once Over Lightly—please stand here by the curtain. You go on first," the attendant barks sharply. She is talking to four girls who look a lot older than us—maybe about nineteen—and are wearing brown leather jumpers and kneesocks.

"I hope they're crispy," whispers Galleria, who is standing between me and Chanel.

"Their earrings sure look like plates—big enough to hold a few strips," I whisper back.

"Ladies and gentleman," booms the announcer, "we've got four sisters from Buttercup, Tennessee. Let's give a hand to Bacon, Once Over Lightly!"

Sisters. They must not be sisters for real, 'cuz they don't look very much alike. Maybe that's just a stage act or something. We hold our breath, waiting for the girls to start singing.

First we hear the track for the Sista Fudge song, "I'll Slice You Like a Poundcake," booming on the sound system. They'd better be real good singers to mess with that song, I think, shaking my head.

Pulling down my jumpsuit, Galleria slaps my hand and mouths, "Stop it!" but I don't even care, 'cuz I can't believe my ears. These poor girls are more like Spam than bacon—they sound like the noise from an electric can opener!

All of a sudden, the noise from the audience is even louder than their singing.

"Omigod—are they booing them?" Angie asks, bobbing her head around to see if maybe she can sneak a peek through the curtain. But we can't see a thing. The attendant is standing right near the heavy curtain, and it's not budging.

Suddenly I start sweating. There is no air back here. It's hot, and I'm nervous. Those girls are getting booed out there! Are *we* gonna get booed too? I can't believe how blasé the attendant is acting! She must be used to all this.

"I think they're awright. They didn't have to boo them like that," Dorinda says, folding her arms. Her lower lip is kinda trembling, and I can tell she feels sorry for Bacon, Once Over Lightly. Ms. Dorothea puts her arms around Dorinda's little shoulders and gives her a squeeze.

All of a sudden, we hear this funny music, and the audience laughing real loud. We just look at each other, like, "Where's Freddy?"

"That means the Sandman went onstage," Ms. Dorothea tells us.

That really did sound like *clown* music or something. I have to catch my breath and say a prayer to God. *Please give us the strength to perform after all this. And please don't let the Sandman take us!*

Then I get the strangest thought: What if High Priestess Abala Shaballa *did* put a spell on us? What if we go out there and start croaking like bullfrogs?

No! That's so silly! We had rehearsal today, and we sound just as good as we always do. And at least we're singing original material, I remind myself. Galleria writes songs—she's *real* talented like that, even if we did fight in the beginning 'cuz she likes to have everything her way.

She wrote the song we're singing tonight, "Wanna-be Stars in the Jiggy Jungle." When we performed it for the first time at the Cheetah-Rama, everybody *loved* it!

They'll probably love us tonight, too. That's right, I tell myself. Angie and I look at each other, and I know she's thinking the same thing.

Two more acts go on—the Coconuts and a boy named Wesley Washington, who tries to sing falsetto like Jiggie Jim from the Moonpies, one of my favorite singers. (He just gives me goose bumps, his voice is so high and beautiful.) This boy sounds like he has been inhaling helium or something. He is definitely singing too high for his range.

"I think we're the only ones singing an original song," I whisper in Galleria's ear.

She pokes me in the stomach and says, "No diggity, no doubt!"

Now it's our turn. The walkie-talkie attendant motions for us to hurry up and stand by her.

I whisper to Chanel, "Ain't you scared? We don't know what's waiting for us beyond that curtain!"

"Fame!" giggles Chanel, grabbing my hand.

"Ladies and gentleman, our next contestants are five young ladies from right here in the Big Apple, and they got a whole lot of attitude!"

How come he didn't say two of us are from Houston? I feel kinda mad, but I just smile when he says, "Give it up for the Cheetah

Girls!" What counts is, he got the name of our group right.

We run out onto the stage, and everybody starts clapping. I guess they like our costumes, 'cuz who wouldn't? We stand side by side, and hold our cordless microphones in place, waiting for the track to begin. We smile at each other, and our eyes are screaming, "Omigod, look at all these people!"

Then the music comes on, and we start to sing:

"Some people walk with a panther
or strike a buffalo stance
that makes you wanna dance.

Other people flip the script
on the day of the jackal
that'll make you cackle . . ."

People start clapping to the beat. They like us! We even get our turns down, 'cuz Angie and I have been working real hard to improve our dance steps. I just wanna scream when Dorinda does her split—and gets right back up without splitting her pants. *Go, Dorinda!*

Hey, Ho, Hollywood!

By the time we take our bows, to a huge round of applause, I feel almost like crying. *This* is why we love to sing—Angie and I have dreamed about moments like this all our lives!

"You were *fabulous*!" Ms. Dorothea screams when we get backstage. "I didn't hear one jackal cackle!"

"That's 'cuz he's in prison, eating his own tough hide right about now," Galleria humphs.

We all laugh at her joke. We know she's talking about Mr. Jackal Johnson—our brush with a real-live jackal. Mr. Johnson wanted to be our manager, but he didn't have good intentions. Lucky for us, Ms. Dorothea got wind of it before he had some Cheetah Girls for lunch. Like I told you, she doesn't play.

"I just *know* we're gonna win!" Chanel says, dancing around in the back while we wait for the rest of the performers to go on.

Pushing up the sleeves on their satin baseball jackets, those two annoying boys, Stak Chedda, posture like *they're* ready for Freddy, then walk out onstage like they think they're all that and a bag of fries.

"I know *you* ain't gonna win!" I say under

my breath, sucking my teeth behind their backs. We all start giggling, then huddle against the end of the curtain so we can hear them when the rap track drops.

"I *know* they got weak rhymes," Angie says, egging us on as they start to do their thing.

> "Well, I'm the S to the T to the A to the K
> Stak's my name and you know I got game.
> When I'm on the mike, I make it sound so right
> I rip the night till it gets way light
> I think I'm gonna do it right now
> So let's get to it—and if you wanna
> Bust a rhyme, go ahead and do it!"

Even though the audience is doing a call and response with these cheesy rappers, we aren't worried about the competition, because their rap is, well, kinda like the alphabet—it starts with A, ends with Z, and gets real corny by the time they get to M.

Stak Chedda does get a lot of applause, but we're still not sweating it. "Get ready for Freddy, *girlitas!*" Galleria says. We do the Cheetah Girls handshake again, and wait for our cue to come out.

Hey, Ho, Hollywood!

"Okay, ladies and gentlemen. It's that time again—time to pick the winner of this month's world-famous Apollo Amateur Hour contest. Come on out! Come on out!"

There's a drumroll, and we are all waved back onstage by the attendant. The lights are so bright, and there are so many people, it's kinda scary.

The announcer calls the name of each group in turn, and they step up to the center of the stage, so the audience can decide who should win the contest. Whoever gets the most applause wins.

"Lord, we need that prize money!" I say, grabbing Galleria's hand. "Just for once, I'd like to pay for my own tips."

Of course, I'm exaggerating, because we did spend some of the prize money we earned from the Cheetah-Rama show. But Daddy usually pays for us to get our hair and nails done twice a month. Maybe if we earned our own money, he wouldn't complain so much about having to pay the garage bill every month for two cars.

I'm getting so jittery I grab Angie's hand real tight. We both look at the front row, to see if we can spot Daddy. We were too nervous to look while we were performing.

Omigod, there he is! Angie and I give him a real big grin. Mr. Garibaldi is waving at us so hard, you'd think he was at the Santa Maria Parade in Houston.

I can't believe how many people are in this theater! I try not to look too far into the crowd, because the lights are so bright they almost blind me.

When the announcer calls our name to come up to the center of the stage, I really do think I'm gonna faint. We step forward, and I can see the little beads of sweat on the announcer's shiny forehead. He's wearing a red bow tie and a white shirt. His hair is slicked down, and his teeth are whiter than the neon sign outside.

I look around, trying to catch a glimpse of the Sandman. Where does he hide at, anyway?

"Okay, ladies and gentlemen. *You* decide. What did you think of the Cheetah Girls!" he bellows into the microphone.

The audience is clapping—louder than they did for Wesley Washington; Bacon, Once Over Lightly; or any of the other performers!

I'm so excited, I can't believe this is happening! We stand together at the back of the stage, and I can feel how excited all of us are by the sparkle in our eyes.

Now there is only one group left—and we know we got them beat by a bag of bacon bits!

"Okay, ladies and gentlemen—what did you think of the rapping duo, Stak Chedda!"

Of course, Popeye and his brother step forward like they own the place, but we know they ain't the cat's meow, as Big Momma would say.

All of a sudden I can't believe my ears. We look at one another in sudden shock when the audience claps louder for these bozos than they did for us!

The announcer's voice echoes like something right out of a horror movie—"And the winner of tonight's Amateur Hour contest at the world-famous *Apollo* Theatre is—STAK CHEDDA!"

"That's what I'm talking about!" Popeye yells into the mike, holding up his hands like he's Lavender Holy, the boxer, and he's just won a title bout.

I can feel the hot tears streaming down my face. *Why did tonight have to turn into Nightmare on 125th Street? Why?*

Chapter 5

Dorinda is crying, and she's not even trying to hide it. Bless her heart. She's probably kicking herself and thinking, Why didn't I take that job as a backup dancer for the Mo' Money Monique tour?

I can't blame her. For me and Angie, singing is our life. We *have* to sing—but Dorinda can *dance*. Maybe she doesn't even *want* to sing, but she's doing it for us, because *we* want her to.

Galleria looks so mad her mouth is poking out. I can't even look at Daddy right now. I feel so ashamed.

"Stak Chedda. They wuz more like Burnt Toast. This competition is rigged, yo!" Dorinda blurts out through her tears when we get backstage.

Ms. Dorothea doesn't say anything. She just holds Galleria, and then we all start crying.

"I can't believe we didn't win, Mommy," Galleria moans, tears streaming down her cheeks. She doesn't seem like herself at all—more like a little girl.

The attendant is now directing traffic, and sending everyone back up to the dressing rooms to get their belongings. "If you don't have anything in the dressing rooms, just move toward the rear exit. Do not try to exit in front!"

"Can we just stay here a minute?" Ms. Dorothea asks the attendant very nicely.

"Yes, go ahead, but you're gonna have to move shortly," she says briskly. She must have seen a million people like us, crying like babies just because they lost.

I don't know what we're gonna do now. We just can't seem to get a break! Angie and I wanted to sing gospel in the first place, but we got into pop and R&B music, because everybody kept telling us that was the only way to break into this business. Dag on, it seems like *rappers* are the only ones who are getting breaks now!

Mr. Garibaldi is waiting outside for us. "Your father went to get the car," he tells me and Angie, then turns to Galleria with his arms outstretched.

"Daddy! *Ci sono scemi.* I hate those people! Take me home!" Galleria is crying so hard, I can't believe it.

Angie is holding me now, because she is crying too. Chanel is holding Dorinda. People are standing around, looking at us. "Y'all were so cute!" this girl says to us as she walks out of the theater.

"Don't say nothing, Aisha. Can't you see they're crying? Leave them alone," her mother says, grabbing the girl's arm.

I look away from them. I don't care if we never come back here again!

Daddy pulls up outside the theater in the Bronco. Why couldn't he pull up down the block where no one could see us? Doesn't he understand how embarrassed we are? I don't want people looking at us, then laughing behind our backs.

I wish we hadn't worn our costumes here.

Hey, Ho, Hollywood!

Then we could have changed back into our street clothes, and no one would have noticed us—the losers. "The Cheetah Girls."

I can't even look Daddy in the face when we get into the car. I try to sit in the back, but Chanel pushes me up front. She and Dorinda are *real* quiet now, slumped down in the back seat. They don't say a word.

"Those boys weren't that good. I don't see what all the fuss was about. You girls shoulda won," Daddy says, to no one in particular.

"Well, we didn't," I say, then sigh.

This is the worst day of my life. Worse than when Daddy first moved out of the house, and Ma stayed in bed crying for a week. Worse than when Grandma Winnie died from cancer. Worse than when I fell from the swing, and got seven stitches in my knee.

If you ask me, it doesn't really look like the Cheetah Girls are meant to be. I mean, we knew it would be hard, but not *this* hard. Every time we turn around, something is going wrong! "We can't get a break to save our lives," as Big Momma would say.

"Anybody want to go to Kickin' Chicken?" Daddy asks.

"No, thank you," we all say, one by one. I don't feel hungry at all. I just want to go home and get in bed, and pray to God to help us find some answers.

"You're cryin' all over your costume," Ms. Dorothea says to Galleria, reaching for a tissue out of her purse.

"I don't care about this stupid costume anymore!" Galleria blurts out between sobs.

We all get real quiet until Daddy stops in front of Dorinda's house at 116th Street. I feel bad that Dorinda has to live here, with all these people living on top of one another like cockroaches and always getting into each other's business.

Dorinda turns to ask Ms. Dorothea one more thing before she closes the car door. "How come they didn't like us?"

"They *did*," Ms. Dorothea tells her. "But one day, they're gonna *love* you. You'll see. The world is cruel like that sometimes."

Ms. Dorothea gets out of the car, and gives Dorinda a big hug, and she doesn't let go for a long time. Ms. Dorothea looks like a big cheetah, and Dorinda looks like a little cub who is happy to be loved.

I hope Galleria doesn't feel jealous. She can be that way. Now she's acting like she doesn't even see them hug, and she doesn't even look up to say good-bye to Dorinda.

"Come here, *cara*," Mr. Garibaldi says to Galleria, then holds a tissue to Galleria's nose. She blows into it so hard it sounds like a fire engine siren.

Galleria is such a Daddy's girl—just like me and Angie—but her dad is a lot nicer than ours. I can't imagine Mr. Garibaldi getting as mean as Daddy gets sometimes. Now I feel more tears welling up—and these tears have nothing to do with the Cheetah Girls.

"Can I have one, Mr. Garibaldi?" I ask him, reaching for a tissue.

"Call me Franco," Mr. Garibaldi says, smiling at me with tears in his eyes as he hands me a tissue.

That is so sweet. He feels bad, just 'cuz his baby feels bad. He's always calling Galleria *cara*. I think that means *baby* in Italian. She's so lucky she gets to speak another language and all. That's one reason why she and Chanel seem so mysterious to us.

It gets real quiet again when it's just us and

Daddy in the car. He doesn't know how to say a lot of things to us. That's just how he is, 'cuz he has a lot of things on his mind—even though he does seem happier now that he has that girlfriend of his. He sure is crazy about her. Too bad we don't like her at all! Angie and I hold hands all the way home.

When we get home, Daddy lets us go right upstairs to bed, without saying anything. Good. I'm too tired now to even try to talk.

"I'm real proud of you girls," Daddy calls after us as we climb the stairs to our bedroom.

"Good night, Daddy," I say.

Daddy goes over to the stereo and puts on an LP. He loves this time of night. He likes to sit by himself, and smoke his pipe, and drink brandy while he watches television or listens to some music. He likes to listen to the legends like Miles Davis, Lionel Hampton, and Coltrane late at night, 'cuz, he says, that's when you can really hear "the jazz men trying to touch you with their music."

"Good night, Daddy," Angie says, and we continue on upstairs.

Angie is real quiet as we change into our pajamas. She doesn't even make any jokes about the shoe boxes in the closet. I wish Mr. Teddy Poodly could come out of his shoe box and dance with us right now. Anything would be better than this misery.

I go to my shoe box and look at it, then decide to take the Scotch tape off it. If Mr. Teddy Poodly wants to come out and dance, let him—he just better not bother Porgy and Bess, our pet guinea pigs.

After I throw the Scotch tape in the wastebasket, Angie and I kneel down by our beds. Tonight, it's Angie's turn to lead our prayer.

"God, please help us see why you didn't let us win the contest tonight," she says. "If you don't want us to be singers anymore, please let us know. Just show us the signs. We'll do real good in school so that we can go to college, like we said. If you don't want us to quit singing, then please give us strength to do better, so we can stay in New York and not let Ma down.

"Please look over her in Houston, and Big Momma, and Granddaddy Walker, too, because his blood pressure is acting up, and he didn't sound too good on the phone. Oh, and please tell us if High Priestess Abala Shaballa is a witch—and if she is, if she is a *good* witch. Just give us the signs. We'll understand. Amen."

After we say our prayers, Angie and I curl up in our beds. We reach out to each other, and hold hands across the space between—just like we did when we were little, and would get afraid of a lightning storm.

"I wish Ma was here," I whisper to Angie.

"Me, too."

"I wish Grandma Winnie was here," I add, crying.

"Me, too."

And that's the last thing either of us says before going to sleep.

The next morning, when I wake up, I feel bad already. That's when I realize that what happened last night wasn't just a bad dream— it was a waking nightmare! If somebody came to me right now with an Aladdin's lamp or something like that, I would wish that last night never happened, even if it meant that Freddy would have to visit me in my dreams.

How could God let all our dreams get shattered just like that?

Hey, Ho, Hollywood!

On Sunday mornings we are usually so happy to get up, because we go to church and we go to Hallelujah Tabernacle, and they let me and Angie do two-part harmony songs on "teen Sundays." Also, during convocation season, we get to sing in the choir sometimes.

Right now, my hair looks a mess. I was so upset last night, I forgot to put the stocking cap on my head to keep my wrap smooth. I hate when I do that!

"Angie, those are my shoes!" I yell, as she tries to sneak her feet into my black pumps instead of hers. She can be such a copycat sometimes—trying to act like she doesn't know her things from mine. She's always trying to switch stuff—especially when she loses a button, or scuffs her shoes bad.

I know Angie is real upset, because she doesn't even pretend like she *didn't* know she was putting on my shoes. She just sits on the edge of the bed and waits for me to put on my clothes.

I reach for the navy blue dress with the gold buckle, because that's what we decided we would wear. When we go to church, we *always* dress alike, and we can't wear pants. "Do you think Daddy is gonna let us be Cheetah Girls anymore?" Angie asks, real quiet.

"I don't know, Angie, but I bet you he's gonna call Ma and tell her we lost." I open the bottom drawer of the white chest of drawers to get out a pair of navy blue panty hose. I feel so bad, my head hurts when I talk. I hold up the panty hose and run my fingers through them.

"Dag on, Angie, these have a run in them!" Sucking my teeth, I throw the panty hose in the white wicker wastebasket under the night-stand. "It's a good thing I checked before I wasted my time putting them on. I told you not to put tights *back* in the drawer if you put a run in them!"

"I musta not noticed!" Angie exclaims, get-ting real defensive. Then I give her that look we have between us, and Angie cracks a little smile. She knows I know when she's lying. I don't know why she even bothers sometimes.

"Don't forget," I mutter. "It's your turn to clean Porgy and Bess's cage."

I can smell the bacon frying downstairs. High Priestess Abala came over this morning, and she's cooking breakfast for us. She's going to *church* with us, too, believe it or not! I think that's pretty strange, considering all her weird rituals and stuff. To tell you the truth, I wish she wasn't here, because I don't feel like being nice to anybody this morning.

"What if we had been on that stage by ourselves, Angie?" I ask, as walk out the bedroom door to go downstairs and eat breakfast. "We woulda frozen solid like a pair of icicles!"

Angie just nods at me. I know that means we're both thinking the same thing—what will we do if we aren't the Cheetah Girls anymore?

The spiral staircase in our duplex is *real* steep, so we always come downstairs slow and careful. (I'm afraid of heights. So is Angie.)

"Omigod!" Angie gasps when we get to the bottom landing. "I *know* the Evil One is in our house now."

"What's the matter, Angie?" I ask, trying not to bump into her from behind.

"What *is* that thing?" Angie asks.

I take a few steps forward, so I can see what it is she's talking about. Then I let out a loud, surprised scream. This ugly thing—some kind of huge, horrible mask—is hanging on the wall in front of us. It gave me such a fright it almost scared me to death—right into Granddaddy Walker's funeral parlor back home!

"Good morning, ladies," High Priestess Abala Shaballa says, walking from the kitchen into the living room. Angie and I get our manners back *real* fast, because we know that Abala musta had something to do with this strange thing hanging on the wall. It's just as weird as she is.

"Good morning, Abala," I say politely, making myself be nice to her, even though I don't want to. I hope Daddy didn't tell her that we lost the Apollo Amateur Hour contest. How *could* we lose that? I *still* can't believe those boys won! "The devil is a liar," just like Big Momma says.

"Do you know what this is?" High Priestess Abala Shaballa asks, pointing to the thing on the wall.

"No, I—we—don't," I say, looking at Angie for some support. Now that Abala is Daddy's girlfriend, it just seems like we never know anything anymore.

It's not like before. At least, in the old days, Daddy, Angie, and I got to learn things together. Now it seems like everything new he knows, he learned from her.

"It's a Bogo Mogo Hexagone Warrior Mask," Abala says proudly.

No wonder it's strange, I think. It's something named after *her*.

"You see the markings here," Abala continues, pointing to the bright red marks across the cheeks of the big mask, which looks like the head of a space alien.

"Yes, I see them," I respond, trying to act interested, even though I know there is something deep-down weird about this thing.

"When the markings change colors, it means it's time for Hexagone to reign once again, and the world will become a magical place. With Bogo Mogo here, you will have someone to watch over you all the time now."

Oh, *great*. Now we not only have Daddy, we have this thing's beady eyes watching us, too. I try not to look scared.

"You *do* believe in magic, don't you, Aquanette?"

"Yes, High Priestess Abala," I say. I don't tell her what I really think—that she needs some more magic lessons, because Mr. Teddy Poodly didn't come out of his shoe box to help us win the contest. So why should this mask do anything—except maybe scare me in the middle of the night when I come downstairs to get a snack?

"Well, let's go eat. I've fixed a divine feast for the two of you," High Priestess Abala says, outstretching her arms the way she does, like a peach tree with big ol' branches. (Grandma Winnie had one in her backyard, with the biggest, juicy peaches we ever ate . . . then it just withered up and died when Grandma did.)

"Good morning, Daddy," I say as we join him in the kitchen. I'm still not able to look him in the eye. I wonder if he told High Priestess Abala that we lost the contest. Dag on, how *could* we?

Angie and I sit down at the dining room table real quiet, and High Priestess Abala serves us some ham, eggs, biscuits, and fried apples. Then, for herself and Daddy, she pours some green stuff from the blender into two glasses.

I can't believe that's all Daddy is eating for breakfast! He used to eat a whole plate of bacon and tin of biscuits, with a whole pot of coffee! Daddy looks into Abala's eyes all goo-goo-eyed, and they clink their glasses of green goo together. Yuck!

"To you, my divine Priestess—because I've never felt younger," Daddy says, then gulps down his shake.

I just hope he doesn't start looking younger, or I'm gonna call Granddaddy Walker to come up here and make sure Abala's not slipping embalming fluid in Daddy's blender! (Granddaddy Walker says that's why dead people look so good—sometimes even better than they did in real life!)

Thank God, the phone rings before these two lovebirds fly over the cuckoo's nest together. Daddy answers, then hands the phone to me. "It's your friend," he says.

"Hello?" I say, taking the receiver.

"Aqua, you're not gonna believe this," Galleria says, without even saying hello. I can't believe how much better she sounds!

"What?" I reply.

"Mom just had her hair done at Churl, It's You! and Pepto B., her hairdresser, told her that *he's* hooking up Kahlua Alexander's braids later!"

"Really?" I answer, but I still don't understand why Galleria is so excited.

"So guess who he's gonna hook *us* up with?"

"No! *Kahlua?*" I gasp. You *know* I'm surprised, but now I'm getting excited, too.

"That's right, dee-light. We have hatched a plan. Mom says for you and Angie to be ready by six o'clock, 'cuz 'Operation Kahlua' is in full effect."

"Okay," I respond, even though I'm still not sure what she's talking about.

"And Aqua—don't wear the same clothes you and Angie wear to church, okay?"

"I know that, Galleria."

"Wear the cheetah jumpers and the ballet flats, okay?"

"Okay, Galleria. Bye!"

When I hang up the phone, I'm smiling from ear to ear. Angie, of course, knows something is up.

"Galleria is picking us up at six o'clock," I say, smiling at Daddy. "We should thank God we have Galleria, because I've never seen anyone rise from the dead faster than her!"

Now Abala is looking at me like she approves, but I don't want to give her the wrong idea. "That's just an expression Granddaddy Walker uses," I explain. "She didn't *really* rise from the dead."

Hey, Ho, Hollywood!

"Your granddaddy is wise, because there are more ways than one to levitate your fate," Abala says, sipping on her witches' brew. "There is nothing for you to worry about, my dears. Bogo Mogo magic is working for you. If not today, then surely tomorrow."

Well, I sure hope Mr. Bogo Mogo can do his wonders from the bottom of a garbage can, 'cuz that's where he's ending up.

Chapter 6

It's so nice of Galleria's folks to offer to pick us up and take us to Pepto B.'s salon, Churl, It's You! Otherwise, Daddy would have probably insisted that *he* drive us. He thinks seven o'clock is kinda late for us to be out without a chaperone! Dag on, even Chanel can come home unescorted up until nine o'clock on school nights, and her mother is kinda strict. Our Daddy takes the cobbler, though.

I shoulda known something was up, though, when Galleria rings the bell at six o'clock. We're not due at the salon till seven thirty, and it only takes ten minutes to get there.

"Toodles to the poodles! You *fab-yoo-luss*

Walker twins, *we've* got a surprise for you!"
Galleria says in her funny Southern accent.

She is definitely feeling better because she's
acting like herself. And when Galleria acts like
herself, the whole world is a brighter place.
Even the cheetahs in the jungle are probably
smiling right now.

Angie and I have been feeling better too,
because Reverend Butter's sermon at church
today did us a world of good. We crowd
the front doorway of our building, waiting
for Ms. Dorothea, Chanel, and Mr. Garibaldi
to come in.

"You're so lucky you don't live in an elevator
building," Dorinda comments, coming in and
kissing us hello.

That's the truth. I would be scared to have to
go up in an elevator every time I wanna get to
my apartment. Like I told you, Angie and I are
afraid of heights. That's why Daddy got a
ground floor apartment in a town house.

It's quiet on our block, and we got a nice
view of Riverside Park, so at least it feels a little like back home. I don't know if I could take
all that noise over where Dorinda lives.

It's good to hear a pigeon chirping every now and again.

Ms. Dorothea is taking some garment bags and stuff from the van, and Chanel is helping her carry them inside. Chanel works part time at Toto in New York . . . Fun in Diva Sizes, 'cuz she has to pay her mother back all the money she charged on her credit card.

See, I think Chanel lost her mind after we did that first show at the Cheetah-Rama. She started shoppin' till we wuz *all* droppin'! I guess Chanel thought everything was gonna come real easy. But it's not—you gotta work *real* hard just to hold onto your dream. By the time she came to her senses, Chanel owed her mother a whole lot of money! Lucky for her, Ms. Dorothea offered her the job at her store.

"What's that?" Angie asks, pointing to the garment bags.

"You didn't think we were gonna let you wear just plain ol' anything to meet the biggest singer in the world, did you?" Galleria asks, batting her eyelashes.

"Now, I was gonna surprise you girls with your new outfits after you won the Apollo Amateur contest. But that was their loss. And anyway, now we have bigger prey to pounce on," Ms. Dorothea says, all optimistic and funny like she is. Opening the garment bag, she pulls out matching fake-fur cheetah miniskirts and vests.

"Oooh!" Angie exclaims, putting her hands on her cheeks, like she does after she opens her Christmas presents.

"We're gonna go in there looking like a *real* group," says Galleria, all proud. Then she pulls a tube of lipstick out of her cheetah backpack. "Look at the new shade of S.N.A.P.S. lipstick we got. It's called Video."

"Oooh—it's got silver sparkles!" I say, grabbing the tube. I never saw silver lipstick like this before. "So what are we gonna do at the hair salon—act like we're getting our hair done?" Knowing Galleria and Ms. Dorothea, there has to be some plan.

Galleria, Chanel, and Dorinda look at each other like I just ate a whole peach cobbler pie without offering them a slice.

"No, silly, we're gonna go in there and *sing* while Kahlua's getting her hair done," Galleria pipes up.

"Ohhhhh," Angie and I say in unison.

"That's right. That's a good plan. Then what?"

"Then Miss Kahlua Alexander will be so inclined to wave her magic wand—and have her fairy godmother help us . . . I don't know, get a record deal . . . or at least a Happy Meal!"Galleria says, waving her hand like it's a wand.

"We know that's right," I chuckle. Kahlua Alexander is the *biggest* singer, and she can do just about anything with all her "magic powers."

"Operation Kahlua will be in full effect," Galleria says, smiling. Then she whispers to me, "Ask your Dad if it's okay for us to practice here."

"Right here?" I ask, smiling. That's Galleria—when she has a plan, there is no telling *what* she'll do to make it happen!

"Come on. We can sing two songs—'Wanna-be Stars,' because we know it so well, and the new song, 'More Pounce to the Ounce.'"

I hesitate a little, because I don't know if we're ready to sing Galleria's new song yet.

"Come on, Angie. We're ready. We've been practicing it for two long weeks!" Galleria begs me, reading my thoughts.

Hey, Ho, Hollywood!

"*I'll* ask Daddy!" Angie says all excited, running toward the den, where Daddy is sitting with High Priestess Abala Shaballa.

Dag on, she's over here a lot now. Doesn't she have some new spells to practice at home?

Daddy and his High Priestess come into the living room with Angie tagging behind them. "Greetings, sacred ones," Abala greets our guests.

She gives Ms. Dorothea a little bow. Those two met at Dorinda's adoption party, and I don't think Ms. Dorothea likes the High Priestess too much. High Priestess is even taller than Ms. Dorothea, if you can believe that— even with Dorothea's new hairdo, which is higher than a skyscraper! Abala is so tall she looks like a weeping willow tree, ready to sway if the wind blows in her direction!

Abala turns to Galleria, Dorinda, and Chanel. "Tell me, sacred ones," she says. "Did the Vampire Spell work?"

Abala does look real pretty today—kinda like a . . . well, a High Priestess I guess. She does have real pretty eyes too. I guess I can see why Daddy likes her so much.

"No," I volunteer sourly. Daddy *musta* told

her by now that we lost the contest. Why is she asking us if the spell worked?

"Then either you didn't follow my directions, or High Priestess Hexagone has bigger plans for you," High Priestess Abala Shaballa says solemnly.

Galleria mumbles under her breath, "Whatever makes you clever."

Finally, Daddy senses the situation is a little tense, because he pipes up, "Listen, girls, I know you have to get ready. My home is yours, and do whatever you need to do to get ready. We'll be in the kitchen if you need anything. Come on, Abala," he says, touching her arm gently.

That makes me feel real proud. Daddy still believes in us! He never says much, but I guess that's just his way.

"*Aah, che bella!*" Mr. Garibaldi says, looking at Daddy's snow globe collection. "May I touch?"

"Go ahead," I say with a smile, looking at Galleria, who is rolling her eyes to the ceiling. I think her Daddy still loves the snow.

"Just don't start collecting them, Daddy," Galleria giggles.

Hey, Ho, Hollywood!

* * *

After we practice for one hour, we climb into the van. I guess, you could say, we are ready for Freddy—and definitely for Kahlua Alexander!

"I can't *believe* how high Pepto teased my wig this time!" Ms. Dorothea says, looking in the mirror on the dashboard. "It looks like a torpedo ready for takeoff!"

We just chuckle and look at each other. I mean, Ms. Dorothea's hair does look a little like a skyscraper, but if anyone has the personality to carry it off, she does.

"Honey, he is so lucky I didn't pull a diva fit! But then he let the glass slipper drop—that Miss Kahlua is in town, to make a movie called *Platinum Pussycats*, with Bertha Kitten. He *also* let it slip that he is giving Kahlua a new 'do, because Bertha, or 'Miss Kitten' to you, said 'those braids have to go.' So I just started pouncing instead of pouting."

"But how did you angle an intro?" Dorinda asks.

Angie and I look at each other, like, "there they go again, saying things we don't understand!"

"Pepto was complaining about how his

mother just couldn't find the right dress for her thirtieth wedding anniversary," Ms. Dorothea explains. "So, naturally, I volunteered to make the dress of Ms. Butworthy's dreams—*for free!* Darling, Pepto and I have played this cat-and-mouse game for *years*, and believe me, his mother is no Happy Meal. She's such a pain, she's probably banned from every diva-size department in the country."

"Ohhhh, so that's what the B stands for," Dorinda says, smiling.

"Mr. B. speaks way too fast to get his whole last name out!" Ms. Dorothea says smiling. "You'll see."

As we pull up in front of the Churl, It's You! hair salon on 57th Street, Ms. Dorothea takes a deep breath, and announces, "Okay, girls, it's time to give them more 'pounce for the ounce!'"

"Ooh, look at how *la dopa* this place is!" Chanel exclaims as we approach Churl, It's You! "I'm gonna bring Princess Pamela here!"

The pink lights in the Churl, It's You! sign are so bright they sparkle like stars. In the window, there are floating brown mannequin heads with pink, blue, yellow, green, and purple wigs!

"Ooh, Angie—look at the heads!" I say, ogling the window display. "Look at the beautiful sign! We don't have anything like this in Houston."

"A blue Afro?" Angie says, smiling. Blue is our favorite color, but neither of us would have the nerve to wear a wig like that on our head. Galleria and Chanel would, of course. I wish we were more like them. They have so much style—but I have to admit, we *all* look fierce in our matching Cheetah Girl outfits.

Of course, Chanel runs to the door first, and we have to hurry to catch up to her. "Wait up, yo!" Dorinda snaps.

"Chuchie, we have to make an entrance *together*," Galleria says, taking the lead.

When Galleria opens the big glass door, musical chimes go off, and a recording starts playing: "Churl, It's You! Work the blue! Think pink like I do! Get sheen with green! We love—guess who!"

"Ooh, that is so dope!" laughs Dorinda.

"*Ay, Dios mío*, the whole place is pink. *Qué bonita!*" exclaims Chanel, looking around the salon like she's in a candy store. Pink is one of her favorite colors, and her whole bedroom is pink. She even has a pink cheetah bedspread!

"Wait till Kahlua sees your braids," I say to Chanel proudly, because she *looks* like Kahlua, with her braids and pretty eyes and all—she's just a lighter complexion.

"Welcome to Churl, It's You!" says a nice lady wearing a pink dress with an apron over it. Even her *shoes* are pink—and so is her *hair*!

"Hi, darling," Ms. Dorothea says, extending her hand to the pink lady. "We have an appointment with Pepto B."

"Yes, of course. So nice to see you again, Mrs. Garibaldi. Right this way. You must be the Cheetah Girls," she says, looking at us.

"Yes, ma'am," Angie says, giving the lady a big smile.

We look around the salon in wonder as we walk to the back. There are two huge cases with pink cotton candy, pink soda, and bags of pink popcorn! The hair dryer helmets are pink, and so are the chairs—even the sink where you get your hair washed!

"Oooh, look at the pink jukebox," I exclaim. The salon we go to doesn't have a jukebox. It's *boring* compared to this. "We have to ask Daddy to let us come here and get our hair done!" I whisper to Angie.

"It's even doper than Princess Pamela's!" Angie whispers back. "But don't tell Chanel I said so."

"I can't believe we're gonna meet Kahlua!" I say. We grab each other's hand and give a quick, tight squeeze, and I know Angie's thinking the same thing.

All of a sudden, a brown-skinned man with a short, pink Afro comes running over to us. He kisses Ms. Dorothea on both cheeks. I've never seen anyone do that before, except in the movies. He must be French or something. Then he turns real quick, and says to us, "Pepto B., that's me!"

We are just tickled—well, pink, I guess! As we introduce ourselves to Pepto B., I suddenly don't feel so nervous anymore.

Pepto B. grabs Ms. Dorothea's arm and whispers loudly, "Churl, your timing is *purrfect*. I just finished putting in Kahlua's weave. Wait till you see it. Churl, it took two hours to get those braids outta her hair! You woulda thought they were stuck on with Krazy

Glue! But you know those *Hollywood* hair-dressers—you need a magician to fix your hair after they get through with you!"

Pepto B. and Ms. Dorothea dissolve into fits of giggles. Angie and I are just staring at them.

"Close your mouth, Aqua and Angie!" hisses Galleria. She says we watch people with our mouths open sometimes. I guess we do, but she has to understand—we're not used to all the ways of the Big Apple, the way she and Chanel are!

After the two grown-ups finish "cutting up," as Big Momma calls it, Pepto B. puts his hand on his chest and says, "Churl, you're killing me. Can you believe Bertha Kitten is coming out of her hermetically sealed coffin to do a movie? *Churrrl*, believe it!"

Then he turns to us, and says the words we've been waiting to hear—"And now, if you all are ready, it's time to meet the one and only . . . Kahlua!"

Chapter 7

When we get to the back of the salon, Kahlua is seated in the beauty parlor chair, reading a magazine. Standing next to her by the counter is a lady in a light-blue sweat-suit. That must be her mother, I figure. I heard she's managing Kahlua now, and that they even started a production company called "Kahlua's Korporation."

All of a sudden, I feel *real* nervous again. My stomach starts getting queasy, while my brain is screaming: *"It's really her! "*

Kahlua looks up at us, all curious, and says, "Hi!"

Oooo, she's even prettier in person than in her music videos! Staring at Kahlua, I wonder

The Cheetah Girls

how she keeps her skin so smooth like that. It's the prettiest chocolate shade I've ever seen. She must be about a shade lighter than me and Angie. No, maybe two shades lighter, because she's got a lotta makeup on.

"Close your mouth, Angie!" Galleria whispers behind me, and pokes me in the butt.

Then Kahlua's mother introduces herself to Ms. Dorothea. "Hi, I'm Aretha Alexander. And who are all these cute girls?" she asks, smiling like a curious cat.

"We're the Cheetah Girls!" Galleria bursts out, giggling.

"Do you sing?" Kahlua asks, smiling now from ear to ear.

"Yes, churl, they do," Pepto B. offers, butting in. "And you should let them sing while I finish. I could sure use some entertainment, after fixing this tragedy that was up in yo' hair!"

We all giggle—even Kahlua—and she has the cutest dimples when she smiles, just like Dorinda's.

"Pepto, you are so *wrong*—but you are *right*," Kahlua says, all bubbly. "After putting up with *you* for four hours, I could use some entertainment!"

"Oh, don't let me take this comb and use it like a forklift on your head, churl!" Pepto B. warns, putting his hands on his hips.

After we all finish giggling, Ms. Dorothea clears her throat and says, "I guess it's time for growl power, girls!"

"'Growl Power!' Oooo, that is so cute!" Kahlua exclaims.

Ms. Dorothea takes our cheetah backpacks and puts them in the corner. Then the five of us huddle together, right there in the middle of the beauty salon, and sing *a capella* (that means without our instrumental track) the song we have practiced fifty million times, "Wanna-be Stars in the Jiggy Jungle."

I wish Ma could see us now—singing in the beauty parlor again, just like we used to when we were three years old, sitting in the double stroller next to her while she got her hair done.

Everybody claps when we're done—even the customers under the hair dryers!

"You wrote that song yourselves?" Kahlua's mother asks, and you can tell she is real impressed.

"*She* did," I say excitedly, pointing to Galleria.

Galleria looks like she's blushing, and I can tell Chanel feels a little bit jealous. Those two fight like sisters—more than Angie and I do—and we *are* sisters!

I think Chanel wants to be the leader of our group, and that's why she's jealous. I guess she's gonna have to learn how to write songs, instead of charging up clothes on her mother's credit card!

"Do y'all have another song?" Kahlua asks excitedly.

"Churl, I hear they got more songs than my jukebox!" Pepto B. says as he teases Kahlua's hair.

Ms. Dorothea looks at us, and motions for us to sing again. "We haven't performed this song before," Galleria says, then looks at us. "I, um, just finished writing it a few weeks ago."

"Go, ahead, we love it!" Ms. Alexander says, egging us on.

On the count of three, we then sing "More Pounce to the Ounce." I can feel my hands sweating, because singing a capella is a lot harder than singing with tracks—especially when you have five-part harmonies. See, you have to make sure everybody sings on the same level, and my and Angie's voices tend to be a little stronger than theirs are.

> *"Snakes in the grass have no class*
> *but Cheetah Girls have all the swirls.*
> *To all the competition, what can we say?*
> *You had your day, so you'd better bounce, y'all,*
> *While you still got some flounce, y'all,*
> *'Cuz Cheetah Girls got more pounce to the ounce*
> *y'all!!"*

After we finish the song, I look over at Angie. She leaned a little too hard on the chorus, I think—but I'll tell her that later. I think we still sounded good, though, because Kahlua and her mother are grinning from ear to ear.

"I love y'all!" Kahlua exclaims. "You got a record deal?"

We shake our heads "no."

I just wanna scream, *Get us a deal, please!*

"Momma, let's talk to Mr. Hitz about them," Kahlua says to her mother. Mrs. Alexander nods her head in agreement. "He's the president of the label I'm on—Def Duck Records," Kahlua explains.

"That would be groovy like a movie!" Galleria says, jumping up and down, she's so excited. Then she kisses Kahlua on the cheek, and gives her a big hug.

"You have so much energy—doesn't she, Momma?" Kahlua asks, her slanty eyes getting wide. "She reminds me of Backstabba a little, don't you think so?"

People have always thought Galleria looks a lot like Backstabba, the lead singer of Karma's Children. That band comes from our home-town—and Angie and I have decided we're not going back until we become as big as them!

"How did y'all become the Cheetah Girls?" Kahlua asks.

We tell Kahlua all about the jiggy jungle, growl power, and our Cheetah Girls rules and council meetings. She just loves it—especially when Galleria tells her about the dream she's had since she's a little girl:

"We wanna go to Africa and start a Cheetah conservancy. When we get rich, we're gonna get lots and lots of acres of land, so all the cheetahs in the jungle can live there and just chill, without worrying about anything. Then we'll travel all over the world, singing to peeps on two legs *and* four!"

"You are *too much*," Kahlua says, crossing her legs and waving her hand at Galleria. Kahlua has nice nails. I bet you they're tips, though—like mine.

I'm looking at the chip on my nail when I hear Galleria blurt out, "We performed at the Apollo Amateur Hour Contest Saturday night—and we lost!"

How could she say something so dumb? I wonder. Why is she telling Kahlua that?

But Kahlua's reaction is the last thing I expected. "Honey, that's nothing. *I* lost it, too!" she says. "You know, the record company doesn't let me talk about it in interviews, but Momma will tell you—I cried like a baby for two weeks after I lost!"

Kahlua is beside herself laughing now. "You know how many famous recording artists have performed at the Apollo Amateur Hour Contest and lost?"

"How many?" Dorinda asks, her eyes wide with wonder.

"Let's see—Toyz II Boyz, The Moonpies, even Karma's Children lost!" Kahlua says, nodding her head like she knows things we don't.

"*What!?*" I say, all surprised. "I didn't know that!"

"No—no one is gonna tell you about their failures, but you have to stick to your dreams in this business, girls—'cuz people will trample on them like elephants!"

Kahlua sips her soda, then looks at Galleria's lips real close. "What color lipstick is that you're wearing?"

"Video. It's dope, right?" Galleria says, beaming.

"Oooo, I haven't seen this one yet! Can I try it?"

"Wait, I'll get it." Galleria runs to get her cheetah backpack, to show Kahlua the new shade of S.N.A.P.S. lipstick we're all wearing.

"Y'all look so cute in those outfits," Kahlua says, putting on the lipstick. Then she and Galleria start "ooohing" and "aaahing" up a storm.

"Tell us about your cheetah-licious movie," Galleria says, egging Kahlua on, now that they're like two peas in a pod.

"It's *such* hard work, you can't believe it! I

have to get up at five o'clock in the morning tomorrow to start shooting," Kahlua says. Then she starts playacting a yawn, and leans on Pepto B.'s shoulders for a hug.

"How are they going to get that 'Mummy' Bertha Kitten to the set on time?" Pepto B. quips. "Churl, she better be *grateful* she got this gig, 'cuz the only thing *she's* been doing for the last thirty years is her nails! She gives you any trouble, we'll sic these Cheetah Girls on her!"

We all hug each other good-bye, then do the Cheetah Girls handshake with Kahlua, Pepto B., and Mrs. Alexander—which they all just *love*. Ms. Dorothea gives Mrs. Alexander her business card, and they hug good-bye.

"We'll let you know what happens," Mrs. Alexander says, "but you don't have to worry, Dorothea. Your Cheetah Girls have 'more pounce for the ounce,' just like they said. The other girl groups won't stand a chance, once the Cheetahs show up."

Mr. Garibaldi is waiting for us outside in his van. "How did it go? *Bene?*" he asks Galleria as we get in the car. But he already knows the answer, from our big grins. "I knew it. That's why I made you girls a fresh batch of chocolate cannolis—Aqua's favorite," he says, handing us a big box of Italian pastries.

We all look at Galleria and burst out laughing. I munch on my dee-licious treats, which I shouldn't be eating, because Daddy doesn't like us to eat anything two hours before we practice—and I *know* we have to practice tonight before we go to bed. He let us off the hook last night—but lightning doesn't strike twice in the same place!

I give Angie a look, and she knows what I'm trying to say—*Don't tell Daddy we ate these!* The one thing I love about Angie is, she sure can keep a secret.

"Darlings, isn't this place something?" Ms. Dorothea says to me and Angie. She points to a beautiful skyscraper with a tiny, brightly lit tower topped by a steeple.

"It sure is," I respond, ogling the tower like it's a secret place in a castle or something. "You know, Ms. Dorothea, I thought for sure it was all over for us when we lost that contest."

"I know," Ms. Dorothea says with a sigh. "You take one wrong turn on the road to your dreams, and all of a sudden, you're in hyena territory. Then you stumble upon a right turn, and there it is right before your eyes—"

"—that magical, cheetah-licious place called the jiggy jungle," Galleria pipes in. Then, chuckling, she adds, "Your one-way ticket to *get-paid paradise!*"

Chapter 8

Biology class is my favorite class at school, besides vocal, but I have no interest today in cutting open a frog—and that's not like me at all. I know we shouldn't expect anything to come from our meeting with Kahlua, but dag on! We can't think about anything else!

We pray to God every night to please give us one itty-bitty sign—*anything*—even a shoe falling from the sky and hitting us over the head would be good enough!

It seems like *years* since "Operation Kahlua," and now we're down in the bottom of the crab barrel again, just moping around, trying not to get bit by the other crabs.

Look at this poor little frog, I think. He is just

lying there dead, on his back, waiting to be cut open. "I wonder if you can tell if someone tried to choke it and murder it or something. You know—'frog autopsy,'" I chuckle to Paula Pitts. She's my biology classmate, and we record all our experiments together.

"The eyeballs *are* kinda big—it does look like something scared it a little before it—you know—croaked," Paula says, all sad. "I don't know what you find so interesting about looking inside of bodies, Aqua. I think it's creepy."

Paula is a drama major, and she wants to be an actress, so she can be a little dramatic at times. "I hardly call opening a frog cadaver *The Night of the Living Dead*," I quip back. "Miss Paula, you are acting like the Pitts again."

I always tease her. She gets so squeamish, and she just doesn't like biology class or science projects the way I do. She likes to slink around, "like she's the cat's meow on Catfish Row," as Big Momma would say. Opening her big brown eyes wide, Paula asks, "You heard anything from Kahlua yet?"

She just loves to talk about show business. *Everybody* at school knows about our meeting with Kahlua—including JuJu Beans Gonzalez, who really cuts her eyes at us now.

I can't blame her for being so jealous of us. Angie and I are kinda popular at LaGuardia, I guess, because we're twins and come from Houston—even though there are kids at our school from all over the country.

The kids here nicknamed us SWV—Sisters With Voices—because, I guess, we do sing up a storm, if I say so myself. We're getting real good training here at LaGuardia, too—singing pop and classical music, which is good for our range. When we were younger, we kinda had our hearts set on singing gospel, but like I said, it just seems like pop and R&B music get more attention in the business.

That's why we got together with the Cheetah Girls. We thought about it real hard, and talked to Ma, and Big Momma, and everybody else about it before we made up our minds. Now we just don't know if we made the right decision.

Letting out a big sigh, I turn to Paula and moan, "This whole thing is like a big roller coaster ride. When you're on top, it's the greatest feeling in the world. But when you get ready to roll to the bottom, you'd better strap yourself in and start screaming your head off again, because it feels so *scary*."

"Yeah, you gotta kiss a lot of frogs in show business before you get anywhere," Paula agrees with a sigh. "That's how I feel in drama class sometimes, too. I give until it hurts, and it never feels like enough." Now she's fiddling around with the knob on the microscope, and her face is pained, like she's getting ready for her monologue. She is so *dramatic*.

"Ooh, look at his little lungs," I exclaim, finally getting excited by Freddy the frog's insides.

Then I feel a wave of pity come over me. "Freddy, I hope your little dreams came true before you left this earth," I mutter. "I hope all of our dreams come true. . . ."

After school, Angie always waits for me outside, and I can tell by her long face that she's still feeling down at the bottom of the crab barrel. "I wish we could go to Pappadeux's and get some Cajun crawfish right about now," I moan.

She nods her head like she could put a bib on

and chow down, too. They've got everything in New York except Pappadeux's—and *I'm sorry*, but nobody makes crawfish like they do. You get a big ol' pot of Cajun crawfish, with pieces of corn on the cob, and small red potatoes, and all this spicy juice. Then you just crack the itty-bitty shells in your hands, and suck out those tasty "chil'rens," as Big Momma calls them. Those were some of the best times we ever had as a family, going there on Friday nights for dinner. Everybody would come—Uncle Skeeter, Big Momma, Grandma Winnie, Ma, and all our cousins, too.

"I don't understand why we have to go to Drinka Champagne's Conservatory today," Angie says sheepishly. "What's the use of practicing if we're not performing anywhere?

"I know that's right, but you know what Galleria says. We should be practicing more, just in case we get to perform somewhere, for somebody, *somehow*."

My voice trails off, because I see the newspaper in Angie's hand, and I realize we haven't read our horoscope today.

"What's it say?" I ask, as we cross the street to catch the subway.

Hey, Ho, Hollywood!

I hope it's not real crowded today, I think, as we wait to ride the IRT down to Drinka's. Dag on, there are so many people on the sidewalks and subway platforms in New York, you feel like you're gonna get trampled or something!

"Dag on, don't you know what page it's on by now?" I say, getting annoyed at Angie, who is still fumbling with the newspaper as we get on the crowded train. But why I'm really upset is because this man with a big ol' briefcase keeps knocking into me like I'm a rag doll.

"Here it is," Angie says, all serious, like she's getting ready to give a sermon in church. Sometimes she is so *slow*! "Let's see. 'Get ready for a big unexpected trip. You're gonna be flying the friendly skies real soon. Pack your party clothes!'"

"Oh, great, that just means we gotta go home to Houston for Thanksgiving, and do something *real* exciting, like work in Big Momma's garden. We know that," I say, curling my upper lip. (Angie and I both do that sometimes when we get mad.)

Angie gets quiet and closes the newspaper. She doesn't have to tell me. I know she feels disappointed, too.

The Cheetah Girls

We normally don't go to Drinka Champagne's Conservatory on school nights. But they have a new choreographer, and she can only work with us tonight, because she's working on Sista Fudge's new music video all weekend. Sista Fudge is one of our favorite singers, because she can "scream and testify"— back home, that's what we say when a singer can really *wail*, and has vocal "chops."

But we're not here studying singing. We're here to get our *moves* down. See, Galleria is always fussing at us to get the dance steps right. It's very important when you put on a show to have real good choreography—to give people something to watch. That's just as important when you perform as how you sing.

Since Angie and I are the background singers, we don't have to dance as much as Dorinda, Chanel, and Galleria, but we all have to do the same dance steps.

"Hi, Miss Winnie," I say, smiling to the receptionist at Drinka's as we enter the building. I like Miss Winnie, because she's real nice, and she has the same name as our grandma who passed.

The rest of the Cheetah Girls have already

changed into their leotards, and are waiting in Studio A for us. They are huddled together in one corner, while the rest of the class is on the other side.

After we do our Cheetah Girls handshake, which just tickles me to death, Galleria hugs us. "Smooches for the pooches!" she says. Every day she has a new saying, and we never know *what* to expect.

Galleria and Chanel are wearing such cute leotards! Angie and I look so plain, in our white shirts and black jeans. It'll be so nice when we can all dress alike all the time, like a real girl group. Yeah, right . . . like that'll ever happen.

"How's Porgy and Bess?" Chanel asks. She thinks it's cute that we have guinea pigs, because she isn't allowed to have any pets. She *loves* animals, too.

"They iz fine," Angie says, playing back.

"What do you feed them?" Dorinda asks.

"They love lettuce," I answer.

"Yeah, I bet—sprinkled with hot sauce!" Galleria blurts out, then looks at the door, because our dance teacher has arrived.

"Hi, I'm Raven Richards," says the teacher, who is real tall and skinny. She is wearing a red leotard and skirt, with a big black belt in the middle. None of us are tall like that. It must be real nice, having those long legs!

"Okay, let's get some combinations down," Raven says, moving her hips. "The movement in the hips is to a one-two, one-two-three combo. Okay, girls?"

Raven looks at me and adds, "Slink, don't bounce."

Raven? She looks more like Wes Craven! I say to myself, because she makes me so mad, embarrassing me like that in front of everybody. It's bad enough that Galleria is always on us about dancing, and Daddy is always on us about practicing more . . .

Dag on, I suddenly realize—she's right. I *am* bouncing!

After class, I feel real tired and sick. "Forget about buffalo wings—I could eat a whole buffalo right about now," I moan.

"That's funny. I thought you were on a seafood diet, Aqua," Galleria quips, pushing me with her backpack.

"Seafood?" I say, squinching up my nose. I just wanna go home and get into bed. I don't care if Kahlua never calls.

Hey, Ho, Hollywood!

"Yeah, you *see* food, and you *eat* it!"

Galleria always makes me laugh. She is *real* funny.

"Don't be down, Aqua and Angie," she says then, holding my arm. "Operation Kahlua is in full effect. We just keep doing our thing, so that we're ready for Freddy. You know what I'm sayin'?"

"Yes, Galleria. We know what you're saying!" I answer, feeling a little better—at least good enough to get on the subway again and go home.

Chapter 9

Daddy is grinning from ear to ear when we get home. His job interview this morning must have gone well. See, he wants to leave his job as senior vice president of marketing at Avon. He and Ma decided that, since he used to be her boss, it wasn't a good idea that they work at the same company anymore.

"Daddy, how did the job interview go?" I ask. Angie and I sit down at the kitchen counter, and wait for Daddy to give us our dinner.

"I took the job," he says smiling. "Now I'm a SWAT man."

"That's real good, Daddy," I exclaim, then kiss him on the cheek. SWAT is the biggest bug repellent company in the country, he told us. They make all kinds of sprays for crawling insects, flying insects, lazy insects—you name it, they got a spray for it.

"Here's the campaign I'm gonna be working on," he says, pushing a black folder toward us. On the folder it has the company's slogan, *Flee, Flea, you hear me?*

Now Daddy is grinning and looking at us. I guess he wants us to say something funny about the slogan or something.

"What?" I ask, looking at him.

"That's not the best news I had all day," he says, still smiling like a Cheshire Cat who ate an insect.

"No?" Angie asks sheepishly.

"No. The best news I got just arrived in a phone call," he says, still smiling.

Daddy sure knows how to drag things out. When we were little, it used to take us two hours just to open our Christmas presents, because he would have to hand them to us first, then wait till *he* said to open them!

"Well, girls, maybe you should call your friend Galleria and find out for yourselves. She just called."

"Daddy, how could you wait so long to tell us?" I whine playfully. He always gets us real good with his tricks.

Angie and I jump up and down and hug each other, then I dial the phone, and she listens at the receiver.

When Galleria picks up the phone, she is yelling so loud, I can hardly understand her.

"Stop screaming, Galleria!"

Trying to catch her breath, Galleria says between gasps, "They're gonna give us a showcase in Los Angeles!!!"

"Hush your mouth!" I exclaim—the same thing Big Momma always says when she gets excited. "For real?"

"Wheel-a-deal for *real*!" Galleria retorts. "Kahlua and her moms told the Def Duck Records peeps that we were 'off the hook, snook,' and they said, 'Well, come on with it!'"

I'm not exactly sure what Galleria means, so I have to ask again, "Does that mean we got a record deal?"

"No, Aqua—just try and go with my flow. It *means* they'll fly us to Los Angeles, and arrange a showcase for us. They'll make sure all the right peeps are in the house to get a read on our

Hey, Ho, Hollywood!

Cheetah Girl groove. There are no guarantees, but at least we get a free trip to Hey, ho, Hollywood!"

"Omigod, I think I'm gonna faint!" I scream into the phone receiver. Angie grabs it from me, to talk to Galleria herself. I stand in the middle of the kitchen with my hand on my forehead. Then I just hug Daddy, and start crying tears of gratitude. I can't believe I ever doubted what God had in store for us! Now, the rest is up to us.

"How'd you find out?" Angie asks Galleria, then yells to me and Daddy, "They called Ms. Dorothea at her store, and asked her if *we* would be *interested*. Can you believe that?"

"*Please*, I'll pack my bags and fly the plane right now myself!" I yell, so Galleria can hear me—and trying to sound like I'm not scared of airplanes, which I *am*.

Daddy gives me a look, like "We'll see how you feel when you get up in the air." That's all right—I'll take a whole box of Cloud Nine pills if I have to, to keep from getting sick on the plane. Hallelujah, thank you, Jesus, we are going to Hollywood!

Chapter 10

After we finish talking with Galleria, we go over the whole story again with Ms. Dorothea. Then, of course, we call Chanel, and after that, Dorinda. But we're only just crankin' up. We call Big Momma to share the news. And finally, we reach our Ma, who is in Seattle on business.

She is surprised to hear from us, because unless it's an emergency, we usually only talk on Sunday after church.

"But this *is* an emergency, Ma," I tell her, "because if I wake up tomorrow and find out this is all a dream, I'm gonna need mouth-to-mouth resuscitation!"

"Hush your mouth, Aqua," Ma says.

Hey, Ho, Hollywood!

"You're gonna let us go, right?" I ask Ma nervously. She gets mad if we do things without asking her permission, even if we are living with Daddy. She says she's "still the boss of this house," no matter what Daddy thinks.

"You just make sure you do your homework while you're there, so you don't fall behind in school," Ma warns us. "But you go and have a good time. It's a shame the two of you haven't really been anywhere before this."

I feel like the whole world is right outside our front door, waiting for us. "That's all right, Ma—if things work out, we're going to be going *everywhere*—and we'll send plane tickets for you to come see us perform!"

"Well, for now, I think you'd better just get off the phone and go to bed, it's past your bedtime," Ma says sternly.

"Yes, ma'am, we're going right now. You wanna speak to Daddy?" I ask, hoping our good news will help them not be mad at each other—for at least a little while. As it is, I have to bite my tongue half the time, not to blurt and tell Ma about High Priestess Abala Shaballa.

"No, Aquanette, I don't have the time. I have

to finish some reports before I go to bed. I'm real proud of you, though. *Real* proud."

I don't even look at Daddy when I get off the phone, because I feel so bad Ma didn't want to talk to him.

"Good night, Daddy," I say, kissing him on the cheek.

"Good night, Daddy," Angie says, then kisses him on the other cheek. When I pass that scary-looking Bogo Mogo Warrior Mask on the way upstairs, I stick my tongue out at it, then poke Angie in the stomach, and we both start giggling.

"That's enough, y'all," Daddy says, leaning over his record collection in the living room. Daddy doesn't like us playing around before we go to bed—he wouldn't care if God came to the door and said it was okay. He likes peace and quiet when he's getting ready to play his music.

Angie and I spend another hour yakking in whispers about this most incredible day. When we're finally lying in bed, trying to get some sleep, I suddenly hear a noise in the bedroom closet!

"Angie, you hear that?" I whisper, sitting upright in my bed. "Lawd, you think that thing got out of the shoe boxes or something?"

We hear more scratching noises in the closet, and we both sit real quiet. "I don't care if it did, 'cuz I ain't going in there to find out!" Angie says, then hides under her covers.

It figures. That scaredy cat. Well, I ain't getting out of the bed either. They'll have to *drag* me out the bed before I get up and go look in that closet.

All of a sudden, I have the strangest thought. "Angie! You don't think that Teddy Bear Poodle thing brought us good luck, do you?"

"Maybe," Angie says, real quiet. "But I don't care—I'm just going to Hollywooooood!" she says, imitating Galleria.

"Not without me, you ain't!" I retort, and hide farther under the covers, till my feet are hanging out the bed. Feeling the cool air on my toes, I get a creepy feeling, and scrunch them back under the covers real quick. I'm not taking any chances—I mean, what if that thing in the closet is *hungry*?

Please God—make it stop raining! If it keeps

raining this hard much longer, Mighty Mouth Airlines will cancel our flight for sure!

Daddy keeps coming up to our room, to give us the latest weather report—like he's Sonny Shinbone, the weatherman on television. Daddy used to travel all over the country with his job at Avon, so I guess he *could* be a weatherman, but right now, he is "getting on our last good nerve," as Big Momma would say. I wish he would just stay downstairs with the "sacred one," so we can pack our suitcases in peace.

"'Furious Flo' is heading north," he says, hovering over us in our bedroom. Furious Flo is this terrible tropical storm that started a few days ago in Florida, and is wreaking havoc all over the place.

She must be mighty mad, because she's making people lose their homes and everything, with all the water she's sending their way. Thank God, Big Momma called and says everything is okay in Houston. Daddy is pacing back and forth, wearing out our rug. He's making us more nervous than we already are!

"What if you don't have enough material to

perform?" Daddy asks, smoking his pipe. He must be *real* nervous, too, because he usually only smokes his pipe late at night, when he's listening to his music or watching television. I hope he doesn't drop any ashes on our white carpet. He's always fussing at *us* to be careful about staining the carpet, because it costs a lot of money to get it cleaned professionally.

"Daddy, we're not the only singers performing in the New Talent Showcase," I explain to him. "The record company does this all the time. They have scouts all over the country looking for new artists. Then they fly them to Los Angeles, and put them in a showcase in front of industry people. There'll probably be a lot of other singers there. We'll be lucky if we get to perform three songs."

"That's right," Angie adds. "They told us to have three songs to perform."

"Okay, okay, I'm just trying to understand how all this works," Daddy says, puffing on his pipe quietly—which means he's thinking about *something*. "You think maybe that magic spell Abala prepared for you girls had something to do with this stroke of luck?"

"Daddy!" I yell. "This is no stroke of luck! If

it wasn't for Galleria and Ms. Dorothea, we'd be packing to go to Big Momma's, and playing 'Tiptoe Through the Tulips' in her garden—*again*!"

Daddy gives me that stern look, like, "Don't get too grown for your britches."

"I'm just asking a question," he says. "Maybe the spell worked just a little late, that's all I'm saying."

Angie and I get real quiet.

"What's the name of the place where you're performing?" Daddy asks for the *hundredth* time!

"The Tinkerbell Lounge," I say quietly. "It's in West Hollywood, and we wrote down all the information on the paper on the kitchen table—*and* we gave it to Ma, too."

I carefully fold the leopard miniskirt and vest that Ms. Dorothea made for us, and put it in the suitcase. I'm just waiting for Daddy to say something else.

"You know, maybe you should bring the navy blue dresses you wore to church last Sunday."

I don't want to fight with him anymore. "Yes, Daddy," I mumble, then go to the closet to get the dresses he wants us to wear.

Thank God, Daddy walks out of our bedroom then, to go downstairs. Angie and I stop packing, and just plop down on our beds.

I'm so nervous, I'm sweating like a tree trunk. Angie and I look at each other, and I know we're thinking the same thing. Giggling, she jumps up and takes the navy blue dresses and sticks them back in the closet!

"No, silly willy," I exclaim, imitating Galleria, "stick those things in the *back* of the closet, so he doesn't see them if he comes snooping around our room while we're gone!"

"Yeah, that's if we get to go," Angie sighs, going over to the window to look at the rain.

"Well, let's pack our bathing suits just in case. Maybe they'll have a swimming pool or something."

Angie runs to the closet and gets out our bathing suits.

"Did you see anything strange in the back of the closet?" I ask her, kinda joking. But inside, I'm kinda serious. What if Daddy is right about Abala's magic spell? What if Mr. Teddy Poodly is running around in there?

That's when I remember something *real*

strange. "Remember, Angie, I took the Scotch tape off that shoe box?"

"Yeah," she says, smiling at me. "Maybe that's what High Priestess Abala Shaballa meant, when she said the Vampire Spell didn't work 'cuz we must not have followed her instructions."

"I don't get it," Angie says, shrugging her shoulders.

"I put Scotch tape on the shoe box in the first place. She didn't tell us to do that. Maybe that's why the spell didn't work! Maybe Mr. Teddy Poodly could only do his thing when he was able to get out of the box!"

"Well, there has to be *some* reason why those boys won, because they sure weren't *that* good. Not as good as we are," Angie says, sitting on the bed and crossing her legs Indian style.

"Yeah. I know that's right. When did I take the Scotch tape off my shoe box?"

"I don't know. After we came home from the Apollo, I guess," Angie says.

"That's right. It *does* seem kinda strange that this happened—"

"Well, nothing *has* happened, Aquanette. I mean, we don't know what's gonna happen when we get out there. They didn't say they're gonna give us a record deal or anything."

I can tell Angie is getting exasperated. And I know what's wrong, too. She is being stubborn because she wants to stay mad at High Priestess Abala Shaballa.

Neither one of us is happy about Daddy getting a girlfriend so quick. Dag on, he and Ma just broke up! Okay, it's been a year, but that's *nothing*. And why did he have to pick *her*?

"I'm just saying, Angie, that maybe we're wrong about Abala," I say, giving my sister that look.

Angie just drags the suitcase off the bed. "We going, or what?"

"Let's ask Daddy and find out," I say, trailing behind her down the stairs. "Daddy! Can you help us with the luggage, please?"

High Priestess Abala Shaballa comes to the bottom of the stairwell. "Your father is on the phone with the airline, checking to make sure your flight isn't canceled," she says, looking like she feels bad for us if we don't get to go.

When we put the luggage by the front door, she turns and winks at us, "I see the Vampire

Spell worked, no?" Her eyes get real squinty, like a mouse's! I never noticed that before.

"Let's go, before the airline changes their mind," Daddy says chuckling, then hustles us out the door and into the Bronco.

The traffic is so bad going to the airport, I don't think we're ever going to get there! I'm really sweating now. "Angie, are you hot?"

"Yeah," Angie says, then sighs. "It's the traffic in New York. It makes me *nervous*, too. I didn't even know they made so many cars!"

"I don't know. It gets pretty crowded in Houston around rush hour," Daddy says, not looking up from the wheel.

Finally, we arrive at the airport, and by now, I'm dying of thirst.

"Did you pack some water, Angie?"

"Yes, Ma!" she says all huffy.

"Daddy, don't forget to feed Porgy and Bess," I mumble. All of a sudden, I'm feeling real jumpy. "They're real particular about their food—they only like fresh lettuce, and they don't like their water too cold."

"Yes, Aquanette, I'll take them for walks too," Daddy says, rolling one of our suitcases through the airport terminal.

Hey, Ho, Hollywood!

"There's Ms. Dorothea!" I say, waving my arm so she can see us. She has on a cheetah coat and big cheetah hat, and is standing with Mr. Garibaldi.

Then she moves aside a little, and I see that they're not alone. "Oh, there's Galleria, too!" Galleria looks so small next to her mother. She is wearing a cheetah coat and hat, too.

"Don't they look like a cheetah and a cub together?" I joke to Angie.

"They sure do!"

"My, she is tall," High Priestess Abala Shaballa comments about Ms. Dorothea.

I wanna say to her High-Mightyness, "Yeah, well, at least she don't put hexes on people like you do!" But I keep my mouth shut, because I'm not so mad at her anymore.

People are looking at us, probably because of all the fabric Abala has wrapped on her body and head. They probably think she's African royalty or something like that.

"There's Chanel and Dorinda," Angie says, pointing to where they're standing by the window. When Chanel and Dorinda see us, they come running over with Galleria and Ms. Dorothea.

"*Pooches gracias* for showing up!" Chanel giggles, then we all hug each other, screaming and carrying on.

Everybody is looking at us now. Daddy gives us a look, like, "calm down."

"Let me check at the reservation desk and make sure the flight is on time," he says, holding the High Priestess's arm.

"You didn't pack any crawfish in there, did you?" Galleria asks, teasing us.

"No, because Porgy and Bess ate 'em!" I chuckle back.

"I miss Toto already," Galleria whines.

"How come you didn't bring him?" I ask.

"We're going to Los Angeles for a singers' showcase, not a poodle convention, darling," Ms. Dorothea quips, but I can tell she feels guilty about leaving him behind. Galleria told us her mother gets hysterical if Toto chokes on a dog biscuit or anything.

"Dad is gonna take care of him," Galleria says, then turns to Mr. Garibaldi, "right, Dad?'

"*Sì, cara, sì!* " Mr. Garibaldi chuckles. He has on one of those real funny hats that looks like a raccoon, or something furry like that.

Hey, Ho, Hollywood!

I look away, to see that Daddy is walking toward us wearing the longest face.

"Oh, no," I moan.

"The flight is canceled," Daddy announces.

I just want to fall on the floor and pull a temper tantrum. Dag on, we can't take any more disappointments!

"But they've put the six of you on standby, in case they can get you on a later flight," Daddy says, delivering the bad news like Granddaddy Walker does when he's telling a family he can't make a corpse at the funeral parlor look real good.

"Whatever makes them clever," Galleria says, disappointed. "I guess their mouth ain't mighty enough for Furious Flo."

"Well, we ain't going home," I announce adamantly. "I don't care if we have to stay in the airport all night."

"I know that's right," Angie pipes in.

"Don't worry, darlings," Ms. Dorothea says, putting her arms around us. "It's just another wrong turn on the road, and we've landed in hyena territory once again—but when the hyenas have eaten their fill, they'll leave us alone, and then we'll be on our merry way.

All's we gotta do is click our heels and *pray*."

Chanel starts clicking her heels together. They are real cute vinyl sandals, and have goldfish in the heels that you can see—but they do make her feet look kinda wet.

"I don't know how you could wear those goldfish on your feet in this weather, Chuchie," Galleria says, rolling her eyes. "Oh, I get it, maybe you'll be able to swim upstream if the water gets too high!"

Chanel is too crestfallen to care what Galleria says. "I hope we have somewhere to swim to," she mumbles.

We all drag our luggage to the check-in storage room. Galleria and Ms. Dorothea's cheetah luggage is so pretty. Ours looks kinda ugly next to theirs. It's just plain ol' blue vinyl. When Angie and I get some money, we're gonna buy ourselves pretty luggage too. I wonder if we are ever gonna get some money of our own. Not soon enough, that's for sure!

After we eat some hamburgers and french fries at Pig in the Poke Restaurant, we get real sleepy, and head to the waiting area, where we sit on the ugly vinyl chairs. "How come they don't have real velvet chairs or something?" Chanel moans.

I put my coat on the floor so I can lie down. "Sweet dreams," Chanel coos. She seems so sad.

I can't take the noise anymore. People are walking around like they're in a hurry, but I know they're going nowhere. All this is making me *real* sleepy.

I don't know how long we've been sleeping, but I hear a loud noise, and I think it's in my dreams, but then I realize it's an announcer's voice on the loudspeaker. "Mrs. Gari-bolda, please come to the reservation desk. Mrs. Gari-bolda, please come to the reservation desk."

"Mom, wake up!" Galleria says, shaking her mother. Ms. Dorothea jumps up, like one of the creatures from *Night of the Living Dead.*

"Wait here!" she orders.

"What time is it?" Chanel says, rubbing her eyes open.

"It's ten o'clock. We've been waiting for four hours," Galleria answers. Then, humming aloud, she sings, "Rain or shine, all is mine. . . ."

We look at each other real quiet. It feels like we're waiting to see if we won the $64,000 prize on the game show *My Dime, Your Time!*

Running toward us, Ms. Dorothea announces, "Come on, Cheetah Girls! It's time to head for Hollywood!"

We all jump out of our chairs and let out a cheer. Then we gather our stuff, and say good-bye to Daddy and Abala. The High Priestess kisses me on the forehead, and says, "Look for the Raven when she opens her wings."

"I will, Abala," I say. Yeah, right. Whatever.

Galleria is trying not to smirk, and as we're running through the terminal to keep up with Ms. Dorothea, she spreads her arms out and coos, "Caw! Caw! I'm the raven! Nevermore! Nevermore!"

Everybody is looking at us as we give our tickets to the attendant, giggling up a storm.

"Oh, and by the way, darling, tell that dreary announcer of yours it's Mrs. *Garibaldi!*" Ms. Dorothea tells the attendant.

"Ooh, this is dope!" Dorinda says, looking at the red velvet seats we pass in the first-class section. She has never been on a plane before.

Hey, Ho, Hollywood!

"This is where all the rich people sit," I whisper in Dorinda's ear. The flight attendants are giving out newspapers and bubbly-looking drinks in plastic cups to the first-class passengers.

"Momsy poo, can we sit in first class?" Galleria asks, giggling.

"Do you have first-class money? You can sit there, darling poo, when *you're* paying."

We go back farther, and get to a section where there are more seats—and they're a *lot* smaller.

"Hold your breath, girls, and tuck it in," Galleria giggles as she sits down.

"Do' Re Mi, *mamacita*, you take the window seat," Chanel says to Dorinda. Bless her heart, she won't be able to see much out the window, even though the rain has stopped. It's so dark out now. But it was still nice of Chuchie to give her the seat. After we settle in, a pilot's voice comes over the loudspeaker and welcomes us aboard.

"*Hola, hola*, everybody, the Cheetah Girls are in the house!" Chanel coos. The lady in the row across from me and Angie looks at us in curiosity. How'd she get her hair teased so high in this weather? I wonder.

"She looks like she's ready for takeoff!" Galleria whispers to me. She is seated in the row behind me.

A screen gets pulled down by the flight attendant, and a movie explains all about safety, and what to do if something happens.

I start getting *real* scared, and my hands are sweating. But I have plenty of time to calm down. We sit and wait in the plane for *two hours*!

Finally, the captain announces that we are "ready for takeoff." Everyone in the plane starts clapping.

"We're ready for Freddy, yo!" Dorinda says, and lets out a hoot. She is so excited. For someone who's never been on a plane before, she seems so much calmer than we do.

I reach down to get my Cloud Nine pills out of my carry-on bag, and put them in the flap in front of my seat. Just in case I get sick, I don't want to be barfing up a storm and embarrassing myself in front of my friends.

Galleria starts singing: "Snakes in the grass have no class/But cheetah girls have all the swirls."

We join in, singing together, and people start clapping all around us, cheering us on.

Hey, Ho, Hollywood!

When the plane finally starts ascending into the air, though, we get real quiet. I think we're all pretty scared.

When we finally reach cruising altitude, I let out a sigh of relief. "We're going to Hollywood!" I yell.

"Hey, we never did get to see the Sandman at the Apollo, did we?" Galleria turns and asks me, then chuckles. "I was kinda disappointed."

"Don't be, Miss Galleria," I say, laying on my Southern accent and fluttering my eyelashes, "If we turn 'stinkeroon like loony toons' at the Tinkerbell Lounge, neither Freddy nor the Sandman is gonna be able to help us—'cuz *Captain Hook* is gonna yank us off the stage himself!!!"

But I just know that ain't gonna happen. We all know it. Maybe it's High Priestess Abala Shaballa's spell, or maybe it's God's Way, just that we know we're due—whatever. It really doesn't matter. What matters is that we're the Cheetah Girls, and we've got growl power. It's only a matter of time till the whole world knows it.

So hey, ho, Hollywoooood, the Cheetah Girls are looking gooood!

More Pounce to the Ounce

We wuz walking down the street
eating Nestlé's Crunch
when a big babboon
tried to get a munch.
Please don't ask for bite
'cuz that's my lunch
Times are hard and
you should know the deal
So please stop breathing
on my Happy Meal.
Here's the wrapper
take the crumbs
Next time you try to sneak a chomp
you won't get none!!!
Snakes in the grass have no class
but cheetah girls have all the swirls.
Big baboons don't make us swoon
'cuz Cheetah Girls can reach the moon

To all the competition, what can we say?
You'd better bounce, y'all

'cuz every Cheetah has its day
You'd betta bounce, y'all
While you still got some flounce, y'all
'cuz Cheetah Girls are gonna pounce, y'all
and we got more pounce to the ounce y'all

More Pounce to the Ounce
We don't eat lunch
More Pounce to the Ounce
Come on with the brunch!

The Cheetah Girls Glossary

Angling for an intro: When you're cheesing for the purpose of an introduction to someone.

At the bottom of the crab barrel: When you're down in the dumps.

Churl: A word made up by combining "girl" and "child" together.

Corpse: The body of a dead person. A cadaver.

Crispy: Supertasty "flow" or food.

Diva size: Size fourteen and up.

Flounce: Show off.

Groovy like a movie: Dope. Cool.

Heffa: A girl who thinks she's all that and a bag of "juju beans."

Hex: A witchcraft spell.

Hush your mouth!: An affectionate response that's really asking, "Is that right?"

Monologue: A dramatic sketch performed by

an actor—or a "drama queen" kind of person.

Off the hook: Dope. Cool

Outtie like Snouty: When a situation gets a little cuckoo and you need a time-out break.

Passed: When someone dies.

Pouncing: A very important Cheetah Girl skill for taking control of a situation and making things happen.

Ready for Freddy: Ready for anything. Ready to do your thing.

She takes the cobbler: When someone is really too much. Can also be used like, "He gave me a C in math. That really takes the cobbler!"

Stinkeroon like loony toons: When you're having an off day with your "flow."

Wefties: Weaves that are so tick tacky the tracks are showing!

Wreckin' my flow: When something is interfering with your ability to talk, sing, think, or whatever it is you're trying to do.

PHOTO BY CHARLIE PIZZARELLO

ABOUT THE AUTHOR

Deborah Gregory earned her growl power as a diva-about-town contributing writer for ESSENCE, VIBE, and MORE magazines. She has showed her spots on several talk shows, including OPRAH, RICKI LAKE, and MAURY POVICH. She lives in New York City with her pooch, Cappuccino, who is featured as the Cheetah Girls' mascot, Toto.